To Ma

Blessings –

Helen Jordan

2-2-2016

The Leather Satchel

Helen K. Jordan

This book is a work of fiction. Names, characters, businesses, organizations, places, events, and incidents either are the product of the author's imagination or are used fictitiously. Any resemblance to actual persons, living or dead, event or locales is entirely coincidental. Laws mentioned in the book are designed to fit the narrative and are not necessarily accurate.

ISBN: 1503032035
ISBN 13: 9781503032033
Library of Congress Control Number: 2014955827
CreateSpace Independent Publishing Platform
North Charleston, South Carolina

ACKNOWLEDGMENTS

After writing my first book, *The Journal,* my intentions were not to write a second book, but with requests from so many for a sequel, I joyfully relented . . . thus, The *Leather Satchel.*

I want to thank my attorney son-in-law, Tom Ostenson, for his advice pertaining to the court cases and my doctor son-in-law, Jerry Cunningham, for helping me describe a heart attack. Thanks also go to Rodger Williams who kindly answered questions about stun guns.

Heartfelt thanks go to my friends and family who read, made suggestions, and encouraged me as I wrote. These were, Margaret Karr, Vann Williams, Joan Mitchell, and my two daughters, Becky Lowe and Carolyn Cunningham.

My granddaughter, Ann Seale, and her husband, Ben, suggested that I use the satchel she brought from Italy as a model for the cover picture. They graciously offered to photograph and photo-shop it so that it would fit well with my story.

My friends often ask how long it took to write the first book, and I tell them between three and four years. When I tell them it took me only four months to write this one, they wonder why so quickly. I tell them when you are eighty-eight years old, you don't have time to tarry.

ONE

Sarah Davis stopped at the open door of the laundry room at Washington Arms, the assisted living facility in Arlington, Virginia. She peeked in and watched the woman at the ironing board. What was she ironing? People didn't iron clothes in 2009. Everything was wrinkle-free, or so they said. Sarah squinted, trying to see what was on the board. It looked like a pile of handkerchiefs. The woman ironing turned and smiled at Sarah. Sarah smiled back and shook her head slightly. It was old Mrs. Livingston's maid. Mrs. Livingston never left her suite without a clean handkerchief.

Sarah chuckled. Who was she to call someone old when she herself would be ninety-one her next birthday and Mrs. Livingston was still in her eighties?

Sarah struggled to turn her walker and then headed back to her suite. She had not ironed in a long time. There was a time when she loved to iron. Ernst accused her of ironing his underwear. He said it was foolish. Sarah stopped and glanced in the large parlor where some of the residents sat. It was too early for dinner. She would go back to her small two room-suite and let her mind remember the olden days. Actually, that was what she remembered best. She couldn't remember everything they had served for breakfast, but that didn't matter. It was the days of her youth that she loved, not the moments of today.

Sarah stopped suddenly when the front door opened and Dr. Bradford brought in an elderly man in a wheel chair. Her own doctor had retired, and Dr. David Bradford was kind enough to take her on as a new patient. Sarah smiled, and Dr. Bradford smiled back, but she could tell that he didn't have time for a conversation. Sam, the black orderly, hustled forward to help, and Mrs. Smith, their director, also appeared from nowhere. They soon moved forward, all the way to the end of the hall, to the suite next to her own. It had belonged to Mr. Grey—the poor man had been moved to a nursing home.

Sarah stopped at her door and stood there a few moments; then she opened it and pushed her walker through, slowly making her way to her recliner. She sat down and breathed deeply several times. She then reclined her chair and closed her eyes. What would she let her mind dwell on today? As if she had many choices. Maybe back in October of 1938, when she was twenty years old and had been married to Ernst for a little over two years. It was the most memorable day she could remember. They lived in Berlin, Germany, in a modest apartment. She was in the kitchen ironing, and she heard the key turn in the lock and the front door open.

"Where are you, Sarah?" Ernst called.

"In the kitchen, ironing. Why are you home so early?" Sarah tried to hide the anxiety in her voice as she called back to her husband. Surely he had not lost his job.

Ernst burst into the kitchen, excitement showing in his blue eyes and a big smile on his face. "Put the iron away, honey. I want to tell you something, and you need to be sitting down for this." Ernst reached over and unplugged the iron, and then took Sarah by the arm and led her into the living room and onto the sofa.

He took her hand and patted it. A slight frown formed on Sarah's face. "What is it, Ernst? I hope good news this time. Surely you are not changing jobs."

"No, no—nothing like that. In fact this is the job of a lifetime. Not for me but for you."

"What in the world are you talking about, Ernst? Do you want me to go to work to help pay off your gambling debts? Is that what you want?" Sarah sat back against the sofa and pulled her hand from Ernst's, her brown eyes flashing.

"No, it's nothing like that. Now, just calm down and let me explain. First of all, this cannot be discussed outside the confines of this apartment." Ernst's blue eyes darkened slightly as they locked with Sarah's.

"Mr. Weinberg called me into his office today, and we had a long talk, mostly about business. Then he began to talk about the political situation here in Berlin and wanted to know if I was aware of the seriousness of everything—you know, the Jewish situation. I nodded my head and didn't say much. What could I say, Sarah?" Ernst paused a moment, as if Sarah might comment, but then continued. "He knows there's a possibility that I'll be called to serve in the Wehrmacht. I thought maybe he wanted to assure me that I would have my job after I did my tour of duty. But it wasn't that."

Sarah sat quietly, waiting for Ernst to continue. She finally said, "What is it, Ernst? Tell me now."

Ernst swallowed hard and reached again for Sarah's hand. "Sarah, Mr. and Mrs. Weinberg want us to have their fourth child, who is to be born the second week in January, just a little over three months from now."

Sarah's other hand flew to her mouth. "What are you talking about, Ernst? Nothing you are saying makes sense. Why would they give us their fourth child? Surely you misunderstood Mr. Weinberg."

"No, there was no misunderstanding. Let me explain further. Mr. and Mrs. Weinberg want you to start immediately to look as if you are pregnant. When the baby is born, the midwife will bring it

to you, and she will act as though you have given birth to the baby. I know this doesn't make sense, but that was the proposal. Now, before you say anything, let me tell you the rest. There will be a very, very large sum of money given to us if you agree to do this."

Ernst released Sarah's hand and sat back against the sofa. He watched Sarah's facial expression, her eyes unblinking, staring into space.

Sarah finally turned and spoke. "I still don't understand. What will the Weinbergs say about the birth of their baby? What will they tell people?"

Ernst's voice softened. "They will tell everyone that the baby died."

Sarah sat forward and frowned. "Why are they doing this? Surely the Jewish situation is not that bad."

"Mr. Weinberg has inside information. He says it's worse than we think. He fears for their lives and knows a new baby could not survive what lies ahead."

Sarah sat back again, silent.

"Sarah, the baby will be ours. Mr.Weinberg does not want the baby to have a Jewish name."

"Are you saying that the baby's name will be Hoffman?"

"Yes."

"Tell me, Ernst, why did Mr. Weinberg choose you out of the hundreds of people he has working for him?"

"I asked him that. His answer was: that 'we fit the bill.'"

"Surely you did not tell him that I'm half Jewish. You promised you would tell no one." Alarm had entered Sarah's voice.

Ernst shook his head. "Oh, no. I would never do that. But, Sarah, he probably knows. Mr. Weinberg has connections. He knows everything."

"How much money, Ernst? How much did it take for you to agree to this...this unbelievable scheme?"

Ernst reached again for Sarah's hand and squeezed it. He breathed deeply and let it out before quietly saying, "One hundred thousand marks, Sarah. That's what he offered."

TWO

David helped Carol out of the car and started to say something but then stopped, pulled his cell from his pocket, looked at it, and smiled. Putting the phone to his ear, he said, "Welcome home. We're outside the terminal." After listening a few moments, he deposited the cell in his pocket and turned to Carol. "That was William. He said they just landed and will go straight to baggage, and we should meet them there."

Carol breathed deeply and smiled. "Oh, it seems like they have been gone forever when actually it has only been two weeks. Let's hurry, David. We don't want to keep them waiting."

David laughed and caught Carol's arm. "Slow down, honey—William said they just landed. It'll take them ten or fifteen minutes to get to baggage, and then they'll have to wait for their bags to come. I seriously doubt we'll keep them waiting."

Carol slowed her pace and turned anxiously to David. "What do you think William and Susan will say when we tell them about Mr. Kroft?"

"They'll probably ask why we didn't tell them the one time we talked on the phone."

Carol shook her head slightly and sighed. "I wanted to, but it was Leonard himself who said not to ruin their honeymoon with bad news of his broken hip."

"Yes, and I agreed. There was nothing William and Susan could do in Hawaii, and any postcards they sent would probably not arrive before they did. You know how resort places are."

"Yes, but at the time, it just didn't seem right to withhold the news from them."

David patted Carol's arm. "Honey, don't worry about it. They'll understand. Leonard's had the best of care. And his being in Washington Arms with Della and Emma has been a real blessing. The three of them are as compatible as anyone I've ever seen."

Carol nodded. "You're right. I think Della and Emma were a little awed at first, wondering how Leonard would take being confined here in the United States. He might give the appearance of being the elderly, reserved gentleman from Germany, but he's far from that when he starts talking."

"Yes, and we're fortunate that he has such a good command of the English language. I doubt there is anyone connected to the assisted-living facility who could translate the German language. Now, that really would be a problem. Look, honey, here come William and Susan."

William made sure Susan was buckled and then quickly pulled his strap and fastened it before asking for the details. "When did it happen, Mother, and how?"

"William, it was Wednesday, as we were leaving a restaurant after having lunch. I think I told you that we had snowfall the Sunday night after your wedding on Saturday. One of those late winter snowfalls that we often have. Well, the snow had melted, but there were still a few icy spots left on the sidewalk. It was just one of those freak accidents. Mr. Kroft happened to step on some ice and slipped. David and I hated it worse than anything. Thank goodness Kurt and Greta didn't fall. David called an ambulance immediately and had him taken to Arlington Memorial. One of

David's friends, an excellent orthopedic surgeon, is caring for him."

"You said he is now in assisted living—the one Aunt Della's in?"

"Yes, Washington Arms. Susan, Della and Emma have made sure that he is not lonely. In fact, I think Leonard is quite happy there. He is up on a walker and can get around very well. Of course Della has her walker. I don't think Emma needs one yet."

David interrupted. "Well, it won't be long. I've discussed it with her, and she's promised me if she feels the least bit unsteady, she'll let me order one."

"What about the Winemans, Mother? Did they fly back with the others?"

"Yes, they all left Friday a week ago. I know Kurt and Greta hated leaving Leonard, but it couldn't be helped."

"How long will Mr. Kroft be confined?"

"I don't know for sure. William, I assure you that Mr. Kroft is content. Greta and Mr. Schmitt promised that they would attend to all of the estate matters in Germany and told Leonard not to worry."

William quieted for a moment and turned to Susan. He caught her hand, pulled it to his lips, and kissed it.

Susan smiled and then yawned. She drew her hand up to cover her mouth and said, "Our honeymoon was wonderful, but it's good to be home."

Carol glanced over at David and smiled.

Not wanting to take his eyes from the interstate, David asked, "Well, which house will it be? Ours or your new home?"

William quickly answered, "Thanks, David, but Susan and I discussed it. We want to go to our home."

THREE

Sarah heard the laughter coming from Mr. Kroft's suite. She had learned his name was Leonard Kroft and had written it down for fear she would forget it. And he was from Germany. Sarah smiled to herself. She had watched him in the dining room. He sat with Della Downing and Dr. Bradford's stepmother, Emma, and old Mr. Andrews. They talked constantly and also laughed a lot. The ones at Sarah's table were quieter. Well, it suited her fine. She couldn't always keep up with the conversation. Her short-term memory often failed her.

Sarah had wanted to see who all was in his living room so she took her walker and acted like she was getting a little exercise. Being at the end of the hall, he kept his door open a lot. Someone said he was not used to the temperature at the assisted-living facility. Sarah could see a young couple sitting on the sofa. Had to be the young married couple whose wedding he was in. Della and Emma were also there.

Sarah walked a few steps farther and then turned around and returned to her suite. She wondered how she could get Mr. Kroft to visit her—just by himself— without Della and Emma. They were always together. She wondered if Mr. Kroft shared her memories. The ones about the war...and before the war.

Sarah pressed the button that would recline her chair. She then rested back and closed her eyes...and remembered.

"Sarah, when are you going to give me an answer? Mr. Weinberg is waiting." Ernst glared at Sarah. He had been patient long enough. She had hardly spoken to him for the last three days. He had to know now. He caught her arm and pulled her to the sofa.

"Please, Sarah, won't you say yes? Think of the money. We'll be out of debt. You can have some of the nice things you've always wanted."

"Ernst, do you realize the danger you are putting us in? Something could go wrong. Can we trust this midwife?" Sarah had hardly slept the past few nights. Her pretty face looked drawn.

"Trust the midwife? Sarah, Mr. Weinberg says she is the most trustworthy person he knows. She has been a loyal friend of his family for almost forty years."

Sarah sighed and sat back. She finally looked at Ernst and said, "All right, Ernst, I'm giving my consent, but if this gets us killed, you can blame it on yourself."

Ernst pulled Sarah over into his arms, hugged her, and whispered in her ear. "Nothing will go wrong. I promise." He then released her and said, "You'll love this little baby, Sarah. You have always loved children, and look, we've been married a little over two years, and you have not gotten pregnant. As you would say, 'this baby is a gift from God.'"

Sarah smiled, thinking about Maria. She truly was a gift from God. Ernst had been right. Nothing went wrong. Nothing, but the terrible things that happened to the Jewish people.

Sarah closed her eyes again and thought about that terrible night a month later on November 9. A night she would never forget. It was the night that violence against the Jews broke out across the Reich. In two days, over 250 synagogues were burned; thousands of Jewish businesses were trashed and looted; dozens of Jewish people were killed; and Jewish cemeteries, hospitals, schools, and homes were looted while police and fire brigades stood by. The pogroms became known as Kristallnacht, the "Night of Broken Glass," for the shattered glass from the store windows that littered the streets.

Mr. Weinberg's department store had less damage than most, probably because the German people loved shopping there and there were so many German people working there. Their large department store was the first to install an escalator.

Ernst said Mr. Weinberg stayed confined to his office. He had to step down as manager and let Mr. Werner, a pure-blood German, take control. It was the new law. Many Jewish men were arrested and sent to concentration camps just for being Jews. Ernst assured Sarah that things would eventually get better, but they didn't.

Sarah opened her eyes and realized all of a sudden that everything was quiet. She looked at her watch and saw that it was almost time for dinner. She hardly had time to go to the bathroom and wash her hands. She certainly did not want to be late.

FOUR

It was the next day, after William and Susan had visited, that Mr. Kroft asked Della and Emma about his next-door neighbor, Mrs. Davis.

Della looked at Emma and said, "Emma, since you have been here longer than me, maybe you can tell Leonard something about Sarah Davis."

Emma thought a minute and then shook her head and said, "I really don't know a lot about Sarah Davis. I do know that she has a granddaughter and a great-granddaughter who visit her at least once a week. I was told that Mrs. Davis lost her husband several years ago and when she couldn't live alone, she agreed to move here. I was also told that her only daughter and the daughter's husband were killed in an automobile accident, and Mrs. Davis finished raising her granddaughter."

Della interjected, "And, Leonard, the picture gets even sadder. We were told that the granddaughter's husband was killed in Iraq two years ago. Her little girl is eight years old."

Leonard nodded. "That is sad. I guess the granddaughter lives here in Arlington; otherwise she could hardly visit so often."

"Yes," Della responded quickly. "She teaches school—I think she teaches in a grammar school."

Leonard cleared his throat. "I couldn't help but notice that Mrs. Davis almost stopped yesterday when she walked past my suite. I wonder if she wanted to come in and visit with us."

Emma and Della looked at each other. Della raised her eyebrows and said, "I doubt it. She's rather strange. She doesn't seem to mix well. Emma and I have reached out to her, but we can't get much of a response. Now, the granddaughter is real friendly. I think she worries that her grandmother stays to herself too much."

Mr. Kroft nodded again. "Does she watch a lot of television? I've never heard it on, but then, I haven't been here very long, and then, too, she could have it on very low."

"I doubt the volume would be that low," Emma said. "I don't think her hearing is the best. Sometimes when I speak to her, she's slow to respond. I often have to repeat myself. But, then, I understand she's almost ninety-one years old. That might account for it."

"There is another interesting thing about Sarah Davis." Emma looked at Mr. Kroft and smiled. "Leonard, I understand she speaks German. Now, I've never heard her, but that's what our hairdresser told me."

"Hmm, that is interesting," Leonard said with a twinkle in his eye. "I just might call on Mrs. Davis."

FIVE

Leonard Kroft stood at Sarah Davis's door a few moments; then he raised his hand and knocked twice. He stood quietly, listening for movement beyond the door and wondering if she might be out or asleep. He would be patient and give her more time. No one at their home moved fast. Finally, he heard the faint sound of Sarah pushing her walker and then positioning it so she could open her door.

Mr. Kroft smiled. "I hope I'm not disturbing you, Mrs. Davis. I'm Leonard Kroft, your new neighbor next door, and I wanted to meet you."

Sarah's face registered surprise, and her hand flew to her gray hair. She pushed back a few wisps that had fallen from her bun and nodded her head. She finally spoke. "Do come in, Mr. Kroft. I've wanted to meet you and should have called, but..." Sarah didn't finish her sentence. She maneuvered her walker around, leading Mr. Kroft to the sofa and motioning for him to sit down.

Sarah settled in her recliner, adjusted her glasses, and waited for Mr. Kroft to speak again.

Mr. Kroft cleared his throat. "As I said, I've only been here a short time, and I've wanted to meet all of my neighbors. Emma Bradford said you have resided here for several years."

Sarah was slow answering. She finally nodded and said, "Yes, I can't remember the exact day I moved in, but it has been several years." Sarah reached again for the wisps of stray hair and pushed them back.

Leonard looked around the room and said, "Our suites seem to be similar in design. They are very convenient, don't you think?"

"Oh yes," Sarah said, "very convenient." She blinked her eyes a couple of times and then asked the question that was on her mind. "Mr. Kroft, are you from Germany?"

Mr. Kroft nodded. "Yes, I came over with a large party to participate in a wedding and had a little accident. My friends all returned to Germany, and I'm here to recuperate from a broken hip. But I'm not complaining, mind you. I've found this place to be very nice and the residents all very friendly."

Sarah shook her head. "Yes, I agree."

There was silence again, and then Leonard spoke. "Mrs. Davis, I was told that you speak German. Is that true?"

Sarah smiled. "Yes, I was born in Germany. My first husband and I lived in Berlin. He served in the Second World War but was killed in Normandy." A slight look of nostalgia crossed Sarah's face, and she paused a few moments before continuing. "It was some years later that I met an American military officer who was with the occupational forces. I married him and came back with him to this country. It was so long ago that I can't remember the exact date." Sarah frowned and looked down at her fingers, thinking, as if they could tell her the exact day, month, and year. She finally looked up.

"Mr. Kroft, did you serve in the Second World War?"

"Oh no, ma'am. I was born in 1930. I was too young to serve."

Sarah looked disappointed. "I see. Well, it was a terrible time for Germany, with the Jewish problem and all..." Sarah's voice faltered.

Mr. Kroft said quickly, "Yes, it was. I certainly know my history well enough to agree with you there."

Sarah fell silent again.

Mr. Kroft struggled from the sofa and stood. He held on to his walker and smiled again at Sarah. "Now, don't get up, Mrs. Davis. I can let myself out. You stay seated. I just wanted to say hello and to let you know who I am. It's been nice talking to you." He stopped at the door and turned slightly. "We'll visit again soon." With that, Leonard opened the door and pushed his walker out and back to his suite.

Sarah sat in her recliner and stared at the closed door. She had not wanted Leonard Kroft to leave so soon, but it was like her tongue was tied. She could not even carry on a conversation with her new neighbor. There were questions she wanted to ask him and things she wanted to tell him. Maybe next time her tongue would loosen up.

Sarah reclined her chair and closed her eyes. She wanted to think about Maria. Sweet baby Maria.

Ernst said that after Kristallnacht, the Weinbergs were careful about being seen in public. They lived in a very exclusive neighborhood with other wealthy Germans as neighbors. They had been well liked by all, and it seemed that some of their neighbors were sympathetic to their situation and tried to shield them as much as possible from any harm the Nazis might inflict.

Mr. Weinberg had immediately provided Sarah with maternity clothes...

Ernst quietly closed the door and put the large box on the sofa. He could hear the music from the radio in the kitchen. Sarah was getting dinner ready. He sneaked in behind her and put his hands over her eyes.

Sarah jerked and turned quickly, dropping the spoon on the floor. "Ernst, you scared me to death. Don't ever do that again." She leaned over, picked up the spoon, and glared at Ernst.

Ernst ignored her scathing remark and smiled. "Honey, come in the living room and see what I have."

Sarah stood a moment, still perturbed, then turned, lowered the flame under the pot, and followed Ernst into the living room.

Ernst motioned to the sofa. "Go ahead. Open it up. Mr. Weinberg sent you this." He eased into the chair across from the sofa and watched Sarah.

She sat down and lightly rubbed her hand across the paper and the ribbon that encircled the large dress box. "This is wrapped so beautifully that I hate to open it." Sarah smiled at Ernst.

"Go ahead, honey. You can save the paper and ribbon if you want to."

Sarah hesitated only a moment longer, and then she carefully unwrapped the box and lifted the top off. "Ernst!" was all she could say as she held up the maternity dresses, one after the other."These are beautiful," she finally exclaimed. " Who selected them?"

"Mrs. Weinberg selected them. Do you really like them?"

Sarah smiled, thinking about how excited Ernst had been over the dresses. She and Mrs. Weinberg wore the same size, which made it easier to carry out the deception. Mr. Weinberg had also given Ernst 50,000 marks, half of what he had promised him. Ernst was able to pay off his gambling debt, raising little suspicion, as so much loose money was floating around due to the Jewish situation. Sarah took a portion of the 50,000 marks and hid it, knowing that they would have more expenses after the baby was born. Only one of their neighbors even asked Sarah about her pregnancy. Sarah gladly told her the baby was due the second week of January.

The weeks passed quickly. Sarah enjoyed shopping for the baby. Ernst plied Sarah with gifts at Christmas and promised her again that he would gamble no more, but Sarah knew better. She was careful not to let Ernst know where the hidden money was.

A light snow fell on January 10, and Sarah prayed that it would not hinder their plans. It was the next afternoon that Ernst came home thirty minutes early.

"Sarah," he called, bursting into the living room. Where are you?"

"Here in the bedroom," Sarah answered as she dropped the baby blanket on their bed and quickly turned to meet Ernst. "Is it time? Has Mrs. Weinberg gone into labor?" She whispered this, feeling a quickening of her heartbeat.

"Yes. Mr. Weinberg slipped word to me and sent me on an errand. There must be no suspicion raised." Ernst kept his voice low.

"How long do you think it'll take? Oh, I need to do a few more things to get ready." Sarah patted the large bundle under her dress.

"Mr. Weinberg said that since this was their fourth child, the baby should come quickly. I'll help you. Just tell me what to do."

Sarah thought back to how nervous she and Ernst were. But there was no need to be nervous. The midwife had already told Sarah and Ernst what to expect and how to take care of the baby. She had spent one whole afternoon at their apartment going over the details. Sarah was impressed with the elderly woman and knew she could trust her.

It was eight o'clock at night on January 11, 1939, when Mrs. Graff, the midwife, came with her satchel. She mentioned that she had not had time to document the circumstance of Maria's birth—something that she meticulously did for every baby she delivered. Sarah suspected it would be a most unusual entry, and she wondered what the woman would write.

Mrs. Graff reported that baby Maria slept the whole time and no one was the wiser to what was in her satchel. Mr. and Mrs. Weinberg had picked the name, Maria, should the baby be a girl. Maria Hoffman. Sarah loved the name and said it, silently, over and over.

Sarah opened her eyes and glanced over to the picture sitting on her table. The maid had dropped it while dusting one day, and there was a tiny crack at the bottom of the frame. Maria was eleven years old in the picture. Sarah and Robert had just moved back to the United States. Maria was standing next to her new bicycle. It was such a cute picture. Sarah sighed. She needed to quit thinking about the past, but somehow she couldn't. In some ways it was all she had. Oh, it was true that she had Rachel and little Sarah Beth. But as much as she loved them, they could not take the place of Maria.

Sarah shook her head, fought back the tears, and looked at her watch. It was almost dinnertime, or was it lunchtime? She took her glasses off and wiped her eyes. She then looked at her watch again. Yes, it was almost dinnertime. She would have to hurry.

SIX

Rachel parked her car and sat a moment, thinking about her grandmother. She seemed to be spending more time in her suite each day. Rachel had discussed it with the director, Mrs. Smith, but Mrs. Smith didn't seem to think it was a problem. She said aging had different effects on people. Some became more outgoing and others more withdrawn. The social director offered things to entertain the residents like music programs and even games like bingo. Beyond that, it was hard to please everyone.

Rachel sighed. Mrs. Smith was probably right. If Grandmother was happy sitting in her recliner, then so be it. She would not agitate her. After all, being ninety, or almost ninety-one, years of age did have its idiosyncrasies.

Rachel got out of her car and entered Washington Arms once again. How many times had it been? She had lost track. Grandmother had moved back in the spring of 2005, almost four years ago, two years before Jonathan was killed in Iraq. She glanced around, pleased to see Sam, the orderly, pushing a resident, probably to get a haircut. It was Thursday, hairdressing day. His infectious smile always warmed her heart.

"Good afternoon, Mrs. Lewis. I hope your day has gone well."

"Thank you, Sam. It has. And good afternoon to you. And to you, too, sir."

The elderly man smiled at Rachel and nodded. Sam continued on with his charge.

Rachel stopped and looked in the large parlor, hoping Sarah might be there socializing with some of the women, but she wasn't. It was four o'clock, an hour before dinner. She would hurry to Sarah's suite. They would have only an hour to visit, and maybe before she left she could encourage her to walk around the halls for a little exercise.

Rachel stood a moment with her hand on the handle and then pressed it and stuck her head in. "Hi, Grandmother," she said with a big smile.

Sarah's face lit up. "Is that you, Rachel? I've been sitting here waiting for you since lunch. Did you have to stay after school?"

"Grandmother, you know I don't get out until three-thirty. I dropped Sarah Beth off at a friend's house and came as quick as I could." Rachel leaned over and kissed Sarah on her cheek, and then she sat on the sofa. "Now tell me what you've been doing since I was last here."

"Rachel, you know I can't tell one day from the next, but I do have something to tell you. I had a visitor one afternoon." Sarah's brow furrowed, and she narrowed her eyes as if making an effort to think. "I'm not sure which day it was, but it was my new neighbor next door. His name is...wait a minute now. I've got it written down." She pulled a small piece of paper from her pocket and adjusted her glasses to look at it. "His name is Leonard Kroft. And guess what, Rachel? He's from Germany."

Rachel raised her eyebrows and looked surprised.

"From Germany? Well, the two of you should have a lot in common. How did he end up here, or did he tell you?"

"He came over to be in a wedding, but while he was here, he slipped on some ice and broke his hip. He'll stay here while he's healing. Dr. Bradford is his doctor, and I think he's friends with Emma, Dr. Bradford's stepmother, and also Della Downing. You know, the two women who live on this hall and are always together."

"That's interesting. I'm looking forward to meeting him. You said he called on you?" Rachel grinned. "Mr. Kroft must recognize beauty when he sees it."

"Now Rachel, don't start that. I don't know who it was, but someone told Mr. Kroft that I speak German. I think that was the main reason he came to meet me."

"How interesting. Did the two of you have a conversation in German?"

"No, Rachel. Not one German word was spoken by either of us."

"Well, that's strange. Maybe your next visit will include some German words."

Rachel stood. "Come now, Grandmother, let's take a little walk down the hall. I think you need some exercise...and maybe we'll run into your new neighbor. I want to meet him. By the way, how old is he?"

Sarah chuckled. "Honey, he's too old for you. He said he was born in 1930. It took me a while, but I figured that makes him seventy-nine years old."

Rachel started counting her fingers and said, "I just turned thirty-five. I guess a forty-four-year difference is a few years too many." Rachel's eyes twinkled as she helped her grandmother up from her recliner and onto her walker.

Sarah pushed her walker aside and plopped into her recliner. She was worn out. The exercise Rachel had forced her to take sapped every bit of her energy. She had even lost her appetite and eaten very little of her dinner. Well, young people just didn't understand old people and how tired they get.

Sarah reached for her controller and pushed the little button that would recline her chair. That was more like it, she thought, as she closed her eyes and smiled. It was too early for bed, but not for a little daydreaming.

It was February 1, 1939. Maria was three weeks old and had just taken her bottle. Sarah had wrapped the receiving blanket tighter around Maria and pulled her close as she rocked and sang a lullaby.

The shutting of a door caused Sarah to stop rocking. Was that Ernst coming home already? She had lost track of time. Well, he would have to wait awhile for his dinner. They now had Maria, and she came first.

"Sarah?" he called.

Sarah tried to keep her voice low. "I'm in the bedroom with Maria, honey."

Ernst stood in the doorway and smiled. "How are my two girls doing? I hope Maria has not slept all day. I really need to get some sleep tonight."

Speaking hardly above a whisper, Sarah said, "I've tried to keep her awake some this afternoon. I think maybe she'll sleep better tonight." Sarah's eyes moved from Ernst's face over to his shoulder and down to his side. "What do you have there, Ernst? It looks like a shoulder bag. Is it new?"

"It's a satchel, Sarah. Mr. Weinberg gave it to me." Ernst slipped it off his shoulder and held it in front of him. "I'll show you what's in it if you'll put Maria down. I think she's asleep." Ernst stepped closer to Sarah and peered around her shoulder."Yes, she is asleep. Put her down and come into the kitchen and I'll show you what is in this satchel."

Ernst began to unbuckle the two straps on the satchel as Sarah sat down at the kitchen table. He opened it and took out two large manila envelopes and a black lacquered box.

Sarah's eyes opened wide and she reached for the box, exclaiming, "What a beautiful hand painted box." But Ernst caught her hand and shook his head. "Wait a minute, Sarah. I want to first show you these documents." Ernst picked up one of the large envelopes and began to unwind the little string from the button.

Sarah's brow furrowed slightly. "Whose are they, Ernst? Surely not ours."

"No, Sarah, they belong to Mr. Weinberg."

Sarah sat back with a look of alarm. "Ernst, what are you doing bringing home Mr. Weinberg's documents? Don't you know we can get in trouble if the authorities find out?"

"Ernst put the envelope down and patted Sarah's hand. "Just settle down now and let me explain. Sarah, Mr. Weinberg called me into his office this afternoon. He looks like he's lost twenty pounds in the last three months...you know...since that awful night in November."

Sarah nodded. "Yes I can imagine. I feel sorry for him and Mrs. Weinberg. Ernst, does he ask about Maria?"

"He's very careful and always speaks as if Maria is ours. His questions are casual, as if he is being polite to a new father."

Sarah sighed and shook her head. "I wish we could let them see Maria, but it's too dangerous. We cannot bring attention to ourselves or little Maria. It's best that we stay in the background." Sarah glanced at the envelope and box. "But, Ernst tell me about the documents and this beautiful box."

Ernst picked up the envelope and pulled out several papers. He placed them on the table and said, "These are deeds to property that Mr. Weinberg owns. He said if they should not survive this war, all of this property will belong to Maria."

Sarah sat silent, trying to absorb all Ernst was saying, her eyes shifting from Ernst's face to the contents on the table. "What's in the other envelope, Ernst?"

"There are several personal things, like World War I medals that belonged to Mr. Weinberg's father and civic certificates that were bestowed on Mr. Weinberg. There are also pictures of the family and lastly two typewritten papers: one explaining the circumstance surrounding Maria's birth with the signatures of the midwife and the Weinbergs. The other is a brief will listing Maria as heir to everything."

"And the hand-painted box, Ernst? What's in that?"

Ernst took a big breath and let it out before answering her. He put his hand gently on top of the box and said, "Three generations of the Weinberg's most beautiful jewelry you've ever seen, Sarah. I could not believe Mr. Weinberg would trust me with this valuable jewelry."

Sarah's hand flew to her chest and she whispered, "Have they given up all hope, Ernst?"

"I asked Mr. Weinberg that very question, Sarah. He didn't answer me, but I could see tears in his eyes as he turned and looked out his window. I knew then that is was hopeless."

Sarah sat forward suddenly and grabbed Ernst's arm. "Did anyone see Mr. Weinberg give you this satchel?" she frantically asked.

"No, Sarah. He's too smart for that. He had it hidden in a dress box under a dress. No one knows."

SEVEN

The voices in the hall woke Sarah. She glanced at the clock. It was two in the morning. She could hear what sounded like the heavy footsteps of boots coming up the stairway. Surely they were coming for Maria. Sarah sat up and reached for Ernst, but he wasn't in bed next to her. She tried to call him but couldn't. There was something wrong with her voice. She couldn't make a sound.

Sarah finally opened her eyes and realized she was having a nightmare. It was not 1939. It was 2009, and she was in her bed in an assisted-living facility in Arlington, Virginia.

She lay back down and tried to relax, hoping the trembling would soon stop and she would feel no chest pain. This was not the first time she had dreamed about that night. It was a terrible night. It was exactly two weeks after Ernst had brought home the satchel. They had decided to hide the satchel in the secret compartment of the antique chest that had been handed down in Sarah's family. That's where they had the second 50,000 marks hidden. Ernst had promised he would not touch them. It would probably be their life savings. Little did they know that the marks soon would have little value.

"Ernst, wake up," Sarah whispered, clutching and shaking his arm. "I hear people in the hall. They're coming for Maria."

Ernst let out a little moan and pulled his arm away. "You feed the baby tonight," he murmured. "I can't."

Sarah squeezed his arm tight and whispered in his ear. "You've got to wake up Ernst. There are people out in the hall. I hear footsteps and voices."

Ernst turned over, opened his eyes, and listened. "Be very quiet, Sarah," he whispered. Don't make a sound." Ernst eased out of the bed, tiptoed into the living room, and stood at the door listening. Sarah soon followed, holding on to his arm as they tried to hear what was going on outside.

They could hear a child crying and a mother trying to comfort it. Was that the Stein family across the hall and one door down? They were the only Jews living on her floor, and they had lived there for a very short time, maybe three months. Sarah remembered when they moved in. It was the middle of November. She had taken them some cookies. The wife's name was Sophia. It was Sophia who had asked Sarah when her baby was due.

The commotion did not last long—only long enough for Sophia and her husband to get dressed and dress their child. The Gestapo then herded them out.

Sarah and Ernst heard muffled voices and a man laughing and then the sound of the party descending the stairs. Quietness soon settled on their floor, and Ernst turned and wrapped his arm around Sarah and led her back to bed.

Sarah had quit trembling, but she could not will her mind to release the memories of that time. Mr. Weinberg was a wise man. He knew what was coming. He and his family had been taken within a week after he had given Ernst the satchel. Ernst had come home the next evening and told Sarah what Mr. Werner had said.

Mr. Werner had called all the employees together and announced that they were under new management but that nothing would really change. All job descriptions would remain the same. He would clean out Mr. Weinberg's office and occupy it himself. Mr. Werner's office would go to the next in line, and so on. His announcements were without emotion. If he felt remorse, no one knew it. Ernst was careful to keep his thoughts to himself.

Sarah turned over in bed and hugged her pillow close to her body. She had to quit thinking and get some rest. After all, she might have another visit from that nice German man next door, and she didn't want to be bleary-eyed.

EIGHT

Sarah stood in front of Leonard Kroft's door and glanced back down the hall. She didn't see anyone. Hopefully Mr. Kroft would be alone. She wanted to talk to him, but he had not called on her since his first visit. She raised her hand, tapped gently on his door, and waited.

She could hear movement beyond the door and, with relief, watched the handle as it moved, opening the door. Mr. Kroft looked surprised, but then a smile formed on his lips.

"What a nice surprise," he said. "Please come in, Mrs. Davis." Leonard backed away from the entrance so Sarah could maneuver her walker through. "I was just sitting there in my chair wondering whether to watch television or read a book. I'm so glad you came for a visit." Leonard ushered Sarah to the sofa, where she sat down.

"Yes, well, I had been wanting to repay your visit and thought this afternoon would be a good time." Sarah smiled at Leonard and reached up to push back a few stray wisps of hair.

"Mrs. Davis, I looked for you yesterday when the music program was presented. Did you not feel like attending? I think the woman who sang did a nice job."

"You're talking about Mrs. Linden? I always thought she was a tad off-key, but then, maybe she has improved. No, I did not attend. I decided to stay in and rest."

Mr. Kroft suppressed a smile, cleared his throat, and changed the subject. "Mrs. Davis, I was wondering—do you still have any contacts in Germany?"

"Not really. The few close relatives I had are all deceased. There may be a very distant cousin or two somewhere, but I never hear from them." Sarah hesitated a moment and then blurted out, "Mr. Kroft, are you a lawyer?"

Mr. Kroft looked surprised at her question. "No, I'm not. My profession was in accounting. I worked for the Haydn Steel Company and other related businesses the Haydns owned." Leonard sat silent a moment, reading the disappointment on Sarah's face. He finally asked, "Do you need a lawyer?"

Sarah glanced out the window before answering. She didn't quite know how to answer Mr. Kroft. She finally said, "I was hoping you were a lawyer...the fact that you can speak German and all..." Her voice trailed off.

Leonard sat a moment, not sure if he should pursue the subject, but then thought about William. "I have a young friend who speaks fluent German. In fact, he spent the last sixteen years in Germany, three of them working in the oldest law firm in Berlin. He's now married to an American girl and decided he would relocate to the States. He lives here in Arlington and is a partner in a law firm here. If you need a lawyer, I'm sure he would be glad to take you as a new client."

"Is he the one whose wedding you were in?" Sarah asked.

Leonard smiled. "Yes, William and Susan are very dear friends of mine. In fact, I was the one who gave Susan away."

"How nice." Sarah smiled. She sat silent.

Leonard could tell she was thinking. He finally said, "Maybe you would like to think about what I said and get back to me at a later date. I will have no problem contacting William."

"Oh, no," Sarah said quickly. "I don't want to wait. I need to talk to him now."

Mr. Kroft raised his eyebrows. "Well, give me a day or so. I assure you that I will contact William and let you know what he says. I'm sure you will like him. He's smart and kind, and he has a great personality."

Sarah smiled and said, "Thank you, Mr. Kroft. I really appreciate that." She then turned and reached for her walker. "Well, I guess I must go now. But before I do, I have a favor to ask."

Leonard raised his eyebrows again and said, "Of course."

"Would you please call me Sarah? My friends call me by my first name."

"Indeed I will. And my first name is Leonard. That's what my friends call me."

Sarah and Leonard both pulled up on their walkers, and he followed her to the door.

Sarah turned and said, "Thank you, Leonard. I do appreciate your help. You will let me know when you have contacted the young man?"

"You know I will, Sarah, just as soon as I can. Now you have a nice afternoon, and I'll probably see you at dinner."

Sarah smiled as she pushed her walker next door to her apartment. She had finally made the first step toward something she should have done long ago.

NINE

Sarah pushed her door open and made straight to her bedroom and the antique chest. She had taken the first step, and now she would continue. It had been months, or maybe years, since she had opened the leather satchel. And she had never told anyone about it—that is, no one but Rachel. But Rachel did not know what it contained. She assumed it was some of Sarah's memorabilia.

Sarah pulled a chair in front of the chest and sat down. She then opened the bottom drawer and removed the lightweight blanket. Next she felt for the small, flat metal head that rested on the inside edge of the bottom drawer and carefully pulled it up. Keeping a tight hold of the shank, she then pulled up the false drawer bottom and lifted it out. Underneath was a secret compartment. That was where the satchel was hidden.

Sarah felt for the shoulder strap and then lifted the leather satchel out, put it on the floor next to her chair, and sat back to get her breath. She had exhausted her strength and wondered why she had not found a more accessible place for the satchel. It was not that she did not trust the maid. It was the fact that no one but Ernst and she had ever seen it. Not even Robert, her second husband, had seen it, and she had never told Maria the satchel existed.

Sarah remembered the day that Robert came into the kitchen and announced that he wanted to adopt Maria.

"Sarah, I think it's time Maria took my name. We've been married three years, and we have not had a child. I want to give Maria my name."

Sarah turned from washing dishes, dried her hands, and sat down at the kitchen table. Robert pulled out one of the other chairs and sat down.

Sarah glanced around and then, speaking softly, said, "Robert, you have taken me by surprise. I had no idea that it made any difference to you. I mean the fact that Maria's name is Hoffman. After all she is eleven years old. I think it's too late for a name change."

"Why do you say that, Sarah? Robert gestured with his open palms."It's never too late to change your name. And the fact that we have just come back to the States makes the timing perfect. When Maria starts attending school this fall, no one will know the difference. It will create fewer problems for her. She'll feel more secure not having to explain why her name is different."

"But you don't understand." Sarah looked frustrated. "What I mean is...well, it's just not that easy."

"What are you talking about, Sarah? Changing one's name is not complicated. I promise I'll handle everything. I even have a friend who is an attorney. He'll help us. You'll see." Robert smiled and sat back in his chair.

"It's more than that, Robert. There are things I have not told you." Sarah furrowed her brow, locking eyes with Robert.

"What are you talking about, honey? What are you keeping secret?" Robert leaned toward Sarah, his expression darkening a little.

Sarah turned and looked behind her. "Where is Maria? She and Julia were in her room awhile ago."

"Oh, I forgot to tell you. She said she and Julia were going to Julia's house. Her mother was making homemade ice cream. I told her you wouldn't mind. You don't, do you?"

"That's fine, Robert. I just didn't want her to overhear this conversation."

Robert sat, waiting for Sarah to continue.

Sarah nervously picked at a loose string on the cotton placemat and then finally looked up at Robert. "I probably should have told you this before we married but, somehow, it didn't seem to be an issue, or maybe I just didn't want it to be."

"What is it, Sarah? You can confide in me. I'm your husband, or have you forgotten?" Robert's voice was strained.

Sarah hesitated only a moment; then her eyes locked again with Robert's. "I did not give birth to Maria. She was given to me and Ernst when she was born."

Robert sat back, speechless, taking in what Sarah had said. He finally sat forward and reached for Sarah's hand.

"Sarah, adoption is not something to be ashamed of or to keep secret. Surely you didn't think it would make any difference to me if you and Ernst had adopted a baby. You must know now that I love Maria as if she were my own."

"It's not that, Robert. It's just complicated, and I've never wanted Maria to know."

"Know what, Sarah? That she has other family?"

"She has no other family, Robert. Her family was murdered by the Nazis."

Showing surprise, Robert thought a moment and then said softly, "So our sweet Maria is Jewish. But, Sarah, that doesn't bother me. And what you and Ernst did was wonderful. You saved Maria's life. I think she's old enough to be told. She'll understand."

Sarah looked down and continued to pick at the string on the placemat. She finally spoke. "I'm not sure she would, Robert. I could not bear to have her know the horrible things that her family suffered. Why tell her that her family suffered and died with the six million Jews Hitler murdered during World War II? Can you imagine her reading about the Jews who were gassed and whose bodies were burned or thrown in mass graves, with a bulldozer shoveling dirt over them? No, I felt it best to leave it alone. I still do. She's been supremely happy with her situation, thinking I'm her real mother. Why change that?"

"But Sarah, what does that have to do with a name change now?"

"Robert, what I have not told you is that Maria's real father was very wealthy and left documents and deeds that she has inherited. The name that is listed on some of those documents is Hoffman. I think changing her name would complicate everything, especially if she is able to someday claim her inheritance." Sarah hesitated a few moments and then said, "And when that happens, I'll tell her everything."

Robert thought a minute and then asked, "Where is her inheritance located, Sarah? Is it in a bank somewhere...maybe in Switzerland?"

Sarah shook her head."No, it's tied up in property in East Germany...behind the Iron Curtain."

Sarah raised her hand, rubbed the side of her head, and thought hard to remember how many years ago she and Robert had that conversation. It was 1950, fifty-nine years ago. The Berlin Wall had come down since then, but not until after Maria and her husband were killed in that terrible automobile accident in 1988. Rachel was fourteen years old.

It was no surprise that Robert never mentioned adoption again, and he never asked to see the papers or any of the things Mr. Weinberg had left Maria. Maybe it was because the Iron Curtain had gone up after the war was over. Robert was a lieutenant in the military. He understood what it meant to have Europe divided into two separate areas with the Soviet Union's Communist influence leading in the east.

Robert knew Maria's inheritance might be gone forever and conveyed that to Sarah. Robert was a Christian—a fine Christian man—and he had had a tremendous influence on Maria and Sarah. He taught Sarah to trust the Lord and said if it was the Lord's will for Maria to own the property, it would work out.

Sarah reached up and wiped a tear that had escaped from the corner of her eye. She missed Robert terribly and wished he was here now. He would know what to do. There had been an article in one of the papers about a lawsuit over property in East

Germany. Some Jewish descendants had begun to sue to recover the property that had been stolen from their grandparents and great-grandparents. Yes, it was definitely time to tell someone about the satchel. Every document in there was written in German. The Lord had moved Mr. Kroft into the assisted-living facility at just the right time.

Sarah gripped the arms of her chair and pushed up. She reached down, caught hold of the strap, picked up the satchel, and balanced it on the tray on her walker. She would keep it out of the drawer for now. Her mind was made up. She would continue to move forward.

TEN

Sarah thanked William and Leonard again for coming and closed the door. Leonard was right. The young lawyer was patient and kind, and oh so tall and handsome with his blond, curly hair and blue eyes. But she needed to get to her recliner and rest. She was emotionally drained and feeling some pain in her chest. Showing William and Leonard the contents of the leather satchel and explaining about the Weinbergs and the baby was extremely difficult.

And now she faced another hurdle. Tomorrow she would have to tell Rachel the truth. What would Rachel say? Would she be hurt? Sarah didn't want to think about tomorrow. She sat down and looked at the table beside her chair. The deflated balloon lay where she had put it last night after opening the satchel. She did not know why she had saved it all through the years or why she had put it in the satchel. Sarah reached over, picked it up, and toyed with it. The balloon was very old—too old to stretch. Sarah closed her eyes momentarily, remembering the day Maria played with the balloon.

"Mother, please. All I want for my birthday is a helium balloon. That's what Marta had at her birthday party."

"Maria, I have no idea where to find a helium balloon. Why would you select something like that? Wouldn't you rather have a book of paper dolls that you can cut out or a new box of crayons?"

"No, Mother. I want a balloon," Maria begged. "Please, Mother, please."

"Well, we'll see. I do have some errands to run this weekend. You find out where the helium balloon came from, and I'll get one for you."

Sarah smiled thinking about Maria and the balloon. Sure enough, Maria knew the exact store where Marta's mother had purchased it, for Marta's mother had written it down on a slip of paper. Come Saturday afternoon, Sarah took little seven-year-old Maria shopping with her and purchased the helium balloon. The man who sold it to her took the string and tied it around Maria's wrist, and Maria swung around in the store, squealing and laughing, watching the balloon bounce around in the air.

There were several customers in the store who stopped what they were doing and smiled at Maria with her helium balloon. There was an American lieutenant standing close by who really seemed to be amused at Maria's antics. Sarah quickly caught Maria's hand and ushered her out before the distraction disrupted sales in the store.

The day was rather windy, and the balloon continued to bounce around in the air. Then all of a sudden the string came untied, and the balloon pulled loose from Maria's wrist and sailed high up in the sky. Maria began to cry.

Maria looked up at her mother with tears streaming down her face and begged to get another balloon, but Sarah had no more money except the money for the bus ride home. Maria would not be comforted. She continued to cry. Sarah leaned down and whispered to Maria that maybe she could have another balloon when Sarah received her next paycheck. Sarah took her handkerchief and wiped Maria's tears from her face, still talking softly to her. Maria began to smile, and Sarah straightened up, pleased that she had comforted Maria. But Maria was not smiling at what Sarah said. She was smiling at the lieutenant holding the helium balloon.

"Wie bitte. Verlieren dein kleiner madchen ballon?"

The lieutenant stumbled through some German words, and Sarah smiled. He had begged Sarah's pardon and asked about Maria losing her balloon. When he finished with his broken German, Sarah smiled again and carefully answered him, making sure he understood what she said and how grateful she was. He spoke better German than she did English, for the only English words Sarah knew were *yes, no,* and *thank you.* The kind lieutenant tied the new string so securely to Maria's wrist that it was only later, after Sarah and Maria returned home, that she could remove it with a pair of scissors.

That was how Sarah met Robert. Sarah smiled, thinking about that afternoon and the balloon. Robert introduced himself to Sarah and insisted on riding home with her on the bus. But before they did that, he took them to a sandwich shop, and they had an early supper. From that day on, Robert was an attentive admirer of Sarah. He proposed six months later.

Sarah sighed, thinking about those years and of struggling to learn English. Robert never criticized her efforts. Maria learned easily. She was very smart, graduating magna cum laude from the University of Virginia. Maria was not only smart, but also a good wife and wonderful mother. She loved Rachel more than life, having given birth to her at the age of thirty-five. Maria had suffered two miscarriages before having Rachel. Sarah thought back to the day Rachel was born. She came a month early but was a healthy baby.

"Mother, look," Maria said, holding baby Rachel's tiny hand. "Look how small her fingers are. Isn't she a beautiful baby?"

Sarah smiled. "She is a beautiful baby, Maria. She reminds me of you when you were born. You were the most beautiful baby in the world."

Sarah sighed again. Then, bringing her attention back to what was left of the old, faded balloon, she dropped it in the waste-basket. As much as it meant to her when Maria was small, there was such a thing as keeping useless things too long.

ELEVEN

William pulled out a chair for Susan, and then he pulled out his own. They both bowed their heads, and he said the blessing.

"I'm hungry as a bear, and this looks wonderful," William said, reaching for the dish that held the hot, steaming stew. "I didn't know I married such a great cook."

Susan grinned. "Maybe you should taste it before giving me such a great compliment." She took a sip of water, obviously pleased, and watched William over the rim of her glass as he took his first bite. "Anyhow, I can read a recipe. And I did learn a few things from Aunt Della. Making a good stew was one of them. But to change the subject, how was your day?"

"You would not believe my day," William said, buttering a piece of cornbread. "I met a very interesting person this afternoon, and you'll be surprised when I tell you that she's a resident of Washington Arms, actually living in the apartment next to Mr. Kroft."

"Really? Is she a new client, or did you just happen to be visiting Mr. Kroft when you met her?"

"She's a new client, soon to be ninety-one years old. Mr. Kroft told her about me. Her name is Sarah Davis. She lost her husband a few years ago."

"I probably shouldn't ask, but I can't resist. Did Mrs. Davis call you to write a will? If she did, she's waited a long time." Susan reached for a piece of cornbread.

"It's a little more involved than that. I don't mind telling you because I'm going to ask a favor, seeing as you have extra time on your hands." William smiled at Susan.

Susan looked surprised. "Really? I was not aware I had any extra time. But since it's a favor for you, I'll make the time. Now, see how nice I am?" Susan took a bite of her stew and chewed silently, trying to keep the smile from forming and dimple from showing.

William ignored her comment and said, "You realize that what I tell you is in confidence. You cannot share this, even with Aunt Della, Emma, David, or my mother." William took another bite of the stew and watched Susan.

Susan stopped eating and said, "This must be important to be that secretive. Now you really have me curious. Tell me, what does an almost ninety-one-year-old woman residing in an assisted-living home have going on that is so important?"

"She has a seventy-year-old leather satchel that she has had hidden in a secret compartment of her chest of drawers for just that long."

Susan put down her fork and sat back, her green eyes sparkling. "William, what is in that satchel? Why has she kept it hidden so long?"

"She has documents and jewelry that are over a hundred years old. It's no telling the value of the contents of that satchel." William stopped talking to take another bite of the green beans on his plate. He chewed and swallowed before adding, "And she's turning the contents of the satchel over to me." William watched Susan's reaction.

Susan blinked a couple of times and then picked up her glass of water and took a few sips before remarking, "My, that sounds intriguing. But, tell me, how am I involved?"

"I took the documents to our firm, but I left the jewelry with her. What I want you to do is take a picture of each piece of the jewelry. You'll have to create a background so the pieces will show up well. Each piece needs to be numbered and described. In other words, they need to be cataloged. We need a complete list of the jewelry that Mrs. Davis can sign, showing her as custodian. She will keep the original, and we'll have copies made. The jewelry needs to be appraised. It looks very valuable."

"You're saying that you do not want the jewelry removed from her presence without her signature."

"That's exactly right. And she has given her permission for you to take pictures and catalog it. I have already copied the documents and will give her a copy of each one. I have the originals in my office safe. I'll work with copies."

"You have not told me what the documents are about."

"Susan, they are old land deeds for property in east Berlin."

"William, are you telling me that she is Jewish?"

"Mr. Kroft says she's half Jewish. Her first husband was not. They both grew up in Berlin before the Second World War. Her story is very interesting. I will tell it to you later. I just wanted to know if you are willing to do this for me."

"Well, of course I'll do it. I've been wanting to get my camera out of storage. When do you want me to go?"

"As soon as you can."

"I can't go tomorrow, but I can the next day. Will you call her?"

"No, I'll let Mr. Kroft inform her. He's as interested in her situation as I am."

"Do you mind my asking if she has heirs?"

"She has one thirty-five-year-old granddaughter who is a widow with an eight-year-old daughter. The granddaughter's name is Rachel Lewis. Her husband was an officer in the army and was killed in Iraq."

"Oh, how sad. I guess she's making a will and leaving Rachel the contents of the satchel."

"No, Susan. The contents of the satchel do not belong to Mrs. Davis. They belong to Rachel."

"I don't understand."

"Look, if you'll just let me finish my dinner, I promise I'll explain. OK?"

Susan held up her hands and grinned. "OK."

After dinner, William pulled Susan onto the sofa and into his arms. "Hmmm," he said. "Now this is more like it." He then gave Susan a long kiss and murmured, "Have I told you lately that I love you?"

"I think so," Susan murmured back.

He kissed Susan a second time. "You know I love you more than anything, don't you?"

"Yes," Susan murmured, "but have you already forgotten?"

"Forgotten? Forgotten what?" William replied softly, his lips still close to hers.

"You were going to finish the story about Sarah Davis," Susan said softly.

"I was?" William kissed Susan a third time.

"Are you trying to kill my curiosity?" Susan asked softly.

"No. It's just that I think romance is more interesting than other people's problems. Don't you?" William's voice was still soft.

"Not always." Susan's dimple showed.

William sat back and sighed, releasing his tight hold on Susan. "OK, you win. Where did I leave off?"

"You said the contents of the satchel belonged to Rachel. I didn't understand."

"Oh, yes. Well, I'll try to make the story short. Jacob Weinberg, the Jewish man whom Sarah's first husband, Ernst, worked for, paid Ernst and Sarah one hundred thousand marks to take their fourth child at birth and raise it as their own."

"That's strange. Are you saying they just gave their baby away?" Susan asked.

"Susan, remember your history. It was 1938, a critical time for the Jews in Germany. The Weinbergs were desperate." William hesitated a moment and then continued. "Now, Sarah actually wore maternity clothes. She would act as if she were pregnant. When the baby was born to Mrs. Weinberg, the midwife quickly took it to Sarah and Ernst's apartment, and everyone thought Sarah had given birth to the baby. That way it could be registered as pure Aryan, not Jewish."

"What did Mr. and Mrs. Weinberg tell people? How did they account for having no fourth child?"

"They told everyone the baby died."

"Oh, how terrible."

"Yes, but If they had kept the baby, she really would have died. The Weinberg family was taken and put in a concentration camp not long after the baby was born, and they were never heard from again."

"Oh, William, every time I think about what happened back then, I want to cry. How could people be so cruel?"

"Mrs. Davis said it was satanic."

"And she's right. But back to the baby. You said *she*. What did they name her?"

"The Weinbergs had already selected a name. She was named Maria."

"What happened after that?"

"Sarah's husband, Ernst, was killed at Normandy, and she eventually married an American soldier, an army lieutenant stationed in Berlin. They moved back to America a few years later. Since the Weinberg property was behind the Iron Curtain, Mrs. Davis never told Maria about it. Maria and her husband were killed in an automobile accident in 1988, shortly before the wall came down."

"That is so tragic. It must have been a sad time for Mrs. Davis. I guess Rachel inherited everything in her mother's satchel."

"This is the strange part, Susan. Mrs. Davis said Rachel knows about the satchel but not what's in it. She thinks it's some old memorabilia that her grandmother brought back from Germany."

"You said Maria never knew about the property, but she did know she was adopted, didn't she?"

"No. Mrs. Davis never told her."

"Well, surely she told Rachel that her mother was adopted, didn't she?"

"No. Rachel knows absolutely nothing about her mother's adoption, the Weinbergs, or anything. Mrs. Davis said she had her reasons but that Mr. Kroft and I wouldn't understand. I didn't press her."

Susan's brow furrowed. "That's strange. When is she going to tell her?"

"She said she would tell her tomorrow. I surely hope she does because Rachel needs to be involved in everything we are doing. After all, the leather satchel belongs to her."

TWELVE

Rachel stood, waiting for the elevator to take her to the intensive care unit. The call had come just as the children were leaving, shortly after the last bell. Mrs. Smith, at Washington Arms, had called to say that her grandmother, Sarah Davis, had been taken to Arlington Memorial. The medics did not say, but they were treating her grandmother as if she had had a heart attack.

Rachel kept her cell off during school hours. Mrs. Smith apologized and said there was so much confusion that finding the number to her principal's office was delayed. Rachel was wondering why elevators were so slow, as the door finally opened and she quickly entered the empty elevator and pressed the button to the third floor.

Mrs. Smith assured her that Dr. David Bradford had been called but Sarah would be treated by doctors in the emergency room. Dr. Bradford would come immediately after his last patient. Rachel stepped out on the third floor and hoped the nurses in charge would let her see her grandmother. She wasn't sure about visiting hours. They were usually strict in the ICU.

Rachel eased the door open and stepped inside the large, quiet, intensive care unit. She stood a moment looking around the room, her eyes finally settling on the nurse's station. The nurses were busy at their computers and were not aware that she had come in. Rachel walked anxiously to the station and to the nearest nurse who looked up with a slight frown. She said, "I'm sorry but you'll have to wait outside. You cannot visit now."

Rachel said, "I know, but my grandmother was admitted a short time ago and I just received word that she may have had a heart attack. I'm Rachel Lewis, her only living relative, and I cannot wait any longer to see her. Please tell me how she is."

"Ms. Lewis, we cannot give out patient information. You will have to get that from her doctor. What is your grandmother's name?'

"Sarah Davis. Dr. Bradford is her doctor."

The nurse scrolled on her computer and looked at the information, then up at Rachel. "Dr. Bradford's nurse called and said he will be here shortly. I suggest you wait for him. He'll tell you the condition of your grandmother."

"May I see her for one minute? I promise I will stay no longer than one minute."

The nurse dropped her eyes a moment then looked back up at Rachel and said, "I'm really not supposed to do this, but if you will stay no longer than one minute, I'll allow it this time. Next time you must follow our schedule. Your grandmother is in room three-fourteen."

"Thank you so much," Rachel said as she turned and scanned the numbers above the doors and then quickly walked to Sarah's room. She stopped and looked through the window. Sarah had an oxygen tube in her nose and IVs attached to her arm. Her eyes were closed. Rachel opened the door, walked slowly to her bed, and stood looking at her grandmother and thinking about the telephone call the previous night.

Sarah had called and asked that she come after school the next day. Rachel could always tell when there was a problem. Her grandmother had a hard time keeping the anxiety out of her voice. But she would not give even a hint as to what the problem was. Rachel touched her grandmother's wrinkled hand. There was a coolness to it. Tears formed in Rachel's eyes, and she reached over to the table next to Sarah's bed, pulled out a tissue, and wiped her eyes.

Rachel stood a moment longer and then glanced out the front window. The nurse was watching her. It was time to go, as she was sure her minute was up. She would wait in the small waiting room outside the ICU until Dr. Bradford came. He would tell her what to expect. Rachel gave another gentle touch to her grandmother's hand and then turned and left.

After waiting almost thirty minutes, Rachel pulled out her cell, scrolled to her friend's number, and lightly tapped the surface. She needed to make sure Sarah Beth could stay until Dr. Bradford came and they had a chance to talk. Martha's cell was busy. Well, she would try again in a few minutes. The girls were probably playing and having a good time. What would she do without Martha? Rachel put her cell back in her purse and looked up to see Dr. Bradford coming down the hall. She quickly stood.

Dr. Bradford nodded and offered his hand to Rachel. "It's good to see you, Rachel, though not under these circumstances. I'm so sorry about your grandmother."

"Sir, could you tell me how she is? Did she have a heart attack?"

"Yes, that's what Dr. Jones, the emergency doctor, said."

"How bad was it?" Rachel anxiously asked.

David nodded toward the two chairs and said, "Let's not stand. I think it might be best if we sit and discuss this."

Rachel sat rigidly in the chair, holding tightly to her purse in her lap, trying to keep her hands from trembling.

Dr. Bradford's voice was calm. "Rachel, I'll be completely truthful. It was bad. Your grandmother had a severe myocardial infarction. Now let me explain. The main artery in the front of her heart is occluded, causing severe damage to a large portion of her heart. The pumping capacity in her heart has decreased significantly."

"Will she live, Dr. Bradford?"

"Her prognosis is very poor, especially in view of her age."

Rachel slumped back, silent.

Dr. Bradford patted her arm. "Rachel, I wish I could be more optimistic, but you need to know the truth."

"Yes, Dr. Bradford, I appreciate that. I didn't know grandmother was having problems with her heart. She rarely complained."

"Yes, well, I discovered a problem and prescribed medication when I last examined her. I believe it was shortly before Christmas."

"She never mentioned it to me. Her mind has been slipping a little lately, and I wouldn't be surprised if she neglected to take her medicine on a daily basis. She was asleep when I saw her less than an hour ago. Will she wake up enough for me to speak to her?"

"I think she will. You might have to stay close by. I'll leave orders that you may see her whenever she awakens.'

"Thank you, sir."

Rachel glanced at her watch and sighed. She had waited an hour with no word from the nurse. Thank goodness Martha had called and reported on the girls. She insisted that Sarah Beth spend the night with Mary Elise. Rachel had consented, knowing that she might have a long wait at the hospital.

She stood up and wiggled her shoulders. She didn't realize how taut she had been. Anxiety caused that, and she could not help worrying about her grandmother and also the future. Her grandmother and Sarah Beth were all she had. Her late husband, Jonathan, had been an only child like herself. His mother was deceased, and his father had remarried and was involved with his second wife and her family. She rarely heard from him.

Rachel looked at her watch again and wondered if she had time to slip down to the cafeteria and get a cup of coffee. Maybe she should notify the nurse as to where she was going. Rachel stood debating when the ICU door opened and the nurse beckoned. "Mrs. Lewis, your grandmother is awake now."

Rachel nodded and said, "Thank you."

She walked quickly to Sarah's room, eased the door open, and walked in.

Sarah turned her head slightly when she saw Rachel. Tears formed in her eyes, and her lips quivered.

"Grandmother, I'm here now. Please don't cry." Rachel patted Sarah lightly on her arm. She gently brushed back the wisps of hair that had fallen on Sarah's forehead and blotted the tear that ran down her cheek. "There, now. I bet that feels better."

Sarah smiled and gave a faint nod. Her lips quivered, and she whispered something Rachel could not hear. Rachel leaned closer. "That's all right, Grandmother. You don't have to talk. I don't want you to strain yourself."

Sarah barely moved her head from side to side, her eyes focused on Rachel.

Her lips quivered again, and she whispered, "I'm so sorry."

Rachel frowned. "Please, Grandmother, you should not be talking. You need to rest."

Sarah blinked her eyes, gave Rachel another slight shake of her head, and repeated, a little louder, "I'm so sorry."

"Grandmother, there's nothing to be sorry for. You can't help being sick." Rachel picked up Sarah's hand and patted it.

Sarah closed her eyes momentarily and shook her head again.

"It's all right, sweetheart. Everything is going to be fine. You'll see," Rachel said, smiling and continuing to gently pat Sarah's hand.

"Mrs. Lewis." The nurse's voice caught Rachel's attention, and she turned.

"It might be best if you let Mrs. Davis rest. She really doesn't need to be talking."

"Yes, I understand. Thank you for letting me see her." Rachel leaned over, kissed Sarah on her cheek, and whispered, "I'll see you tomorrow."

Sarah's eyes followed Rachel as she left.

THIRTEEN

Sarah's heart had stopped beating shortly before seven o'clock the next morning, and she slipped quietly into heaven. Rachel had been called an hour earlier and was by her grandmother's side when she passed away.

Rachel knew that Sarah had preplanned her funeral and even paid for it. Assisting their residents in that area was one of the services Washington Arms provided. Sarah would be buried before the memorial service that was held at the little chapel in the church Rachel attended. Sarah had become a shut-in the last six months, preferring to watch the Sunday morning services from her television at Washington Arms. She had outlived all of her peers, and other than Rachel's friends and a few residents from Washington Arms, the memorial service was small.

Mr. Kroft and William were among those who attended the Saturday-morning memorial service. It was after the service that they were able to have a few minutes with Rachel.

Mr. Kroft moved his cane to his left hand and extended his right hand to Rachel. "Mrs. Lewis, I'm Leonard Kroft, a friend of your grandmother, and this is William Handel, her attorney." Mr. Kroft motioned to William. William gave a slight nod and offered Rachel his hand.

Rachel looked surprised as she shook their hands. "It's nice to meet both of you, but I'll have to confess that I'm a little surprised. I had no idea that my grandmother had engaged an attorney."

William smiled. "It was the day before she had the heart attack that we met with her. Please let us extend our condolences. I know it must be difficult to give up someone you've loved for such a long time."

"Thank you. Yes, this has been a very difficult time, I guess because everything happened so quickly. I'm still trying to absorb the shock." Rachel looked from Mr. Kroft to William. "Was there something I needed to know, Mr. Handel? You said you met with my grandmother. Did she have a legal problem?"

"I wouldn't put it exactly that way, Mrs. Lewis, and I realize this is not the place to discuss our meeting with your grandmother. Could you possibly meet with us the first part of next week?"

Rachel hesitated, still a little surprised. "Well, yes, I guess I can, but it might have to be after school. I'm a teacher, and I don't get out until three thirty."

"That will be fine," William said, handing Rachel his card. "How soon can you come?"

Rachel thought a minute and then said, "Will it be all right if I come Tuesday after school? There are things I'll need to attend to on Monday."

"Yes, Tuesday will be fine. Mr. Kroft and I will be waiting for you whenever you can get there. And if there is anything that we can do for you in the meantime, I hope you will let us know." William smiled.

"Thank you. You're kind to offer."

William and Mr. Kroft nodded and left, leaving Rachel standing, still slightly confused and wondering how she could pay a lawyer's fee. She turned and walked over to the beautiful flowers on a stand and picked up the card and looked at it, hardly reading the names.

FOURTEEN

Rachel thought back over the weekend. She couldn't focus. She had attended to business on Monday, yet her mind was elsewhere. Why had her grandmother hired a lawyer? What did she have that was so important or valuable that a lawyer was needed? The funeral home would supply Rachel with death certificates for anything deemed necessary. But Rachel couldn't think of a need even for a death certificate, other than the small burial policy that Sarah had owned that would pay for her footstone. The funeral director would even notify the Social Security Administration of Sarah's death. As for Sarah's checking account, Rachel was joint owner to that, and there was only a modest amount of money there.

The light turned red, and Rachel slowed and stopped. She glanced at her watch. It was quarter to four. The young lawyer said he and Mr. Kroft would be waiting for her. What was the young man's name? She had left his card at home. Rachel jogged her memory and finally remembered—William Handel. Mr. Kroft's name was not hard to remember because her grandmother had mentioned him several times. The light turned green, and Rachel pressed the accelerator.

Rachel thought about Washington Arms. She had decided that she would keep a few pieces of furniture that belonged to her grandmother. The rest she would donate to a needy family.

Mrs. Smith said she would take care of that for her. And most of Sarah's clothes were well worn. Those, too, would be sent to a charitable organization. And other than a few pictures and books that Rachel would keep, there was little else to worry with.

Rachel slowed as she approached the law office and turned into the well-landscaped parking area, pleased to find several open spaces. Most of their clients had probably already transacted business and gone home, she thought. The receptionist smiled as Rachel entered the waiting room.

"May I help you?" she said.

"Yes, my name is Rachel Lewis, and I have an appointment with Mr. Handel."

The receptionist scrolled on her computer, typed a few words, and then picked up her phone and pressed a button. She spoke only a few seconds and then hung up and said, "Mr. Handel's waiting for you in the conference room, Mrs. Lewis. I'll show you where it is."

Rachel followed the receptionist down the hall and thanked her as she opened the door and stood aside for Rachel to enter.

William smiled and held out his hand. "Good afternoon, Mrs. Lewis. I hope you did not have a problem finding our office building."

"Oh, no. I was born here in Arlington and am rather familiar with this part of town." Rachel's eyes scanned the elegant room. "I must say, you have a beautiful building, inside and out."

"Thank you." William motioned toward Mr. Kroft, who was seated at the conference table. "Mrs. Lewis, I know you will understand. I've asked Mr. Kroft to stay seated. He's still recovering from his hip surgery."

"Indeed I do." Rachel smiled, walked over to Mr. Kroft, and held out her hand. "How are you feeling, sir?"

"I'm feeling stronger each day, thank you. And it's good to be able to use a cane. I love my walker, but it can become cumbersome when I go out."

Rachel nodded. "Yes, my grandmother often said the same thing."

William cleared his throat. Mrs. Lewis, I know you have wondered what this meeting is all about."

"Yes, Mr. Handel, to be perfectly honest, I have. I wonder, though, would you mind addressing me as Rachel? I hear Mrs. Lewis all day long at school. You can imagine, with twenty-five children, it gets rather old." Rachel smiled.

"Certainly. We'll be glad to," William said, pulling out a chair. "And most everyone calls me William. I think being on a first-name basis sometimes makes communication easier—more relaxed." William patted the top of the chair.

"Rachel, I want you to sit here on my left. I'll sit at the head. With Mr. Kroft on my right, you won't have to strain your neck looking from one of us to the other."

William helped Rachel and then sat down and glanced to Mr. Kroft and then to the leather satchel on the table. He turned to her and said, "Rachel, are you familiar with this satchel? It belonged to your grandmother."

Rachel looked surprised; then her facial expression relaxed, and she smiled.

"Yes, but only vaguely. Grandmother told me about it and where she kept it years ago. She said it contained some old papers and things she brought back from Germany. I figured it was memorabilia, you know, things she didn't want to part with." Rachel thought a moment. "I was a junior in college when she told me about the satchel. I don't speak German, so I quickly forgot about it."

"Well, this satchel is what our meeting is about. The documents inside are all written in German, but I have translated some of them for you. I think it's time you read them," William said, opening the satchel and removing its contents.

William set aside the satchel and the black lacquered box and then picked up a folder. He placed the folder in front of Rachel, his hand on top of it. "Rachel, these papers are personal, and if you would rather read them in private, Mr. Kroft and I will certainly understand." William sat still, waiting for Rachel's reply.

Rachel looked at the folder questioningly and then at William. "I don't know what to say, William. This has certainly taken me by surprise. But, no, I don't mind you staying here; in fact, you might be able to answer some questions." Rachel's eyes again dropped to the folder.

William nodded. "In that case, I think I'll pour us a cup of coffee. Mr. Kroft, would you like one?"

"Yes, that sounds good. And if you can remember, I use only cream."

"I remember," William said, standing. "Rachel, would you like coffee?"

Rachel looked up. "Thank you, William, but I think I'll pass."

Rachel stared at the folder a moment longer and then slowly opened it. She picked up the top two papers that had been clipped together and then removed the paper clip and held them side by side. There was the old, faded paper with the typed version of her mother's birth and a freshly typed English version.

Rachel laid the German paper down, sat back, and began to read the one William had translated. After reading a few moments, she sat forward and looked up, her brow slightly furrowed. "William, who are the Weinbergs?"

William sat his cup down before he answered. "Your grandmother said Mr. Weinberg was the owner of a large department store where her first husband worked. Mr. Weinberg and his family were Jewish."

"Oh," Rachel said, as she looked at the paper and continued to read.

William took another sip of his coffee and glanced at Mr. Kroft. Mr. Kroft closed his eyes momentarily. The slight side-to-side movement of his head was barely noticeable.

William and Mr. Kroft watched the color drain from Rachel's face as she continued to read and the truth of the message registered. Her hands slowly fell to the table, releasing the paper, and she sat back in the chair, staring at nothing.

There was complete silence. William and Mr. Kroft waited for Rachel to speak, but Rachel continued to stare into space. Then her eyes began to glisten, and a tear escaped and trickled down the side of her face.

William reached over to pat her arm as she dropped her head into her hands and began to sob.

William dropped his car keys in the small pewter bowl, shed his jacket, and loosened his tie and his top collar button. He then collapsed on the sofa and picked up the remote control to the large sixty-inch television.

"Honey, I'm home," he said, loud enough for Susan to hear if she were downstairs.

"Yes, I heard you come in," Susan said, coming into their large keeping room and leaning over to plant a kiss on William.

"Now, that's the way to greet your husband," William said with a smile, as he pulled Susan onto the sofa close to him and gave her a long kiss.

"How was your day?" Susan said, reaching for a tissue and wiping the lipstick from William's lips.

"Emotionally draining."

"I figured that. How long did you spend with Rachel?"

"Almost two hours."

"William, what did she do when she read the papers you translated?"

"She went into shock and then cried. Mr. Kroft and I felt so sorry for her."

"I can imagine. Did she say anything about her mother's adoption and the fact that her mother was Jewish?"

"She couldn't understand why her grandmother kept it a secret for so long and asked us if she had told us why. I told her Sarah's reason was that she didn't want Maria to know how her parents died. Other than that, she said we would not understand.

My guess is that Sarah loved Maria so much that she really wanted her to be her birth-child, but I didn't tell Rachel that. After Rachel settled down, she was intrigued by the pictures of the Weinberg family and agreed that her mother looked just like Mrs. Weinberg."

"I wish I could see the pictures. William, does Rachel also look like Mrs. Weinberg?"

"She does resemble her some, but not as much as Maria does. Rachel is a very pretty young woman. I think I told you that she is thirty-five. She has that same thick, slightly curly, brown hair and the big brown eyes that Maria and Mrs. Weinberg had. Mrs. Davis said Mrs. Weinberg and Maria were both petite. Rachel is a little taller but slender and has a beautiful light-olive complexion. I would describe her as a 'head turner.'"

"Hmmm. I can't wait to meet her. But what did she say about the jewelry?"

"She almost went into shock again. Mr. Kroft explained that her grandmother had given the satchel to him on Wednesday, shortly after lunch, when she started having chest pains, and after the ambulance left, he called me to come get the satchel and lock it up. I told Rachel that Mrs. Davis had, on the day before, entrusted several documents to me, and they were also locked up in my safe."

"Do you think Rachel wants me to catalog the jewelry?"

"I mentioned that to her, and she thought it was a good idea. She wanted me to keep it in our safe for the time being and then probably have it appraised. Susan, Rachel was so overwhelmed that she could hardly make a decision."

"I can imagine. But you haven't told me what she said about the property in Germany."

"Now, that took some explaining. I let Mr. Kroft tell her about the situation there. He also told her about Paul Abraham and the East German Economic Development organization he heads. Susan, I told Rachel there was no way she could reclaim that property without a trip to Germany. She asked if you and I could possibly go with her."

"Well, what did you tell her?"

William grinned. "I told her I would have to ask my wife."

Susan chuckled. "Surely you didn't tell her that."

"No, I'm just kidding. But a question for you. How would you like a trip back to Berlin?"

"I'd love it."

"OK, but in the meantime, could I please have some dinner? I'm as hungry as a bear."

FIFTEEN

William read the fax again and then looked at his watch. It was almost nine o'clock. Mr. Kroft should be back in his room after having breakfast. He punched in several numbers, put it on speaker, and sat back against his chair, his eyes focused on the fax he was holding. There were three rings before Mr. Kroft answered.

"Hello? William, is that you calling?"

"Yes, Mr. Kroft. Don't you love caller-ID?"

"It is convenient, to say the least. But I know you didn't call to talk about caller-ID." Mr. Kroft gave a soft chuckle.

"No, sir. I didn't. I'm calling to tell you that I just got a fax from Paul and wanted to read it to you."

"He must be back in Berlin"

"Yes, he got back yesterday."

"I've been anxious to hear from him. What did he say?"

"He starts off, 'William:

It was good talking to you and Leonard and learning that he is healing well and is content in Washington Arms. But I hope that Leonard is not so content that he would consider becoming a permanent resident of the United States. Now, that would be a great loss for all of his friends here in Germany.'"

William paused, and Mr. Kroft chuckled again. "William, it sounds like Paul is more concerned about my situation here in assisted living than the deeds you faxed him."

William laughed. "I'm not sure about that, Mr. Kroft. Maybe that was just a little warning. I don't think he wants you to entertain any thoughts of staying here in America. He does acknowledge the deeds. I'll read on.

'I did receive the copies of the deeds that you faxed and must say I've rarely seen any that old. I am fascinated by them. In fact, everyone in my office is fascinated by them. But I must be honest and tell you that doing the research on documents that old will take considerable time. I know you understand.'"

"Well, it looks like we'll have a little wait on the deeds. What about the jewelry? You said Susan cataloged it. Has it been appraised yet?"

"I'm glad you asked. After a little research, I suggested to Rachel that we take it to Wattenberg Jeweler's for appraisal. We did that two days ago after Rachel got off from school. Mr. Kroft, I wish you had been with us. We created quite a stir. Mr. Wattenberg said he had never seen jewelry any prettier than Rachel's."

"Yes, I can imagine. Did he ask her for any history?"

"Yes, and I had cautioned her that she might be asked that question. All Rachel told him was that it had been in her family for a very long time."

"Did he say how long the appraisal would take?"

"He said, with that many pieces, it might take as long as two weeks. He asked Rachel if she wanted to sell any of it, and she said she was thinking about selling two or three pieces."

"William, I imagine she has a limited income. A teacher's salary is modest, or so I've been told. And didn't Mrs. Davis say that Rachel's husband had served in the National Guard before being sent to Iraq? I don't imagine Rachel has a great income from that source. Now, with the trip to Germany coming up, she could certainly use extra money. Yes, I think it would be wise to convert a few pieces of that jewelry to cash."

"I agree with you, Mr. Kroft. And how much jewelry can a person wear, anyhow?"

Mr. Kroft cleared his throat. "Well, William, we had better not tread there. You know how women are when it comes to things like that."

"Thanks for the reminder, sir. But changing the subject. How are things at Washington Arms? Do you have everything you need?"

"Everything's fine, William. This place is feeling more and more like home. And having Della and Emma to keep me company makes the days pass quickly. Yes, I can honestly say that I'm quite content."

"Well, don't tell Paul that. He might make a trip over here just to take you back." William's chuckle was light.

"Oh my! Good-bye, William. We'll talk again soon."

"Good-bye, Sir."

SIXTEEN

Rachel sat at the intersection, behind four cars, waiting for the light to change. Her head was still in the clouds. She had received a message from Mr. Wattenberg, and she had called him during her lunch period. The appraisal was complete, and she was shocked at how wealthy she had become—almost overnight. But she would have to sell a few pieces of her jewelry for the trip to Germany. She had spent so little time with the jewelry—how could she make a decision about which to sell? Rachel sighed.

And then William had also called and wanted her to come to his office as soon as school was out. Rachel looked up to see the car ahead move forward, and she pressed the pedal, moving in tandem with it.

These past two weeks had flown by. Maybe it was because she had so much to accomplish. William and Susan had helped her with a to-do list. First on the list were passports for her and Sarah Beth that she had to apply for. Then there was her wardrobe. William told her what to expect with Berlin weather. She had not bought any new clothes in quite a while so she had spent all last Saturday shopping. And in between, she had attended to a few last details pertaining to her grandmother's death.

Rachel's heart seemed to take an extra beat just thinking about what William may have found out. He said the property search would take time and for her to be patient. Be patient? Rachel had learned patience a long time ago. The Lord had taught her that.

She slowed and turned into the law office's parking lot, again admiring the landscaping. Arlington was beautiful in the springtime, and the law office had its share of beauty. Their beds were bright with mounds of flowers, clusters of alternating colors that complimented one another. Rachel felt a longing to be at home digging and planting in her own flower beds. But that might have to be put on the back burner until she had crossed off everything on her list.

Rachel turned off the engine, unhooked her seatbelt, and looked at her watch. It was ten minutes until four. She had come as fast as she could. She got out and pressed her remote to lock the doors and then quickly walked toward the building.

The receptionist smiled as she stepped inside. "Mrs. Lewis, just go on back. Mr. Handel is waiting for you in his office."

"Thank you," Rachel said, returning her smile.

Rachel walked quickly down the hall and into the secretary's office. Mrs. Noel smiled, pressed a buzzer, and motioned with her hand. "Just go on in, Rachel. William and Mr. Kroft are waiting for you."

Rachel opened the door, and William immediately got up from his desk and strode forward to meet her. "Thanks for coming on such short notice, Rachel. Mr. Kroft and I were just sitting here mulling over the information that Paul sent us."

Rachel nodded. "When I read your message, I felt like this was important, so I made arrangements to come as quickly as I could."

She then turned to Mr. Kroft and motioned for him to stay seated. "Good afternoon, sir. It's good to see you again."

"Thank you, Rachel. I'm always glad to be included in your meetings. It's a real pleasure to be with you."

Rachel smiled as she sat down in the empty chair next to Mr. Kroft and then turned again to William. "I also received a message from Mr. Wattenberg saying that the jewelry has been appraised and he has a buyer for any piece I want to sell."

"Well, that's good news. And especially that you have a buyer. But Rachel, don't be pressured into making a decision overnight. Just take your time. But you must rent a lockbox at your bank, at least for the time being. You can't keep that valuable jewelry in your house. Did Mr. Wattenberg give you any figures?"

"Yes, and I'm overwhelmed. He said he gave it an overall appraisal of close to half million dollars."

"That is wonderful, but I'm not one bit surprised. I suspected it to be that much. Didn't you, Mr. Kroft?"

"Well, William, I'm no authority on jewelry, but the appraisal doesn't surprise me. Rachel, you have some beautiful pieces of jewelry. I imagine the Weinbergs were very wealthy and could afford the best. And, too, they were in the retail business and could buy jewelry wholesale."

Rachel nodded. "Yes, I'm sure that was an important factor."

"William, Mr. Wattenberg wants to go over each piece with me and tell me how many carats are involved and the quality of the stones and so forth. I'll be prepared to spend at least an hour with him, maybe two. I wonder if Susan would like to go with me tomorrow after I get out of school."

"I'm sure she will. She can help you decide which pieces to sell. But now, about your property in East Berlin. I got a fax from Paul Abraham this morning." William paused a moment, as he picked up the fax. "Paul says the good news is that he finally discovered where your property is located." William hesitated and then locked eyes with Rachel. "But the bad news is that it has just been built on. Rachel, there is a multimillion-dollar—almost a billion-dollar—complex sitting on your property."

Rachel's mouth dropped in shock, and then disappointment clouded her face and she slumped back against the chair and stared at William. She finally spoke.

"But William, how did they get a clean title?"

"That's what I called Paul to find out."

SEVENTEEN

William put the fax aside and picked up another paper. "I jotted down some facts that Paul gave me over the phone. He's going to send me a full report in a few days. He said he's still investigating the matter."

Rachel shook her head. "I don't know what to say. I know nothing about real estate and certainly nothing about property laws in Germany. William, I'm depending completely on you and Mr. Kroft."

"And that's exactly what you're supposed to do, Rachel. But I think we need to wait and see what else Paul comes up with. We won't be hasty. There's absolutely nothing we can do about the complex. It's sitting there on your property, and it's certainly not going anywhere."

Rachel gave a rueful smile. "I guess that is the one thing we can be sure of."

"Yes, and now that we're over the shock, let me tell you a little bit about the situation." William looked at his notes.

"Paul did research and discovered that the Konrad Neumann Development Company owns the deeds to the land but not the complex. Paul is not sure, but he thinks that Neumann may have partnered with the group that built the complex."

"The group who built the complex is made up of four investors and they have formed a limited partnership. The person in charge is a forty-year-old man named Luke Hartmann."

"Is he a German? The name sounds German." Rachel glanced from Mr. Kroft to William.

"Paul didn't say what his nationality is, but he did find out a little of his background." William glanced again at his notes. "Hartmann grew up in Oxford, England, and graduated from Oxford University, afterward earning an MBA there. Then he came to the States and got a doctorate in business economics from Harvard. He worked four years for UBS Financial Services here in the States and then asked for a transfer to Germany. After a year in Germany, he left UBS and started his own investment company. He's been dealing in commodities for the last nine or ten years and has made a fortune. He speaks five languages fluently and two more partly."

Rachel raised her eyebrows. "He sounds smart. I thought taking three years of French was an accomplishment. I'm already intimidated."

"Yes, he sounds very smart. I just hope he is the type of person we can deal with—you know, someone amiable."

Rachel nodded. "William, did Mr. Abraham say where he lives now? And if he has family?"

"I asked him that. He said he's living in Berlin and is divorced with no children. Paul said rumor was that he was not married long. He did not know any details—only that the girl was Canadian. Paul was told that both of his parents are living and they reside in London. It seems, Rachel, that the whole family is smart. Paul said both parents taught at Oxford University. They are now retired."

"That's interesting." Rachel thought a moment and then asked, "Did Mr. Abraham say whether Mr. Hartmann has been made aware of the situation? I'm talking about the fact that he has built on my property."

"Paul said he has not approached him yet. He has only uncovered this information in the last few days and wants to do a little more research to find out what the connection is between the Neumann Development Company and Hartmann's group. He wants to be sure of all his facts before he meets with Hartmann. And he also wants to tour the building first."

"Is he going to wait until we come over?"

"I'm not sure. He asked me when exactly we are coming. You did say you will be out of school in three weeks, didn't you?"

"Yes. And I'm free to go any time after that."

EIGHTEEN

"I'm home, honey," William called out as he dropped his keys in the small pewter bowl. He quickly removed his sports jacket and laid it across the back of the chair and then loosened his collar and tie and relaxed on the sofa.

"What's this?" he said, reaching for the delicious-looking drink Susan was offering on a tray.

"It's Aunt Della's non-alcoholic cocktail."

William raised it to his nose and took a sniff and then gave Susan a questionable look.

"Go ahead and taste it, William. I think you'll like it."

William took a little sip and rolled his eyes.

"It's really good for you, honey. It destroys the free radicals in your system."

"Are you sure that's all it destroys?" William took another sip and swallowed hard.

"It might take a little getting used to, but once you do, you'll find yourself looking forward to this cocktail." Susan gave William a big smile.

"What does Aunt Della call this? Does it have a name?" William took another sip and grimaced.

"Now that you mention it, she did name it. She calls it 'the Answer.'"

"The Answer? That's a stupid name. Why does she call it that?" William was frowning.

"I asked the same question. She said this drink is the answer to good health."

"Oh—well, let's hope it works. But don't get your feelings hurt if I don't look forward to it." William sat the drink on the end table, pulled Susan close to him, and gave her a big kiss. "Now, this is what I look forward to." He kissed her a second time and then leaned back on the sofa and asked, "What's for dinner?"

William relaxed against the back of the sofa, and Susan sat in the chair close by. She said, "Did you notice that I have waited until after you've had dinner before asking about an update on our trip to Germany?"

"Yes, and I'm surprised. I wondered when the subject would come up."

William reached over to the end table for the remote.

"William Handel, please, I've been so patient. I cannot wait another minute."

William laughed. "I love teasing you, and I love to see that dimple showing or either those green eyes flashing."

Susan couldn't help grinning. "OK, you've seen my dimple; now let's get on with an update. Please tell me—what's the latest on our trip?"

"OK, here it is. I booked our plane tickets today. We'll fly out the fifth of June. That will give Rachel a few days after school is out to get packed."

"You did get first-class tickets, didn't you?"

"Of course. Now that I've flown first-class, how can we go back to coach?"

"Did you call Rachel and tell her about the tickets?"

"Yes, and she told me what she received for the pieces of jewelry she sold. I think she was very pleased. Did she call you?"

Susan nodded. "Yes. I don't think she'll have a problem paying for her trip to Germany, do you?"

"Not with fifty thousand dollars, she won't."

Susan hesitated a moment and then said, "William, I have a secret to tell you. Can you keep a secret?"

"What kind of a question is that? Of course I can keep a secret. I didn't tell anyone about the journal, did I? Susan! Don't you realize? That's what lawyers do. They keep secrets."

"OK, honey, I believe you, and now I see why you are such a good defense lawyer. You put heart in your argument." Susan's eyes were twinkling.

William chuckled. "Let's not get sidetracked, Susan. What's this big secret you've been holding in?"

"Well..." Susan took a big breath and with a show of drama, said. "I'm the one who bought the pieces of jewelry Rachel sold. Mr. Wattenberg and I had a confidential agreement."

William looked surprised. "Why would you do that, honey? Weren't you complaining about all the Haydn jewelry you had locked up? Why buy more...and especially Rachel's?"

"It's a girl thing, William. I don't expect you to understand. If you could have been with us when Rachel was trying to decide which pieces to sell, you might understand. I could tell by the way she handled it, and the way she kept changing her mind that she did not want to sell one piece of it."

"Surely you're not planning to wear it in front of her. That would be unkind."

"No, William, I would never do that. I'm keeping it safe for her. I plan to let her buy it back when she gets her inheritance. It'll be a wonderful surprise for her."

"You women are something. I never would have thought of doing that."

"You probably would have had it been me."

William reached over, caught Susan's arm, and pulled her onto the sofa. "You're right, sweetheart. I would do anything for you because I love you so much." William kissed Susan on the side of her neck.

Susan pulled back slightly and said, "I love you too, William, but I haven't finished asking about our trip. Has Mr. Kroft decided to go with us?"

"He said he has struggled with the decision but his better judgment tells him to forgo this trip." William pulled Susan close again.

Susan could feel William's warm breath next to her cheek. "What did the orthopedic surgeon and David tell him?"

"They both said it was up to Mr. Kroft. Dr. Smith said his hip has healed well but, at his age, he shouldn't put a lot of stress on it so soon after surgery."

"I'm sure Dr. Smith knows best, but I bet Mr. Abraham will be disappointed. You haven't told him, have you?"

"No, because I wasn't sure whether Mr. Kroft would go or not." William kissed the side of Susan's cheek.

"Have you found out any more about the situation with Rachel's property?"

"Hmm. No, not really. I think Paul is supposed to have a meeting with Luke Hartmann sometime next week, but he was not sure of the exact day. I'll hear from him when he does." William drew up Susan's hand and kissed it.

"I almost forgot to ask. Have you booked hotel rooms for us?"

"Yes, I have a suite of three rooms: two bedrooms with two baths and a lovely sitting room in between. You said it would be nice if we had a suite of rooms in case you have to keep Sarah Beth for Rachel. And it's in the Mitte district."

"That sounds perfect."

"Now, what is my reward for tending to all of this?"

"What would you like?"

William's eyes twinkled. "Surely I don't have to tell you!"

Susan's brow furrowed for only a moment, and she said, "Oh, William!" trying but failing to hide her dimple.

NINETEEN

William patiently listened as Susan told him what the repairman said about their underground watering system. It was when his secretary, Mary, tapped on his door and stuck her head in and said, "William, Mr. Abraham is on line one," that he told Susan he had an important call to take and he would get back to her later.

William turned his recorder on and reached for his notepad and pen before switching lines.

"Paul? It's William. I've been eager for your call and to hear what you found out."

"Good talking to you, William. Well, I hardly know where to start except to say that these last few days have been busy and, fortunately, productive ones. I did get to see the complex. And by the way, it has a name: Hartmann Plaza."

"Well, that rolls off the tongue nicely. Hartmann must have the controlling interest to have it named for him."

"Yes, that's what I've been told. I think you'll be impressed by the variety of businesses and the upscale apartments housed within the complex. It really is a beautiful place. Of course, I didn't see all of it—just a part. Luke Hartmann has half a floor dedicated to his investment firm. There is a bank on the first floor and also a five-star French restaurant—even an Olympic-sized swimming pool. The complex covers half a city block. It's very large."

"It does sound impressive. I can't wait to see it. Did you meet Hartmann?"

"Yes. I had an afternoon appointment. I spent a couple of hours looking around the building, had lunch in one of their delis, and then met with Hartmann at two o'clock. William, you are going to be surprised when I tell you that Hartmann has leased the land owned by the Neumann Development Company and there is absolutely no connection between Hartmann's group and Neumann's company. This was strictly a business arrangement."

"They leased it? Why would they do that, Paul?"

"I don't know, but Hartmann says they have a fifty-year lease. With him being forty years old, I guess the lease will outlive him." Paul suppressed a chuckle.

"And something else, William: the lease seems to be clean, not like some of the other property that Wolfgang Mueller tampered with. By the way, the latest news on Wolfgang is that he has declared bankruptcy because of all of the suits brought against him since the indictment."

"Yes, I've been keeping up with that situation. But tell me something about Hartmann. How did you size him up? What does he look like?"

"Well, he looks to be a bit over six feet and in great physical condition, and he has light brown, wavy hair—no gray whatsoever—and the most penetrating green eyes you've ever seen. I felt like I was under an X-ray machine."

"That bad, huh?"

"Well, let's put it this way. He is not one to manipulate. You can tell he is shrewd; maybe I should rephrase that and say he is as smart as they come.

Another thing. I found out that he is quite wealthy—possibly two billion or more."

"I guess he made it in commodity trading. You know, in that business, it doesn't take long to go broke or get rich. And it's obvious that he knows what he's doing."

"Yes, I think we can assume that."

"How did you break the news to him? I'm talking about Rachel."

"I told him that I was representing an American widow who was heir to the property he had built on. I showed him the copies of the old deeds and the paper trail that led us to his property. You could tell that he was surprised, but his reaction was very calm. He hardly blinked his eyes. He, obviously, has great self-control.

"He sat silent a few moments, and then he told me about their lease with the Neumann Development Company. He said that, with all of the Jewish lawsuits abounding, he demanded proof that the titles were clean and was satisfied with what they produced. But then he added that he had even researched the deeds himself. I think that tells you something about the man. His final analysis was that the matter was between the American woman and Neumann and that he wouldn't be surprised if the woman turned out to be an imposter.

"I didn't comment on that but changed the subject and asked him if he would mind showing me his lease. He said I would have to speak to his lawyer—that all business transactions were confidential."

"Well, Paul, it looks like we'll be dealing with two companies rather than one."

"Yes, this situation is getting a little complicated."

"When are you going to approach Neumann?"

"I'm not sure. I'd like to know more about him and if there are any other owners involved. I'm going to do a little more research, find out if he is the one in charge and make an appointment. I'll keep you informed."

"Good, I'll be eager to hear from you. But before you hang up, I want to tell you that I've asked Greta Wineman to help us. We need a German law firm involved, and Greta readily agreed. She said she would file any papers with the court that we wanted her to. I'll call her after talking with you and tell her to go ahead and file. Oh, another thing, Paul. Greta also said our suit will probably be treated as a hearing, somewhat like Susan's. We'll not have a jury involved, only a judge and expert witnesses. She said that, with the brevity of a hearing, we shouldn't have to wait long to be put on the docket."

"William, I wish you had some DNA to tie Rachel to the Weinbergs."

"That would be the icing on the cake, but as you well know, Hitler didn't give Holocaust victims private burials in beautiful caskets encased in vaults." William paused a moment, but Paul was silent. He then continued. "Yet, on the other hand, I think you'll be pleased with our proof."

"I'm sorry, William. You lost me when you said the words *Hitler* and *Holocaust*. I guess I'll never get over the six million innocent people who lost their lives simply because they were Jews."

"Yes, Paul, I agree. It was a terrible time for Germany—a part of history, I'm sure, they would love to delete, but it doesn't work that way, does it? Let's hope we learned something from it." William paused. "Look, I've said enough, and I know you need to get on with your work, so I'll just..."

"Wait, William, before you hang up, tell me about Leonard. Is he coming with you?"

"No, he decided that the trip might be too stressful with his hip just healed. I don't think his doctors encouraged a long flight this early. Mr. Kroft said he hoped you would understand."

Paul was quiet. William could hear him sigh.

"I'd be lying if I said I was not disappointed, but I certainly don't want him to go against his doctor's advice. Maybe he can come a little later."

"I'm sure he will, Paul. He really wants to see you."

PART TWO

TWENTY

Luke Hartmann got up from his desk, walked to one of the large windows in his spacious, lavishly furnished office, and looked out onto the street below. There was a steady stream of traffic, but he was not aware of it. His mind was elsewhere.

Though the elderly Jewish man's visit had been unnerving, Luke had stayed cool. He had not shown any emotion. That was the only way he could keep control of any situation and he learned that early in life. His parents were strict disciplinarians and had taught him the value of self-control. They said the one who had self-control always had the edge.

Luke walked back to his desk and sat down. He glanced at the lease papers in front of him and then opened the file he had created and turned the first few pages, not reading the type. There was absolutely no way the Neumann Development Company had missed anything. He himself had researched everything from before World War II until 2005. The Nazi records were accurate. There were absolutely no surviving members of the Weinberg family. And the Russian records and the East German records were also accurate. There was not one single thing to indicate that the deed had ever been tampered with. Surely this woman in America was not an heir, and especially not a blood granddaughter.

Luke sat back, rested his elbows on the arms of his chair, and made a steeple with his fingers. He wondered what he would tell his partners. They had trusted him with the lease. Actually, he had not trusted any one of them to ferret out the truth. There had been too many suits, brought by Jewish heirs of the Holocaust victims, attempting to regain what had been stolen from their parents and grandparents. It was easy to overlook something. Just one little detail could ruin the whole picture. And, when it came right down to it, he had to admit that he had entertained doubts about Neumann's deed. Thus, his own investigation.

The buildings on the property had little value. The damage done to them during World War II had received the least possible repair. The Russians were not known for restoring old property they had controlled at that time. Razing the buildings had been costly, but that had been one of the stipulations in the lease. His group had also trusted him with that project.

Luke sat forward. He reached over and picked up Paul Abraham's card, fingering it. He read the name again and the initials: EGED. Paul Abraham had been appointed chairman of the East German Economic Development organization. Frank Rhueman had stepped down when he and Wolfgang Mueller had been indicted for falsifying hundreds of East German land records.

Luke sat back again and thought about the next step he would take. He had no choice. He would call Jeffrey Alston and Timothy Abbott in London, but he would wait to tell Andre Broussard this evening. He would tell all three members the truth: that they were possibly going to be embroiled in a lawsuit.

Truthfulness was another attribute that his parents emphasized. From an early age, he was taught to always be truthful. Truthfulness was the better part of integrity. And his integrity was intact. He was forty years old, and at forty years, one did not change.

TWENTY-ONE

William checked twice to make sure Susan, Rachel, and Sarah Beth had their carry-ons before leading them onto the jet bridge and out into the terminal. There were a few English signs marking the way to baggage, and William smiled when he saw Susan and Rachel giving each other confused looks as they passed numerous other signs written in German. Susan had learned very few German words during the months she spent in Berlin, as all of her German friends spoke English.

"Just follow me," William said, smiling and slowing his pace to be sure little Sarah Beth could keep up. "We'll get our baggage and then work through customs and find a taxi. Rachel, how are you and Sarah Beth holding up?"

"We're fine, William. As long as we have you and Susan, I feel secure, but please don't leave us by ourselves. I know absolutely no German."

Susan turned to Rachel. "I wonder why your grandmother never taught you any German words. You said you took French in school. I'm surprised that your grandmother or your mother didn't influence you to learn German."

"I've often wondered the same thing. Mother said she took to English quite easily but Grandmother struggled. Once they learned English, German was never spoken again. At least, not around me. I never remember Mother or Grandmother speaking

German. French was the popular language at my high school. All of my friends took either French or Spanish. I don't remember a German class being taught."

"I love the French language," Susan said, "and even spent a semester in Paris while in college. It was fun and a challenge communicating with so many French natives. If we're not going to learn German, I guess you and I will have to hone our French while we're here in Germany." Susan paused a moment and looked ahead. "Oh my, I need to stop talking and start concentrating on staying with William, or we'll end up lost." Susan motioned to Rachel, who was holding Sarah Beth's hand, and they picked up their pace.

Maneuvering through the crowd in the terminal was easy for William, and upon getting their luggage and going through customs, they soon found themselves in a taxi and approaching their hotel.

"Well, girls, how do you like our suite of rooms?" William turned and gave the hotel attendant a tip after he removed their luggage from the rolling cart.

"I think you did a great job, William," Rachel said, looking around the spacious sitting room and then walking to the window to look out. "Which bed-room is ours?"

"You have the twin bedroom." William motioned to the open door on the right. "Susan and I will enjoy the king-size bed." William winked at Susan.

Susan grinned. "Ok, lover boy, let's get our bags into our room. You haven't told us what's on our agenda for this evening."

"I have interesting dinner plans, but before we get on that subject, I want to remind you that Rachel and I will spend Monday morning at Greta's law firm with her and Paul."

"Yes, I remembered, and I will keep Sarah Beth. Now, tell us about this evening."

"Paul says there is a fancy restaurant in Hartmann Plaza. Are you and Rachel game for going there?"

"Sounds good to me, William. What about you, Rachel? Are you game?"

"Why not? I really want to see what's sitting on my property."

William paid the taxi driver and helped the girls out of the cab. They stood a moment on the sidewalk, looking at the entrance to Broussard's: Français et Allamand á Manger, a five-star restaurant. Following William, as he opened the door for them, Susan proudly explained that the French words translated to "French and German Dining."

William spoke to the hostess and she scanned her reservation list and motioned for a waiter to seat William and his party. The waiter led them through the north end of the formal dining room and into what looked like a dimly lit, very large stone-walled terrace. The floor was covered with dark bluish-gray slate and the wall between the formal dining room and terrace was primarily glass. Going clockwise, the next wall provided large arched entrances opening to a wide corridor that led to the bar-room, kitchen and restrooms. At the base of the other two stone walls were raised, softly lighted slate beds planted with exotic greenery, some of it climbing on the walls, almost to the balconies above. The balconies off the second-and-third-floor rooms were secured with beautiful, wrought-iron guardrails the color of the floor. William smiled when he glanced up to the third floor and saw the couple standing, looking down onto the terrace.

There was a fountain in the center of the terrace accented by soft lights, and when William and the girls looked up, they saw the sixty-foot ceiling held miniature lights that gave the appearance of stars twinkling in a midnight-navy sky. It was magnificent.

The waiter seated them at a round table for six on the side of the terrace that joined the formal dining room. After handing them their menus, he lit the candle under the glass hurricane globe, righted their goblets, and removed the extra place-sets. The table was covered with a white cloth, each place holding white, matching monogrammed napkins, handsome stainless monogrammed flatware, and stemmed water goblets. Fresh flowers encircled the base of the hurricane globe. The glass wall between the terrace and the formal dining room was separated only by an elongated, lighted, partially sunken pool filled with small exotic goldfish, making visibility between the two rooms easy, especially for those sitting on the terrace.

Sarah Beth said, "Mother, I can't read this menu. What is this writing?"

Susan and Rachel laughed, and Rachel said, "It's French and German, honey. Don't worry about it. I'll help you order."

After several minutes of silently studying the menu, Susan said, "Remember, now, Rachel, I spent a whole semester in Paris while in college. I know what's good."

Rachel put down her menu and said, "I trust you, Susan. You order for me and Sarah Beth. But, I must say, these are some pricey entrées."

William said, "Don't fret, Rachel. I brought my credit card. Hmmm, I've missed my German dishes. I'm ordering German."

Sarah Beth reached over and touched her mother's arm. "Mother, please, may I go look at the fish?"

Rachel smiled and said, "Yes, but don't put your hand in the water."

The waiter returned shortly with a pitcher to fill their water goblets. Susan smiled and commented, "This is a beautiful restaurant, and I see that you have great patronage."

"Yes," the waiter said, speaking fair English and nodding his head. "And we've been open less than a year."

William looked up from his menu. "I see that you have mainly French dishes on your menu along with a few German ones and assume that the owner of this restaurant is French?"

"Yes, sir. Mr. Broussard owns a restaurant in Paris, and he decided to open one here. He has mentioned that several times to some of our patrons."

"I imagine he has his hands full. He must have to fly back and forth a great deal."

"Well, I don't think so. His son runs the one in Paris, and Mr. Broussard would tell you himself that he also has excellent managers."

The waiter glanced through the glass partition and casually said, "Mr. Broussard is sitting in the main dining room at the table with his wife and Mr. Hartmann—the table next to the large potted plant."

William turned slightly and glanced through the glass partition. He recognized Luke Hartmann from Paul's description. Mr. and Mrs. Broussard's faces were more difficult to see.

William nodded and then gave the waiter their order, and the waiter left, promising to bring their iced teas on his return.

William rolled his eyes and reached into his pocket when he felt the vibration of his cell. He had meant to turn the darn thing off. Pulling it out and looking at the caller ID, he smiled. It was Beck.

"How did you know we were in town, Beck?" William grinned, speaking in German. After a pause, William said, "Look, man, I'm going to be tied up the first of the week, but I'll get back to you after that, and we'll play some tennis." Another pause. "Sure, Susan and I want to meet her. And we have a friend with us we want you and Thomas to meet." Another pause. "Forget that, Beck. She's a widow with a little eight-year-old daughter. She's not interested in dating you." William laughed. "Where am I staying? At Hartmann Plaza in the Mitte district." A long pause. "I guess you could say that. Well, don't hold your breath." Another pause. "OK, we'll talk later." William chuckled as he turned his cell off and put it in his pocket.

Susan said, "Well, aren't you going to tell us what Beck said?" She turned to Rachel. "Beck is William's best friend, or one of them. Thomas is the other. They are both bachelors and live here in Berlin."

"Same old Beck, Susan. Still chasing the girls and playing a lot of tennis."

"What were you laughing at?"

"He asked where we are staying, and when I told him Hartmann Plaza, he said he really wants to see us but Hartmann Plaza was too rich and too far away. He would wait until we could meet him at Stout's Sports Bar."

TWENTY-TWO

Sixty-five-year-old Andre Broussard had a habit of clearing his throat when he became nervous, and he cleared his throat three times before his forty-year-old wife, Karla, frowned at him and then dropped her eyes and returned to the menu she was holding.

Luke looked up from his menu and said, "Andre, there is absolutely no use getting upset so early in the game. We haven't even met the woman yet. Making a claim and proving it are two different things. And, keep in mind, we do not own the land—only the lease. Konrad Neumann will have to deal with her first."

Broussard laid his menu down. "When are you calling Jeffrey and Timothy?"

"I've already called them. They'll meet with us this following Monday. That gives them time to fly in."

"Do you have any idea when the hearing will be?"

"Yes, it seems that there were several cases settled out of court, and Neumann's was pushed forward. I think Paul Abraham was influential there. He notified me that it will be the week after next. I think he said on Friday."

"I surely hope your confidence proves true and that our lease stays intact."

Hartmann thought a minute, his eyes sweeping across the dining room and then back to Andre. "Even if by some bizarre circumstance this woman prevails, she'll own nothing but the deeds to the land. And we'll have to negotiate with her for a new lease or purchase the land." Luke shook his head. "But I don't see that happening."

"What do you know about this woman?"

"Very little. Paul Abraham said she is a thirty-five-year-old widow with an eight-year-old daughter. I think she's a schoolteacher. Paul also mentioned the fact that she recently buried her grandmother, who, I think he said, was her only living relative."

"Do you know if she's coming for the hearing?"

"Yes, Abraham said she and her little girl were flying over with her lawyer and his wife. He didn't give me the lawyer's name, but the woman we're dealing with is Rachel Lewis."

Andre Broussard wanted to clear his throat again but decided against it. Instead he smiled and said, "Is everyone ready to order?"

TWENTY-THREE

Greta Wineman was sitting at the long conference table poring over papers. She held a long yellow pencil between her second and third finger, and the pencil's fast up-and-down motion caused a slight tapping noise on the table. At the sound of the knock, she quickly put down the pencil and stood up to see the door open, revealing Paul Abraham with William and Rachel close behind.

Greta smiled and nodded at Paul and then walked forward, taking William's outstretched hand in both of hers. "Welcome back to Berlin, William." She then turned to Rachel and said, "Now I want to meet this pretty young woman from America." Greta offered Rachel her hand, not waiting for an introduction. "Rachel, I'm Greta Wineman, and I've looked forward to meeting you ever since William told me about you and your very interesting case."

Rachel smiled. "I've also looked forward to meeting you, Mrs. Wineman. Both William and Susan have spoken so fondly of you, and I'll say at the outset how much I appreciate your help in taking my lawsuit. William has assured me that I'm in very capable hands."

Greta's eyes twinkled. "I think William might be my best cheerleader. We won't get ahead of ourselves, though. There's still work to be done, and I'm just thankful that you have the evidence William has told me about. William and I both feel like we have a pretty solid case. Now, let's have a seat and get to work. William, I trust you brought all of the Weinberg original papers with you."

"You know I did, Greta. They're here, still in the old seventy-year-old leather satchel that Mr. Weinberg gave Ernst Hoffman back in the early part of 1939." William laid the satchel on the shiny conference table, and there was a moment of silence before Greta spoke.

"You know, I've been thinking. How could a judge resist this evidence?" Greta reached over to the satchel, fingering the straps and rubbing the ancient leather lightly with her hand. "I definitely think we should have an expert witness testify to the age of this satchel. It's in perfect condition, and we shouldn't have any problem proving its age. Yes, I definitely think we should do that."

William nodded and said, "I thought the same thing, Greta, and you'll probably laugh when I tell you that I've gotten attached to this old satchel and wouldn't mind having one just like it. It fits my shoulder just right."

Greta grinned. "Go ahead and open it up, William. If you're lucky, maybe Rachel will give it to you after you win her lawsuit—that is, if you can get it away from Judge Krause. I understand he collects antique satchels."

William stood up, pulled his arms back in a stretch, and said, "I don't know about all of you, but I'm a little stiff. We've been working now for almost two hours. What about a break, Greta? I think we should take a break and drink a cup of that delicious-smelling coffee your secretary just brought in."

"I think that's a great idea, William. Why don't you do the honors? And, Paul, while William does that, why don't you tell us a little about the East German development company and what you found out?"

"I wondered when it would be my turn," Paul said good-naturedly as he opened his small notebook. "At my age, I don't trust my memory, so I've learned to take notes. I've written down the names of the two owners. Of course we know that the name of the company is Neumann Development Company and the manager is Konrad Neumann himself. Neumann has a partner. His name is Karl Kirsten."

"That's interesting. Does Mr. Kirsten work in the company?"

"I asked Mr. Neumann that, and he said no—that Kirsten was more or less a silent partner. He was actively involved in other businesses that he owned until the last few years. He is unable to work now and resides in a nursing home.

"Greta, Neumann didn't give me much time but was willing to show me the papers he transacted with an investment company that had acquired the deeds from the German Trust agency in 1990. A west German investment company by the name of Holderman bought the deeds and rented the property out, thinking they would hold it and make a mint of money. But development was slow in East Berlin, and they decided to sell the land to Neumann in 1996.

"Now, let's fast-forward to 2004. Hartmann approached Neumann with an offer to buy the property, but Neumann was unwilling to sell it. After a few months of negotiating, Neumann agreed to lease it to Hartmann. I tried to find out the terms of the lease but got the same answer from him that I got from Hartmann—'see his lawyer.'"

Paul looked up from his notebook, took a sip of his coffee, and said, "That seems to be the situation, Greta. It looks like we'll have to go after Neumann and void that lease."

"Yes, I agree, Paul. And he's going to fight us with everything he has."

TWENTY-FOUR

The morning of the hearing was rather cool, and Rachel put on her long-sleeved knit dress, which was the rich color of apricots. The neckline had soft folds that accentuated her slender neck, and she wore one of the Weinberg diamond cluster pins at the center where the seams met. The belted dress fit her slender frame perfectly, and the skirt just covered her knees. Her brown pumps were made of Italian leather, and she carried a matching Medici leather handbag. William whistled when she came into the sitting room.

Rachel laughed. "Susan, you had better come get your husband. I'm not sure if he's making fun of me or not."

Susan stepped into the sitting room and exclaimed, "Make fun of you? Rachel, you look beautiful. I'd whistle too, except I never learned how. Where is Sarah Beth?"

"She is standing in front of the mirror, making sure her hair is just right. She said you and she are going out on the town."

"We are," Susan said, checking both earlobes to see if her earrings were secure. "Rachel, I'm sure you remember me telling you about Rolfe, our friend who worked for my grandfather, Mr. Haydn. Well, he is going to take us sightseeing. William arranged this last night. Rolfe knows every place in Berlin that would appeal to a little eight-year-old girl. So don't worry about us. We'll have a great time."

"I'm not worried about you and Sarah Beth, Susan. It's this hearing that I'm worried about. I just hope I won't get too nervous. I'm one woman against—how many men, William?" Rachel gave William a bewildered look.

"Oh, Rachel, there are, altogether, about six men, but don't worry—only two of them will be there. Anyhow, a good-looking woman like you will have the edge with the judge. It usually works that way." William chuckled.

William paid the cab driver and ushered Rachel into the courthouse and down the hall to the courtroom where their hearing would take place. William opened the door for Rachel, and they stepped inside and looked around. Paul Abraham was standing down front talking to Luke Hartmann. Greta was at the plaintiff's table immersed in her notes and talking to the two expert witnesses. William looked at the defendant's table but didn't recognize the two men sitting there. He guided Rachel down the aisle toward Paul and Luke Hartmann.

Paul smiled when he glanced back and saw William and Rachel, and he turned to greet them, speaking in English. "Good morning, Rachel, and to you, William. It's good to see you." Paul turned again to Luke and said, "Mr. Hartmann, I want you to meet friends of mine. This is Rachel Lewis and her attorney, William Handel."

Luke didn't smile but politely nodded his head and, speaking with a slight British accent, said, "It's nice to meet you, Mrs. Lewis, and you, too, Mr. Handel."

Rachel nodded and said, "Yes, it's nice to meet you, Mr. Hartmann."

William put out his hand, smiled, and said, "I've been looking forward to meeting you, Mr. Hartmann, but please call me William. I'm not a very formal person."

Luke couldn't help but smile at the young man's unpretentiousness and friendliness, and he gave William a firm handshake, suspecting that, in spite of the circumstances, he would come to like him. And if somehow the woman won and his intuition was right, Handel might be easy to deal with. Luke's voice softened a bit, and he said, "Yes, William, I'll remember, and I hope your stay in Germany will be a pleasant one."

William said, "Thank you, sir." He and Rachel then turned to talk to Paul while Luke stood silent, glancing again at Rachel and wondering if there was a mistake. She certainly did not look like any of the Jewish people he was acquainted with. Most of the ones he knew had jet-black hair and a dark complexion, whereas Rachel's hair was brown and she had beautiful skin, as if she had just developed an early summer tan to go with her large brown eyes and thick lashes. Her profile featured a straight, very slender nose, and her neck was also slender. In fact, everything about the woman was slender—well, almost everything, Luke thought, as his eyes traveled down her body to her stylish shoes. She was lovely, but she looked ill at ease, and Luke almost felt sorry for her... almost.

He wondered what her true background was. Well, he would find out soon enough. In the meantime, he would keep reminding himself that this woman was an enemy, obviously someone set up to take what did not rightfully belong to her. But weren't most women, to a certain degree, enemies, he thought, as his mind flashed back ten years to Kate, his divorced wife?

There was little doubt: Rachel Lewis had to be an imposter. Luke caught her eye, and with a frown, hardly noticeable, he nodded again and then moved over to the defendant's table.

Rachel turned when she heard Greta call her name. The expert witnesses had moved farther down the table and were looking at their notes, and Greta was motioning for her to come sit next to her.

"I see you met Luke Hartmann." Greta's expression bordered between one of amusement and one of inquisitiveness.

"Yes, and I wouldn't describe him as being friendly." Rachel then quickly added, "Not that I would expect him to be. After all, I am his adversary."

"Why do you say that, Rachel?" Greta put her pen down.

"Maybe it's my perception of what he thinks of me. I got the impression he wants nothing to do with me. I could tell by the way he spoke to us. He certainly gave us a cool reception."

"I really can't see any difference in whether the lease is with Neumann or with you. As long as you are not out to take advantage of Luke Hartmann's limited partnership, I cannot see where it would bother him." Greta glanced over to the table where Luke and the other two men sat.

Rachel opened her purse, took our her cell, put it on mute, and said, "I don't know. There's just something about him. I get some vibes that he does not like women. Paul told William that his marriage was of short duration. Maybe that is his problem—an unhappy marriage."

The door to the judge's chamber opened, capturing Greta's attention, and she made no further comment.

Judge Krause walked out and paused, letting his eyes sweep around the courtroom before coming to rest on Rachel. He looked at her for only a moment, and then he continued on to the bench.

The bailiff asked everyone to rise and then be seated as the judge took his seat.

Judge Krause was slightly over six feet and in his mid-sixties. He still had a head full of dark hair with a touch of gray at the temples, and he wore dark rimmed glasses. Some in the legal profession thought him rather handsome. Greta had never given that much thought. What she had admired about him were his courtroom manner and the impeccable way he handled his cases.

Judge Krause adjusted his glasses and cleared his throat, and when he spoke, his English was flawless, and his voice resonated across the room.

"Let the record show that this is a bench hearing. We will not have a jury. I will render a decision, hopefully today." He looked at the court reporter and then continued. "I expect both parties to be courteous, with no outbursts. I am not hard of hearing, so you can keep your voices moderate. Mrs. Wineman asked that we conduct this hearing in English as the plaintiff does not speak German. The defendant has agreed to this."

Judge Krause looked over to the defendant's table and then continued. "Let the record show that the court has looked at pictures of jewelry with individual appraisals. The court has also read a deposition by Walter Wattenberg, a Registered Jeweler and owner of Wattenberg's Fine Jewelry in Arlington, Virginia in the United States of America. The deposition was taken by William Handel and submitted by Greta Wineman. Mr. Beckle, I see that you did not take a deposition from Mr. Wattenberg. Is that correct?"

"Yes, Your Honor. The defendant accepts the appraisal of the jewelry as truthful."

"Very well." Judge Krause looked back at his paper and said, "Let the record show that the court has read the analysis of the leather satchel, given by Ralfe Coupp, owner of The Leather Company here in Berlin." Judge Krause looked again at the defendant's table and said, "Mr. Beckle, I see no deposition pertaining to the satchel from you. Is that correct?"

"Yes, Your Honor. The defendant accepts the satchel's age as truthful."

"Very well." The judge looked at Greta. "Mrs. Wineman, do you have any opening remarks?"

"Yes, Your Honor." Greta stood and walked toward the center of the room, slightly past the end of the table.

"Your Honor, the plaintiff was not aware until the death of her adopted grandmother that she had inherited property in East Germany. She has documents to prove that she is the rightful heir to this property and wants to exercise her rights according to the German Restoration Law passed in 1990. The plaintiff is petitioning the court to allow her to exercise this right to reclaim the property that was unlawfully taken from her grandparents by the Nazi government in 1939."

After a moment of silence, the judge said, "Are you through, Mrs. Wineman?"

"Yes, Your Honor."

Judge Krause watched as Greta returned to her table, patting Rachel on her shoulder. He then turned his eyes to the defendant's table and said, "Mr. Beckle. Do you have an opening statement?"

"Yes, Your Honor, I do." Beckle took one last look at the paper in front of him and then stood and moved back from the table.

"Your Honor, the defendant will prove that Rachel Lewis is not the granddaughter of Jacob and Rebekah Weinberg and is not entitled to exercise the German Restoration Law. Moreover, we will show evidence to prove that the defendant has not only purchased the property legally but has paid taxes on the property for over seven years and comes under the German Adverse Possession Law. Therefore, we are asking the court to recognize the defendant as sole and legal owner of the East German property that the plaintiff claims is hers."

Mr. Beckle glanced over to Rachel and then pulled out his chair and sat down.

Judge Krause made a few notes and then looked at Greta and said, "Mrs. Wineman, you may call your first witness."

"Your Honor, the plaintiff, Rachel Lewis, will be the first to testify."

After Rachel was sworn in, Greta approached her and said, "Would you please tell the court your name and where you are from."

"My name is Rachel Matthews Lewis, and I am from Arlington, Virginia, in the United States of America."

"Rachel, would you please tell the court why you are here today."

"Yes. I am here in Germany to reclaim the property that was illegally taken from my grandparents, Jacob and Rebekah Weinberg, by the Nazi government in 1939."

Beckle stood up and said, “I protest, Your Honor. The plaintiff has not proven that she is the granddaughter of Jacob and Rebekah Weinberg.”

Greta turned to Judge Krause. “Your Honor, neither has the defendant proven that Mrs. Lewis is not the Weinbergs’ granddaughter. All the plaintiff has testified to is her name and why she is here.”

Judge Krause looked at Beckle and said, “I’m going to let the plaintiff’s answer stand. This is her perception of who she is and why she is here. The defendant will have plenty of time to prove otherwise.”

Greta turned back to Rachel. “Rachel, did your adopted grandmother have a satchel?”

“Yes, she did.”

“When did you learn about her satchel?”

“I was a junior in college when Grandmother told me about the satchel.”

“Did she tell you what was in the satchel at that time?”

“Somewhat.”

“Please explain.”

“She said it contained old German papers she brought with her when she moved to America.”

“Did she tell you the nature of the papers?”

“No.”

“Did you ask to see the papers?”

“No. I do not read German and thought the papers were memorabilia that Grandmother had brought to the States. I was not interested in them and soon forgot about the satchel.”

“Did your adopted grandmother tell you about the other contents of the satchel?

“No, she mentioned the papers only.”

“When did you discover that the satchel held deeds to the East German property?”

“After my grandmother died.”

"Thank you, Rachel. That will be all."

"Mr. Beckle? Do you want to cross-examine?" the judge asked.

"Yes, Your Honor. I do."

Beckle approached Rachel, stood silent a moment, and then said, "Mrs. Lewis, did your grandmother tell you that your mother, Maria Hoffman, was adopted?"

"No."

"Why do you think she didn't tell you that?"

"I—I don't know," Rachel stammered.

"Could it be because your mother was not adopted?"

Greta stood. "I object, Your Honor. The defendant is asking Mrs. Lewis to read her adopted grandmother's mind."

"Strike the defendant's last two questions from the record," Judge Krause said as he quickly made a note.

Beckle glanced down to the floor and then up again. "Maybe I should rephrase my question. Mrs. Lewis, when you were finally told that your mother was adopted, did you wonder why your grandmother never told you?"

Rachel looked at Greta.

"Answer the question, please."

Rachel nodded her head and whispered yes.

"Please speak louder, Mrs. Lewis. The court cannot hear you."

Rachel held her head up, her eyes glistened with tears, and she said yes.

"Thank you. That will be all."

Judge Krause said, "You may step down now, Mrs. Lewis."

"Mrs. Wineman, would you call your next witness, please."

Greta stood up and said, "The plaintiff calls Daniel Medlik."

Mr. Medlik was sworn in, and Greta said, "Sir, would you please tell the court who you are, where you are from, and what your credentials are."

"Yes. My name is Daniel Medlik, and I am from Los Angeles, California, in the United States of America. I have been in the photography business for forty years. I am former president of Advertising Photographers of America, consultant on Licensing and Copyright, professor of photography at the Art Center College of Design." Medlik paused a moment, took a deep breath, and continued. "I am a leading consultant, speaker, and author on legal, business, and technical-photography topics. I am a respected and acknowledged authority on all forms of commercial, editorial, and stock photography and a consultant and testifying expert on all issues related to photography and imaging."

Greta looked at Judge Krause and said, "I ask that the court accept Daniel Medlik as an expert photography witness."

"So ruled."

Greta handed Medlik the group picture of the Weinberg family.

"Mr. Medlik, you have already examined this picture. Would you tell the court what the conclusion of your analysis was?"

"Yes. First of all, the picture is in excellent condition and has not been tampered with. It is the original photograph made in 1938. The date on the back of the photograph has not been altered. The identifying names written on the back are authentic. The ink agrees with the age of the picture. Whoever wrote the names on back wrote them at the time that the picture was taken."

"Thank you, Mr. Medlik." Greta handed Medlik another smaller picture. "Mr. Medlik, I realize that you have also examined this five-by-seven-inch picture of a woman. Would you please tell the court what your analysis of this picture was?"

"Yes. This picture is also in excellent condition, considering its age. The date is on the back, and it was taken at the same time the group picture was taken. The name is also written on the back and the age of the ink tested to be the same as the age of the picture. It is my opinion that the same person who wrote on the back of the group picture also wrote on the five-by-seven-inch picture. And the woman in the five-by-seven-inch picture is also in the group picture."

"Now, Mr. Medlik, would you please tell the court about the jewelry that the subject of the five-by-seven-inch picture is wearing."

"Yes. The woman is wearing diamond earrings, a diamond necklace, and a diamond bracelet."

"How can you be sure that they are diamonds?"

"Because I have compared them to the pictures of the jewelry that have been submitted to the court. I have technical ways of comparison that are foolproof."

Greta handed the witness a third picture and turned to the bench.

"Your Honor, the third picture that Mr. Medlik has in his hand is a copy of an original picture that was submitted to the court in discovery. The defense was given a copy along with a copy of the deposition taken from Michael Raines, Maria Hoffman Matthews's pastor in Arlington, Virginia." Judge Krause nodded and Greta turned back to her witness.

"Mr. Medlik, comparing this picture with the five-by-seven-inch picture made in 1938, would you say the two women resemble each other?"

"Absolutely. I have studied the two pictures for several hours and have concluded that they must be mother and daughter. In fact, if it were not for the hair styles, I might get them confused."

"Thank you."

"Your Honor, as I said earlier, this third picture is a picture of Maria Hoffman Matthews. It was made when she was approximately the same age as the woman in the five-by-seven-inch picture. If it pleases the court, I would like the two pictures added to the five-by-seven-inch picture of Maria Hoffman Matthews and all three entered as evidence for the plaintiff."

"Very well," the judge said, handing the pictures to the clerk. "Are you through with this witness, Mrs. Wineman?"

"I am, Your Honor."

"Mr. Beckle, you may cross-examine now."

Beckle walked briskly to the witness stand, looked intently at Mr. Medlik, smiled, and said, "Mr. Medlik, you testified that the picture and the writing on the back of the group picture were circa 1938. I have no argument with that. But I do have a question.

Could you determine that the person who wrote the names on the back was a member in the picture itself?"

"No, I have no way of determining that."

"Thank you. That will be all."

Judge Krause said, "You may step down now, Mr. Medlik. Mrs. Wineman, your next witness, please."

"I call James Klein to the stand, Your Honor."

Greta glanced at her papers as James Klein was being sworn in. She quickly approached the witness stand and said, "Mr. Klein, would you please tell the court your name, where you live, and your qualifications as an expert witness."

Klein nodded his head and said, "I will. My name is James Klein and I am from the Washington, DC, area in the United States of America. I am a certified and court-qualified forensic handwriting expert. I graduated from a two-year resident training program in Forensic Document Examination conducted by the US Army Criminal Investigation Laboratory in Fort Gillem, Georgia. They prepared me for the comparison of handwriting and hand printing, the detection of forged signatures and handwriting, the examination of inks and papers, and the decipherment of erased entries and also indented writings.

"I have testified as an expert witness in forensic document examination in federal, state, and military courts and by deposition on more than one hundred fifty occasions."

Greta turned to the bench. "We would ask the court to accept Mr. Klein as an expert in forensic handwriting."

"So ruled." Judge Krause nodded at Greta and glanced at the court reporter.

Greta handed Klein the typewritten document telling of the birth of Maria and the typewritten will listing Maria as heir to the estate of Jacob and Rebekah Weinberg.

"Mr. Klein, you have already examined these documents. Would you please give us the conclusion of your analysis?"

"Yes. I found these documents in exceptionally good condition, considering their age. They had not been tampered with, and the ink used in the signatures was compatible with the age of the documents."

Greta then handed Klein a copy of the group picture.

"Mr. Klein. You have already compared the original group picture with this copy. Is it your expert opinion that the signatures on these documents match the handwriting on the back of the group picture that you examined?"

"Yes, I would say they are as perfect a match as you can get."

"Thank you, Mr. Klein."

"Your Honor, realizing that the court is familiar with the documents explaining the birth of the Weinberg baby, Maria, and the will leaving Maria her parent's estate, and also having given copies of the documents to the defendant in discovery, if it pleases the court, I will refrain from reading them out loud."

Judge Krause nodded and said, "Let the record show that Mrs. Wineman is excused from reading out loud the two typewritten documents pertaining to the Weinberg will and the birth of Maria Weinberg."

"Thank you, Your Honor."

Greta handed Judge Krause the two documents to be joined with the other evidence for the plaintiff, and the judge passed them on to the clerk.

"That will be all," Greta said and returned to her table.

Jude Krause made a quick note and looked up. "Mr. Beckle, you may cross-examine now."

Beckle, already standing, glanced one more time at the paper on his table and approached the witness stand with a smile on his face.

"Mr. Klein." Beckle paused. "You said the signatures were as perfect as you can get. What exactly does that mean?"

"Well, it means that a match with something of that nature is not exactly like a matching DNA analysis. With DNA, you can get a one hundred percent match. With handwriting, I've been taught that the best you can get is ninety-nine percent, and I would say the signatures that I just testified to are in the ninety-nine percent range."

"But let's talk about that one percent. Is it possible...I'm not saying probable...but is it possible that the one percent could apply to this case?"

Mr. Klein thought a minute. He raised his eyebrows and said, "Anything is possible, I suppose, but I would stand by my analysis and say that the signatures were written by the same person."

"Thank you, sir. That will be all."

James Klein returned to the plaintiff's table, and Judge Krause said, "If there are no more witnesses, we will have a short recess. Upon my return I will expect both sides to be prepared to give their closing arguments." He gave a light tap with his gavel and left the courtroom, taking his notes with him.

Rachel turned to Greta. "What do you think, Greta?"

"I'm not sure. It's the one percent that bothers me. Beckle's shrewd. I hope Judge Krause didn't fall for that. Let's wait and evaluate after our closing arguments." Greta patted Rachel's arm. "In the meantime, let's get a cup of coffee."

Judge Krause looked once more at his notes and then turned to Greta and said, "Mrs. Wineman, your closing argument, please."

Greta picked up her notes, stood, and moved over to the middle of the room, standing back a respectful distance from the judge's bench.

"Your Honor." Greta paused and then continued. "The plaintiff admits that she was thirty-five years old before she was told of her true grandparents, their daring plan to save the life of their unborn daughter, the sacrifice they made to do that, and the couple who willingly agreed to help them.

"Rachel grew up thinking that Sarah Davis was her blood grandmother and loved her dearly. We do not know why Sarah never told Rachel the truth. We do know what Sarah told Rachel's attorney: that when the property fell behind the Iron Curtain, she decided it might be lost forever and didn't want Maria to know about the way her real parents had died in the Holocaust.

"But that did not explain why she kept the truth from Rachel. It is obvious that she died with a heart attack before she could tell Rachel the truth; nevertheless, all evidence points to the fact that Rachel is the blood granddaughter of Jacob and Rebekah Weinberg. The court and defendant are aware that Rachel's mother, Maria, and her father, Steve Matthews, were killed in an automobile accident in 1988, leaving Rachel in the care of her step-grandmother, Sarah Davis.

"That makes Rachel the second-generation descendant of the Weinbergs, who were murdered in the Holocaust during World War II, and heir to her grandparents' estate. Her claim falls under the German Restoration Law, passed in 1990. This court now has the opportunity to right a wrong that happened seventy years ago. We are asking the court to grant Rachel Lewis title to the East German property that she makes claim to." Greta stood a moment and then walked quietly back to her chair and sat down.

There was a silence in the court; even those at the defendant's table were silent, with most of their eyes cast downward. Finally, Beckle stood up, waiting for Judge Krause to acknowledge him.

TWENTY-FIVE

Judge Krause looked up from his notes and said in a quiet voice, "Mr. Beckle, you may address the court with your closing argument."

Beckle nodded, stepped out from the table, and walked toward the center of the room.

"Your Honor, looking back in history, as Germans, I'm sure we all have regrets over what happened to the Jewish people in our country. I know I do. However, we cannot let our emotions control the decisions we make concerning any legal case. I think the defendant would be perfectly willing to relinquish the property to the plaintiff if he felt one hundred percent sure that she was truly the granddaughter of the Weinberg family, but there are too many holes in her case.

"The foremost question is why Sarah Davis failed to tell Maria or Rachel about the satchel and its contents. And if Maria was truly adopted, why didn't she tell her?

"There is another question that we can address. Who knows what the Weinberg family looked like? The plaintiff claims that the pictures are of the Weinbergs, but there is no proof to verify that fact. No other pictures to compare them to. All we know, from Nazi records, is that every member of the Weinberg family died in the Holocaust. That is documented evidence.

"The jewelry the plaintiff claims belonged to the Weinberg family could have been jewelry confiscated from many Jewish people during that time.

"But let's say this jewelry really did belong to the Weinberg family. Let's concede that Jacob Weinberg did give Ernst Hoffman his deeds and some personal things such as the World War I medals belonging to his father and his own civic awards for safekeeping. For some reason, unbeknownst to us, Mr. Weinberg probably trusted Ernst with their family jewelry. Maybe it was Sarah he had faith in, knowing that she was half Jewish. Could Sarah have been related to Rebekah? There are those who think there is a family resemblance there.

"And Jacob Weinberg may have promised Ernst a part of the jewelry after they attained their freedom. But he did not give him their fourth child. There is no record of them having a fourth child. This was a scheme that Ernst Hoffman hatched. He would have had no problem getting pictures of the Weinberg family. Surely if they were close enough for Mr. Weinberg to entrust his deeds and jewelry to him, he would have given them pictures of his family.

"No, I contend that Ernst Hoffman probably typed both the paper and the will and practiced writing Jacob Weinberg's signature for as long as it took to make it identical to Jacob Weinberg's actual signature.

"Sarah Hoffman was the one who gave birth to a baby girl on the eleventh of January in 1939, and her birth was registered at the courthouse. Ernst knew if the Weinberg family did not survive, he would claim their estate for his daughter.

"The plaintiff claims that the pictures of Mrs. Weinberg and Maria Matthews are almost identical. The defendant submitted pictures of Sarah Davis to the court that also showed how she resembled Maria Matthews. Mrs. Davis also had brown eyes, brown hair, and an olive complexion and was petite. In discovery our research found that people in Arlington, Virginia, never doubted that Maria Matthews was Sarah Davis's daughter. Early in the case, the defendant submitted several brief depositions to that effect. Interestingly, the plaintiff never rebutted these depositions." Mr. Beckle paused a long time, dropped his head, and then looked up and over to Rachel. He shook his head slightly and said, "We wonder, had the plaintiff not known about the beautiful, almost billion-dollar building that was recently completed on the East German property, would she have chosen this property to claim heir to?

"Your Honor, we have proven that the defendant bought the deeds to the East German property from a reputable company and has paid taxes on the property for over seven years. If nothing else, the defendant claims legal rights to the property under the German Adverse Possession Law. We ask the court to rule in favor of The Neumann Development Company." With a brisk nod, Mr. Beckle looked straight at Judge Krause and said, "Thank you."

He then took a deep breath and walked calmly back to his chair, focused only in the direction of the defendant's table.

Judge Krause looked at the large clock at the back of the courtroom and said, "This court will recess until two this afternoon, at which time I will render a verdict." He tapped lightly with his gavel, gathered his papers, and left the courtroom.

The humming of low voices stopped as the door to the judge's chamber opened and Judge Krause walked out. Those few in the room did not wait for the bailiff to ask them to rise; they automatically stood up and watched as the judge took his place at the bench. They then sat down, and the bailiff called the court into session.

Judge Krause let his eyes sweep around the courtroom and then to the paper on his desk. All was silent, and he finally looked up and said, "After two hours of studying the facts and law of this case, I have come to the conclusion that it is too early to render a verdict. I will postpone ruling until I am totally convinced that I am making the right decision. This is a very unusual case involving millions of dollars, and I do not take it lightly. I am asking both parties to be patient and give the court time to render a fair decision. Who knows? In the meantime there may be more evidence that will come to the surface." Judge Krause paused a moment and glanced at the two parties and then at the court reporter. He spoke slowly and clearly.

"I am postponing a decision for three months and taking the case under advisement. I'm receptive to any new evidence, in the meantime, through a new trial. I hope this does not create a hardship for anyone. If it does, the court apologizes for that. Should I come to a decision before the three-month period is up, I will notify both parties a week ahead of the final ruling. Thank you for your understanding." With that, Judge Krause stood and quickly left the courtroom, leaving a strange silence and everyone looking at one another.

Greta turned, took Rachel's hand between both of hers, and said, "Don't despair, Rachel. Just because Judge Krause has postponed his ruling does not mean that you will lose. He's giving both of us more time to gather evidence."

"But Greta, I don't have any more evidence. I brought everything I have."

Greta patted Rachel's hand. "I still don't want you to worry. I'm sure there is something we can do to strengthen our case. We might get another expert witness. We have plenty of time. You heard the judge say he was giving us three months."

Rachel gave a big sigh, withdrew her hand from Greta's, and picked up her purse. "Greta, I know you and William, and also Paul, have worked hard...I just hate to think this case is going to be prolonged. I really need to get back home and get ready for school."

"Rachel, listen to me." Greta's voice was stern. "My advice to you is to call your principal, tell her your situation, and ask her to get someone to take your class, at least for the first semester."

Rachel looked alarmed. "Greta, are you telling me that I'll be over here until Christmas?"

"Well, I'm not sure how long you will be here, but if you win this case, then there is still Luke Hartmann's group to deal with." Greta smiled and gave Rachel a couple of gentle pats on her arm. "Honey, legal matters don't move very fast. Trust me. It was a miracle that we had this hearing as quickly as we did."

Rachel sat quiet, trying to absorb what Greta was saying. She turned and looked around the courtroom. "Where is William? I want to hear what he has to say."

Greta turned and also scanned the room. "He was here a minute ago. Maybe he stepped out to take a call. I don't see Paul, either. He must have gone out with William." Greta motioned with her eyes. "Well, the defendants are still here, all huddled together across the room."

Rachel turned and followed Greta's eyes. "Yes, they must be relieved that the judge did not rule in my favor. I wonder what their lawyer will come up with in these next three months." Rachel's eyes narrowed. "Beckle sure made my grandmother and her first husband sound like villains."

"Some lawyers will do anything they can to win, Rachel. One gets used to that in the courtroom. Try to forget what he said. I doubt he believed it himself."

"Well, he must have convinced the judge; otherwise this case would be over."

"I doubt seriously that Judge Krause believed everything their lawyer said. Judge Krause is not only smart but also fair. That's one reason he has delayed his ruling. Look, here comes William."

TWENTY-SIX

William pressed the numbers above the handle and then opened the door for Rachel to enter. Sarah Beth jumped up from watching television, rushed to her mother, and gave her a big hug.

Susan turned, gave Rachel a sympathetic look, and mouthed, "I'm sorry." She then got up from the sofa and also gave Rachel a hug.

William said, "OK, girls. I want your attention as I have an announcement to make. I received a call from my firm today, and I'll need to fly back to the States. But I don't think I'll be there for more than two weeks. I have a real important case that needs my attention."

Susan frowned and said, "Honey, do you have to go? Can't your uncle take care of this for you? Or can't you work from here?"

"No, Susan, Tom's buried in his own work, and anyhow, he's not familiar with this case. I have no choice but to fly home. I need to meet with my clients." William paused. "Now, I have something else to tell you. I have a six-month lease on a beautiful apartment in Hartmann Plaza, and I'm moving you there this afternoon. Both of you have remarked about the great sports complex and the restaurants and delis, not to mention some of the other shops in the plaza. I really think living there for the time being will be very convenient. What do you think?"

Susan laughed. "Well, since you've already leased it, what difference does it make what we think? But I really think it's a great idea. William, I can't wait to try out that sports complex and the Olympic-sized swimming pool." Susan turned to Rachel. "How about it, Rachel? Does this suit you?"

Rachel hesitated, looking from Susan to William. "Well, I had no idea we would be staying this long." Her brow furrowed. "William, I imagine an apartment in Hartmann Plaza is quite expensive. I doubt my money will hold out for something that pricey, but I certainly do not want to interfere with your and Susan's plans."

William walked over, put an arm around Rachel's shoulders, and gave her a gentle hug. "Look, Rachel. Susan and I are picking up most of this cost. She'll tie up some final work on her estate while she's here, and that will be a partial write-off. We don't want you worrying about finances. We'll settle up after the case is finished. I've paid for the lease, and Luke Hartmann says if we finish early, he'll have no problem subleasing the apartment and he'll give us a refund. I want you to relax and enjoy the plaza. It truly is a beautiful place. And anyhow, I'll feel better with the three of you staying there. You'll be safe. Actually, you'll hardly have to leave the complex as I've been told there's great shopping there."

Rachel smiled and shook her head. "After I pay my share of the lease, William, I doubt seriously that I'll have any money left for shopping. But I'm not going to worry. I'm going to relax and enjoy my stay there. Actually, I have not had a real vacation in four years—ever since Jonathan left for Iraq."

There were six elevators in the lobby of Hartmann Plaza, and when William and the girls stepped into the nearest one and pressed the button for the tenth floor, Susan caught her breath, Rachel grabbed Sarah Beth's arm, and Sarah Beth laughed. The ride up was so fast and thrilling that Sarah Beth wanted to ride down and "do it again."

They were all laughing when the door opened and who should be standing there but Luke Hartmann.

Luke smiled and held out his hand to shake William's. He nodded at Susan and Rachel and said, "William, I wanted to check with our housekeeper to see if your apartment was ready. Everything is so new that some of our apartments lack a few things here and there. But not yours. Our housekeeper assured me that it's ready to go."

"Thanks, Luke, that's good to hear. Look, I'm flying back to the States for a couple of weeks, and I'm leaving my girls here by themselves. I would appreciate it if you'd keep an eye on them for me."

"Of course." Luke nodded. He glanced down at Sarah Beth and said, "We have a great children's library on the second floor. Your little girl might enjoy going there. We employed a young librarian to help the children select books and even help with schoolwork if necessary."

"I think this complex has everything." William gave a wave of his hand. "A person could settle here, with all his needs met, and be perfectly content."

"Well," Luke said, chuckling as he stepped inside the elevator, "I'm not sure I would go that far, William." He glanced at Rachel and sobered before the door closed.

Rachel was holding Sarah Beth's hand and following William and Susan as the waiter led them to the terrace and to their table.

Sarah Beth looked up at her mother and said, "Mother, are we going to eat under the stars tonight?"

"Yes, darling. William thought it would be fun before he flies out tomorrow."

"I can't wait to see the little fish again. This is my favorite eating place."

Rachel smiled down at Sarah Beth. "Mine, too, honey."

William and the waiter pulled back the chairs and seated Susan and Rachel and then Sarah Beth. It was the same waiter who had served them on their first visit. He handed the three adults a menu and lit the candle under the hurricane globe. He then turned all four water goblets right-side up and left to get the water pitcher.

William looked a few moments at his menu and said, "Well, girls, what are you ordering this evening?"

Susan said, "I can't decide whether to stay with the French dishes or switch to German. What about you, Rachel?"

Rachel laughed softly and said, "I think I'm going to get a child's plate and split it with Sarah Beth. Every time I look at these prices, I think about how many meals I could cook for just one of these entrées."

Susan lowered her menu and said, "Oh, Rachel, don't worry about the cost. William has his credit card, and that's sufficient. Anyhow, I'll tell you like William told me one time. You need to learn to go with the flow."

Sarah Beth looked up at Rachel and said, "Mother, may I have a hamburger?"

William grinned. "Now there you go, Rachel. You can split a hamburger with Sarah Beth."

William's teasing helped Rachel to relax, and she began to laugh. Susan put down her menu to join in the fun, and the three adults were laughing when the waiter came back to fill their water goblets and take their orders.

When he left, Sarah Beth patted Rachel's arm. "Mother, may I be excused to look at the fish?"

"Yes, but remember—don't stick your hand in the water."

William watched Sarah Beth as she walked over and sat down on the ledge of the fishpond, wondering if she would resist the temptation to touch the water. A woman's laughter caught his attention, and he glanced over to the three people following the waiter. It was Luke Hartmann and Mr. and Mrs. Broussard. Luke caught William's eye and said something to the Broussards and to the waiter and then led his friends over to William's table.

William pushed his chair back and stood. Luke smiled and said, "William, I want you to meet Andre Broussard and his wife, Karla."

They exchanged handshakes, and then William said, "Mr. and Mrs. Broussard, I want you to meet my wife, Susan, and our friend Rachel Lewis." He paused. "And the fourth member of our party is over guarding the fish."

Andre smiled and said, "Yes, we saw her when we came in." He turned to Rachel. "Mrs. Lewis, you have a cute daughter."

Rachel smiled and said, "Thank you, sir."

Andre looked from Rachel to Susan. It's nice meeting all of you. Luke told us that you moved in just this afternoon. I hope you'll enjoy your stay here."

Susan smiled. "I'm sure we will. This is the second time we have dined at this beautiful restaurant. We were told that you are the proprietor."

Andre nodded. "Yes, and I hope you'll enjoy your meals. I think we have an excellent chef. If you want anything special, just let us know."

Rachel entered into the conversation. "I wonder if you've yet had a request for a hamburger. That's what my daughter asked for."

Andre laughed. "I'm not sure, but if that's what your little girl wants, I'll see that she gets it."

After the waiter poured their tea and left, Susan said, "Karla Broussard must be on the quiet side. She had very little to say. How old is she, anyhow? She looks twenty-five years younger than her husband."

Rachel nodded and kept her voice low. "I noticed the same thing, but every time I looked her way, she was staring at me. I wonder why."

William stirred his tea. "Maybe she's impressed by your looks, Rachel."

"Oh, William, I doubt that."

"I'm sure her husband has told her about your case. Maybe that's the reason."

"That's probably right. She might be wondering if I'll end up with the deeds and how it will affect her husband."

William shook his head. "Don't worry about that...Oh, I almost forgot to tell you and Susan something. Paul says there is a small chapel within walking distance that you might like to attend. He really thinks you'll like the pastor there."

Susan asked, "Did he tell you anything about him or the denomination of his church?"

"He said he and his wife are middle-aged, in their early fifties, and the church is nondenominational. The pastor's name is Peter Grenfell, and his wife's name is Nancy. Paul also said the church has a screen with captioning in English."

"I was wondering if Rachel and I would have to search the tube for a sermon this Sunday. Now we won't have to. Thanks for remembering, sweetie."

"No problem. Look, here comes our food. Rachel, you might call Sarah Beth."

TWENTY-SEVEN

Susan stepped inside the small chapel with Rachel and Sarah Beth following closely behind. It was a quarter until eleven, and the chapel was already three-fourths full. An elderly man greeted them and led them to a pew amid the sounds of soft voices and music that the organist was playing from the hymnal. Sarah Beth sat between Susan and Rachel, and the young couple sitting next to them smiled and, speaking German, introduced themselves to Susan and asked if they were visitors. Susan shook her head and said, "English," and the couple quickly nodded and greeted Susan and Rachel with their limited English and pointed out the overhead electronic screen with English translations for the hymns and the pastor's message.

Everyone quieted when the pastor walked to the podium and led in prayer. He then greeted his congregation and asked the newcomers to please raise their hands so the ushers could give them cards to fill out. The couple, knowing that Susan and Rachel did not speak German, raised their hands in their stead and gave them the cards.

After singing two more hymns, Pastor Grenfell again stood in front of the podium to preach while the electronic screen displayed what he was saying in English.

It was after the service, when the pastor was standing at the door shaking hands with the members as they left, that he introduced himself to Susan and Rachel. They were surprised at his command of the English language, and he apologized for the closed-captioning screen. "Ladies, I wrestled with our language barrier for months and finally decided that an overhead screen with the English translation was the only solution."

"There is no need to apologize," Susan said. "We're used to closed-captioning, aren't we, Rachel?"

"Indeed we are, and even Sarah Beth could read some of it on the screen."

Peter Grenfell said, "Wait, here comes my wife. I want you to meet her." Peter motioned with his hand. "Nancy, we have some visitors from the United States I want you to meet."

Nancy Grenfell smiled and held out her hand. "I'm Nancy. You probably saw me at the organ. We're delighted that you visited with us today. What are your names?"

Peter patted Nancy on her shoulder. "Honey, if you'll just give me a chance, I'll introduce you. This is Susan Handel and Rachel Lewis and, of course, Rachel's little girl, Sarah Beth."

Nancy smiled and said, "I certainly hope you'll come again. Where are you staying while you're here in Berlin?"

"We have an apartment at Hartmann Plaza." Susan said.

"Oh, you're staying at a beautiful place. We're acquainted with Luke Hartmann but have not seen but a couple of the shops in his complex. We are very impressed with what we've seen."

Rachel said, "We just moved in Friday afternoon and are still getting adjusted. Sarah Beth is so fascinated by the fast elevators that she's constantly begging to go to the lobby. I sure hope the newness wears off."

Nancy smiled again. "I'm sure it will, but that's a child for you. She reminds me of our little granddaughter who lives in Stuttgart, though our granddaughter is much younger. We really miss seeing her and our grown children."

"Do they visit you often?"

"Yes, as often as they can. But now onto another subject. Peter and I would love to have you for lunch next Sunday after the service. Do you think that would be convenient for you?"

Rachel turned to Susan, and Susan said, "I don't know why we can't. That certainly is kind of you. Are you sure that it will be convenient for you, what with the church service and all?"

"Indeed it will. We have Sunday company for lunch all of the time. Just let us know if something comes up and you cannot come." Nancy opened her purse and pulled out a small card. "Here is our e-mail address. Just e-mail us if you cannot come, but I hope you can."

Susan nodded her head and smiled. "I assure you our social calendar is empty. We'll be there. You can count on that."

TWENTY-EIGHT

"The last one in is a sissy," Sarah Beth announced, holding her nose and jumping in a slightly deeper part of the beautiful Olympic-sized swimming pool in Hartmann Plaza.

Susan laughed and held her hand up in front of her face to keep the water from splashing into her eyes. She and Rachel were sitting on the side of the pool with their feet dangling in the water, watching Sarah Beth as she swam to the opposite side and back again.

"Sarah Beth's a good swimmer for her age." Susan said. "You can see that she's a natural in the water."

"Yes, I've worked with her and she's coming along." Rachel said. "I was on the swim and diving team in college and I would like to think she could achieve that?"

"Now, I'm really impressed." Susan looked at Rachel in awe. "I was on the tennis team, but my swimming leaves a lot to be desired. Oh, I can swim well enough, but I'm no speed swimmer."

"Well, I used to be. But diving was my better sport. I love the high diving board." Rachel turned slightly and glanced up at the high board.

"Rachel Lewis, to look at you, I would never guess that. I always thought it took a lot of nerve to dive off a high board."

"I think the secret is starting young. My dad was a great diver, and he started me young. After he died, I had extremely good coaches in high school and college. So many people have a fear of water. Fortunately I never did. I even served as a lifeguard during the summer months from the time I was sixteen years old until I finished college. It was an easy way to make spending money." Rachel glanced again at the high board.

"For you maybe, but I'm not sure I could save anyone drowning." Susan adjusted the clip in her hair, and when Rachel didn't answer, she said, "Rachel, you're not listening to me. You're thinking about that high board, aren't you? Tell me, when are you going to fly off of it?"

Rachel grinned. "It won't be long, Susan. I can only resist a high board for so long before I have to try it out. Oh, I hope I haven't lost my skill. It's been a little over two years since I've been on a high board—actually before Jonathan died."

"I know you must miss him."

"I do. But time has a way of healing the hurt. It's been four years altogether since Jonathan was with us—two years in Iraq and two years since his death."

Susan started to comment but instead caught Rachel's arm and said, "Look who I see, Rachel. Isn't that Luke Hartmann on the other side of the pool? He must have just come in. I wonder whom he's talking to."

"I don't know. Maybe it's one of the lifeguards. Luke Hartmann must not work a full day. It's only three o'clock."

"William says his business consumes half of the third floor. He probably employs a lot of people and can take off whenever he wants to. William also said he's rich as Croesus."

"It must be nice." Rachel gave Susan a coy look. "Susan Handel, you're one to talk about being rich. Didn't you inherit a lot of money from your grandfather?"

"Yes, but I'd rather people not know about it. I've always thought it dangerous to be very wealthy—you know—kidnapping for ransom and that sort of thing. Anyhow, most of my money is tied up in investments and endowments, plus I've given a lot away, especially to orphanages in Africa."

"That's commendable. I've always said if I were rich, there are many things I would contribute to." Rachel picked up her swim cap and began to put it on.

Susan grinned. "I was wondering when you were going to put that cap on. I'll watch Sarah Beth. You go on and have fun. What's your first dive going to be?"

"I hope it won't be a back flop. I'm not sure; maybe I'll do a jackknife and then a swan dive."

Susan watched as Rachel climbed the steps. Rachel was wearing a black one-piece swimsuit that hugged her slender body, and she looked like a million dollars. Susan glanced over to see if Luke Hartmann had noticed her. He had just come out of the water and was sitting on the side of the pool, running his fingers through his hair, when he looked up and saw Rachel. Susan tried to read the expression on his face. It was something between surprise and pleasure, but then, in a moment, it changed, a slight scowl appearing, and he returned to running his fingers through his hair. Susan wondered what was going through his mind and if the hair thing were a nervous habit.

Rachel stood at the back of the board a few moments and then went forward and bounced a few times, stopped and returned to the back of the board. The second time she went to the very end of the board, bounced to attain the height she wanted, and then sprang up from the board, touched her toes in a jackknife, straightened out, and hit the water as smooth as a sharp pencil going in lead first.

Three teenagers who were watching her clapped as Rachel surfaced. Rachel grinned, held her hands up, and clapped two times; then she swam to the side ladder and got out. She stood a moment and looked back at Susan. Susan gave her a thumbs-up, and Rachel climbed to the board again.

Susan glanced over to Luke Hartmann. There was no doubt. He was mesmerized. Susan didn't know whether to watch him or Rachel. This time his expression was one of admiration. Susan figured he liked anything that reeked of success, and Rachel was certainly successful on the diving board.

Rachel's second dive was a swan dive, and she did it perfectly. The teenagers clapped again, and Susan glanced over to Luke. He started to clap but caught himself and instead rubbed his hands across the waist of his swim trunks and then leaned back on the palms of his hands and shook his leg, watching the water drip off of his foot.

"I'm starving, Mother. Please let's get something to eat."

"I know, honey. Swimming always makes one hungry, but it's so close to dinner that I don't want you filling up on junk."

"I'm hungry, too, Rachel," Susan said, looking at her watch. "It's a little after five. Why don't we go and put our wet suits in our apartment and come back down and eat Italian this evening? I overheard someone at the pool say there is a great Italian restaurant in this complex and it's on the first floor."

"Suits me," Rachel said. "I'm hungry, too. I had forgotten how much energy it takes to swim and dive."

"Yes, and I'm still amazed at the exhibition you put on. It was beautiful, and I don't know if you were aware of it, but Luke Hartmann was watching, and I think you really impressed him."

"I don't think there's anything I could do to impress that man, Susan."

"You might be surprised."

"*Surprised* is certainly the right word."

"Well, anyhow, I wish I had the nerve to dive off of the high board."

"Don't worry about it. You can have just as much fun on the lower board. It boils down to one's perspective, believe me. And speaking of having fun, when are you going to try out the indoor tennis courts? Can you believe this complex?"

"I keep pinching myself and wondering if I'll wake up and find out it's a dream. I'm so glad William moved us here."

"Have you talked to him since he arrived home?"

"Yes, he called last night." Susan thought a minute and remembered that it was afternoon for William. "Rachel, this time difference where we're six hours ahead of Arlington has me confused. He said his trip was fine. He had texted me earlier to let me know he arrived safely, but last night was the first time I talked to him. I told him all about meeting the Grenfells and their church service, and he was pleased." Susan pressed the elevator button and said, "OK, Sarah Beth, here we go."

The aroma of Italian cooking met Susan, Rachel and Sarah Beth as they entered the restaurant, and they smiled. The restaurant was dimly lit with each table hosting a candle held in an interesting, old, colored bottle. Wax had run down and built up on the candles and the bottles, hinting at past lingering dinners and intimate conversations. There were also booths for those who preferred them. Sarah Beth wanted to sit in a corner booth. It had a round table and round seating. The booths had high backs, providing privacy for the restaurant's patrons.

"Mother, please, I want pizza," Sarah Beth said with a pleading look.

"Of course, Sarah Beth. You may have pizza. What about you, Susan? What are you ordering?"

"I'm having lasagna. There was an English-speaking couple at the pool talking about how good it is." Susan paused. "This menu is also in English, Rachel. I just noticed it."

Rachel looked again at the menu and nodded. "They must have known we were coming. Yes, lasagna sounds good. Make that two of us." She looked up and said, "Uh-oh, Susan, I see the Broussards coming in, but don't turn around and look. They are so engrossed in conversation that neither one has even looked our way." Rachel eased over closer to the center of the seat, completely out of the Broussards' sight.

"Where are they going to sit? I can hear them. They're speaking French," Susan whispered.

Rachel leaned over slightly to see. "Two booths from us. They are in a world all their own, and I'm glad. I don't know what we'd talk about if they came over to our booth. We have nothing in common but the lawsuit, and that's not a suitable subject for a conversation. Anyhow, here comes our waiter."

Susan gave their selections and spoke softly. After taking their order, the waiter moved to the Broussards' booth. Susan and Rachel could hear them give their order in German, reverting back to French when the waiter left.

Susan kept her voice low. "Isn't it amazing the way everyone today speaks multiple languages? The Broussards speak French and, obviously, fair German and English."

"Yes, and I regret that you and I cannot speak German."

"I agree, but we do understand French. They ordered in German, and the only word I understood was *pizza*."

"I guess their fine-dining restaurant doesn't serve pizza," Rachel remarked, barely above a whisper.

"No, you would never find pizza on their gourmet menu," Susan said with a low chuckle.

"Susan, they don't realize that their voices are loud enough to be overheard, especially since we're the only ones on this side of the restaurant."

Sarah Beth turned, patted Rachel on her arm, and whispered, "Mother, why are we talking so low?"

Rachel suppressed a laugh and, speaking in a low voice, said, "We don't want to disturb the people in the other booth." She rolled her eyes at Susan.

Sarah Beth looked confused and finally said, "Oh. And they're talking in that funny language, aren't they?"

"Yes, honey. They're speaking French."

It was then that Andre's voice rose even higher. "Have you lost your mind, Karla? What would Luke say if he heard you talking like this?"

"I think Luke might agree with me, but lower your voice, Andre. People all over this restaurant can hear you."

"No one is listening to us. Most of these people speak German. They don't speak French."

"You don't know that. Even waiters today speak multiple languages."

"All right, I'll lower my voice if you'll get off the subject of that woman. That's all I've heard for the last three weeks, and I'm sick of it."

"You could be sicker down the road if you don't address it now, believe me."

"I'm warning you, Karla, if you persist in talking about this, I'm going to get up and leave."

There were a few moments of silence, and then Karla's voice could be heard. It was not loud, but it carried all the way to the end booth.

"You don't have to leave, Andre. I will."

Karla Broussard moved out from her side and stood up. She held her head high and walked quickly across the tile floor to the door, leaving behind only the staccato sound her stiletto heels made. Andre sat for two or three minutes longer before also getting up and leaving. Neither one ever glanced in the direction of Susan and Rachel's booth.

"What was that all about, Susan? What woman were they talking about? Andre asked Karla if she had lost her mind. I hope they were not talking about me."

"No. I doubt they were talking about you. But Andre was really hot under the collar, wasn't he?"

"Yes, and do you think it was Luke Hartmann he mentioned? He said something like, 'what would Luke say if he heard her talking like that?' And she said he might agree with her."

"I don't know any other Luke he could have been talking about, but then I know very few people here in Berlin."

"Well, she really got in a huff and left her husband sitting there. She was going to show him, I guess."

"Well, I'm glad they're gone. Maybe we can enjoy our meal. Look, here comes our waiter with our food."

TWENTY-NINE

Luke Hartmann stood at his office window, watching the five o'clock traffic and munching on a health bar, calories needed to tide him over until dinner. He had made four laps before leaving the pool, and those laps had drained his energy. He would not neglect his swimming. Four laps were not enough but a good start. He saw a familiar figure down below and kept him in sight until he turned the corner. Most of his employees had left for the day, leaving a quietness that he enjoyed. He often did some of his best work after hours.

But he couldn't seem to get his mind on business at the moment, instead thinking about that woman—the one in the black swimsuit—the one who gave the beautiful diving exhibition: Rachel Lewis.

As hard as he tried to dislike her, there was something alluring about her, and that bothered him. His dislike did not necessarily come from the fact that she was the plaintiff in the lawsuit that involved Hartmann Plaza. He didn't know what it was. Or maybe he didn't want to admit what it was.

He would admit that he still felt bitterness every time he thought about Kate and the way she had just one day up and walked out on him and their marriage. Oh, he had stopped loving her years ago; in fact, she was not worthy of his love. No woman who walked out on her marriage was worthy of a man's love.

And the fact that they had no children was, in a way, a comforting thought. At least he did not have to worry about how divorce would have affected his child. His parents were disappointed that they never had the opportunity to become grandparents, and he was sorry for that, but being married to one's work did not produce children, and he was definitely married to his work. At least his work had been faithful to him. Look at the success it had created.

Luke walked back to his desk and sat down. He sat back in his comfortable chair, resting his arms on the leather arms, and continued to think. It was apparent that Rachel Lewis and Susan Handel were Christians, for William had asked for specific directions to the small church not far from the plaza. Luke smiled when he thought about Peter and Nancy Grenfell. They had invited him numerous times to their church services, but he never accepted. He didn't have time for religion. His work was all-consuming, and he had tried to make that clear to them.

Peter probably thought that the fact that he had learned to speak German in Luke's father's German classes at Oxford University would, in and of itself, give reason for Luke to respond to his church invitation. And maybe it should have, but he was glad he never got involved.

He would respect the Handels' and Rachel Lewis's right to get involved. That was their business. But he would not join in. Luke sat forward and looked at the digital clock on his desk. He had been daydreaming long enough. It was time to put in at least two hours of work before he went to dinner.

THIRTY

Karla Broussard looked at her speedometer and slowed. She was not on the autobahn and could not afford to get a ticket. She was still fuming from Andre's and her disagreement last evening and had lain awake most of the night. She thought back over the ten years of their marriage and realized that it had not worked out as well as she had hoped. He was rich enough, she conceded, but he was getting old and developing habits that were common to old people.

Karla sighed. A twenty-five-year difference was a lot, but she thought having beautiful clothes and jewelry would make up for the age difference. It did for a while. But now Andre cleared his throat all of the time and had lost interest in going out at night. His idea of a perfect night was dining at the plaza. He no longer liked to stay out until midnight dancing and sipping wine and laughing with the crowd. And he had pretty much lost interest in sex.

Karla could see the nursing home in the distance and again felt satisfaction in having not told Andre about the discovery of her father. At the time, she did not know what made her want to keep it secret, but now she was glad she had. If she could just be patient and things worked out as planned, she would be wealthy... and independent. Karla smiled.

Karla thought back to the day, almost two years ago, that her mother died and she had to return to Paris for the funeral. Her mother died in a nursing home, and she had gone through her mother's private papers, searching for her insurance policy, and discovered the shocking truth. Karla's name was not Dowd. That was her adopted name, taken at the time she was one year old, when her mother remarried. Her birth certificate gave her name as Karla Kirsten, daughter of Rhonda Bouchon Kirsten and Karl Leo Kirsten.

Her mother was married to Karl Kirsten in Paris, France, in 1964, and she divorced him in Berlin, Germany, in 1969, seven months before Karla was born. Apparently her mother and father moved to Germany after they married, and when they divorced, her mother moved back to Paris, where Karla was born. Karla searched further and found the certificate for her mother's marriage to Phillip Dowd. They were married in Paris, France, in 1971, and Phillip adopted Karla in 1971, before she was two years old. Phillip Dowd had been dead ten years. Karla wondered, at the time, if her real father were still alive.

After the small graveside service, Karla gathered her mother's few personal things and flew back to Berlin. She never showed Andre the papers or told him the truth about her adoption. She rented a lockbox in her maiden name, Karla Dowd, and placed all of the papers there. Her key was well hidden.

Karla slowed her car and turned into the well-landscaped parking area for the high-scale nursing home that provided care for her father. She turned off her engine and sat, continuing to think about her past. She had pulled up a website that offered a broad-based people-search program and discovered that Karl Kirsten was still alive. She remembered her excitement as she rang the doorbell to her father's condo, only to discover that he no longer lived there. He now resided in a nursing home and was suffering with early-onset Alzheimer's disease. His mind would come and go.

The first day she visited her father and told him who she was, he cried and cried, and she cried with him. Some Alzheimer's patients were known to cry a lot. Her father said he never knew Karla's mother was pregnant when he left her for another woman he lived with but never married.

It was shortly afterward that she put two and two together and came to the shocking realization that her father was Konrad Neumann's silent partner and he owned 40 percent of Neumann Development Company. Karla kept her closely guarded secret and had her father sign a will making her his sole heir. The will had a clause declaring any previous wills null and void.

Karla relaxed against the back of her seat and thought about the turn of events and the suit filed against Neumann Development Company. The woman was going to ruin everything unless she and George could stop her. But how much trust could she put in George? He had worked at the nursing home less than a year, yet long enough for her to see the shady side of his character. Would he react favorably to her suggestion? she wondered. After all, his hours at the nursing home had been cut, and he said he desperately needed supplemental work.

Karla reached over to her glove compartment, opened it, and took out the folder she had so carefully prepared. She looked again at the forms and let out a deep sigh just thinking about her plans. But she couldn't sit any longer in her car and daydream.

Karla removed the key from the ignition, opened her purse, and slipped the fourteen-karat-gold key ring, with the attached keys, inside. She removed her small cosmetic bag, fumbled for her lipstick, and then flipped down the sun visor to reveal the mirror on the back side. She applied a small amount of fresh lipstick and smoothed back her beautiful coiffure, making sure the few strands of blond hair were in place.

She then picked up the folder and hesitated a moment, looking at the magazines on the front seat of her car. Why had she brought those? Her father could not read them, but maybe he would look at the pictures.

Karla's mind flashed back to Andre again, and she frowned. What if he somehow found out about her visits to the nursing home? What would she tell him? Karla's frown eased off, and she smiled. She would tell him that she was a volunteer helper there. She would start bringing magazines for the residents who could still read. He would probably be proud of her. Andre had always been a soft touch for charities and those sorts of things.

Karla tucked the magazines and folder under her arm and quickly got out of her Mercedes, pressing the button on her remote to lock the doors. She walked briskly to the entrance that would admit her to the depressing place that was home for her father.

THIRTY-ONE

Luke Hartmann spared no expense with his beautiful state-of-the-art kitchens that featured luxurious granite tops on all of the surfaces. Susan and Rachel, attired in their pajamas, sat at the spacious bar on cushioned, wrought-iron stools eating cereal and sipping their coffee. Susan reached for the cream and said, “OK, we swam yesterday. What are we going to do today for exercise?”

Rachel chewed slowly and then swallowed and said, “I vote for the gym, the large room with all of the exercise equipment.”

“I had that on my mind also but didn’t know whether you would want Sarah Beth to go.”

“I think I’m going to drop her off at the children’s library. She’s been begging to go there. And you heard Luke Hartmann say they employ a young librarian. I think Sarah Beth will be safe. I’m sure there are rules to abide by.”

“Yes, that sounds like a great idea.”

Rachel poured herself a second cup of coffee. “I wonder whose idea it was to have the children’s library. Whoever thought it up is smart.”

“I agree, and I wonder who the architect was that designed Andre Broussard’s restaurant. That high ceiling with the tiny lights is breathtaking, and the wrought-iron balconies, the exotic greenery climbing up the walls, the fishpond in front of the glass wall, the beautiful slate floors...I could go on and on.” Susan gestured with a wave of her hand. "Actually, the entire restaurant is magnificent."

"I agree. And as long as we're on the subject, I wonder if Andre and his wife made up. They were both mad as hornets."

"I imagine we'll find out soon enough." Susan cocked her head. "Rachel, I think your daughter's up. I hear her coming, so you had better put the bacon in the microwave."

Rachel stood in awe as she stopped inside the door and looked around the children's library. Being an elementary school teacher gave her an appreciation for educational tools that the average person might overlook. The young librarian appeared to be in her mid-twenties, and she looked up and smiled at her first patrons of the morning. She quickly walked around the counter and introduced herself.

Rachel made note of her name. Actually, her name was all she understood because the librarian spoke in German. Rachel said, "I'm sorry. I don't speak German. I'm Rachel Lewis, and I hope you speak English."

Shannon smiled and nodded. "Yes, Ms. Lewis, fortunately, most people in Germany do speak English. I think you will find that many of the younger generation speak almost fluent English. We start very early in school learning English." Shannon smiled at Sarah Beth and said, "What is your name, young lady?"

Sarah Beth moved a little closer to Rachel and shyly said, "Sarah Beth Lewis."

Shannon said, "Well, Sarah Beth, are you going to spend some time with me this morning?"

Sarah Beth nodded her head up and down, smiled, and said yes.

Rachel said, "This library is all she's talked about for the last two days. And it is beautiful. I'm so glad you have something like this for the children."

Rachel turned toward Susan and said, "Shannon, this is my friend, Susan Handel."

Shannon acknowledged Susan and then took the three on a quick tour of the library, afterward recording Rachel's name and cell number and assuring her that she would look after Sarah Beth while they were at the fitness center.

"It's nice not having to show your card, isn't it?" Susan said as she and Rachel inserted their cards in an electronic receiving device and walked into the large exercise room.

"Yes, but where do I keep mine? These leggings are too snug for a pocket, and I've been told that electronic cards shouldn't share space with a cell."

"You have a tiny waist pocket, don't you? That's where mine is."

"I hope we don't lose them. These pockets are hardly large enough for a little change. My card is sticking out the top."

"They'll probably be all right," Susan said, letting her eyes sweep around the room. "Where do you want to start?"

"How about the recumbent bikes?"

"I was thinking the same thing, and there are several not being used."

After twenty minutes on the recumbent bikes, Susan and Rachel moved over to the treadmills. "It was while they were on the treadmills that Rachel heard her name called over the loudspeaker.

Rachel quickly pressed the stop button and said, "Susan, wasn't my name just called over the loudspeaker?"

"Yes, and I wonder why." Susan stopped the motion on her treadmill.

"I'll see. I hope it's not a call from Shannon," Rachel said, turning and quickly walking back into the large reception area and to the main desk.

"What was it, Rachel?" Susan asked when Rachel returned.

"Can you believe my card fell out while we were on the recumbent bikes and someone turned it in?"

"Well, I'm glad they turned it in, but we'll need to make better provisions for our cards."

"Yes, and do you know who was at the main desk when I got there?"

"The Broussards?" Susan said with a chuckle.

"No. Luke Hartmann. And I was so embarrassed. He looked at me as if I were a child and couldn't even keep up with a little card."

"Was he here to exercise?"

"Not unless he plans to exercise in his street clothes."

"Did he speak to you?"

"No he just nodded with that nondescript look on his face, the one that's hard to read. And then when he overheard the desk clerk telling me someone had found my card, I could tell he wanted to roll his eyes, but he didn't. He probably thinks I'm incompetent."

"I doubt that. He's probably anxious about his lease and wondering what you'll do if you are awarded the property this building sits on."

"He needn't worry about that, and anyhow, the judge might not rule in my favor." Rachel glanced at her watch. "Well, we'd better finish our exercise. Time's getting away, and I'll need to pick up Sarah Beth shortly."

"I have a good idea. While you are getting Sarah Beth, I'll stop at the deli and pick up some sandwiches."

"Sounds good to me..." Rachel said, glancing over to a couple of machines for building upper-body strength.

Susan stood at the counter of the deli, looking up at the sign on the wall and wondering which sandwiches she should order. Actually, Sarah Beth would probably enjoy a peanut butter sandwich more than the ones offered on the deli's menu. Susan thought a minute and then decided it might be nice to get a turkey, ranch, and Swiss sandwich and one of the interesting-looking salads. She and Rachel could split the sandwich and salad and make Sarah Beth the peanut butter sandwich themselves.

Susan gave her order, took the card with the number, and stood back to let the next person order. She glanced around at the people in the booths and smiled, thinking how quickly people took to a deli and glad that this one was popular, especially with the younger generation.

Susan's eyes swept all the way to the corner booth and stopped when she saw who was eating a salad and talking incessantly. But who was the man with her? It certainly was not her husband, Andre. Maybe it was Karla Broussard's brother. The man looked nearer her age, maybe five or no more than ten years older than Karla. Susan was glad she was partially hidden behind the teenagers standing in front of her waiting to give their order.

Susan watched Karla and wondered what her conversation was about. The way she would hold up her fork and gesture with it gave the impression that whatever she had to say was pretty important, for she didn't think Karla had it in her to be so demonstrative. Karla laughed and put her left hand on the table, and the man reached over and patted it, letting his hand rest on Karla's for a few moments. Karla's laughter waned into a smile, and she finally blinked her well-made-up eyes a couple of times and withdrew her hand from the table, put her fork down, and rested back against the back of the booth. She sat like that for a full two or three minutes, just looking at the man across from her. She finally picked up her fork and began to eat again.

Susan turned to the counter when she heard her number called for the second time. She relinquished her number and took her deli package and left, making sure she could not be seen from Karla's booth.

"No, Rachel, I didn't know who the man was," Susan said, putting salad forks next to their plates. "He appeared to be a lot younger than Karla's husband, though. I wondered if he was her brother until I saw him put his hand on top of hers and her expression. No, I'm sure he was not her brother."

"What did he look like?" Rachel asked, putting Sarah Beth's sandwich down in front of her.

"He had blond hair, blue eyes, and fair skin. It looked like he had a few freckles on his face. Oh yes, he also had a small mustache. And I would guess that he's about six feet tall and on the slender side. It was his blond hair and blue eyes that made me think he might be Karla's brother."

Rachel looked at Susan and rolled her eyes. "Susan, you are describing Konrad Neumann to a tee. That man had to be Konrad Neumann, the person I have a lawsuit against."

Susan picked up her glass of tea and held it a minute, thinking, and then took a sip and said, "Well, apparently they know each other rather well. At least it appeared that way to me. I wonder where Andre was today. You'd think he would be having lunch with them."

"Maybe he had other plans, or maybe he wasn't invited."

Susan took a bite of her sandwich, chewed slowly for a minute or so, and swallowed. She gave Rachel a mischievous grin and said, "I think we need to drop this subject."

THIRTY-TWO

Nancy Grenfell was sitting at the organ when she saw Susan and Rachel coming down the aisle with Sarah Beth. She had a delicious chicken casserole in the oven on time-bake, and she couldn't wait to get better acquainted with the attractive young women from the United States. She nodded a warm greeting, and they nodded back.

It was after the service that Nancy led her three guests to the back of the chapel, through an outside passageway, and into a charming two-story parsonage. The first floor consisted of a small foyer with a spacious parlor on the left. The parlor had a large stone fireplace on the outside wall, flanked on each side by ample bookcases. Large windows took up most of the front wall, and they were positioned a foot and a half off the floor, making it easy for Nancy to enjoy the flowers that she planted near the house. The furniture was arranged attractively, using the fireplace as the focal point. Peter's lounge chair was easy to identify next to his side table holding several books, a good reading lamp, and a small glass jar of lightly salted peanuts. Nancy apologized for what she called the preacher's comfort zone. All in all, the room had a beckoning feel, and Rachel thought how nice it would be to curl up on the sofa after lunch, with the colorful afghan, and take a nap.

Sarah Beth quickly became acquainted with the family cat and was content to sit at the back of the room, with the sun shining through another set of large windows, and let the cat sleep in her lap while she gently stroked it.

Susan and Rachel helped Nancy get the food on the table, and after Sarah Beth washed her hands and joined the others at the table, Peter said the blessing.

Seeing that everyone was served, Peter glanced at Susan and Rachel and said, “I was hoping you ladies would bring Luke to the service with you.”

Rachel looked surprised and quickly said, “But Reverend Grenfell, we hardly know the man. I'm not sure I would even have the nerve to invite him to your service. And if I did, I feel sure he would not come. William, Susan's husband, was told that he is not interested in religion and is married to his work.”

Peter chuckled. “That's what Luke says now, but I suspect the day will come when he'll change his mind. Nancy and I have prayed faithfully for him and his mother and father.”

“Have you known him a long time?” Susan asked.

“I first met him many years ago. I had several German classes under his father at Oxford University. Luke was just a boy but would occasionally come to the university and to his dad's classroom. His mother and father are fine people. They are not spiritual but some of the best people I've ever known. Mrs. Hartmann, also with a doctorate, taught at the university—in the law school. The Hartmanns would often have students over for cookouts at their home. Luke was an only child and would join in the fun. That's how I got to know him.”

Rachel nodded. “You said you took German classes. Were you planning to spend your career here in Germany, sir?”

“My ambition was always to work at the British embassy here in Germany, and I knew how much language figured in. I studied hard and mastered the German language and also had a minor in international studies, and I ended up with the job.” Peter chuckled and shook his head. “I often think back to Dr. Hartmann's classes. He was a unique teacher. Once we stepped across the threshold into his classroom, we were allowed to speak only German. It was quite a challenge, and we couldn't use the excuse of being tongue-tied. Needless to say, he kept us on our toes."

"I can imagine," Susan said, with a soft chuckle. "But what happened if you had a lapse of memory and spoke English?"

"He would make us write a paper in German. I assure you, after that, we were very careful with our words. Actually, his class was a great class for learning discipline."

"I bet Dr. Hartmann was proud of you. It's quite an accomplishment to work at an embassy in a foreign country. That's how William's father met his mother. William said his father spent fifteen years in the United States working in the German embassy. But how did you end up in the ministry, and in Germany, of all places? Please tell us how that came about."

Peter looked at Nancy and smiled. He was buttering a roll and playfully pointed his knife her way and said, "Blame it on her. I guess love will make a person do most anything. You see, I fell in love with Nancy during my first year at the embassy. Her father was a pastor here in Berlin. That's how I came to know the Lord. Being nurtured by Nancy's godly father had a strong impact on my life. And, of course, sitting under his teaching every Sunday, and also at times during the week, contributed to my spiritual growth. I was thirty-two years old and married to Nancy with two children when God called me into full-time service. I left the embassy and went to seminary, and here I am. This was the chapel that Nancy's father preached in. He retired, and God so graciously gave the little chapel to me, and I have some lovely Christians to pastor. Nancy and I have been very happy."

Rachel smiled. "Your testimony has warmed my heart. Really, it's as effective as a sermon, Reverend Grenfell."

"I would be pleased if you young ladies would call me Peter, and I know Nancy feels the same way. Most of our young members call us by our first names." Peter chuckled. "It keeps us young."

It was after dessert and after the dishwasher had been loaded that the four adults relaxed in the living room and continued getting acquainted with one another. Sarah Beth returned to the sleeping cat and settled down next to it.

"Are you girls here on vacation?" Nancy asked.

Susan looked at Rachel, and Rachel said, "No, this trip was a legal one. I don't know if you have the time or the interest for it."

Nancy sat forward and said, "Of course we have the time. Time is about all we do have these days. Our children no longer live here, and most of our church members work so we are not able to visit them in the daytime. Other than visiting those in assisted living and nursing homes and an occasional member in the hospital, we have time on our hands. And that means we have plenty of time to pray. Maybe you could give us a prayer need."

Rachel sighed. "Nancy, I hardly know where to start. But maybe I should start in Germany where my grandmother Sarah was born and raised—right here in Berlin. She married straight out of high school, and it was during the turbulent time of the Nazi regime.

"The Jewish man my grandmother's first husband was employed by worked out a scheme to save the life of his unborn baby girl, which was his fourth child. Pardon me for speaking of my adopted grandfather, Ernst Hoffman, as being her first husband, but he died in the Normandy Invasion, and I never knew him. My grandmother later married a lieutenant from the United States who was stationed in Berlin after Germany surrendered, and they eventually relocated to America. Robert Davis was the only grandfather I ever knew.

"Anyhow, my grandmother wore padding and pretended she was pregnant. When the little Weinberg baby was born, the loyal midwife immediately took the baby to my grandmother's apartment, and everyone thought my grandmother had given birth to the baby. My mother's name was Maria, and she was registered as pure Aryan and given the name Hoffman. Before the Weinberg family was sent to a concentration camp, Mr. Weinberg, my real grandfather, gave my grandmother Sarah and Ernst a satchel with deeds to a lot of East Berlin property. They also gave them beautiful jewelry from three generations of the Weinberg family for safekeeping. In the satchel were family pictures and two typewritten documents, one explaining the birth of their baby and the other a will leaving their estate to baby Maria should the whole family fail to live through the Second World War." Rachel paused. "And, of course, they didn't.

"My mother and father were killed in an automobile accident two years before the Iron Curtain came down. And what I've failed to tell you is that I've inherited the land that the Hartmann Plaza resides on."

Nancy and Peter were shocked and speechless. Peter finally spoke. "Rachel, I have never heard such an intriguing story. So you are over here with a lawsuit trying to reclaim land that was stolen from your grandparents."

"Yes, sir. And I'm afraid it's turning into a nightmare. For some strange reason, my grandmother, Sarah Davis, never told my mother she was adopted, and she never told her about the satchel. Her excuse was that the property was behind the Berlin Wall and she thought it was a lost cause. And also she didn't want my mother to know how her real family died in the concentration camp.

"But I suspect my grandmother loved my mother so much that she did not want to reveal the truth to her. She actually wanted to be my mother's real birth mother and probably convinced herself that she was. I know that sounds strange, but I've been told that the brain can be swayed to think most anything a person wills it to."

Nancy said, "Yes, we've known people like that, and I'm sure Peter could relate to experiences of that nature in his years of counseling, but I have a question. Did Luke Hartmann purchase the deeds to the land?"

"No. He's leasing them from an East German development company by the name of Neumann. Are you familiar with the name?"

Nancy and Peter shook their heads. "No, dear," Nancy said, "I'm afraid we're not."

"Well, to continue my story, we've had one hearing, and the judge has postponed ruling on our case for three months. Greta Wineman, my lead attorney, and William, Susan's husband, thought we had an airtight case, but the defendant's lawyer punched holes in it. They claim I'm an imposter because there are no legal records showing that my mother, Maria, was born to Rebekah and Jacob Weinberg, my true grandparents. They also claim that I'm the blood granddaughter of Sarah and Ernst Hoffman and that Ernst typed the two documents and forged the Weinberg names on them."

Rachel paused and shook her head. "Isn't that ironic? I'm talking about the fact that grandmother probably convinced herself that she was truly Maria's mother, and that's exactly what I'm trying to disprove." Rachel paused again. "We're hoping something will surface in the next few weeks to strengthen my case."

Peter sighed and shook his head again. "I am so sorry that you are having this problem. I have an interest in the Jewish claims, mainly because I'm a firm believer in God's Word and have a love for the Jewish people. I also believe what Nancy's father taught me in the study of prophecy. And, on top of that, I'm a World War II history buff. I love the study of that period."

Nancy gave her husband an affectionate smile and said, "Girls, that's an understatement. I'm ashamed to take you upstairs to see the room Peter calls his World War II room. He has so many books, magazines, and paraphernalia pertaining to that period that I've given up on cleaning it. I just close the door and concentrate on the rest of the house. He loves all of his junk, though, so I let him keep it."

Susan looked over to Peter and said, "I hope Nancy will change her mind and let us have a sneak preview of your famous room, for I, too, love the study of that period." She then looked at her watch and said, "I hate to break up our visit, but I think it's time to leave. William will be calling shortly, and I left my cell in our apartment. I don't want to miss his call."

"Of course, dear, we understand. Peter and I will be praying for both of you and especially for Rachel and her lawsuit."

Nancy and Peter accompanied their guests as they walked out and around the side of the chapel, pointing out things of interest, and Nancy showing them the landscaping that she and Peter had recently completed.

Thanking them again for the lunch and fellowship, Susan said, "Nancy, would you and Peter consider being our guests one evening this week for dinner? We would love to entertain you in the plaza."

"I'm sure we would, wouldn't we, Peter?"

"Indeed. E-mail us the day and time, and we'll be there."

THIRTY-THREE

At breakfast the next morning, Susan poured Rachel and herself a cup of coffee and said, "Rachel, I think we should have Nancy and Peter for dinner at Broussard's."

"But, Susan, it's so expensive."

"I know, but I bet they'll never see the inside of that place if we don't invite them. Anyhow, I've got my credit card. I'll just add the cost of our meal to it. That's what William told me to do."

"I feel bad about you and William picking up so much of the expense here at the plaza. I certainly want to pay my share."

Susan grinned. "We'll let you do that when your ship comes in."

Rachel grunted. "Have you given a thought to the possibility that my ship might not reach harbor?"

"No, Rachel. You are going to win that case. Please stay positive." Susan gave Rachel a pleading look.

"OK, I'll really try. I promise. Now, are you going to e-mail Nancy?"

"Yes. What evening should we choose?"

"I've been thinking about it. Let's say Thursday. That'll give them and us something to look forward to. Anyhow, don't they have prayer meeting on Wednesday night?"

"I think they do, but William has forbidden us to go anywhere by ourselves at nighttime. Don't you remember?"

"Yes, and even if we had someone going with us, Sarah Beth would probably fall asleep. She's worn out at the end of the day."

Susan nodded and said, "After I e-mail them, I think I'll go to the indoor tennis center and hit some balls. Maybe I can find someone to hit with; otherwise I'll have to hit the backboard. What are you going to do?"

"Oh, I don't know. I think I'll just hang around here, maybe wash and dry a few things. I promised Sarah Beth that we would watch a cute movie I bought her right before we moved here. We'll do that this morning. You go on to the tennis center. We'll be fine."

"Mother, I hear the doorbell. Someone's at the door."

"I hear them, honey," Rachel said, getting up from the sofa, walking quickly to the foyer, and pressing a keypad to see who was outside. The screen showed a man in a Hartmann Plaza uniform with a woman in a maid's uniform standing next to him. Rachel pressed a button and asked, "Who is it, please?"

"Service call, Mrs. Lewis," the woman said. "Mr. Hartmann wants all of the electrical boxes inspected. We're having a few outages in some of our apartments. This man does not speak English so Mr. Hartmann sent me to explain."

Rachel frowned. She wished Susan were here, but if Luke sent this man, then she had better let him in; otherwise she would be in trouble. And she certainly didn't want their power going off, especially during the evening and night hours.

Rachel opened the door to the man in service uniform who was holding what looked like a small tool carrier. He smiled, stepped inside, mumbled something in German, and headed to the utility room.

Rachel stood a second and then started to follow him, but her cell rang, and she had to stop a moment and think where she had put it. Rachel walked quickly to the bar in the kitchen and answered the call. A woman said, "Mrs. Lewis, did your little girl leave her purse in the children's library?"

Rachel thought a moment and then said, "No, she didn't. It must have been another little girl, but thank you for asking."

"Yes, well, I'll just leave it here. Whoever left it will be back, I'm sure."

"Is Shannon there?" Rachel asked.

But whoever was on the line had hung up.

Rachel stood, her brow slightly furrowed, looking at her cell a few moments. She then walked back into the living room and put it on the end table next to the sofa. She started back to the utility room but met the serviceman coming out. He mumbled something else in German, handed Rachel a card, and left. Rachel looked at the small card. It read, *Hartmann Plaza Service Department. On call twenty-four hours a day*. It was printed in English and German. The phone number was printed at the bottom, and there was a place to fill out the name of the service person and the time, but it was blank.

She laid it down next to her cell and sat back down on the sofa with Sarah Beth, hoping that she could forget the strange interruption and focus back on the movie.

THIRTY-FOUR

Rachel looked up from the book she was reading and said, "Susan, did you think to invite Nancy and Peter up to see our apartment before we have dinner?"

"I thought since we are eating a little early, they might like to come up after our meal. That way we can relax and visit as long as they want to stay. They won't mind you putting Sarah Beth to bed."

"You're right. Afterward would be best. I hope you told them what the dress code is so they wouldn't be worried about what to wear."

"I did. I'm sure Peter already knew to wear a coat and tie. You can tell he's not a country bumpkin. And if he was with the British embassy for several years, you know he was used to more formal attire. William said his dad was so used to wearing ties that he could put one on blindfold and with most of his fingers tied together. His dad was with the German embassy in the States."

"Yes, I heard you tell Nancy and Peter that. I knew his mother's name was Bradford but never gave much thought to William having a different name."

"William's father was killed on the autobahn shortly before William graduated law school, I think, in 2005. A drunk driver plowed into his car going about ninety miles an hour. Mr. Handel was killed instantly."

"That was a tragedy."

"Yes, and it really affected William. William's mother married Dr. David Bradford almost a year ago. Actually, it was William who introduced them. But, changing the subject, I was dusting this morning and found a card on the end table. Did you have to call the service department for something?"

"Oh, I forgot to tell you. They were having electrical problems in some of the apartments and were checking the electrical boxes on this floor."

"Well, I noticed that the repairman did not fill out the card, and I wondered why."

"I don't know why he didn't. Susan, he only spoke German."

"And you let him in?"

"Luke Hartmann sent an English-speaking maid with him to explain the problem. Otherwise I never would have let him in. He had on a Hartmann Plaza uniform, Susan. I'm sure he was legitimate."

"Did he find any problems with our box?"

"I don't think so. My not speaking German, I had no way of asking."

"William says we can't be too careful in dealing with strangers. Maybe I'm gun-shy, having inherited so much money. It's scary, really."

Rachel tried not to smile. She shook her head and said, "I'm sorry, Susan. I don't understand. I've never had that problem."

Susan picked up a small decorative pillow from the chair she was sitting in and threw it at Rachel. Rachel laughed and caught it.

"Susan, I don't only swim and dive but also used to play basketball—never quite as well as I can dive, but I could catch the ball."

"Rachel Lewis, you are full of tricks, aren't you?" Susan bantered. Glancing down at her watch, she jumped up and said, "Oops—time's getting away, Miss Olympian. I think I'm going to shower and get dressed. Nancy and Peter will be coming before you know it."

Peter looked up at the ceiling with the tiny lights twinkling and exclaimed, "I'm overwhelmed with this beautiful restaurant. I wonder who designed it."

Susan and Rachel looked at each other and laughed. "Peter, you just quoted me. I said the same thing to Rachel the other morning. Whoever thought up the design for this restaurant is extremely gifted."

Nancy added, "And the owner of this restaurant is quite wealthy. You don't build something this elaborate without deep pockets. I can't imagine what the cost of renting it would amount to."

Rachel smiled. "We thought you would like it. Sarah Beth says it's her favorite eating place. But you know why, don't you? Because of the exotic goldfish. I assure you it's not the gourmet food. Everything takes second place to the fish—oh, and the hamburger that the chef so graciously prepared for her." Rachel glanced over to Sarah Beth. "And I keep reminding her that she's not to put her fingers in the water."

Nancy glanced to the fishpond and smiled. "Rachel, I know Sarah Beth brings you a lot of pleasure. Little girls have a way of capturing your heart."

"Yes they do, and I realize that more and more. It seems like it was yesterday that she was toddling around."

"OK, ladies, I hate to interrupt good conversation, but I see the waiter coming and wonder if you have made your selection." Peter looked at Nancy over the rim of his glasses.

"Almost, dear, almost." Nancy said, quickly scanning the menu again. She laid down the menu and smiled at her husband. "Peter, would you please order for me? You know what I like."

Peter respectfully gave their order, and after the waiter left he shook his head and laughed. Susan and Rachel looked at each other and laughed also. They could tell that eating out with the Grenfells would prove to be a delightful experience.

"What's so funny, ladies?"

Rachel looked up. Standing to the side of her was Luke Hartmann, dressed for dinner in a beautiful gray suit, obviously tailor-made just for him. His yellow tie was of the finest silk. His hand rested lightly on the back-corner of her chair.

Susan blushed and stammered, "Uh, nothing really. It was just something Nancy said. Mr. Hartmann, you do know Nancy and Peter Grenfell, don't you?"

"Of course I do. I saw you come in and thought I might speak to Peter and Nancy."

Peter stood and shook Luke's hand, and Nancy smiled and said, "Luke, we haven't seen you in a long time, and after seeing this beautiful building of yours, I can see why."

Luke nodded. "Yes, the plaza has kept me busy—I would say very busy—for the last four years or more. It was quite an undertaking."

"I can imagine. I don't think I've ever been in a restaurant as beautiful as this one," Peter said with a slight wave of his hand. "We wondered who designed it."

"Andre Broussard, the proprietor, said a young French architect designed it. There is none like it in all of Europe. Your compliment will please Andre."

There was a moment of silence, and then Peter said, "Have you had dinner?"

Luke shook his head. "No, and I did not come over here to disturb yours. You have ordered, haven't you?"

"Yes, but we would like, very much, for you to join us. Wouldn't we, girls?"

"Indeed," Nancy and Susan chorused. Rachel smiled and nodded.

"Well, your table is certainly large enough for six. I see five settings. Where is your fifth?"

"Where else but the fishpond?" Rachel said, glancing up at Luke.

Luke smiled at Rachel and said, "It takes me back to my childhood. The fishpond, I'm talking about. The best days of my life were spent fishing with my grandfather."

Peter spoke up. "Did your grandfather live in London?"

"No, about a hundred miles from Oxford, where I grew up. I would visit him during summer vacation."

"Making memories, no doubt."

"Yes, very good ones."

Susan looked up. "We insist that you join us, Mr. Hartmann?"

"Only if you call me Luke."

Susan smiled. "Then Luke it is." She glanced around the terrace. "I wonder if a waiter could bring another chair."

"That will be no problem."

Luke turned and motioned to a waiter nearby, and a sixth chair was added between Susan and Peter. "Now, Luke," Peter said, "we need to get your order in."

"That, also, will be no problem. I'll call the kitchen and have my order added to yours." Luke pulled out his cell, pressed a couple of numbers, and ordered in German.

Susan looked at Rachel and could tell that she was impressed, or maybe a better word would be *intimidated.* Rachel turned and motioned for Sarah Beth to return to her seat. She examined her hands to see if they were clean and took out a wipe from her purse and cleaned them. Rachel shook her head. "She didn't put her hands in the water; she just cleaned the top of the slate with them."

Everyone laughed and Rachel looked up to see Luke's eyes focused on her, his expression hinting at feelings of awe and maybe a bit of caution. Rachel dropped her eyes and wondered what was really going through his mind.

Nancy and Peter stood just inside the foyer door on the living room side and scanned the room. Nancy exclaimed, "This is a beautiful room, and if this is an indication of what the whole apartment looks like, I would say you girls are living in luxury."

"Yes," Susan said, "William surprised us with a six-month lease. I'm glad he did. Nancy, the swimming pool and workout center are state-of-the-art. In fact, everything in this building is five-star, and we are still getting acquainted with the shops and other things offered here."

Peter said, "Luke's done a great job. I wonder why he wouldn't come on up with us. But I'm glad he joined us for dinner. It was quite a surprise seeing him this evening and more than generous of him to pick up the check."

"Yes, that was kind of him. William says he's quite wealthy and a workaholic. He has been overheard, numerous times, saying that he's married to his work. I guess he's talking about his commodity business. We understand that a large part of the third floor is dedicated to his commodity business and the management of this building. And another thing. He's known for working after hours. I wouldn't be surprised if he left us and went to his office."

Peter shook his head. "Yes, he's admitted to me that his business comes first. I'm afraid he's consumed with it and now with Hartmann Plaza. I surely hope he'll get someone to manage this large building for him."

Nancy smiled at Rachel and said, "Well, I caught Luke looking at Rachel off and on during dinner. I couldn't exactly read him, but if I were to guess, I'd say it was a look of interest."

Rachel raised her eyebrows. "Nancy, looks of interest don't always mean the interest is favorable. I've had some strange looks from that man ever since my court case. But let's not stand here. You and Peter have a seat. Susan will entertain you while I put Sarah Beth to bed."

Luke sat back in his leather desk chair, his feet propped on his desk, and laced his fingers together, letting them rest on the middle of his torso. He looked at the upper part of his $500 Gucci loafers and thought about Rachel.

There was no doubt she was the prettiest woman he had seen in years, with her long, thick lashes, sparkling brown eyes, and smile that would melt any man's heart. She had a pleasant enough personality—maybe a little on the shy side but not pushy like so many of the women he knew. And as far as the court case was concerned, he had just about convinced himself that Rachel's claim didn't matter that much one way or the other. He knew he could deal with young William Handel. Anyhow, Neumann would probably get to keep the deeds.

Luke reached over to his desk and picked up a pencil, toying with it and asking himself the big question. Why did he go to their table tonight? Was it to see Peter and Nancy Grenfell? Or was that just an excuse to see Rachel? As determined as he had been to keep her at a distance and as diligent as he had been in resisting the slightest romantic emotion that might have arisen, there seemed to be a magnetism that kept drawing him.

He had to admit that being at their table tonight was an enjoyable experience. Susan Handel had entered into every conversation and was never at a loss for words. Peter and Nancy were good people even if they were a little too religious. But that was Peter's profession, and he was dedicated to it, just like Luke Hartmann was dedicated to his, so he had no reason to be critical.

Luke removed his feet from his desk. He rarely ever put his feet there and didn't know why he did tonight. Maybe he could think better sitting back in his chair. Anyhow, he needed to settle down and try to forget Rachel and her cute eight-year-old daughter and go to work. It was eight-thirty, and he could put in two good hours before retiring to his apartment.

THIRTY-FIVE

Rachel came into the living room, picked up the attractive tote with the books in it, and said, "Susan, do you mind keeping an eye on Sarah Beth while I return the books to the children's library? She was reading to me but fell asleep. I won't be gone more than twenty or thirty minutes. Shannon promised to give me some information on a reading program she recommends. I might look at a few websites with her."

"Sure, I'm going to e-mail Aunt Della and then try to finish the book I've been reading for the last week. You go on and work with Shannon—oh, and tell her I said hello."

"I will." Rachel stopped at the door and turned around. "And if Sarah Beth wakes up, let her have a snack but nothing to ruin her dinner."

"Will do," Susan said with a wave of her hand.

Rachel stepped in the elevator and pressed the button for the second floor, hardly noticing the man standing at the back of the elevator, slightly bent, reaching down for his briefcase. She adjusted the tote she was carrying and glanced up to the fast-moving numbers when all of a sudden an arm came around the upper part of her body and something clamped over her nose and mouth. She tried to scream but couldn't. All she could do was inhale the strong solution that quickly overcame her, causing her arm to fall to her side and the tote to slide off. The last thing she heard was the tote hitting the floor before she completely passed out.

Rachel opened her eyes to darkness and lay there trying to remember what had happened and why she was lying on a cold concrete floor. It slowly came to her. She had been drugged in the elevator. There was no one on the elevator but her and one other person, a man she had never seen before and would probably not recognize if she saw again. Why would he want to drug her?

She rolled over on her side and tried to sit up, but dizziness overcame her, and she lay back down. Finally her head began to clear, and she tried again, this time working her way slowly to a sitting position and resting her back against the wall. She felt for her small cell. It was not there. Of course it was not there. Why would she think it would be? No one drugging her would be stupid enough to leave her with a cell.

Rachel felt the wall behind her. It was smooth concrete. She sat still and breathed deeply, trying to relax, and then got on her hands and knees and pushed up, leaning against the wall to keep her balance.

Inching forward, she began to feel around the wall and soon realized that she had to be in an empty closet no larger than five feet square. She found the door, ran her hand across the smooth surface, and tapped on it. It was metal. She groped for the handle, but it was locked, and she stood, holding onto the handle, fighting the tears.

She could not let herself panic if she were going to get out. She had to think but then realized that thinking was futile in a five-by-five-foot, dark, locked concrete closet. Rachel balled up her fist and banged on the door, but her soft hand made little noise. She reached down, removed her sandal, and banged on the door with the rubber sole. But it also made little noise, and after several minutes, she stopped. There was nothing but complete silence.

She slipped her sandal back on and sat down, resting back against the wall once more. Apparently someone or maybe more than one person was out to scare her, or maybe even hurt her. A feeling of panic overtook Rachel, and she willed herself to breathe deeply, again and again. As she began to settle down, she realized that the plan was to put her in the closet until she could be slipped out of the building unseen, and whatever they planned to do to her had to be done somewhere else. She wondered if she was still in Hartmann Plaza, maybe in the basement, which would explain the concrete wall and floor. Could it be possible that they were planning to kill her?

Who hated her enough to want her dead? On the other hand, hate might not have been the motive. It was more likely money, she thought, as her mind raced back to the Italian restaurant and the conversation she and Susan had overheard. Karla said Andre had a lot to lose and, Andre said he was sick of hearing about "the woman." Well, apparently Rachel was the woman. Apparently the Broussards and maybe also Luke Hartmann were involved. But surely Luke was not a killer. And didn't he join them for dinner last night? But was that just a ruse to divert attention from him? Nancy said he kept looking at Rachel. But what was he really thinking—or plotting?

Maybe it was Konrad Neumann. Susan said she had seen Karla Broussard sitting with Neumann in the deli. Neumann had the most to lose. But wasn't Luke Hartmann sitting with Konrad Neumann at the trial? And weren't they huddled together after the judge's decision to delay the ruling?

Maybe it was Luke who hired the man. Luke had access to every movement his residents made. He would have no problem carrying out something of this nature. If that were true, the man would be back, and she had nothing to fight with. How could a 115-pound woman overcome a strong man? It was hopeless. Rachel slumped back against the wall and wept.

Susan glanced at her watch. Sarah Beth was still napping, and Rachel had been gone an hour and a half. Rachel must have gotten more involved with Shannon and the children's reading programs than she had anticipated. Well, it was normal for a schoolteacher and a librarian to let time slip away. But on the other hand, Rachel would have called if she were planning to stay that long. Maybe ten or fifteen minutes more would not merit a call but a whole hour? Susan frowned and put her book aside when she heard Sarah Beth's feet hit the floor.

"Where's Mommy, Susan?" Sarah Beth asked, yawning and rubbing her eyes.

"Honey, she went to take some books back to the library. Come here and let me fix your hair." Susan took the band from her ponytail, brushed her hair back with her hands, and put the elastic band back on. "Did you have a nice nap?"

"Umm." Sarah Beth nodded her head. She yawned again. "When's Mommy coming back?"

"I'm going to call her right now. She should be on her way. Would you like a little snack, honey?"

"Do you have any fudgsicles?"

"Yes, but wait a second until I call your mommy, and then I'll get you one."

Susan scrolled to Rachel's number and called but received nothing but her answering service. That wasn't like Rachel, she thought. She walked to the kitchen and looked up the library number using the in-house directory. Shannon said Rachel had not been in. Susan stood a moment thinking and then realized that something was not right. Rachel would never change her plans without telling Susan. She needed to call for help but could not talk in front of the child.

Susan gave Sarah Beth a fudgsicle, settled her on a bar stool in the kitchen, and then slipped into the bathroom to make the call.

Luke Hartmann looked annoyed when the light blinked on his phone. He had given his secretary instructions that he was not to be disturbed. He waited a few moments before pressing the button. "What is it, Joyce? Have you forgotten that I am not to be disturbed?"

"Forgive me, Mr. Hartmann, but I have a woman on the line, and she is frantic and wants to speak to you. She would not take no for an answer."

"Who is she?"

"Susan Handel, Mrs. William Handel, in apartment ten twenty-two."

"Put her on."

"Yes, sir."

"Susan? This is Luke Hartmann speaking."

"Luke, I did not know who to call. I was afraid if I called security they might not take me seriously, and I'm here alone with Sarah Beth and cannot leave her."

"What's your problem?"

"Rachel Lewis is missing."

"What do you mean she's missing?

"She left our apartment almost two hours ago to return books to the children's library. She said she would not be gone over thirty minutes, and she's been gone almost two hours. I called her cell and got her answering service. I called the library, and she was never there. I'm really worried."

"Could she have changed her plans—maybe run into a friend and lost track of time?"

"No, she would never do that without calling me."

"I see. Susan, I'll need a description of Rachel for security. Would you please give me one?"

"Yes, Rachel is five feet five inches tall, weighs one hundred fifteen pounds, and has brown, slightly curly hair and brown eyes. She is wearing a pair of brown capri pants and a peach-colored sweater with three-quarter-length sleeves. And she's wearing brown sandals. She was carrying three books in one of your children's library totes."

"Thank you. I'll get on this right away. You stay in your apartment with the child, and I'll get back to you shortly."

"Thank you, Luke."

Luke turned to his in-house communication system and punched a button. "Yes, sir? Rudy speaking."

"Yes, Rudy—we have a missing woman." Luke quickly read the information describing Rachel and said, "I want you to run the elevator tapes back two hours and fast-forward to see if you can pick up anything. She entered the elevator on the tenth floor. Get two other men and check three elevators—numbers four, six, and eight."

"Yes, sir. We'll tend to this immediately."

Luke got up, walked to his window, and looked out, oblivious to the traffic, wondering where Rachel Lewis was. There had to be a simple explanation. The faint beeping noise broke Luke's train of thought and he turned and quickly returned to his desk. The call was from security. "Have you found something this soon, Rudy?"

"Sir, I hate to tell you this, but the elevator camera on number six has been tampered with. I checked the floor tracking records and found that the number-six elevator went all the way to the basement. Sir, only our service elevators go there. Someone did an override on number six."

"Rudy, I want you to check the thermal cameras in the basement. Check every one of them. I'll wait."

"Yes, sir."

Luke took a deep breath and rubbed his hand across his clean-shaven jaw. He dropped his hand and leaned slightly forward when he heard Rudy's voice.

"Mr. Hartmann?"

"Yes, Rudy, what did you find?"

"We found a single image and some movement on camera three. It's in the north end of the building. We've pinpointed a closet across from the storage room that we keep the janitorial supplies in. Do you want me to send Sam and Ralph down?"

"No, I'm going myself."

"Sir, do you know where it is?"

"Yes, I already have it on my computer, and I can see exactly where the closet is. Get Sam and Ralph to take the elevator to the first floor then come down the stairs to be sure they are clear and wait there between the elevator and the door to the stairs. They can stand guard."

"Yes, sir."

Luke got on the service elevator and pressed the letter *B*. Surely Rachel Lewis would not be locked up in a closet in their basement. That didn't make sense. Maybe an animal got in there by mistake. The servicemen could have carelessly left the door open when a delivery was made. That had to be it.

The door opened, and Luke got off the elevator and walked quickly to the small closet that had shown the thermal imaging. When he inserted the electronic card and opened the door, a ray of light shone in, revealing Rachel pressed against the back wall, trembling, her eyes wide with fright. Luke stood, shocked. He could tell that she had been crying.

She raised both hands and hysterically began to cry and plead. "Please, Luke, don't kill me. My little girl would be all by herself. She would have no one."

Luke stepped forward and reached for Rachel, but she fought him and became even more hysterical, crying out, "Please, I don't want to die. You can have the land. Please, just let me go."

Luke finally overcame Rachel, caught her arms, and pulled her close. He wrapped his arms around her and held her tight.

"What are you talking about, Rachel? Why do you think I'm here to kill you? I would never do that. I've come to get you out of this closet."

Rachel didn't answer him. She was trembling too badly and had begun to sob again. Luke continued to hold her, his right hand gently pressing her head against his shoulder. He stroked her hair and spoke softly. "Don't cry, Rachel. I promise. I'm not going to hurt you. I do not know where you got that idea. I would never hurt you."

Rachel's sobbing lessened, and she drew in a deep breath, closed her eyes, and relaxed her head against Luke's shoulder. An occasional shudder caused Luke to hold her even tighter while his mind raced, searching for answers as to why Rachel was locked up and why she thought he was out to kill her.

Luke stood still as seconds turned into minutes, and he continued to hold her in his arms. He told her once more, "You're safe now, Rachel. I'm not going to let anyone hurt you."

Luke could feel Rachel's intake of breath and a deep sigh, and he knew that she would be all right. But as for him? He wasn't so sure. For he knew, without a shadow of a doubt, that he was falling in love with her.

THIRTY-SIX

Rachel awakened in her own bed and looked over to the small digital clock on her nightstand. It was eight o'clock. She quickly pushed up on one elbow and turned to Sarah Beth's bed. When she saw the small form under the covers and her hair splayed across her pillow, she breathed out and fell back, wincing at the subtle pain when her head hit the pillow. She felt groggy and her mouth was dry. Yesterday's memories of being drugged surfaced, and she shut her eyes and fought the tears, allowing only one to escape and run down the side of her cheek.

She didn't remember much after Luke brought her home. Why was she calling this apartment home? It could never be a home. After what she had gone through, nothing in Germany could ever be home to her.

She did remember Luke calling his doctor and then being given something to help her sleep. Was it possible she had slept thirteen hours? Rachel wiped her fingers across the dampness on the side of her cheek. She needed to get up, make coffee, and bring some life back to rid herself of that slightly drugged feeling that often follows a heavy, induced sleep. Rachel sat up on the side of her bed a few moments and then got up and put her slippers and robe on. After going to the bathroom and brushing her hair and teeth, she came into the kitchen to find Susan sipping a cup of coffee and reading her Bible.

Susan looked up, pushed her Bible to the side, and put her coffee down. Trying to keep the anxiety out of her voice, she said, "I'm glad you're awake, Rachel. I've been worried about you sleeping so long. Are you all right?"

"I guess. What kind of sleeping pills did Luke's doctor give me? I think I've slept almost thirteen hours."

"I'm not sure of the name. I'll have to look on the bottle. I don't think Luke ordered more than three or four pills. He said you shouldn't need more than that to help you sleep normally again."

"I should hope not." Rachel sighed. "Susan, I need a cup of coffee—something to wake me up. I have a hangover."

"Of course, Rachel. You sit still. I'll get you some coffee, and you need to eat something, also. You have not had anything to eat since yesterday at noon, and that was nothing but a green salad."

"I'm really not very hungry."

"I know, but you still need to eat something or you'll develop a headache and end up nauseated."

"Maybe some toast, then."

"And some jelly."

"OK, if you insist. Toast and jelly." Rachel put her hand on her forehead and leaned on the counter. "Susan, yesterday was a nightmare."

"I agree, Rachel. I'm still in shock from what happened. I'm just so thankful that you were not harmed."

"And I'm thankful Sarah Beth was not with me. I could not stand it if she had been hurt."

"Rachel, let's not think about things like that, please." Susan put Rachel's cup in front of her. "Your toast will be ready in a minute. I might put some bacon in the microwave for Sarah Beth. She'll probably be up shortly."

"Susan, what did you tell Sarah Beth about me? You did say she was with Luke's secretary watching a movie, didn't you?"

"Yes. And that was Luke's idea. He didn't think Sarah Beth should see you in the condition you were in and called with that suggestion before he brought you back up. Sarah Beth was a little reluctant to go with Joyce at first, but I assured her that it was all right. When Joyce told her they were going to watch *Mary Poppins,* she left with a big smile on her face. I understand Luke has a beautiful snack room. That's where they watched the movie."

"Was she upset when she came back and I was asleep in bed?"

"She asked for you and I told her that you had a bad headache and needed to sleep. Rachel, I was not going to scare her with what happened yesterday."

Rachel shook her head. "She would have been frightened to death." Rachel paused and took a sip of her coffee. "How long did Luke stay after I went to bed?"

"He stayed until nine. He ordered dinner, and after I fed Sarah Beth and put her to bed, we talked. He wanted to see what I knew that might shed some light on what happened and why you were locked up in the closet. Rachel, Luke hopes you can identify the man who drugged you."

"Susan, I told him I could not. I never really saw his face."

"You didn't see him when you got on the elevator?"

"No. He was leaning over to pick up his briefcase. I stepped inside and pressed the button for the second floor and then stood, looking up at the fast-moving numbers. I remember the tote slipping a little on my arm and my adjusting it and then the man grabbing me and clamping something over my nose and mouth. I wanted to scream but couldn't. I heard the tote hit the floor, and that's the last thing I remember until I came to in the basement closet."

"I know it must be difficult to talk about," Susan said, patting Rachel on her arm. "Luke called William and told him what happened and that there would be a full investigation. You can imagine how upset William was. He immediately booked a ticket and will be flying in late tomorrow."

Rachel forced a weak smile. "I know you'll be glad to see him, and so will I."

"Yes, I can't wait." Susan hesitated a moment and then said, "I know this is an awkward question, but it's the elephant in the room, and I can't ignore it. Please tell me. Why do you think Luke was trying to kill you?"

Rachel spread a bit of jelly on her toast before answering. "Susan, when you are locked in a five by five foot concrete room by yourself for two hours, you have a lot of time to think. The Broussard's conversation in French that we overheard kept running through my mind. If you can remember, Andre was tired of hearing about 'that woman.' Apparently I was that woman and Karla was complaining about the lawsuit and how much money they stood to lose if I won. Maybe she has money of her own invested with Andre's. Anyhow, I think she wanted to get rid of me and I figured she convinced Luke to help her. She probably planned it."

"That's ridiculous, Rachel. I doubt Karla Broussard could plan a picnic, let alone plot a murder. She doesn't appear to be very smart to me."

"Well, Luke is smart, and he has access to everything that goes on in this building. It wouldn't be difficult for him."

"I don't see how you can think that. Luke is no killer. Rachel, we had dinner with him two nights ago. He was as friendly as could be."

"Well, maybe it was Neumann and Karla. But I doubt that. Susan, if you could have seen Neumann and Luke huddled together at the hearing, you might be suspicious of them also."

"Luke was shocked and upset by what you accused him of and said he had a hard time getting you to settle down. He said you might be small but you can fight like a tiger."

"He told you all about it, didn't he?"

"Yes. He had to. Rachel, he looked like he had been in a fight."

Rachel suppressed a smile. "I got lipstick all over the upper part of his expensive shirt and tie. I doubt it will come out."

"Luke was not concerned about that shirt and tie. He probably has a closet full of shirts and ties. He wanted to know why you thought he was trying to kill you."

"Well, I just told you why. What did you tell him?"

"I didn't know what to tell him, Rachel. I was also in a state of shock. But I did tell him about overhearing the Broussards' conversation."

"What did he say?"

"He was surprised and confided that they were having marital problems, but he didn't elaborate, and I let it drop."

"See? If he wanted to clear the Broussards and himself, he would have at least tried to explain what they were talking about. Susan, I figured the man who put me in that closet planned to come back after dark and move me somewhere far away from the building. Whoever plotted to kill me was making sure that this new building would not be involved and have its reputation tarnished."

"Rachel, by accusing Luke, you are implying that he cares more for the reputation of this building than your life. That is not true, and I don't see how you could come to that conclusion. He said over and over how thankful he was that he was able to rescue you. Believe me when I say that."

"Maybe you're right, yet I still have my doubts. Did he notify the police?"

"Yes, Luke said his security team called the police and they sent out a forensic team early in the evening. They sealed the basement off and worked for two hours taking prints in the elevator and closet and searching for any clues that might have been left by the man.

"And another thing. Luke has set up a meeting at ten o'clock this morning in his office and wants you and me to be there. A detective by the name of Richard Wendall has been assigned to your case, and he's a friend of Luke. He'll interview us." Susan paused. "Rachel, I hope you will not cast any suspicions on Luke."

Rachel shook her head. “No, I wouldn’t do that, Susan. I have more sense than that.”

Susan looked at Rachel and sighed. “This detective is going to prove you wrong. You wait and see.”

“I hope he does, Susan. I truly hope he does.”

THIRTY-SEVEN

"I'm so glad to be back, sweetheart." William said, pulling Susan into his arms and kissing her. "You can't imagine how much I've missed you."

"And I've missed you too, William, more than you realize, and especially these last three days. I sure hope you can talk some sense into Rachel."

"Let's not talk about Rachel. I think when she gets over the scare she had, she'll see things in a different light. And maybe the detective will solve the case quickly, and she'll see that Luke's not her enemy." William gave Susan a lingering kiss.

Susan sighed and relaxed in William's arms. She traced her finger across his chin and said, "You have not told me how long you'll be able to stay. I hope you don't have to rush back so soon."

"No, I plan to stay at least a week or maybe ten days. But then I'll have to return and finish the case I've been working on." William kissed Susan again and said, "Did I tell you how alluring you are early in the morning?"

"Maybe. I can't remember," Susan said, smiling and sliding her fingers down the side of William's neck. "I can't wait for you to meet the Grenfells."

"I know, but that can wait. Right now, I just want to concentrate on us." William kissed Susan on her neck.

"You don't want to talk? You've been gone for three weeks."

"No, I don't want to talk," William said, fumbling with the top button on Susan's pajamas.

William was drinking his second cup of coffee when Susan's cell rang. Susan spoke a few minutes and then turned and said, "William, this is Nancy Grenfell. She wants to know if we can bring Rachel and Sarah Beth over this afternoon. Rachel called and told them about what happened Friday."

"I don't see why not. I'm looking forward to meeting them. What time do they want us to come?"

"She said three o'clock if it's convenient for us."

"Tell her we'll be there."

Rachel was holding Sarah Beth's hand as they walked. She looked up at William and said, "I'm so thankful you're here, William. Susan and I have not been out of Hartmann Plaza since Sunday a week ago, and we miss the fresh air and sunshine. It's delightful walking to the Grenfells. I'm glad you didn't make us take a cab."

"If I thought there would be danger, I would have, but there was no reason to do that. I think you're perfectly safe with us walking together. And I agree that it's delightful being outside, especially after that long flight over here. It's good to stretch my legs. How many blocks is it to the Grenfells, anyhow?"

"I think Sarah Beth counted them. Didn't you say there were six, honey?"

Sarah Beth looked up, smiled and said, "Yes, mother, I counted six."

They walked awhile in silence, and Rachel asked, "Did Luke say when the investigation would be complete?"

"He hopes by the end of the week."

Rachel glanced toward the bus full of children passing by. "I trust the detective will have uncovered the truth by then, but I doubt it."

"Why do you say that, Rachel?"

"Oh, I don't know. Just some vibes, I guess."

"Well, let's be positive. I really think Luke's going to push Wendall hard to get to the bottom of this mystery. Let's give both of them a chance, OK?"

Rachel nodded. She smiled and said, "Look, I see the Grenfells. They are out front waiting for us."

After Susan introduced William, Nancy and Peter ushered the four into the parsonage and to the living room, where the adults settled while Sarah Beth left to search for Tippy, the family cat. The discussion of Rachel's bad experience led to a short prayer session, and afterward, Nancy excused herself and went to the kitchen to get refreshments.

Peter surprised William when he said, "William, I've really looked forward to meeting you, especially since I found out that you were the young lawyer who read Mr. Haydn's journal."

William turned quickly to Susan. Susan shook her head no, and they both turned to Peter when he chuckled and continued, "Susan did not tell me. It was Matthew Maas, Mr. Haydn's pastor, who told me."

William's surprised look evolved into one of curiosity, and he said. "This is interesting. Please tell me, Peter, what is your connection to Matthew Maas? I really don't know him but heard him speak at Mr. Haydn's funeral. His message was dynamic."

"Yes, I was there and agree with you. It was dynamic." Peter thought a moment. "Let's see now...It was twenty years ago that I entered seminary and served something like an internship under Matthew. It was a wonderful experience. He is such a godly man and taught me a lot. That's also when I met Mr. Haydn and Mr. Kroft."

"You know Leonard Kroft?"

"Indeed I do."

"Did you know that he is residing in an assisted-living home in Arlington, Virginia, in the States?"

"No. How did that come about?"

"Well, he came over for Susan's and my wedding. He gave Susan away and a few days later slipped on an icy sidewalk and broke his hip. He's doing fine now. The hip has healed, and he'll probably be coming back to Germany in the near future."

"William, you be sure and tell him that Peter and Nancy Grenfell said hello. He'll remember us from when I served in their church with Pastor Maas. We were there four years before taking this pulpit."

"That's very interesting. I'm sure Mr. Kroft will be pleased to hear from you and Nancy."

"Yes. And I'll tell you something else interesting. I did not know who Susan really was until Nancy's younger brother, Fred, who is an attorney, told me. He keeps up with all of the high-profile cases in Germany. From what he said, the lawyers kept Susan's case pretty much out of the news, but Fred was involved in a case that a Jewish couple brought against Wolfgang Mueller, and it was while he was working on that case that he met Paul Abraham and the facts of Susan's case came out. I was telling Fred about meeting Susan and Rachel, and one thing leading to another, he began to piece things together. Of course, we respect your and Susan's right to privacy and certainly would not discuss this with others."

"And we appreciate that, Peter. When Susan inherited half of her grandfather's estate, her life was threatened. Not many people know this, but she and I were both kidnapped before the case came to trial, and had it not been for the grace of God, we would have been killed by an overdose of drugs.

"Having a lot of money is not always the answer to happiness, as many people may think. Before we were married, Susan and I attended a Christian seminar on wealth management and learned the right perspective to have toward money. We vowed to each other that we would practice what we've learned, and so far, we've done that."

"William, I've discovered, in my ministry, that a large percentage of divorces are caused by couples who have money problems that they cannot resolve. I have put on several seminars pertaining to money management. There is definitely a need for Christian financial counseling in the world we live in today."

"I agree with you, Peter. We entrusted a great deal of Susan's estate to a competent investment company, but I manage some of it and am quick to confess that it is time-consuming and a big responsibility. But don't misunderstand—I'm not complaining. I've learned a lot, and I wouldn't have it any other way. And I wouldn't be honest if I didn't admit that we both enjoy having things that we would not ordinarily have. But we do not go around broadcasting that we are rich."

"That's commendable and a good testimony, William. Sometime, I want you to tell us in detail about that kidnapping experience. I'm sure it was frightening."

"What's frightening, dear?" Nancy said, coming in with a pitcher of lemonade and a plate of homemade cookies.

"Never mind, Nancy, I'll tell you later. Let's let the young folks enjoy your refreshments. Where is Sarah Beth? I know she loves lemonade and cookies."

THIRTY-EIGHT

Luke Hartmann sat at his desk looking at the names that he had compiled for Richard Wendall. Richard's first step had been to have Luke and his three partners take a lie detector test. Richard reported that all had passed.

Andre Broussard had cleared his throat at least ten times within fifteen minutes after Luke told him what Richard's instructions were. Luke chuckled, thinking about Andre's remark. He said, "What about you, Luke? I know you are friends. Is he making you take the damn test, also?"

Luke's eyes moved down the list and focused on Neumann's name. Neumann was the first person Richard targeted. But Neumann had also passed the lie detector test.

Of course, a lie detector test was not 100 percent-foolproof—only 99 percent, much like the expert witness testified to in Rachel Lewis' hearing about the handwriting analysis.

Luke rubbed the pencil's eraser across the bottom of his chin, deep in thought. Rachel certainly had not locked herself in the closet, nor had she paid anyone to lock her in. That was obvious. No one could have faked the show she put on, not even her.

Paul Abraham had nothing to gain. Anyhow, he was close friends with William and Susan. He would never harm his friends.

Karla Broussard had a big mouth and loved to spout off, but she really had nothing to lose. She had no personal money invested in the plaza. In fact, he doubted if Karla had any money of her own. Andre had confided to him the fact that Karla had been a waitress in his Paris restaurant, and he married her after his wife died. Richard had not asked Karla to take the lie detector test, and Luke would feel like a fool suggesting to him that she do it.

That left William and Susan Handel. But what would they gain? Luke sat back in his chair and propped his feet on his desk. He eyed his Gucci loafers, and once more promised himself he would not make a habit of propping his feet on his desk, but he seemed to do his best thinking in that position. And this problem called for drastic measures.

He had not given William and Susan much thought. William was an extremely likable fellow and so was Susan. But thinking about them and how young they were made Luke wonder how they could afford to stay in the plaza at $10,000 a month rent. William, certainly, was not getting the money from Rachel. Rachel was only a schoolteacher with a small pension from her deceased husband's military service.

Luke wondered if they had family money. A lot of young people were rich by inheritance. Maybe that was the case with them. Luke removed his feet from the desk and swung around to the desk arm that held his computer. He would first do a search on William Handel. Maybe there would be something there, but on the other hand, there might be nothing.

Luke typed in William's name and address. He was glad he had paid for a subscription to You Search, a large people-search database operation with headquarters in England. It took a few minutes, but Luke was able to scroll through and get the information he wanted.

William was born in Arlington, Virginia, where his father was assigned to the German embassy. He moved to Berlin, Germany, with his parents and sister when he was twelve years old. William graduated from an elite prep school in Berlin, entered college, and graduated magna cum laude with a degree in accounting. After graduation, he attended law school and graduated summa cum laude in 2005. He was editor of the law journal, and after graduation he was employed as an associate with the Rhueman & Schmitt, et al. law firm in Berlin for three years. The information stopped there.

Luke sat back and thought about William. He had not realized that William had resided in Germany. William's English was perfect, with absolutely no accent. Luke would have sworn that William had spent his twenty-nine years in the United States. Well, that was interesting.

Luke printed William's information and read it again but did not see anything there to indicate that he would have enough money to stay in Hartmann Plaza. Luke frowned and thought. Could Susan have the money? She certainly didn't act like it. Not that she did not have class, for she certainly did. Most wealthy young people flaunted their wealth, but Susan was as down-to-earth as anyone he had ever become acquainted with.

Luke typed in *Susan* but then removed his hands from the keyboard and thought a minute. He did not know her maiden name. There were probably a hundred Susan Handels in the database. Luke propped his chin on his hand and thought. Well, he had no choice. He would type in *Susan Handel* with the same address William had given and see what came up.

Luke waited a moment and then sat forward to be sure he was reading the name right. The name that came up was *Susan Leah*. Her last name was Leah? Luke clicked on last name *Leah,* and two hundred names associated with *Leah* came up, but no Leah with the first name Susan came up. Luke grimaced and left the You Search website.

He decided he would go about it in a different way. He typed in *babies born in Arlington, Virginia, in 1983.* When the long list came up, Luke almost cursed. That was something else his parents taught him. The first time Luke said a curse word, his mother washed his mouth out with soap. And during his teenage years, they reinforced their teaching method with common sense answers to his questions. Mature, self-confident people did not curse. They had self-control, and people who exercised self-control always had the upper hand.

Well, there were plenty of babies born in 1983. He would narrow it down to female babies. That did reduce the list considerably. Then Luke typed in *Susan,* but that didn't help. Apparently the newborn would have been registered under her last name. He would have to be patient going through the list and see if there was a Susan Leah. Leah was probably her middle name. Luke dragged his mouse slowly, blinking his eyes and stopping at intervals, careful not to overlook the right name.

There it was—in the month of June. *Susan Leah Goldman.* Goldman? But Susan was not Jewish. Surely, this was not the right Susan. Nevertheless, Luke clicked on *Susan Leah Goldman.* Her mother was Jennifer Lee Goldman, and her father was Benjamin Carl Goldman Jr. The name Lee was not Jewish. Maybe Susan was half Jewish.

Luke left the Arlington, Virginia website, pulled You Search back up and typed in *Susan Leah Goldman.* When the results appeared on the screen, he smiled. Susan Leah Goldman resided in Arlington, Virginia. She graduated from the College of William and Mary and also held a masters in journalism. She was a freelance writer for several publications. Goldman was listed as defendant to a suit brought by EGED in Germany. The date listed was November 2008. That was less than a year ago.

That was all the information available. Apparently there had not been an update on Goldman since the suit was settled. Luke opened the middle drawer to his desk, pulled out Paul Abraham's card and looked at it. Abraham was chief financial officer for EGED, the East German Economic Development non-profit organization that was founded by the late Randolph Wilhelm Haydn.

Luke, again sat back and propped his feet on his desk, holding Paul's card and unconsciously rubbing his thumb across the smooth surface. He needed to find out how the case came out. Apparently Susan Goldman won. And it had something to do with the Haydn estate. He leaned over, laid Paul's card on the desk, rubbed his hand across his smooth-shaven chin, and continued to think. To his knowledge, there had been no publicity about the Haydn estate. Maybe the results of the case were sealed. But Richard would be able to access the records.

Luke removed his feet from his desk once more and sat up straight. He reached for his phone, wondering if Richard was still at his office or if he had gone home to be with his family?

THIRTY-NINE

Susan reached, patted Rachel on her hand, and smiled. "You look like you're feeling better, Rachel. I see that sparkle back in your eyes."

"Yes, I do. How can you not feel better when Nancy and Peter are praying for you? William, did you enjoy the afternoon?"

"Absolutely. The Grenfells are the real deal. I'm glad they are befriending you and Susan. Knowing that, I feel better about leaving you here in Germany by yourselves."

Susan dropped her voice. "Rachel, I see Luke. He just came in and is talking to the waiter. It would be nice having him join us, but I would never ask him without your permission."

Rachel was slow answering. She finally said, "Go ahead. I don't want to be a killjoy."

"No, I wasn't implying that. I just wanted to be sure I was not creating an awkward situation for you."

"I think I can handle it. I certainly can't avoid seeing him in the weeks to come. Anyhow, maybe he has heard something from the detective. I'll be glad when we can finally have closure—you know what I mean." Rachel picked up her water glass and took a sip.

Susan looked to William. "What do you think, William? Do you want to have Luke join us?"

"I think it would be nice if Rachel doesn't mind."

Rachel nodded and forced a smile. "Sure, William, go ahead. Being with the Grenfells this afternoon convinced me that I might have misjudged Luke. The Grenfells agree with you and Susan. They say there is no way Luke Hartmann could murder anyone. I think they are good judges of character. So I'm going to trust their judgment and stay positive."

"That's the right attitude, Rachel," William said as he pushed his chair back and got up. He walked over to Luke, talked a few minutes, and brought him back to their table.

Luke greeted Susan and Rachel with a smile and said, "I was hoping to see all of you tonight. You're kind to include me in your dinner plans. I told William that I certainly did not want to intrude, but he insisted that I'm not." Luke looked over to the fishpond. "I see Sarah Beth is guarding the fish again. I think Andre may have to put her on his payroll."

William and Susan laughed, and Rachel smiled. Luke could be charming, she thought. There was no doubt about that.

After ordering, William said, "I was wondering, Luke. Have you had an update on Rachel's case? Has Richard Wendall found out anything?"

"Yes, but nothing of substance. All of the fingerprints in the closet were Rachel's. The elevator had so many smeared fingerprints that Richard said it was impossible to get any evidence there. Nothing helpful was found on the floors or stairways."

"What about the lie detector tests? Have you received them?"

"Yes, the results are in and everyone passed."

"Well, that's good news." William paused. "I guess."

"You guess?" Luke gave a half chuckle."What do you mean by that, William?"

"Nothing, really. I think I spoke before I thought."

"You want this thing to have closure. Well, so do I...more than you know." Luke looked at Rachel. "Rachel, I hope you are feeling better. If there is anything I can do personally, I want to do it. Did the sleeping pills help?"

Rachel couldn't help a smile. "Oh yes, they helped immensely. In fact, I slept thirteen straight hours, and when I woke up, I wondered if I had been drugged again."

Luke cleared his throat. "I assure you—that was not my intention. I guess my doctor went a little overboard. You'll have to forgive him for that."

"He's forgiven," Rachel murmured as the waiter began to put their iced teas and salads on the table.

She turned and waved to Sarah Beth, beckoning her to come to the table. "Here we go again," Rachel said, taking out a wipe and cleaning Sarah Beth's hands.

Luke smiled and said, "Rather than asking Andre to add Sarah Beth to his payroll, I might ask him to supply her with a finger bowl."

That drew another bout of laughter from the table and even Rachel joined in.

It was the next afternoon when Richard put the folder down in front of Luke and said, "Here it is. I had to go to the top to get it, but it was worth the trouble. This is the information you wanted on the Goldman girl."

Luke looked up and said, "Thanks, Richard. I'll look at it in a minute. In the meantime, have a seat. Joyce is going to bring us some coffee."

Luke opened the folder and read the information pertaining to Susan's lawsuit, but didn't comment until after Joyce had left.

He looked at Richard and said, "You know, I suspected something like this. Susan Goldman Handel inherited a couple of billion euros from her grandfather, Mr. Haydn. This could possibly put an entirely different spin on what happened to Rachel."

Richard sat his cup on Luke's desk and said, "Are you thinking the same thing that I am?"

"That the man got Rachel mixed up with Susan?"

"Yes, that is the conclusion I've come to."

"This could very well have been a plot to kidnap Susan for ransom. But he mistakenly drugged Rachel. Stop and think about it, Richard. Both girls are brunettes with thick, slightly curly hair. They are the same height and wear the same size clothing, I presume. They have the same complexion. The only difference is the eyes. Susan has green eyes. But, from a distance, you would not notice that. In fact, from a distance, I have even mistaken Susan for Rachel. It's easy to do."

"You're right, Luke. I have gone over this case with a fine-tooth comb. And with everyone passing the lie detector test, I'm at a dead end. We have found absolutely no clues as to who the man is. There was absolutely nothing in your basement—no fingerprints in the closet except Rachel's. It's obvious the man put on gloves after he drugged her."

"Do you think the man was working alone?"

"That's something I've asked myself over and over. It's very possible he was working alone. He must have known about Susan's inheritance. But, you know, that information wouldn't be hard to come by with so many people working in the courthouse. Even though the judge issued a gag order, it doesn't mean everyone abided by it.

"The man probably discovered that she had come back to Berlin and decided to make some easy money. I'm sure it's not hard to get an electronic card for your closet."

"It's not. Our apartment locks are coded with keypads. Storage rooms and storage closets are opened with electronic cards. The electronic cards are more accessible. We close down the basement at one o'clock on Fridays and don't open it up again until Monday morning. This man probably did his homework and knew that."

"I think we're right about the mix-up, Luke. I need to tell the Handels what I suspect. I can't prove this, mind you. But it's about the best explanation I have."

"When you tell William, I doubt he will want to leave Susan over here without him. He'll take her back to the States."

"You know, Luke, this is a hard call to make. I hope we're right in our assumptions. I would hate to endanger the widow's life by my error of judgment."

Luke looked at his friend and nodded in agreement. He said, "Yes, Richard, if our assumption is right, then Rachel is not in any danger. But if we are wrong, then she could very well be harmed again, and I will not let that happen. I will install a security camera in her hall and have it monitored daily. I will also put extra men on the elevator cameras until she gets her case settled. I'll not take any chances with her life."

Richard sat a moment, noticing Luke's deep concern, and said, "I think your concern is well founded. It would be a shame to have this beautiful new building marred by tragedy." Richard stood and pushed back his chair. "I see no reason to prolong this investigation, Luke. Let's call a meeting tomorrow afternoon, and I'll tell the Handels the conclusion I have come to."

Luke stood, shook Richard's hand, and ushered him out. He then walked over to his window and stood, looking out and thinking about Richard's remark about tragedy. The building be damned. It was Rachel he was concerned about.

FORTY

Rachel woke up with Luke Hartmann on her mind. She lay there, recalling the evening before last, when Luke joined them for dinner and displayed so much charm. She had no idea he had that side to him. He laughed a lot with William and Susan. She laughed some but not as much as they did. And she caught him looking at her on several occasions, and she wondered what he was thinking.

Rachel yawned and stretched her arms and then couldn't help smiling as she took her hand and brushed her hair from her forehead. She had gotten past her bad attitude—her thoughts of his wanting to harm her. Looking back, she wondered how she had come to that conclusion in the first place—that he wanted her dead. He had certainly held and comforted her a long time after finding her in the basement closet. Rachel's mouth curved into a partial smile again, thinking about how hard she had fought and what Luke said about her being like a tiger.

She didn't want to admit it at the time, but being in his arms felt good, especially after two hours of mental turmoil in the closet. But she still had to be cautious. The man who had drugged her had not been caught, and apparently the detective was no nearer to solving the case now than he was at the beginning. Rachel stifled another yawn with her hand and relaxed back against her pillow. She was glad Nancy and Peter had convinced her that her suspicions were wrong and that Luke's character allowed him no room for entertaining thoughts of murder, let alone committing the act itself.

She wondered what she would say if he invited her to dinner. Would she accept? Susan would encourage her to go with him. She and William had come to like him. Well, maybe she would go if he asked her, and maybe Susan would keep Sarah Beth.

Rachel glanced over to her clock. What was she thinking about, lying in bed so long and daydreaming about Luke Hartmann, of all people? It was seven-thirty, and she needed to get up and start the day. She could make the coffee and let Susan and William sleep. It was a comforting thought, knowing they were there in the apartment with her. But, in a way, she couldn't help but envy them. They had each other and were so much in love, whereas there she was, single again, not sure of the future, with no one to love but her precious little eight-year-old daughter.

Rachel pushed her feet into her slippers, put on her robe, and headed to the bathroom. She needed to brush her hair and quit feeling sorry for herself.

Rachel turned around and smiled when she heard Susan come into the kitchen. The coffee was hot. There was crisp bacon in the crisper, and Rachel had the toast ready for the oven. She had cut up some fresh fruit and even had the eggs ready to scramble. "Is William going to eat with us?" she asked.

"Yes, he'll be out in a minute. I thought I heard your cell a while ago. Did you have a call?"

"Yes, it was Luke. Richard Wendall wants to meet with us this afternoon in Luke's office. Luke says Joyce will take Sarah Beth to the snack room and keep her until we get through."

Susan looked surprised. "Rachel, I wonder if he's uncovered something new—maybe some clues that have surfaced."

"He didn't say—only that he wanted us to come at two o'clock."

William and Susan were speechless. William finally spoke. "Richard, what proof do you have to back up your conclusion that Susan is the one the man was after?"

"To be perfectly honest, William, I have no proof. It's only a hunch. And I've gone over the reasons why I think Susan was the target."

"You've made some good points, but you can't base something this serious on a hunch."

"Let me explain further, please. I have interviewed all of the men who are directly or indirectly involved with the lawsuit Mrs. Lewis has filed to recover her property. All of these men have been given lie detector tests, and they all not only passed but did so easily.

"The members of the limited partnership would have no motive for harming Mrs. Lewis. The transfer of deed ownership would pose no problem with the lease. Should Mrs. Lewis win the lawsuit, there might be a new lease negotiated and drawn up, or the parties involved might choose a contract to purchase. Either way, I'm sure Mrs. Lewis would be fair, and I know, William, that you would be the first to testify to that. Am I wrong?"

"No, I'm sure Mrs. Lewis would be reasonable to work with."

"That leaves Mr. Neumann. He stands to lose the most. He passed the lie detector test with no problem at all."

"What about his partner in the nursing home? Does he have family who might be involved?"

"You're talking about the man with Alzheimer's. No, he has no family."

"Who looks after his estate?"

"We wondered the same thing and looked into it. A large bank is handling his affairs."

William thought a moment and said, "Well, I'm still not convinced that Susan is the target, but under the circumstances, I have no option but to take her back to the States with me. I cannot leave her here and let her life be endangered."

Rachel's voice had an anxious tone to it. "William? What about me? Where does this leave me? Am I to stay over here by myself?"

"Rachel, my case is still pending, but I hope to have it settled in a week or two; then Susan and I can come back. Richard doesn't seem to think you are in any danger. And I'm sure Luke will be close by to assist you."

William looked at Luke and Luke nodded his head and said, "I've already arranged to have extra security for Rachel and her child. I really don't think she has anything to worry about."

Rachel anxiously listened, watching Luke as he spoke. Luke turned his attention from William and met Rachel's intense look, holding it, until she finally turned and looked out his window.

FORTY-ONE

The doorbell interrupted the movie Rachel and Sara Beth were watching, and Rachel got up and walked quickly into the foyer, wondering who was at the door. The security screen revealed Luke Hartmann standing patiently, his hands by his side, and a look of solemnity on his face.

Rachel opened the door with a questioning look and said, "Good evening, Luke."

"Good evening, Rachel. May I come in?"

"Why, of course," Rachel said, stepping back and opening the door wider.

Luke stepped just inside and closed the door behind him.

Rachel said, "Sarah Beth and I are watching a movie. Would you like to join us?"

"No, thank you. I came mainly to see if you needed anything and also to find out if William obtained a ticket for Susan and if they had left."

Rachel smiled. "Thank you for asking, but we're fine. We have everything we need. And to answer your second question, William did manage to get Susan a ticket, and they flew out this afternoon."

Luke nodded. "That's good. I'm glad William was able to secure a ticket, but I hate that they left under these circumstances."

"I agree."

Rachel and Luke stood, looking at each other, an awkward silence building.

Finally, Luke said, "Well, if you're sure you don't need anything, I'll be going. He turned and reached for the door handle, but Rachel put her hand on his arm and said, "Luke, before you leave, I want to tell you something."

Luke turned back around and waited.

Rachel searched his face, and then after taking a breath, she said, "I owe you an apology."

Luke raised his eyebrows. "For what?"

"For accusing you of harming me."

Luke motioned with his hand. "Rachel, don't worry about—"

Rachel interrupted. "No, Luke, I don't know what came over me. I was so scared, and I guess I let my imagination run away with me."

Luke hesitated a moment and then said. "Rachel, I owe you an apology."

"You do?" A surprised look crossed her face.

"Yes—for the impression I gave you when we first met."

"Oh."

"Will you forgive me?"

"Yes."

An awkward silence once more ensued as they stood and looked at each other. Rachel opened her mouth to speak, but Luke said, "Rachel?"

"What, Luke?"

"I've always taken great pride in my ability to stay in control."

"You have?"

"Yes, but I'm having trouble now."

"I don't understand."

"I don't expect you to. You see, I probably shouldn't, but I can't leave without kissing you goodnight."

"You can't?" Rachel's right hand moved nervously to the top of her chest and she blinked her eyes a couple of times, her thick eyelashes sweeping up and down, as she searched Luke's face.

"No, I can't," he murmured, taking her face between his hands and tilting it to meet his. He leaned slightly and gave Rachel a gentle, lingering kiss. His body never touched hers. Only her hands had come to rest gently against his chest, but somehow he could sense the quickening of her heart and feel her yield to him. Euphoria coursed through his body.

He released Rachel's face and she opened her eyes. They stood, continuing to look at each other until Luke finally said, "Good night, Rachel." He then turned, opened the door and left.

Rachel stood, staring at the door for a full minute, unable to quiet the loud beating of her heart. She finally went back into the living room and sat down again with Sarah Beth, knowing there was no way she could bring her focus back to the movie they were watching.

Luke didn't go to his apartment; rather, he went to his office. He needed to sit back, prop his feet on his desk, and think. He picked up a small paper weight and toyed with it as his mind replayed the scene he had just left.

He would be completely honest with himself. He had wanted to kiss Rachel Lewis ever since he saw her on the high diving board. After a ten-year period of parched, dry living, he felt a glorious awakening, something similar to a spring garden putting forth its first green shoots. He was in love! There was no doubt about it, and it felt wonderful!

And he was not absolutely sure, but he thought he felt Rachel's warm response as he kissed her. But he would have to go slowly. He did not want to scare her away.

Luke removed his feet from his desk and placed the expensive paper weight back where it belonged. He looked at his computer but did not touch it. He made a quick decision not to work but rather to go to his apartment, take a shower, and retire early. He might even down-load a romantic movie and watch it before going to sleep.

FORTY-TWO

Rachel sat on the side of the pool and watched Sarah Beth play in the shallow water with her new friend, Annabelle, and others she had met in the children's library. Rachel smiled. Sarah Beth had been lonely for the past few weeks, and making friends had added a new dimension to their stay at the plaza.

Rachel's eyes scanned the opposite side of the pool. There was a nice crowd today and a lot of teenagers especially. But there was a man who seemed to be staring at her, and every time she looked his way, he would quickly turn his head and focus on one of the diving boards. She could not make out his features, as he was not directly across from her but farther down.

Rachel frowned. Ever since the experience in the elevator, she was conscious of strangers looking at her. But then most people were strangers, and maybe she was too sensitive. She had promised Susan she would not see a demon behind every bush. Anyhow, the man could have been looking at the woman a few feet from her. Rachel stole a glance at the woman in the bikini. She was worth a look from any man.

Rachel focused back on Sarah Beth until she felt the gentle pressure of a hand on her shoulder and looked up. It was Luke. He had on his swim trunks and was smiling down at her. "I thought I would find you here," he said. "Are you going to give us another exhibition on the high diving board?"

"Are you making fun of me?" Rachel asked, wanting to tease him.

"You know I'm not. How could I make fun of something so beautiful?"

"Are you talking about my diving?"

"Why are you asking so many questions?" Luke said, suppressing a grin and sitting down next to her, putting his feet in the water.

"I don't know. Maybe I'm curious."

"You've heard that old adage, 'Curiosity killed the cat.'"

"But, then satisfaction brought him back...or I think it was something like that." Rachel smiled. "Tell me, Luke Hartmann, when do you work? This is the second time I've seen you here in the middle of the afternoon."

"Rachel Lewis, don't you know what day it is? It's Saturday. Most everyone has Saturday off. You would not deny me that, would you?"

"Forgive me. I've lost track of time. No, I would not deny you a day off, especially knowing that you have a penchant for working after hours," Rachel said, cutting her eyes at him, "and a small problem with self-control."

Luke cleared his throat. "I guess I'll have to concede that one," he said, suppressing another grin as he looked over at the children playing in the shallow water. "Your daughter is having fun with the other children, I see."

"Yes, I think she has finally found a few playmates. It's hard being an only child."

"I can testify to that. But then, so can you." Luke turned and looked at her. "You were an only child, weren't you, Rachel?"

Rachel nodded and then picked up her towel and rubbed her hands and arms.

They sat silently, listening to the loud exuberance of the swimmers. Rachel looked across the pool, but the man was no longer there; she dismissed her concern as overkill yet was still glad he was gone.

Luke looked down at the water, moving his foot around in a circle and watching the water swirl. He finally looked up and said, "I wondered if you and Sarah Beth might like to have dinner with me tonight."

"Is that an invitation or just something you wondered?"

Luke grinned. "An invitation. I can see now that I'll have to be careful how I choose my words when addressing you."

Rachel was slow with her answer. She folded the towel and laid it aside and then turned to him and said, "I'll have dinner with you on one condition."

"Oh? What's that?"

"That you go to church with me tomorrow morning."

Luke turned again to the circling of his foot in the water and gave a soft chuckle. "What would the Grenfells think?"

"I'm sure they would be pleased."

Luke's foot came to a standstill, and he looked directly at Rachel and said, "You know that going to church would be strictly out of character for me, don't you?"

Rachel's eyes sparkled, and her lips curved slightly. "You'll live through it. I promise."

Luke took Rachel gently by the elbow and led her and Sarah Beth into Andre's fine-dining restaurant. He stood a moment and then walked over and said something to the waiter, and the waiter smiled and led them into the beautiful enclosed terrace and to a table close to the fishpond. Sarah Beth grinned and looked up at Rachel, and Rachel nodded *yes*. She turned to Luke and said, "You'll capture her heart by way of the fishpond. But then I'm sure that is your motive."

Luke laughed. "Rachel, I was once a child. I know what children like. And, remember, you're only young once."

"I guess you're right. And I've quit telling her to keep her hands out of the water. Actually, I've decided I'm playing a game of futility when I ask her to keep her hands clean. I've learned to take wipes with me when we eat out."

Luke looked over at Sarah Beth and smiled. "Sometimes the simple approach is better, though I'm no authority on raising children—never having had any."

After the waiter lit the candle in the glass hurricane globe and righted their goblets, he left.

Rachel looked up at the twinkling lights and said, "Each time I enter this restaurant, I become enthralled again. It is so beautiful. I hope I never become immune to beautiful things." Rachel thought a minute and then looked down at her menu. "But I must say Andre's restaurant is a bit pricey, don't you think, Luke?"

"I guess so...but then, maybe it's all according to one's perspective. When you deal in large numbers, you soon get accustomed to expensive things. I don't mean it's necessarily the right attitude, I guess what I mean is..." Luke laughed. "Rachel, I'm not sure what I mean."

"Are you apologizing for your expensive taste?"

"Maybe so. Actually, I was not raised that way. Both of my parents taught at Oxford University, and though they had a nice income, they never considered themselves rich."

"Both of your parents are doctors, aren't they?"

"Yes—my father taught German and my mother taught in the law school. They're retired and now live in London."

"I remember Peter Grenfell saying that he took classes under your father and enjoyed being in your parents' home. Having both parents as doctors is quite unusual. Do young people address both of them as Dr. Hartmann?"

"No. Mother always left her doctor-title at the university. When she was home all of my dad's students addressed her as Mrs. Hartmann, but they continued to address my dad as Dr. Hartmann."

"I see. Well, Luke, do you see your parents often?"

"Not as often as I should. It seems that I'm always buried in work. I keep promising myself—and them—that I'll do better, but so far..." Luke shook his head and made an apologetic gesture with his open palms.

"What do your parents say?"

"They don't say much. I think they love me so much that they're willing to overlook my negligence."

Rachel looked thoughtfully at Luke, then finally dropped her eyes and focused again on the menu. "I can't decide what I want to eat. You probably know what's good, Luke; would you be kind enough to order for me? Oh, and let's see if the waiter will bring Sarah Beth a small amount of meat—either chicken or beef—and some mashed potatoes and maybe some english peas."

"Sure, we'll get Sarah Beth fixed up, and I know just what you'll enjoy. It's a favorite of mine."

Luke held Sarah Beth's hand, and they stood back as Rachel put in the code that would open the door to her apartment. They stepped inside, and Luke said, "I hope you remember to put your alarm on every night before you go to bed. You do know that your alarm is connected to our security system and there is always someone on duty?"

"Yes, William pointed that out when we first moved in, and I like the way the keypads are installed—having one here next to the door and others next to each bedroom door, should we forget to set the foyer pad. And, of course, the one at the back entrance."

"We made it a point to put the very best security systems in our apartments. In fact, most everything we built with was of the highest quality, such as hardwood and granite." Luke looked up at the ceiling. "The high ceilings give you the feeling you're in much larger rooms, and the millwork is superb."

"This apartment is beautiful. You'll get no argument there."

Luke followed Rachel into the living room and reached over for the TV remote. "You go ahead and put Sarah Beth to bed. I'll watch a little television"

"I was getting ready to suggest that, Luke. Just make yourself at home."

Luke removed his feet from the ottoman, picked up the remote, and turned off the television when he saw Rachel stifle a yawn. He got up and said, "I don't know why I wanted to see that movie to the end. It's not funny; it's just plain stupid. Anyhow, I can see that it's your bedtime, so why don't you walk me to the door and lock up?"

Rachel blinked her eyes. "Forgive me, Luke. I think that movie was about to put me to sleep. I agree it was rather stupid."

Luke strode to the door and stopped. He stood, looking down at Rachel. "May I say one more time how much I've enjoyed being with you this evening and, I'll include, during the afternoon swim also?"

Rachel smiled. "No more than I have enjoyed being with you. And let me thank you again for the wonderful meal. I agree that the French might have the edge. We tease William about his German dishes, but Susan and I are partial to the French ones."

After a bit of awkward silence, Luke said, "Rachel, would you mind another lapse in self-control? I feel myself losing it again." A smile played on his lips.

"It seems to me, Luke, that someone as successful as you might have to work on that." Rachel paused, trying hard not to smile. "But, under the circumstances, I'll forgive your sudden lapse of control."

Luke searched Rachel's beautiful face for only a moment and then gently pulled her into his arms and kissed her. Rachel's hand moved up and around Luke's neck, and she relaxed in his embrace. The only sound either could hear was the ticking of the wall clock in the foyer.

FORTY-THREE

"I thought we were going to walk to church," Rachel said as she buckled her seatbelt and glanced around the interior of Luke's Mercedes.

"I have plans for us after church," Luke said, giving a backward look to make sure Sarah Beth's belt was secure. "I was wondering, Rachel, if you have seen much of Berlin."

"Not really. I'm afraid Hartmann Plaza has held me captive."

"I figured that. We'll have lunch at a favorite restaurant of mine. After that, we'll ride around."

Rachel smiled at Luke. "Have I told you how thoughtful I think you are?"

"If you have, I can't remember. But tell me again. I love hearing it," Luke said, smiling at Rachel as he pulled out of his private parking place in Hartmann Plaza's garage and onto the inside ramp that would take them outside.

The waiter seated Luke and Rachel at a table in a secluded area near a large window looking out on a serene lake, home to several geese foraging around the edge of the bank for bugs.

Luke broke his gaze from the geese, relaxed against the back of his chair, and smiled at Rachel. "That was kind of Nancy and

Peter to offer to keep Sarah Beth while we have lunch, and afterward, while I show you around."

Rachel nodded. "Yes, Sarah Beth has become attached to them, and even more so to their cat. She loves letting Tippy sleep in her lap." Rachel hesitated. "But I don't want to talk about Sarah Beth. I want to know how you liked the sermon Peter preached."

"I knew you would ask me that, and I'm not sure how to answer you."

"What's so hard about that? I thought his sermon was easy to follow, and if I could follow it with the closed captioning, surely you could with your command of the German language."

"I followed it all right. If you can remember, Rachel, I told you that I'm not very religious."

"Neither am I, Luke."

"What do you mean? You said you are a Christian. Aren't Christians religious?"

"No, Christians aren't religious. They are spiritual, or they should be."

"Well, what's the difference?"

"Unbelievers can be religious, but only Christians can be spiritual."

"Rachel, you're not making sense."

"Luke, when a person puts his faith in Jesus Christ, God sends the Holy Spirit into that person's life, and that's when he becomes a child of God. The Holy Spirit leading him enables him to be spiritual."

"Are you saying that a person cannot be a child of God unless he puts his faith in Jesus?"

"Luke, Jesus is the one who said it and He is God's Son. That's where I get my authority. It's in the Bible. Read it for yourself in the book of John."

"Well, I just might surprise you and do that," Luke's grin was mischievous. A moment later he said, "Rachel, I love it when you get excited about something, and you do get excited about spiritual things, don't you?"

Rachel's laugh was spontaneous and she touched her lips lightly with her fingers. "I'm sorry, Luke. I did not realize I was raising my voice." She sighed and looked down. "Maybe we should focus back on these menus." She looked back up and said, "The only problem is I cannot read German."

"Yes, I remember, and I just might start giving you a few German lessons." Luke watched Rachel for her reaction, and when there was none forthcoming, he set the menu aside and said, "Rachel, have I ever told you how beautiful you are?"

Rachel blushed. "No, I think you mentioned my diving being beautiful, but I don't remember you telling me that."

"I'm telling you now. And, furthermore, I love it when you blush."

Rachel laughed again and shook her head. "You love my getting excited and now you love my blushing. Luke, would you please stop teasing me and tell me what's on the menu?"

"Oh, I almost forgot," Luke said, suppressing a grin as he opened the menu. "We're eating prawns cooked with walnuts and served with rice and the most delicious sweet sauce you've ever tasted. I'm sure you'll love them, especially if you like Chinese food."

"I do. In fact, I love Chinese food." Rachel unfolded her napkin and put it in her lap. She glanced down at her hands and then looked up, thankful to see their waiter approaching to take their order.

Luke helped Rachel out of the car, and they walked around the side of the chapel to the charming parsonage Nancy and Peter Grenfell called home. Sarah Beth was sitting on the floor in the living room playing with Tippy. Nancy and Peter were reading. Peter put his book down, got up, greeted Luke once more with a handshake, and invited him and Rachel to have a seat.

He picked his book up and said, "Luke, did you know that there were approximately eleven million people killed during the

Holocaust and six million of those were Jews? In fact, the Nazis killed approximately two-thirds of all Jews living in Europe. This book says that one point one million children were murdered in the Holocaust."

Luke thought a few moments and said, "You know, Peter, in looking back over those years, it's hard to believe Hitler could have been influential enough to have caused all of those deaths."

"Yes, it goes to show how easily mankind can be influenced to become a partner to evil."

Luke nodded. "I'm glad I was born in a different age."

"What year were you born, Luke? As well as I can remember, you were just a boy when I was in your father's German class."

"In 1969."

Peter nodded. "You and I have lived in a more peaceful era." Peter tapped his finger on the book he was holding and said, "But we must never forget what happened to the Jewish people during World War II."

"I agree, and I hope we've learned something from that war."

"Perhaps we have, but I doubt it."

Nancy spoke up. "Let's change the subject, dear. I want to know if Rachel has heard anything from her lawsuit."

Rachel shook her head. "No, but thanks for asking, Nancy. To be honest, I had almost forgotten my lawsuit. I have not heard a word from Greta Wineman since we were in court." A slight look of worry crossed Rachel's face. "I surely hope she hasn't forgotten me."

Luke cleared his throat. "Rachel, have you so quickly forgotten what Peter said in his sermon this morning? Wasn't it something like, 'You are supposed to cast your cares on Jesus'?"

Peter's mouth flew open. "Well, look who's preaching to us, Nancy. Luke, you are a good listener. Thanks for the reminder. I wish all of my parishioners were as attentive as you were."

Luke laughed. "Please, I'm not trying to impress anyone, and truth be known, that might be all I remember from your sermon. But to change the subject, when are your son and his family coming for a visit?"

"I think in two weeks, or was it next weekend? Nancy can tell you. I get the weeks mixed up."

"I'm asking because I would like to have all of you for dinner one evening."

"Well, Luke, that is kind of you. We'll certainly look forward to that."

Luke shut the engine off, looked at his watch, and turned to Rachel. "I've got a great idea. It's still early. Let's take a swim."

Rachel glanced down at her watch and said, "Luke, it's six o'clock. The pool closes at six today. It's too late."

"Mother, please," Sarah Beth begged, "let's go swimming."

"See, Rachel?" Luke said, releasing his seatbelt. "Sarah Beth wants to go, too. Anyhow, the pool's never closed to me."

"Do you have access to every door in this building?"

"Of course, Rachel. I'm the owner. Wouldn't you expect me to?"

"I don't know. I was just wondering."

"You are not worried about the security of your door, are you?" Luke asked teasingly.

"Not as long as my security system works. And you can be sure I set it each time I leave and every single night."

"Good girl," Luke said, releasing Rachel's seat belt. "You go on up and get your swimsuits. I need to check on something in the main office. I'll get my suit and pick you up on the way down."

Luke ushered Rachel and Sarah Beth into the elevator and pressed the button for the first floor. Rachel looked up at him and said, "Guess who rode up on the elevator with us a while ago?"

"I have no idea."

"Karla Broussard."

"That's interesting. Did she strike up a conversation?"

"Yes, she was very friendly, especially to Sarah Beth."

The elevator stopped and Rachel paused. She stepped out and then continued. "Anyhow, she asked Sarah Beth what she liked best about living in the plaza, and Sarah Beth told her she liked the children's library, the swimming pool and the fish pond, all in that order. Then Karla gave Sarah Beth a big smile and said she just loved the fishpond. A moment later Sarah Beth told Karla we were going to get our swim suits so we could go swimming with you. Luke, I wish you could have seen the surprised look on Karla's face. I wish Sarah Beth had not told her that."

"What difference does that make, Rachel? Children are quick to share."

"I don't know. Somehow, I don't trust Karla Broussard, and I don't like her knowing my business."

"I doubt she really cares that much about what we do. Let's forget Karla Broussard and have a good time." Luke punched in the numbers and opened the door to the reception area that led to the dressing rooms and pool.

After they put their suits on, Rachel looked around the large aquatic room and said, "Luke, it's so quiet in here that you could hear a pin drop, and it's almost like anything above a whisper is in violation of the rules."

"What rules are you talking about, Rachel? I'm not aware of any rules about talking."

"Where is your imagination, Luke? I'm not talking about literal rules but unspoken rules. You know...and look at how beautiful and still the water is. It seems a shame to disturb it." Rachel stopped talking a moment to put her swim cap on and then continued. "Look how clear the water is. I bet if I threw a penny in the pool, you could see it at the bottom."

"Of course you could. Haven't you ever played the money game, Rachel? As a boy, I played it all the time. We'd have a certain amount of coins and throw them, all together, into the deepest part of the pool. Then we would all dive down to see who could find them. The person who found the most was the winner. And with other people in the pool stirring up the water, it wasn't easy."

"I can imagine," Rachel said jokingly, as she handed Sarah Beth her inflatable inner tube, then reaching up to tuck a stray lock of hair under her swim cap. "You haven't said, but I bet you were usually the winner and that was your first introduction to fortune making."

Luke shook his head and chuckled. He then moved over to lay his towel down next to the wall. After putting his cell on top of the towel, he straightened up and said, "If I didn't know better, I would think you're making fun of me, and if I decide you are, you just might have to pay. And it won't be with money." Luke stood, eyebrows raised, rubbing the palms of his hands together and watching Rachel squirm.

Rachel backed up a couple of steps and raised her hands in mock surrender. "I promise, Luke—I won't say another word about your coin game." Her lips were twitching, and she was trying to keep from laughing.

"It's too late," Luke said, grinning, as he reached for Rachel's arms and pulled her to him. He picked her up, and ignoring her pleadings, he walked quickly toward the deep end and threw her in.

Rachel squealed before hitting the water and then came up sputtering and laughing.

Luke stood on the side laughing, and then jumped in the pool with her.

"Now, this is what I call living," Luke said, as he floated on his back next to Rachel. "And, by the way, when you squealed, you violated the noise rules."

Rachel splashed water on him and said, "Now, before you retaliate, I declare a truce."

"Well, aren't you something? You splash water in my face and then declare a truce. I'm not sure I'll buy that. I just might penalize you."

Rachel treaded water around Luke, laughing and saying, "I hate to ask what the penalty is."

"Just a couple of dives off of the high board."

"Oh, is that all? I think I can do that. Which do you want? A somersault with a twist? Or did you like the jack knife and swan best?"

"I like them all. Where in the world did you learn to do that, anyhow?"

"My dad..." Rachel hesitated. "Luke, isn't that your cell I hear?"

"Yes, and I meant to turn that darn thing off."

"Maybe you had better answer it. You might have an important call."

"OK, but promise me you won't go anywhere."

"Where would I go?" Rachel said with a chuckle, as she turned to float on her back.

Luke swam to the edge of the pool and pulled up, got out, and walked quickly toward the shallow end to retrieve his cell. Rachel could hear him say, "Hartmann speaking. Who's calling please?" Then, all of a sudden the lights went out and there was nothing but darkness and silence.

"Hold on, Rachel," Luke called, as he switched on the LED light in his cell. "I'm calling security, and then I'll see if I can find out what the problem is. I may have disrupted the timer when I turned the lights on manually. If that's the problem, it shouldn't take me but a minute or so to have them back on."

"Mommy," Sarah Beth cried from the shallow end, "where are you? I'm scared."

"Don't be scared, darling," Rachel called to her. "Just stand still where you are. Luke will have the lights back on in just a minute."

Luke began to walk toward the reception area, and then stopped and said, "Rachel, I think you should swim to Sarah Beth and both of you get out of the pool. If I can't get the lights back on from the reception area, I will have to go to one of the mechanical rooms. You'll be fine, though. Someone from security should be here shortly to help."

"Yes, I'll do that." Rachel turned and began to swim toward the shallow end. On her third stroke, a hand grabbed her ankle and pulled her under, but she turned and kicked with her other foot and pulled loose. She pushed to the surface, spitting out water and crying out, "Luke, help..." But that was all she could say as an arm came around her neck and she was pulled under a second time. Rachel struggled and fought but was unable to break loose. She held her breath, but pressure on her windpipe caused her to breathe out, and water to slowly seep into her nose and down into her lungs, and she began to lose consciousness.

Rachel opened her eyes to see Luke, on his knees, bending over her and helping her turn and cough up water. She finally lay back on the towel he had folded for her to rest her head on. The lights were back on, and she could hear voices and see shadows of people walking around.

"What happened, Luke?" she whispered in a raspy voice."Who was that who tried to drown me?" She glanced toward the pool and then tried to push up while frantically asking, "Where is Sarah Beth?"

Luke caught her shoulders and eased her back down. "Don't talk, Rachel. Just lie still. Sarah Beth is fine. She's with a member of my security team. The Grenfells are on their way to get her. She'll spend the night with them."

"But I want to see her."

"You are going to the hospital. In fact, I see the medics coming now."

"Why do I have to go to the hospital? I'm all right now."

"Because you might develop pneumonia. We cannot let that happen."

Rachel caught Luke's arm. "You have not answered me. Who tried to drown me?"

"I don't know. I could not save you and subdue the man at the same time."

"He got away?"

"Yes."

Rachel lay still and closed her eyes. A few moments later, she opened them and said, "It looks like Richard's and your hunch turned out to be wrong."

Luke didn't comment, but his sober look and nod spoke volumes.

FORTY-FOUR

The head of Rachel's hospital bed was elevated, and she was sitting up, dressed and waiting for the doctor to sign her release papers. Luke sat next to her bed along with Richard Wendall, as Richard continued to question both of them.

"Rachel, Luke described the man as being large and as having a head full of hair. Other than that, do you have anything to add? I'm thinking about when he had his arm around your neck. Did he say anything to you? Were you able to feel his hands? Did you feel a ring on his finger? Sometimes it's little things that are important in helping us find the perpetrator."

"No, Richard, he did not say one word. And it all happened so quickly. The first time he grabbed me I was able to kick with my other foot and push away from him. The second time he grabbed me around my neck and pulled me back and under. His arm was pressing on my windpipe. I could do absolutely nothing to free myself and I never felt his hand. I agree with Luke that he was large. If he had been a small man, I might have freed myself. I am a good swimmer and was a summer lifeguard during my high school and college years." Rachel shook her head slightly and said, "I wish I could give you some clues, but I can't."

Richard gave a sympathetic nod. "Luke said he managed to break the man's hold, and the minute he did, the man disappeared under the water and got away. He was apparently hiding in one of the mechanical rooms to have been able to slip into the pool so quickly. There was nothing in any of the dressing rooms to indicate he had been there. And that included the room you and your child dressed in. You realize that taking fingerprints in any of those rooms would be a waste of time. There would be no way of eliminating the innocent ones." Richard turned to Luke. "And you can't give any distinguishing clues other than that the man was large and had a head full of hair?"

"No. Once I broke his hold, I was so concerned for Rachel, I couldn't think about him. I knew I had to get her out of the water or she would drown."

Rachel thought a minute and then said, "This might be something that I let my imagination run away with, but Saturday afternoon, on several occasions, I caught a man looking at me from across the pool."

"Describe him, please," Richard said, adjusting his recorder and placing it closer to Rachel.

"That's just it. He was so far away that I could not distinguish his features, but he did have dark hair and a slightly dark complexion. I finally decided that he might not be looking at me, but at a woman near me who was wearing a bikini."

"Did you notice the color of his swimsuit?"

"No, not really. I think his swim trunks were dark. Had they been light-colored, I probably would have noticed them."

"Well, that's something to check out, though I doubt it's enough to identify anyone." Richard picked up his recorder and said, "Rachel, I'm sorry this happened to you. I really thought someone was trying to kidnap Susan for ransom. But this second attack on you changes that. I have reviewed all of my notes and the material our forensic team collected from the basement, and I still come up with nothing. I wish I could tell you that we have a suspect, but I can't."

"I don't mean to interrupt you, Richard," Luke said, touching his arm lightly and then turning to Rachel, "but I want to say something." Luke paused for only a moment. "Rachel, I know this situation has been devastating for you, and it's been awkward for those of us who have come under suspicion. I do not want to sound harsh, but it's not only shocking, but also frightening to wake up one day and be told that you are a suspect in a conspiracy to murder someone. It's not something you take lightly, I assure you."

Luke paused once more before continuing. "And taking a lie detector test is a new experience for all of us, but thank God we passed it. Rachel, I can say this in all truthfulness: I am innocent, and the three men in partnership with me are innocent. Neither they nor I have absolutely any reason to harm you, and I want to make sure that you understand that. And furthermore, Richard was not alone in his conclusion. I was also convinced that the man was working by himself, hoping to extort money from William by kidnapping Susan. This attack on you has both of us baffled. Please believe me."

Rachel's lips trembled slightly. "I do understand, Luke, and I do believe you. I'm not accusing anyone in your group of attempting to harm me." Rachel's facial expression was strained and pale from the near drowning, and she looked like she might tear up, but instead, she swallowed hard and rested back on her pillow. She then turned and forced herself to ask a question. "Richard, I might be out of line asking this question, but it seems to me that the only one profiting from my death would be Neumann Development Company. I know Mr. Neumann has passed the lie detector test, but could it be possible that the machine was not completely accurate?"

"No, you are not out of line, Rachel. I asked the officials administering the test that same question. They assured me their machines were accurate but said they would run another test using a machine from another district. And surprisingly, Konrad was not offended at being asked to be tested again. He took the second test and passed with flying colors. The consensus is that he is innocent."

"Where was he yesterday?"

"He has been out of town all weekend visiting his son in Switzerland. There was no way he could have known you and Luke were going swimming. Luke said himself that he decided on the spur of the moment to swim."

"Yes, I can see your logic."

"Did you see anyone before going to the pool? Who did you spend the afternoon with?" Richard turned to Luke. "Did you mention wanting to swim to anyone, Luke?"

"No. I took Rachel sightseeing. And the only ones we saw were the Grenfells. Peter Grenfell is the pastor of the chapel a few blocks over from the plaza. He and Nancy are friends of ours. I said nothing about swimming to them."

Rachel sat forward. "Luke—remember, I saw Karla Broussard on the elevator, and Sarah Beth told her we were going swimming with you."

"Rachel, Karla didn't attack you. A man attacked you. Andre said that Karla does not know how to swim. And, too, she has no motive. She doesn't have any money invested, and I'm sure Andre has assured her that his investment is secure." Luke shook his head. "I doubt she would get involved for his sake."

Richard asked, "Was anyone else on the elevator with you?"

"Yes, a young man went up with us."

"Could you describe him?"

"Let me think a moment," Rachel said, relaxing back against her pillows again and rubbing her hand across her forehead. She turned to Richard. "I would say he was in his early twenties. He had on shorts, was carrying a tennis racket, and wore a cap with a bill."

"What color was his hair, and how tall would you say he was?"

"I think he was a blond, and I would guess he was six feet tall, give or take an inch."

"Which floor did he get off on?"

"He was still on the elevator when I got off on our floor, the tenth."

"I can check the camera's film. Rachel, can you remember which elevator you rode up on? It will save me some time."

"Yes, it was number four." Rachel hesitated. "Richard, if you are finished with the tennis player, I want to ask a question."

"Go ahead—ask anything you want to."

"What about Konrad's partner? The one in the nursing home?"

"He's seventy-five years old with Alzheimer's disease. You can scratch him."

"Maybe there is someone in his will who doesn't want to chance his losing the deeds."

Luke interjected, "What about that, Richard? Do you think there could be anything to that theory?"

"This is strictly confidential, Luke, but I spoke with the president of the bank, who is handling the man's estate, and he said Kirsten has no will. I figure what he has will be turned over to the government. I've ruled Kirsten completely out of the picture."

Richard sat back in his chair and thought a minute before saying, "There is one long shot that I have not mentioned. Actually, I hate to bring it up."

"What are you talking about, Richard?" Luke sat forward, a slight frown on his face. "If you have any leads whatsoever, say so."

"Well, there has been a recent case where someone from a group that calls themselves the New Progressives attacked a Jewish family suing to regain property lost to the Nazi government. It never could be decided whether it was personal or just a hate crime. I certainly don't want to muddy the waters bringing a group like that into our complicated case."

"Yes, I agree," Luke said. "That does seem a little far-fetched."

Silence settled in the room, and finally Richard put his recorder in his pocket and stood up. "When is Rachel being dismissed?" he asked.

"As soon as the doctor makes rounds and signs her papers. Then, I'll take her back to the plaza." Luke looked at his watch. "He should be by any minute now."

Richard turned to Rachel. "I want you to call me or tell Luke if anything comes to mind. I'm referring to what happened in the pool. Sometimes we remember things later—things that can be important."

Rachel nodded and said, "I will, Richard, but to be honest with you, I hope I can forget this horrible experience." Rachel's lips trembled again; her eyes suddenly began to glisten, and a tear trickled down her cheek. She wiped it away with her fingers and said, "I'm tired of being attacked. I'm ready to go back to my home in America."

Luke got up, quickly moved over to sit on the side of the hospital bed, pulled Rachel into his arms, and began to comfort her. Richard stood a moment longer and then quietly slipped out.

"Please don't cry, Rachel," Luke said. "I promise—I will guard you with my life." Luke held Rachel until he heard knocking on her door. He released her and turned to see the nurse pushing a wheelchair into the room.

Luke drove his Mercedes under the large hospital portico, and the orderly helped Rachel out of the wheelchair and into the front seat, leaning over to help her buckle the safety belt. He said, "Einen schönen Tag, gnädige Frau," and then quickly turned the wheelchair around and pushed it back into the foyer of the hospital.

"What did the man say, Luke?"

"He said, 'Have a nice day, ma'am.'"

"Oh," Rachel said, forcing a weak smile and relaxing against the back of her seat.

Neither Rachel nor Luke said anything else until Luke had driven a ways from the hospital. He glanced over to Rachel and said, "I failed to tell you, but I called William last night and told him what happened."

"You did?" Rachel's eyes met Luke's. "What did he say?"

"He was shocked and said immediately how glad he was that you were all right. He didn't say, but I could sense relief in his voice that Susan was no longer in danger." Luke quickly added, "Not that he wanted you to be endangered. We both know better than that. William and Susan care deeply for you and have shown it by their willingness to assist you here in Germany."

Rachel gave a deep sigh. "Yes, I could have no better friends, and I'll be the first one to say I'm glad Susan can feel safe again."

Luke nodded and turned his eyes back to the busy traffic. Soon slowing for a stoplight, Luke turned again to Rachel and said, "I asked William when they would be back, and he said he would probably be through with his case by the middle of the week. He was almost sure that he and Susan would be able to return this coming Saturday."

Rachel didn't comment immediately but after a short silence said, "Luke, I'm still thinking seriously about canceling my suit against Neumann and flying back home."

Luke's head jerked slightly, and he turned with a frown and said, "Rachel, you can't do that. You'll be doing exactly what they—I'll call them 'the enemy'—wants you to do." Luke shook his head. "This is the most baffling case I've ever encountered. As hard as I try, I cannot fathom who the enemy is—the one or ones who are doing this to you."

"I know, and I'm scared they'll target Sarah Beth next. I cannot endanger my child's life. Surely you understand that."

"Of course I understand, but I don't think they are after Sarah Beth. They would have taken her earlier if they were. It's you, the second generation heir, they want. Sarah Beth is third generation and no threat to them."

"Yes, you're probably right." Rachel thought a minute and said, "You know Luke, it's a miracle I'm still alive." She gave another deep sigh and turned to Luke. "And I have you to thank for that."

Luke reached for Rachel's hand and squeezed it. "If anything happened to you, I don't know what I would do. But this is not the time and place to talk about that." Luke turned his eyes again to the traffic and slowed slightly, careful to stay a safe distance behind the car ahead. They rode in silence, and then Luke turned once more to Rachel. "I have not told you, but Nancy called this morning to let you know that Sarah Beth is fine and having fun with their cat."

Rachel's smile was strained. "I cannot thank them enough. They are so kind and giving."

"Yes, I agree," Luke said, continuing to focus ahead. A few moments later, he said, "Nancy also said she and Peter want you to stay with them for a few days." Luke cut his eyes toward Rachel. "How do you feel about that?"

Rachel frowned slightly and shook her head. "I hate to burden them with my problems, Luke. They might feel that they cannot leave me alone, and I wouldn't want that, seeing as they both minister to the people in their church." Rachel hesitated. "And yet, in all honesty, I'm afraid to go back to the apartment. I don't know what to do."

"I could send one of my security team to stay with you if you would feel more secure at the plaza."

"No, I couldn't relax with a stranger hovering over me."

"Then my suggestion is that you accept the Grenfells' offer. Rachel, they care for you and want to help. Didn't I hear you say that Christians help one another?"

Rachel laughed for the first time since the near-drowning incident. She said, "Luke, if I didn't know better, I might think you were a born-again Christian the way you've been reminding me of spiritual principles. But yes, Christians do help one another, and maybe I should accept the Grenfells' offer. They are such delightful people to be with, and...just maybe, being with them will help me forget what happened in the pool." Rachel looked out her window at the cars riding alongside them. She then turned again to Luke, forcing a smile, and said, "I surely hope so."

FORTY-FIVE

Karla Broussard sat at her dressing table brushing her blond hair. It was when Andre quit reading and said, "Luke says the American woman is depressed and wants to drop the suit and go back to America," that her hand stopped suddenly and she looked at Andre's reflection in the mirror and said, "What happened to bring that about?"

Andre cleared his throat and said, "Luke doesn't want this getting out, but I know you won't say anything about it. There was a problem at the swimming center. It seems that Luke took the woman and her daughter swimming after the pool closed Sunday evening and someone attacked the woman. What is her name, Karla? I cannot remember it."

"Her name is Rachel, and her little girl's name is Sarah Beth. She's a cute child." Karla began to brush her hair again, looking at herself in the mirror and hoping Andre did not notice the sudden flush to her face. She breathed deeply and willed herself to calm down. She said casually, "I wonder who attacked her."

Andre looked up from his paper and said, "Who knows? I'm sick of the whole mess. Taking that damn lie detector test did me in. I hope she goes back to the States. I think it'll be good riddance."

Karla's hand stilled once more, and she stopped brushing but continued to talk to Andre through the reflection of her mirror. "You might think that, but I doubt Luke does. He seems to be smitten with her. I've never seen such a change in a man. I always had the impression that he had no time for women, but this woman has certainly changed his attitude. I would say he's fallen under her spell."

"He'll get over her soon enough if she leaves." Andre cleared his throat two more times and said, "And I'm sick of reading about these Jewish lawsuits in the paper. Here's another one. You can never know whether your deed is clear or not. I'm glad we didn't buy those damn deeds from Neumann. He thought he was so smart leasing." Andre grunted. "But look what he's going through."

Karla put her brush down and turned around. "I saw Konrad in the deli several days ago, and he said there were members of an organization who attacked some Jews over lawsuits they had filed, but I cannot remember the name of the organization. I wonder if that was the case with Rachel."

"I don't know. I do know that Konrad had nothing to do with harming her. Even Richard Wendall admits that." Andre looked up. "I probably shouldn't say anything, but I ran into Neumann today in the deli. He was having lunch with his lawyer, and he looked happier than I've seen him in weeks. I met his lawyer. His name is Beckle."

"That's interesting. I wonder why Konrad was so happy."

"I asked him that same question after Beckle left."

"Well, what did he say?"

"He said he and Beckle were onto something that might insure that he wins the lawsuit."

"Did he tell you what it was?"

"He did not go into detail, but he said it had to do with some old cemetery records."

"That's interesting."

"Yes, I hope he gets to keep the deeds. It'll sure save us the trouble of dealing with that woman."

Andre sat with the paper in his hand. He thought a minute and then said, "You say there is an organization causing trouble for the Jews? You could be right. They might have a list to target, you know, using the scare tactic. But I don't approve of violence. You understand that, don't you, Karla?"

Karla nodded, turned back to the mirror, and picked up her facial cream. She slowly applied it, thinking about her lunch with Konrad and his other comments, ones pertaining to his nursing home partner and how wealthy he was. She had tried not to show too much interest. But news of her father's wealth from other investments almost made her giddy, and she had to change the subject for fear of revealing too much.

With this latest news, she could finally relax. Her eyes narrowed thinking about George. She had not talked to him in several days. She would see him at the nursing home when she visited her father the next day, and she would tell him. She slowly screwed the top back on the jar of cream and wondered what George's reaction would be.

Karla smiled as she stopped in old Mrs. Goddard's room and handed her a magazine. Mrs. Goddard smiled at Karla and said, "Thanks, honey. You are the only one who ever brings me anything."

Karla patted Mrs. Goddard lightly on her arm. "You are certainly welcome, but I can't believe I'm the only one. Where did that pretty vase of flowers come from?" Karla pointed to her bedside table.

"Oh, those?" Mrs. Goddard replied. She thought a moment and said, "I really can't remember, but they're pretty, aren't they?"

"Yes, they are." Karla patted Mrs. Goddard's arm again and said, "Now you read your magazine, and I'll bring you another one next week."

Mrs. Goddard smiled and nodded, and Karla turned and left, closing her door.

Karla pushed the auxiliary cart back to the station and heaved a sigh of relief when she found no one there who might want her to stand and talk. She needed to find George and also check in on her father.

Karla pressed the handle to her father's door and stepped inside. He was asleep in bed, and she stood looking at him. His health had declined considerably in the last six months, and she wondered how much longer he would live. His hair was gray, his face and body were thin, and there was an unhealthy pallor to his skin. A movement to her right caught her attention, and she turned to see George standing at the window, looking out.

He did not turn around but said, "Did you bring my money?"

"Yes," she said.

George turned and walked over with an outstretched hand. "Let me see it, Karla. I hope you brought the full amount."

"Why do you say that? You did not fully complete your job."

"You did not tell me how strong the man was."

"That was your job to find out, not mine." Karla opened her purse, withdrew an envelope, and handed it to George. "I hope you have been attending to my father. He looks like he needs a shave, and I've tipped you well for that."

"At his age, he has little hair on his face. I'll shave him when he wakes up." George opened the envelope and fingered through the bills.

Karla walked over to the window and looked out. She stood a moment and then turned and said, "Consider the plan finished. I no longer need you."

George looked up. "What are you talking about? I'll say when the plan is finished, and I say it's not."

"You have no authority to dictate to me—remember? I hired you."

George ignored Karla as he continued to count the money. He finally looked back up. "You shortchanged me, Karla. I need more than this."

"To feed your drug habit?"

George looked startled. "What are you talking about?"

"You know what I'm talking about. You think you had me fooled, but I know."

George shrugged. "What I do with my money is none of your business."

"It's my business when you steal my father's drugs. I'm surprised they haven't caught you."

George walked to the window and stared out. After a few moments, he turned and said, "Don't worry about them catching me, Karla. Your father's not suffering, but you will unless you give me the rest of my money."

"Are you threatening me, George?"

"Call it what you will. You promised almost twice this much at the beginning. I want the rest of it, and I want it now."

"You'll have to wait. I promise you'll have it when he's dead." Karla looked over to her father.

"Are you hinting that I help him along?"

Karla grabbed George's arm. "Don't you dare touch my father. Do you hear me?"

George laughed and then jerked his arm from Karla's grasp. "Don't worry. I'll not risk my job so you can get your greedy hands on his money. I have ways of making money."

"Your ways had better not include the woman or her daughter. Do you hear me, George?"

"Yeah, I hear you. There are other rich people at the place you call home." George grinned. "And if you don't come through with the rest of my money, I might have a few plans of my own. Have you considered that, Miss Karla?"

Karla stood glaring at George for only five seconds. She then turned and stormed out of the room, walking quickly to the front entrance and leaving.

Karla sat in her Mercedes, breathing deeply. George was out of control, and she didn't know what to do. The weekend job that she had helped him obtain at the plaza had backfired, and there was no way she could interfere and get him fired. It would be too dangerous and raise too many red flags. She thought she could use his drug habit for personal gain, but that had also backfired. Now he wanted more money, and she had none.

Fully frustrated, Karla slapped the steering wheel and then lay back against the seat. Maybe she could get Andre to give her a larger allowance, but he had complained about all of his money being invested, and she doubted he would give her one tenth of a euro.

Karla reached for her seat belt and fastened it. She needed to leave the parking lot before she drew attention to herself. Surely she could come up with a way to obtain more money soon; otherwise George might get both of them sent to prison.

FORTY-SIX

Luke gave the waiter their orders and handed him the menus. He then turned and looked longingly at Rachel. "Do you realize it is Thursday evening and I have not seen you since Monday afternoon? Please forgive my negligence, Rachel."

"You don't have to apologize, Luke. I know how busy you are. But have you considered getting more help? You're burning the candle at both ends."

"Yes, I totally agree with you, and I am trying to find someone, but you don't realize how hard a job it is. I have contracted with an excellent headhunter company, and hopefully they'll find the right person. But there are few who have the experience it takes to run a complex as large as this, and I doubt they'll find someone soon."

Luke's voice took on a more personal tone. "Let's not talk about me and Hartmann Plaza. Let's talk about you. How are you doing at the Grenfells?"

Rachel's facial expression softened, and she smiled. "I'm doing very well. They are very kind to me, and they have a way of lifting my spirits."

"I'm glad to hear that. And, look, you have a built-in babysitter."

"I'm afraid that's going to change, Luke. Their son and his family are coming Saturday."

"Then you'll be moving back to the plaza. That won't be a problem, will it?"

"No, I talked to Susan yesterday, and they are flying back and should be here early Saturday morning. I'll feel safe with them back."

"Yes, William told me that when we talked the first of the week. I have been so busy that I've not had time to check with him since, but changing the subject, I have something to tell you. I had a long conversation with Konrad Neumann yesterday."

"And?"

"And I don't want to upset you, but he's on to something that he thinks will strengthen his case with the judge."

"Luke, I've made up my mind. I'm not going to be upset if it turns out in Neumann's favor. As, I said earlier, I have mixed emotions about the whole thing. If the Lord wants me to have the property, I'll have it. And if He gives it to Neumann, I'll accept that as God's will for my life."

"That's admirable, Rachel. I wish I could feel that way."

"You can, Luke, if you would learn to trust the Lord."

Luke glanced up, relieved to see the waiter with their salads and wondering how he could answer Rachel.

Rachel bowed her head in silent prayer and then looked up and smiled at Luke. "Now, tell me. What has Neumann found that will help him? Did he confide in you?" Rachel took a bite of her salad and chewed slowly.

"He did," Luke said, savoring the first few bites of his salad. "He said that he has access to some old cemetery records that might reveal something about the Weinbergs' history. I know this is serious, Rachel, but I couldn't help but feel a little amused."

Rachel looked surprised, reached for her water, and said, "Amused? Why would you be amused, Luke?"

"Well, Beckle had, at an earlier date, spent a lot of time helping Konrad search for anything that might give them something solid about the Weinberg family, but the fellow in charge of the Jewish cemetery said that all of the records of the old Jewish cemetery were destroyed during World War II. What was not vandalized by the Nazis was destroyed by the bombs the Allies dropped."

Rachel shook her head slightly and said, "I don't see how cemetery records could help. The Weinbergs died in a concentration camp. Or that's what the Nazi records had recorded. Mr. Beckle brought that up at the hearing."

"Yes, but Beckle got wind of a rumor that the Weinbergs really might have had a fourth child and that the child died at birth. He told Neumann that if they could find the burial records, that would be proof enough."

"Luke, are you telling me they've found them?"

Luke chuckled. "This is the amusing part, Rachel, and, I might add, an unbelievable story. It seems that a ninety-five-year-old man who had been living in a nursing home for the past year died recently, and his son came from out of town to clean his house out. He found thirty large boxes in his father's attic. Every box was filled with cemetery records, some going back as far as 1850."

Rachel put her fork down and tried to suppress a grin. "Did you say thirty boxes, Luke?"

"Yes—thirty *large* boxes—and they were filled with records of people buried in two cemeteries: a large cemetery of German ancestry and a large Jewish cemetery. The cemeteries were next to each other. The son said his father had been caretaker of the German cemetery and was a very close friend to the Jewish man who cared for the Jewish cemetery.

"When vandals and the Nazis started desecrating the Jewish cemetery, the man's father apparently offered to keep the Jewish records from being destroyed. I think there was so much damage done to both cemeteries by the bombs during the Second World War that they were abandoned and new cemeteries were opened. Anyhow, the man became caretaker at the new cemetery. Naturally, he did not take the old records with him, for there were no bodies there. The old records stayed in his attic. I imagine the poor Jewish caretaker probably died in a concentration camp."

"Well, how did Konrad or Mr. Beckle find out about the records? Did they know the man?"

"No. I think the son informed someone connected to the cemetery association, thinking they might be interested in the old records, and this person was a friend of Neumann." Luke suppressed a grin. "Neumann said he and Beckle have spent the last three evenings going through the boxes. Rachel, it's no telling how long it'll take them to filter through all of those papers. It might take weeks because the Jewish and Aryan records are all mixed together."

Rachel suppressed a laugh. "I wonder how that happened."

Luke grinned and shook his head. "I have no idea."

"Why don't they hire someone to at least separate the records?"

"I asked the same thing. Neumann said he didn't trust anyone. He wanted to do it himself, with the help of Beckle, and I doubt Beckle's too happy with giving up his nights. But he'll make Neumann pay, and pay dearly. Trust me."

Rachel laughed. "Come to think of it, it is rather amusing. I can visualize these two men going through stacks of boxes. And they are probably not talking for fear of making a mistake. Where do they have the boxes?"

"In one of Neumann's warehouses. I could tell that Neumann is a little weary, but he tries to hide it."

Luke stopped talking long enough for the waiter to serve them their dinner plates; then he said, "I thought you would want to know that."

"Yes, well, the three-month period is not far off. Maybe they won't find it by then." Rachel paused. "Thirty boxes?" Rachel shook her head, dismissing the subject and turning to her dinner. After tasting the first bite, she looked up and said, "Luke, how do you always know what I like? This food is delicious."

"Because, Rachel, we like the same things. I would say that we probably have more in common than you realize."

Rachel gave Luke her hand as he helped her from the car and said, "Luke, you don't have to walk with me to the parsonage. It's just a short walk around the chapel. I know you must have things to tend to back at the plaza."

"Oh, but I would never let you walk alone, Rachel. Anyhow, I must have my good-night kiss. Don't you think I deserve one after the nice meal I fed you?"

Rachel tucked her hand inside Luke's arm and looked up at him. "I think that's fair enough," she said, smiling and walking slowly by his side, savoring the quietness of the night. Neither one said anything until they stopped in front of the parsonage front door and Luke said, "I'm glad Nancy forgot to leave the outside light on. We have more privacy this way." He glanced toward the chapel. "And there's just enough light coming from the corner of the chapel to let me see your pretty face."

"You had better keep your voice low, or she might hear you and turn the light on," Rachel whispered.

"That still would not keep me from kissing you," Luke said, pulling Rachel into his arms. It's been a week—much too long since I've held you in my arms."

"I have not counted," Rachel said, her heart beating faster.

"I could hardly wait for tonight," Luke murmured, searching Rachel's face.

"Then why are you still waiting?" She whispered.

"I'm not," Luke whispered back, his lips touching hers lightly at first and then firmly as he held her closer. He kissed her not once but twice. It was the sudden shining of the outside light that kept Luke from kissing her a third time.

Luke sat at his desk a few moments, and then he reached down, opened the bottom drawer, and removed a box. Inside was a leather bound Bible, a gift from friends of his parents when he left for college twenty-two years ago. He had never taken the Bible out of the box but one time—not to read it, but to write a note of acknowledgement. He sat and stared at the box, then finally removed the Bible and discarded the box.

Rachel had suggested that he read the book of John. Luke glanced up to the framed university degrees grouped together hanging on his wall, pieces of paper that represented knowledge he had learned through years of hard work. Yet, he knew very little about the Bible. Maybe Rachel was right. It wouldn't hurt to do a little reading and learn something. If nothing else, he would be equipped to discuss spiritual issues with her. He flipped through the pages, but soon realized that he had no idea where the book of John was. He turned back to the first few pages of the Bible and smiled, relieved that there was a table of contents.

Luke leaned over and intensified the lighting; then he unconsciously sat back in his chair, put his feet on his desk, and began to read. It was at the end of chapter eleven that he closed the Bible and looked at the clock on his desk. It was late, and he needed to shower and go to bed, but he hated to leave.

Luke finally put the Bible back in the bottom drawer and turned out the light. He sat in the dark a few minutes thinking about what he had read. Rachel was right. There was no doubt that Jesus was the Son of God. Otherwise, how could he have performed so many miracles? And in the third chapter Jesus told Nicodemus that he had to be born again. That was the same expression Rachel had used. But, by far, the greatest miracle was in chapter eleven, the account of Jesus raising Lazarus from the dead.

Luke got up from his chair, knowing that sleep might be long-coming. How could one read of that miracle and drop right off to sleep? Luke knew, for sure, that he could not.

FORTY-SEVEN

"Welcome back, Susan," Rachel said, giving her a big hug. "And you too, William." She turned and joyfully hugged William. "You cannot imagine how happy I am to see you. Berlin was never the same after you left."

"Ah, Rachel, aren't you stretching it a bit?" William said over his shoulder, as he rolled his large upright traveler into the short hall that led to their bedroom. He came back out to get Susan's and said, "I doubt anyone even knew we were gone."

"Well, I did, and believe me, I'm glad you are back."

Susan stood a few moments, looking around the spacious living room. She then smiled and said, "I'm really glad to be back, Rachel, but tell me, where is Sarah Beth?"

"She's down the hall visiting with a little friend of hers. Do you remember our talking about a new family who would be moving in shortly after you flew back to the States?"

"The one from England?"

"Yes, and they have a little girl Sarah Beth's age. Her name is Annabelle, and she and Sarah Beth have become fast friends. They're very compatible and love playing together. Susan, having them on our floor has made a world of difference, not only for Sarah Beth but also for me. I want you and William to meet Margaret and Rodger Springfield, Annabelle's parents."

"Yes, we'll look forward to that, but changing the subject, I want to hear about the Grenfells and how they are doing. I haven't talked to you in the last three days. I bet they hated to see you and Sarah Beth leave."

"Well, I'll have to say yes and no to that. Actually, their son, Pete, and his family are flying in this morning from Stuttgart, and they will be staying a week with them. Sarah Beth and I had to leave so they could have our bedroom. And while I'm thinking about it, Luke wants to have all of us for dinner tonight. The Grenfells will have a sitter for Pete's two children, and Margaret, Annabelle's mother, said she'll keep Sarah Beth for me."

Susan smiled. "That's thoughtful of Luke. Now tell me, how's the romance going?"

Rachel blushed. "What are you talking about, Susan?"

"You know. I'm talking about you and Luke. Luke told William that he has taken you out to dinner. Don't hedge now, Rachel. Tell me the truth."

"I don't know what to say. Really—Luke has been attentive—I mean. Oh, Susan, I wish you had not asked me that question."

Susan laughed. "OK, Rachel, I won't tease you. I'll just observe for myself. I'm a pretty good judge of things like that." Susan stopped talking and turned and looked down the hall. "I wonder what William's doing?" Susan rolled her eyes and shook her head. She dropped her voice and said, "Excuse me, Rachel, while I check on William. He's probably unpacking, and it's no telling where he'll put things."

Karla stood in front of the long mirror and looked at herself. She liked what she saw and smiled. Her pantsuit was very flattering—not that she needed anything to flatter her figure, for Andre kept telling her how perfect it was.

She had paid entirely too much for the outfit. But at the opening of the plaza, Andre wanted her to shop in the exclusive shops there, and they carried the latest designer clothes which were very expensive. Karla turned and looked at the side view. She ran her hand along her hips and was thankful that she never had to have a garment altered, not even the length of the pants. The length was perfect with the wedge sandals she wore.

Karla continued to look in the mirror, wondering what earrings she would wear—and what necklace. She walked into her large closet, brought out her hidden jewelry box, and laid it on her dressing table. The €40,000 diamond bracelet that Andre had given her as a wedding present sparkled when she raised the lid. She put it aside and looked through her earrings, finally deciding on a pair of gold loops. But she might not wear a necklace as she did not want anything to interfere with her neckline and her cleavage. Not that Andre cared. He had lost interest. All he was interested in was his restaurant, the plaza, and making money. Well, that suited her fine, because she liked to spend it. And if ever there was a time that she needed money, it was now.

Karla frowned, thinking about George and wondering if he was loitering outside the building or in the parking garage. She doubted he was truly guarding and regretted that she got him the weekend job. Had she known that Konrad would discover new evidence for the lawsuit, she would not have. But it was too late. Karla closed the lid to her jewelry box when the doorbell sounded.

She walked quickly from her bedroom and into the short hall that led to the foyer and pressed the button that would let her see who was standing outside her door. Karla's hand flew to her throat, and she caught her breath and took a step backward. It was George, in his watchman's uniform, standing as if he were a visitor waiting for her to open her door.

The doorbell sounded again, and then he began to knock. Panic overtook Karla, and she stood only a moment longer before quickly opening the door and motioning him in.

"Have you lost your mind?" she said. "Don't you realize the other tenants on this floor can hear you knocking?"

"Don't fret, Karla. They'll probably think I'm here for security reasons and nothing else." George walked past Karla and began to look around.

"What do you think you're doing, George? You cannot stay here. What do you want?"

"You know what I want. I want the rest of my money."

"I told you to be patient and you would have it in due time. I need more time."

George reached for and picked up an antique figurine from the mantel and began to examine it.

"Put that back, George." Karla glared at him. "Andre would kill me if you broke that figurine. It belonged to his grandparents."

George put the figurine back on the mantel and stood a moment looking all around the living room. He then turned and walked down the hall and into their bedroom, stopping just inside the doorway. It was the sparkling bracelet on the dressing table that caught his eye, and he walked over and picked it up. He turned to Karla with a grin. "Now, this is what I call pretty. Did Andre give you this for Christmas, or was it for your birthday?" George laid it across his wrist and whistled.

"Put that down. Andre gave that to me when we married."

"Really? He must have loved you very much." George walked over to the window and held it up to the light. "I bet this little trinket could be hocked for plenty. What do you say, Karla?"

"I said to put it back, George. It's not for sale."

George walked over, sat down in Andre's lounge chair, and crossed his legs. "Now, I'll tell you what, Karla. You give me this bracelet, and we'll call it even."

"I can't do that, George. Andre would kill me if he thought I no longer had that bracelet."

"OK, here's the deal. I'm taking the bracelet as collateral. You have the money by this time next week, and I'll give the bracelet back to you."

"If you take my bracelet out of this apartment, I'll notify security and you'll be arrested."

"Go ahead, Karla. When they arrest me, they'll arrest you. Can't you figure that out? Surely you're not that dumb."

"Why are you doing this to me, George? Have you already spent the money I gave you?"

George's eyes narrowed. "Drugs aren't cheap, Karla. You don't understand. When a person needs a fix, he needs a fix. And that takes money—lots of money."

"Maybe I could get you some drugs, George. I'm not sure I can get my hands on that much money, but maybe I can get some drugs."

"You're talking crazy, Karla. It takes money to buy drugs. I know—believe me."

"If I came up with half the money and some drugs, would you give me back my bracelet?"

"I'll think about it. You let me know next weekend what you've come up with. Maybe we can make a deal." George winked at Karla, got up from Andre's chair, and shoved the diamond bracelet in his pocket. "I'll find my way out," he said. "In the meantime, just stay cool."

Karla turned and looked at the long mirror, ignoring her reflection. She stood there a long time thinking and then walked over to her dressing table and put the gold loops in her ears.

FORTY-EIGHT

It was while they were finishing their desserts and enjoying a second cup of coffee that Luke said, "Pete, your dad says you are with the Mercedes company in Stuttgart. Do you travel much?"

"I wish I could say no to that question, Luke, but yes, I do travel quite a bit. I love my job though and have become accustomed to air travel."

"Do you travel to the States often?"

"Yes, I recently made a trip to Alabama. Are you familiar with the location of that state?"

"Yes, I lived in the United States for several years. I got my doctorate at Harvard and then worked four years for UBS Financial Services in Atlanta. Alabama borders Georgia," Luke said, chuckling, "and the University of Alabama is known for its successful football team. You probably already know this, but the people in the United States love football like the people in Germany have always loved soccer."

"Yes, I soon found that out. The locals are quite supportive of their teams, and I was amused at the rivalry between the two universities there. I learned early on not to take sides, or else I would have found myself in deep trouble."

After a hearty laugh from the party, Pete looked at his watch and said, "It's getting late, and Liesel and I should probably check on our children. I'm sure they're asleep, but you never know—with a sitter they are not used to, it's no telling what they'll do."

Pete smiled at Luke. "This has been a delightful evening. Thanks for inviting us. And I must say this is the most beautiful restaurant I've had the pleasure to dine in."

"You're very welcome, Pete. I'm glad you and Liesel could be my guests, and I hope we can do this again before you leave. I'll be sure to relay your compliment to Andre Broussard. He'll be pleased to hear another compliment about his restaurant."

Peter put his napkin on the table and looked up at the ceiling. "Well, before we leave I want to say that I think the stars are prettier tonight than they were when we ate here before. What do you think, Nancy?"

Nancy laughed. "Peter, I don't know how you come up with these ideas, but if you say they are prettier, then I'll take your word for it." She turned to Luke and said, "Pay no attention to him, Luke. He just loves to hear himself talk and wants the last word."

Luke grinned and said, "He's probably trying to think of something related to the stars to preach about tomorrow, Nancy. I'll cut him some slack."

"Now, there you go. See, Nancy? I have one person who understands me." Peter turned toward William. "I know we need to leave, but before we do, I wanted to ask William if he settled his case—the one he had to fly back and forth to tend to."

William nodded. "Yes, as a matter of fact, I did, Peter. It was a malpractice suit brought against a doctor in a group we represent. And I'm proud to say we won the case."

"Well, congratulations! I know you must be proud. I understand the medical profession in your country has had to stay on the defensive these past few years, what with all of the frivolous lawsuits."

"It has," William said, nodding his head. "But speaking of lawsuits, Rachel told me that Neumann may have found some new evidence to strengthen his case."

"Yes, Rachel also confided that to me." Peter turned to Luke. "Do you know whether Neumann has actually found what he's looking for?"

"He has a strong lead, but I don't think he's found it yet. The last I heard, he was still searching."

"Well, it looks like everyone knows about this case but me," Pete interjected. "How about letting me in on it?"

Peter looked at his watch. "Son, it's too late to go into all the details now. If Rachel doesn't mind, I'll tell you all about it after we get home." Peter turned to Rachel. "This son of mine took after me, Rachel. He always loved things pertaining to World War II. In fact, he wrote his college thesis on the effect the Second World War had on Germany. I think he'll be intrigued when he hears your story."

"You didn't have to ask my permission, Peter. Of course you can share it with Pete, and you can expect us in church tomorrow morning."

"I'll be looking forward to that." Peter looked at Luke. "Are we going to have the pleasure of your company, Luke?"

"I'm seriously thinking about it. Are you preaching from the book of John?"

"I had not planned to, but if that's what it'll take to get you there, I could pull out one of my old sermons and preach it. I have quite a few I developed from the book of John."

Luke smiled and shook his head. "No, Peter, I wouldn't want you to do that. I'll take your weekly special, whatever that might be."

Handshakes were exchanged by the men, and everyone departed, leaving Luke and Rachel standing at the table.

"Do you have to go yet, Rachel? We could sit and have another cup of coffee."

"If I drank another cup of coffee, Luke, I would not sleep a wink. I must get Sarah Beth and put her to bed."

"Why don't you ask Susan to do that for you?"

"Because she's already gone. And anyhow, she and William are tired. They flew in from the States this morning. Have you forgotten?"

Luke hesitated a moment, and then shook his head. "No, I have not forgotten. It's just that I hoped after the party broke up we would have a little time together—alone."

Rachel stood, watching Luke, as he struggled to hide his disappointment. She thought a minute and then said, "If you can wait until after I put Sarah Beth to bed, we might enjoy a late-night movie. Susan and William will have retired, and we can have the living room to ourselves. Would you like that?"

Luke's face brightened, and the corners of his mouth curved slightly. "Only if you promise to sit close to me on the sofa."

Rachel laughed. "Of course I will. Surely you didn't think I would sit in a chair by myself."

Luke's eyebrows raised slightly. "And let me put my arm around you?"

Rachel nodded. "I suppose so."

"How about an occasional kiss?"

Rachel grinned. "I thought we might watch *Sabrina,* the make with Harrison Ford. Have you seen it?"

"Only a half-dozen times. You didn't answer my last question."

"I know. Do you mind seeing it again?"

"No, I like the idea. I won't have to concentrate on the plot."

"What will you concentrate on?"

Luke laughed. "Now, *you're* asking the questions. I'm not sure, but it won't be *Sabrina.* I suppose it depends on your answer to my last question."

Rachel laughed. "Would you repeat it, please."

"I think you like playing these word games—and you know what, Rachel? You're rather good at it."

Rachel put her arm through Luke's and looked up at him. "I won't ask any more questions."

Luke grinned and patted her hand. "Is that a promise?"

FORTY-NINE

Karla lay in bed thinking. She had made up her mind. She would get rid of George, but it would have to look like an accident—maybe one that involved drugs, since George hungrily fed his drug habit. She sighed, thinking about all of the accidents that happened every day but realizing that it would be almost impossible for her to orchestrate even one of them.

Karla looked up at the ceiling, her eyes moving over and around the deep molding that connected the walls to the ceiling, and continued to think. There had been a near-fatal accident at the Olympic-sized swimming pool yesterday. Andre said a senior adult had developed cramps and almost drowned. Could she somehow use the swimming pool? Drowning was not a frequent occurrence in Berlin, but at the same time, it was not unheard of.

The problem was she did not know how she could accomplish that. George had bragged about being a good swimmer, and she had never learned how. There was no way she could drown him unless he was unconscious or so drugged that he could not defend himself. He was a large man, and it would be difficult enough for her to push his body into the deep end of the swimming pool.

Karla glanced over to the clock on her night table. It was almost nine o'clock. Andre had risen early, had his cup of black coffee, and left. He said he needed to check on the restaurant's inventory and did not want to be disturbed. Well, that was fine with her, as she had a lot on her mind.

Karla rubbed her fingers across her brow and continued to think. The one thing she was good at was injecting drugs into a person's arm, for she had helped her mother do that all through the years when her mother had suffered from migraine headaches. But she would need complete control of George to put a needle in his vein, and that would be the hardest part. She certainly could not knock him in the head—not if she wanted it to look like an accident. Anyhow, she was being foolish thinking she would have an opportunity to knock him in the head. And even if she did, how could she conceal a weapon large enough for something like that?

Karla glanced again at the clock and frowned. She needed to get out of bed and get dressed, but she really didn't want to—that is, not as long as her plans were incomplete. Karla closed her eyes, breathed deeply, and relaxed, willing herself to search every recess of her brain. She had read somewhere that breathing deeply several times and relaxing afterward would cleanse your mind of cobwebs, and maybe if she could do that, she could think better. After that exercise, she lay perfectly still and once more searched for the solution to her problem. It was a few moments later that she smiled. How could she have forgotten so soon? Why had she not thought about this earlier? The documentary she saw on television a month ago was about ways women could defend themselves against male attackers. One of the ways was using a stun gun. And it proved to be very effective. That was her answer. The documentary said small stun guns were convenient to carry in one's purse or pocket, which would make them available for any unforeseen attack one might experience. She would research stun guns on the Internet and find out about the voltage and how they were used. Karla got out of bed with renewed energy and congratulated herself. Ridding her mind of cobwebs had certainly paid off.

Karla made a mental note of the address, closed the website that gave her the information she wanted, and shut down their computer. She could not chance ordering the stun gun. That would be too dangerous. She could not leave a trail for anyone to follow. She would disguise herself, go to the store listed, and pay cash for the gun. The documentary she had watched said the gun had become so popular with women that it was considered a hot item. That was also what the store's ad said. That was good news because she doubted any of the salespeople even noticed who bought them.

Karla looked at her watch. It was almost one o'clock. She might go down to the deli and have lunch. If she were lucky, she might even run into Konrad Neumann and find out how close he was to getting the information he needed for his court case. Karla smiled. Why did she keep saying "his" when she knew it was also her father's court case and, by way of inheritance, her own? And if she were really lucky, he might even bring up the subject of her father and mention again how rich he was.

Karla pulled into the public parking garage and sat a moment. She pulled down her sun visor and looked at herself in the mirror. Her brunette wig was still perfectly in place, as was her lipstick. She had bought lipstick of a special color, suited for someone with dark hair. It was not bright. She did not want to do anything to draw attention to herself. She had put on a black pair of slacks and a light-blue, long-sleeved, polyester blouse. She wore no jewelry except her watch and small ball earrings. She had purchased a cheap shoulder bag. She knew better than to take her new €b3,000 Saint Laurent handbag. Now that would surely draw attention, and she could not have that. Karla got out of her car, pressed her remote to lock the doors, and made her way quickly to the store that stocked the stun guns.

Karla thanked the clerk and put her purchase in her shoulder bag along with her wallet and her receipt. She nodded when the clerk reminded her that their policy included a thirty-day refund but that she had to show her receipt and the gun still had to be in its original wrapper. She turned and reached for her dark glasses that were perched atop her head and settled them on her face as she pushed the large glass door open and left, heaving a sigh of relief.

She walked quickly to the garage, got in her Mercedes, and sat behind the steering wheel, breathing deeply and trying to relax. Now, her final purchase would be the heroin. But she would have to wait until later in the day for that. First, she needed to find a secondhand shop and buy an old pair of blue jeans, a worn sweater, and some worn sneakers. She didn't want to look like a bag woman, but she didn't want to look prosperous either. She had her wig and her cheap shoulder bag. She needed to complete her wardrobe to accomplish her goal. Everyone wore blue jeans. She would blend into the neighborhood with little suspicion, or she hoped that would be the case. Karla put her gear in reverse, carefully backed out into the narrow passageway of the parking garage, and headed outside.

FIFTY

It was two days after their dinner at Broussard's restaurant that Susan suggested to William that they take Pete and Liesel and also Rachel and Luke to see the Haydn mansion. Nancy and Peter graciously offered to keep Sarah Beth with their grandchildren, and William asked Rolfe if he would accompany them and drive the Rolls. Luke said he and Rachel would follow in his Mercedes.

The mansion had been closed since the first of April, after Mr. Kroft broke his hip and was unable to return to Germany. There were twenty-four-hour security guards manning the entrance and a weekly crew who came to care for the grounds. Most of the furniture was still intact, and except for a few personal things, including the walnut desk William sat at to do Mr. Haydn's probate inventory work, the house was much the same as when Susan and William were there in the fall of 2008 preparing for Susan's lawsuit. The mansion had been on the market for three months but had not been sold.

Susan stood at the piano and then opened the keyboard and tapped a couple of the treble keys with her right index finger. She looked up and said, "This piano brings back memories that I promised myself I would not let surface."

"What are you talking about, Susan?" Rachel asked.

"I apologize. What I said was misleading. I did not mean all of my memories. Some of them are good. It was the picture of my dad playing this piano that made me sad—and I don't expect anyone in here to understand except William."

Rachel said, "I'm the one who should apologize. I should not have asked you what you were talking about."

"No, Rachel, I need to talk about it. Sometimes it's a good thing to bring up sad memories. It helps one keep things in perspective." Susan hesitated a moment and then continued. "I doubt any of you, except William, know the story of my father being born to a young Jewish prisoner at the very end of World War II. The American colonel, and those with him, found my grandmother still on the delivery table, having hemorrhaged to death after giving birth to my father. The colonel, who had no children, immediately claimed the baby as his own and had him sent to England on a transport plane with his sister-in-law, the young nurse who accompanied him that morning.

"The colonel arrested the doctor and sent him to Nuremberg to await trial. What he didn't realize was that Mr. Haydn, the young doctor delivering the baby was the father and he was very much in love with Leah, the baby's mother. Since the law forbade a German to marry a Jew, my grandparents said their vows to each other secretly and pledged to marry legally after the war."

"What did your grandfather do when he discovered that the colonel had taken his baby?" Rachel asked with a bewildered look on her face.

"The report the colonel turned in said that the baby died and was buried with his mother. Mr. Haydn, my true grandfather, never knew his son lived until a few days before he died."

"Oh, how terrible," Rachel said, moving over and putting her arm around Susan.

"But that's not the end of the story, Rachel. It was during the Vietnam War in the sixties and early seventies that my grandfather, Haydn, and his wife, who had no children of their own, would entertain soldiers on R & R for the weekend. There were a group of six lieutenants who came one weekend, and one of them was my father. He was the life of the party with this very piano. He played by ear and was a great jazz player. And, of course, Mr. Haydn never knew he was entertaining his own son. Mrs. Haydn took pictures of the men, and that was how I discovered that my father had been here. I had a duplicate picture that I found among his possessions after he died with cancer."

"So Mr. Haydn never knew he had any family?"

"Only a few days before he died did he find out. It's really a long story, and I'll have to tell it to you in detail one of these days, but we don't have time now. William and I want to show you the rest of the house."

"And the grounds, Susan," William said. "The grounds are beautiful, and I think Rolfe was going to see about the golf carts. That's what we tour the grounds in."

"Now, how did you manage this, Mr. Hartmann?" Rachel smiled as she sat down next to Luke on Mr. Haydn's bench by the lake.

"Didn't you notice that I made sure we had a golf cart to ourselves, Rachel? I told Rolfe to go on ahead and that we would catch up with them or meet them back at the house." Luke tried but had a hard time suppressing a mischievous smile. "I know you think I work all of the time, but you might be surprised to find out that I occasionally play. I play golf when I have a chance. In fact, I've asked William and Pete to join me tomorrow morning at the club I belong to." Luke let his gaze sweep out over the lake and then back to Rachel. "I realize that I shouldn't be riding in a golf cart. I should be walking for the health benefits, but because of the time factor, I've found it necessary to own one."

Luke reached for Rachel's hand. "Forgive me. I've failed to ask you if you play golf. William says Susan attempts to."

Rachel grinned. "Poorly, Luke, or as Elizabeth Bennett would say, 'Very ill, very ill, indeed.'"

Luke smiled. "Now I'm finding out more about you. Are you telling me that you love *Pride and Prejudice?* I should have known. There is something about those who follow Jane Austen that's a dead giveaway." Luke chuckled. "But to be perfectly honest, I like her, also. In fact, I've read *Pride and Prejudice* not once but twice and have seen the BBC production several times. I have it on DVD."

Rachel smiled. "Are you trying to prove that we are soul mates?"

"Yes, something like that." Luke brought Rachel's hand to his lips and kissed it.

Luke put his arm around Rachel and pulled her closer, and they both looked out over the lake, enjoying the silence and watching a swan glide by.

"I could sit here all afternoon," Luke said, continuing to gaze at the lake.

"Yes, it's so peaceful." Rachel looked up at Luke. "Don't you wish this bench could talk? I wonder what it would tell us."

"We might be surprised. But, on the other hand, Rolfe said this was Mr. Haydn's special place—the place he came to meditate. Maybe there would be more silence than conversation." Luke smiled down at Rachel.

"You're probably right. Mr. Haydn was a Christian. Maybe this is one of the places that he liked to come in order to be alone with the Lord."

"I figured you would say that."

"You don't mind me bringing up the spiritual, do you?"

"No. I don't mind. I don't know why I have not told you, but I have read the entire book of John in the New Testament. You would probably laugh at me. I had to use the table of contents to even find out where it was."

"I would never laugh at someone hunting for scripture. It thrills me to hear you say that you have been reading the Bible."

A gentle breeze blew through the branches above where they sat, and Luke turned to Rachel and said, "I love you, Rachel. Do you realize that? I love everything about you." Luke took her face between his hands and searched her eyes, hoping she would respond in kind. He finally leaned down and kissed her, not once but twice.

Rachel looked longingly at Luke and said, "I know, and I love you, Luke."

FIFTY-ONE

Karla made sure her automobile had plenty of gasoline, and she looked again at the map before pulling out of the Hartmann garage and into traffic that would lead her to the main thoroughfare. She would save time by using the autobahn that would take her to West Berlin.

Andre was entertaining two men from France. They were old acquaintances of his who had shown up unexpectedly, and Karla marveled at the timing. He had looked a little irritated after she told him she would not be joining them tonight because she had made arrangements to attend a special trunk showing of the new holiday designer clothes at one of the leading department stores.

Karla frowned at his comment. "More clothes, Karla? When is enough *enough*? I've told you how tight money is, so don't run up a large bill on my credit card."

Andre had nothing to worry about, Karla thought. Buying new clothes was the last thing she had on her mind. What would give him a stroke would be his finding out about the €20,000 she had borrowed from the bank. She had taken the papers and filled them out, convincing the loan officer that she would pay the loan back in one week. She had shown him a €50,000 CD in her and Andre's name and made him promise that he would not reveal her loan to Andre.

Karla slowed down. She had to quit thinking about Andre and concentrate on where she was going, as she was not as familiar with that part of Berlin. She picked up the card on her seat and read the address again. She had exited the autobahn and found the right street but was far from the address on the card. She would have to be careful. She did not want to drive right up to the residence. She didn't want anyone to see her Mercedes and her license tag. She had already decided that she would park at least a block away.

It was cool enough outside, but Karla felt a bit of perspiration forming on her forehead, and she blotted it away with her handkerchief and breathed deeply. She had to stay calm if she expected to complete her mission.

This was the address George had hinted at one day when he was tending to her father. George was testing her to see if she was interested and seemed disappointed when she didn't take the bait. She had her own set of problems, but dabbling in drugs was not among them. Karla glanced over to the numbers on the unkempt house on the right and slowed to a snail's crawl. The residence she wanted was on the next block, so she pulled over to the curb and cut her engine, relieved to see very little activity—only an old woman pushing a wobbly grocery cart down the sidewalk.

She wished she could have driven over in an older and less expensive model, but had she rented an ordinary low-end car, they would have asked for her driver's license, and she did not want that on record at a rental company. She and Andre were among the few who had automobiles, as most Berlin residents used public transportation.

Karla put the address card in her purse, got out of her Mercedes, and locked her doors. She wished she had a dog on a leash, something to make her look like she was a local resident out for a walk, but that would have been a nuisance, and she dismissed the thought as she walked the long block, stopping only at the intersection. She unconsciously felt for the small object—the stun gun—that was hidden under the right sleeve of her sweater and attached to her wrist with a narrow strap. She hoped she would not have to use it, but if someone attacked her, she would. She had stood in front of her long mirror, following the instructions and practicing.

Karla glanced both ways before crossing the street. She stopped in front of the corner house to check the address and then walked slowly to the house next door. It was a two-story, rather neat clapboard structure. She glanced up and down the street before walking up the six steps and onto the front porch to press the doorbell. The left end of the porch hosted two cushioned metal chairs that sat opposite a swing that was attached to the beaded ceiling. Karla wondered why drug dealers would have such a public seating area but admitted to herself that it made for a normal appearance.

Karla turned her attention back to the door. She could hear steps and finally the lock slipping back. The door opened to reveal a hard-looking, heavyset woman who looked to be every bit of six feet tall. She stood, unsmiling, waiting for Karla to speak. Karla didn't know what to say. She finally blurted out, "I was told that you might have something for sale that I could use."

"Who told you that?" the woman asked, frowning.

"I can't remember. It was last year, I think. May I come in?"

The woman's eyes narrowed, and she waited a full minute, eyeing Karla from head to toe, and then opening the door wider and letting her in.

The woman closed the door, leaving Karla standing outside looking down at her shaky hands. She then rubbed them up and down the sides of her hips, hoping to still the shaking. Karla breathed in deeply and adjusted her shoulder bag before glancing one last time at the swing set and quickly walking down the steps. Purchasing the heroin had taken only ten minutes, but it had taken most of her cash. She could tell by the looks the woman gave that she was not one to haggle with. Karla paid her what she asked and deposited her small package in the pocket of her blue jeans. If anyone grabbed her purse, they would not get the heroin. She kept her car keys, remote, driver's license, and cell phone in her right pocket and the small package of heroin in her left. Her shoulder purse held a handkerchief, a tube of lipstick, the address card, an ink pen, and what little cash she had left.

The woman did not reveal her name and did not ask Karla her name. No conversation was exchanged—only the bare information needed for Karla's purchase. She paused at the intersection and then stepped off the curb and walked quickly across the street. The sun had sunk behind tall buildings in the distance, and shadows were beginning to play across the yards of houses along the street. Karla picked up her pace.

She could see her Mercedes at the end of the street, but it did not stand alone. There were two men leaning back against it, and Karla's heart began to beat faster. They were smoking cigarettes and talking to each other. She slowed her pace, reached under her sweater sleeve, pulled down the small stun gun, and gripped it in her right hand, thankful that the narrow wrist strap would prevent her from dropping it. She adjusted her shoulder bag once more and walked slowly to her car.

The blond man threw his cigarette butt down and turned to her with a grin. "Well, what do we have here? Honey, is this your car?"

Karla shook her head and said, "Would you mind moving away from my car, please?"

"Now, why would you want us to do that?" he asked. "We thought you might like to take us for a ride."

Karla glanced around, hoping someone would come out and distract them, but there were no lights showing in any of the windows, and all of the doors were shut.

The blond one continued, "What are you doing in this neighborhood, lady? I know you don't live here, and you certainly are not visiting the people in this house." He pointed to the house on his right.

Karla said, "It's none of your business; now move aside before I call the police."

The dark-haired man grinned and said, "Ah, come on. Surely you wouldn't do that. You know why? You would have to answer too many questions, one of them being why you are in this neighborhood. He'd want to know who you were visiting, and what would you tell him? That you were calling on Big Bertha?" He flipped his cigarette butt toward the sidewalk and then pushed away from the car and began to walk slowly toward Karla.

"You don't really want the police, do you? Come on now and relax, baby. We're not going to hurt you. We just want you to come with us. We know a place where we can get a drink and have a little fun. Unlock your car now and be a good sport."

Karla backed away from him, moving slowly around the front of the car to the driver's side and standing with her back to the door. The dark-haired man stopped in front of the car and looked over to the blond. He motioned toward the back of the car with his head and said, "I think she's coming to her senses." He then turned again to Karla and said, "You going to drive us, honey?"

"No, I'm not going to drive you anywhere," Karla said, holding her stun gun down at her side.

"Listen to the woman, Bert. She says she's not driving us anywhere." The brunette chuckled and gave the Mercedes a couple of pats on the front fender as he moved closer to Karla.

"I heard her," the blond said, coming slowly around the back of the car. "Maybe we'll drive her, Joe."

The brunette reached Karla first and grabbed her left arm, but she thrust the stun gun into his stomach and pulled the trigger. He screamed and fell backward. The blond lunged forward but then hesitated just long enough for Karla to stun him in his chest. He crumpled to the pavement, and Karla pulled her keys and remote from her pocket, opened her car door, and quickly slid under the steering wheel. It took her only a few seconds to start her engine and ease forward, careful to avoid running over the stunned men lying in the street. She did not speed but left the neighborhood as quickly as she could without even looking in her rearview mirror.

FIFTY-TWO

Luke punched in the numbers that would open the door to his office. He was glad that he had a private entrance and could come and go as he pleased with his own security system set in place. It was late, but he was not sleepy. He was not sure that he would ever be sleepy again after the wonderful day he had experienced. Rachel had said she loved him. He could hardly keep his eyes on the road as they drove home.

He smiled thinking about the way she looked at him when she told him she loved him, as if it had taken all the courage she had. He had not wanted to leave the lake. Mr. Haydn's bench was, no doubt, enchanted. Kissing Rachel was like being in heaven—not that he knew much about heaven, but Peter Grenfell said it was the most glorious place one could imagine, and he would take Peter Grenfell's word for it. He and Rachel had spent such a long time on the bench that Rolfe sent one of the security men to check on them.

Rachel was a little embarrassed and wondered how they would explain their long absence, but Luke told her not to worry—he would explain. But he didn't actually have to. William and Susan knew. They could tell just by looking at the faces of their good friends. Love has a way of expressing itself in more ways than the spoken word.

Luke sat back in his chair and put his feet on the desk. The rest of the day was a blur. He couldn't even remember what they ate for dinner. He knew one thing: he did not want the day to end. But where would he go from here? He knew without a shadow of a doubt that he wanted to marry Rachel, but would Rachel accept a ring so soon? Maybe it was time for Luke Hartmann to seek the Lord's will for his life. Rachel always said that one would find the truth in God's Word.

Luke removed his feet from his desk and again opened the bottom drawer and retrieved the black book. He rubbed his hand gently across the soft leather and smiled, thinking about the many times Rachel had chided him about spiritual things. Luke reached over, turned his desk lamp on, and sat back and continued to think. He wondered why he had been so resistant to spiritual things. He was forty years old and had lived all of those years running his own life. Rachel said if a person were to have real joy in life, he or she would have to relinquish control and let the Lord run it.

Luke opened the Bible and turned back to the New Testament. He liked the Apostle Paul. He had read two chapters from the book of Galatians. Paul was his kind of man. He didn't mince words, and he told it like it was. Luke smiled again as he turned to the book of Romans. Peter said the book of Romans was meaty stuff. Well, maybe that was what Luke Hartmann needed. Luke pushed back in his chair, propped his feet back up, and began to read. He would read until he got sleepy, and then he would close down shop and go to bed. He glanced at his computer and then back at the book he was holding and chuckled, wondering what Rachel would think if she could see him now.

Luke looked at the digital clock on his desk. It was one. He was still far from sleepy, but he knew if he were to function normally later that day, then he had to get some rest. He put a bookmark where he had stopped reading, closed the Bible, and laid it on his desk. He sat up straight and thought about what he had read. He had not read hurriedly but slowly, even checking some cross-references. There was one conclusion that he had come to: he was a sinner. Paul made that very clear in the first few chapters.

Luke remembered laughing at someone years ago who talked about everyone being sinners. Luke had not wanted to admit that he himself was. After all, he had never been in trouble with the law. His life had been exemplary—or so he thought.

Well, now he knew what his problem was: pride, which had kept him from confessing his sinfulness all of those years He was proud of his successful business. He was proud of his self-control. He was proud that he had never been in trouble. He never really realized just how proud and self-righteous he was until he met Rachel and she began to show him in her own sweet, humble way. And now the apostle Paul explained it so clearly.

Luke sat a few more moments reflecting on his life, and then humbly bowed his head, confessed his sin of pride, and asked for the Lord to forgive him and come into his life.

Leon Beckle put the papers aside, stood up, and pulled his arms back in a stretch. He did an exercise rotation of his head and neck and said, “Konrad, it’s after midnight. We need to hang it up. I have a heavy court case tomorrow, and if I’m going to be any good, I need to get some rest. Anyhow, I’m stiff as a board. Sitting here night after night is getting to me.”

“I know, Leon. I’m stiff, too, but I don’t know any other way to get this information we need. And look, we’ve gone through twenty boxes. There are only ten left. It shouldn’t take us much longer to go through them.”

“Maybe not, but what I can’t understand is why the damn papers are all mixed together. Why didn’t they keep the two cemeteries separated?”

"Who knows? It's possible that the Jewish caretaker brought his papers in sacks and they were all dumped together. I guess we're fortunate we have any records at all."

"Yes, well, I'm leaving. You can sit here and search through the other boxes. I've got to get some sleep."

"Are you going to help me tomorrow night?"

"I guess so. But I can't promise anything beyond this week. I want to make that clear. You know if we find the papers, we'll have to hire an expert witness."

"Why is that necessary?"

"For the authenticity of the papers—someone to convince the judge that they are the original burial documents."

"Oh. Well, that will be another couple of thousand euros, I guess. It never ends, does it?"

"That's the law for you. It's expensive, but look what you'll have in the long run. If the judge awards you the deeds, you'll be fixed for life."

"Yes, and don't think that has not been on my mind."

FIFTY-THREE

Luke held Rachel's arm lightly as they followed the waiter into the beautiful terrace and to a table far in the corner. Luke had made it clear when making the reservation that he wanted a table for two with as much privacy as possible, and that he was not interested in sitting near the fishpond.

Rachel smiled. "You did not tell me we would be by ourselves tonight."

"You don't mind, do you?" Luke asked.

"No. And I love the privacy here in the corner amid the greenery. It's like a little hideaway."

"I thought it would be nice—just the two of us. We've hardly been alone. I think our friends understand."

Luke turned and looked past the fountain. He smiled and said, "There will be a second surprise for you, Rachel. Look, the small combo is setting up. We're going to have music tonight."

"Does that mean we'll have dancing?"

"Yes. Andre rearranged the tables. You do dance, don't you?"

"I do, and I dance a lot better than I play golf."

Luke smiled again and said, "Well, I see that I'm in for a treat, and on top of that, I'll have a wonderful excuse to hold you in my arms."

"You don't need an excuse for that, Luke."

Luke glanced around and said, "You don't mind being the only couple on the dance floor, do you, Rachel?"

"No, as long as you didn't select a fast Latin American tune to dance to." Rachel looked a little alarmed. "You didn't, did you, Luke?"

Luke laughed. "Do I look like the Latin American type? You can relax, Rachel. Our music is strictly the big band kind and with plenty of slow pieces."

"That's good to hear." Rachel relaxed against the back of the chair. She thought a moment and then raised her brows slightly. "When William and Susan hear about this, they will wonder why you did not include them. Susan says they love big band music, and William's favorite song is *Green Eyes*."

"William is the one who suggested this music. We'll include them next time, Rachel. Tonight belongs just to us." Luke's eyes dropped to the menu on the table. "Is there anything special you have a taste for tonight, sweetheart?"

"Why don't you surprise me, Luke. Somehow or another, you make me feel like a young person experiencing her first love affair. Everything you do pleases me."

After giving the waiter their order, Luke said, "You look especially beautiful this evening, Rachel. But then, you always look beautiful."

"You're generous with your compliments, Luke, but you know what they say: 'Beauty is in the eye of the beholder.'"

"Yes, but Rachel, haven't you noticed how often eyes turn when you enter a room with me?"

"No, I have not noticed that. Could they possibly be looking at you, Luke? You are quite the handsome man with your broad shoulders, those green eyes and your wavy brown hair."

"Now, you are teasing me."

Rachel started to say something then stopped. She smiled excitedly and said, "Luke, listen. They're playing *Stardust*. Aren't you going to ask me to dance?"

Luke held Rachel close as they danced to songs from the 1930s and the 1940s. Rachel smiled, looked up at Luke, and said, "I'm surprised the musicians are familiar with songs that were so popular in the United States."

Luke dropped his eyes to meet hers and said, "I think beautiful music is not limited to one country. And I confess that I helped them a bit."

"Are you saying that all of these songs are by request?"

"Most of them are, yes, and they are especially for you."

"You're so kind and thoughtful, Luke. You're not the same person I met the day of the trial."

"No, I'm not."

"What has caused this wonderful transformation?"

"You, of all people, should know." Luke kissed Rachel lightly on her brow and pulled her closer to him.

"I know you have been reading your Bible."

"Could that possibly be the cause, sweetheart?"

"It could be if you wanted it to be."

Luke, again, touched Rachel's brow lightly with his lips and pulled her even closer."

They danced in silence until the song ended and then returned to their table.

"Luke?" Rachel said.

"What, sweetheart?"

"We did not finish our conversation on the dance floor."

"No, we didn't."

"Is there something more you want to tell me?"

"Yes. It's the third surprise I had for you."

"I love surprises."

"You'll really love this one."

"Don't tease me any longer, please!"

"Last night, after reading in the book of Romans, I surrendered my life to the Lord."

Rachel sat speechless, looking at Luke. A few moments later she picked up her napkin and dabbed at her eyes.

"You're not going to cry, are you, Rachel? I thought you would be happy."

"I am happy, Luke. Women often tear up when they're happy."

"I didn't realize that."

Rachel's laugh was hardly audible. "I love watching you when you get that little-boy look on your face, Luke."

"I hope you'll always love me, Rachel, though I doubt you could ever love me as much as I love you."

"Now why would you think that?"

"I don't know. I guess it's because I love you more than anything or anyone I've ever loved before."

"I don't know how to answer that, except to say how happy I am that you love me that much."

"Rachel, I know we have not known each other a long time, but at our level of maturity, I really don't think that is a major factor. I love you, and I want to marry you. This might come as a shock to you, but the moment I saw you, I was drawn to you. It's hard to explain, and I'll be honest and tell you that I fought my feelings for weeks but then decided that I would be honest with myself." Luke stopped and gave Rachel an endearing look. "Do you understand what I'm trying to say, Rachel? I guess what I mean is that I've loved you almost from the time you walked down the courtroom aisle with William. You looked shy and ill at ease, and I didn't want to, but I felt sorry for you."

"I thought you hated me."

"I tried to. But who can hate someone as lovely as you?"

"I'm afraid you've put me on a higher pedestal than I deserve, Luke, and when I fall off, who will catch me?"

"I will, Rachel. I'll always be there for you. Now please tell me that you'll marry me. I could not live without you."

Rachel smiled. "What can I say but yes? I'll marry you, Luke, because I love you and I've seen a wonderful spiritual change in your life. I really think we were meant for each other." Rachel sat back and sighed. "You know it's strange the way the Lord plays checkers with our lives."

"You must be referring to our strange meeting over the lawsuit."

"Yes. I never would have known you if I had not inherited the deeds to the land your building sits on and I had not come to Germany."

"I'm so glad you did."

"So am I."

Luke looked lovingly at Rachel and then reached for her hand. "But there's one thing missing, he said, glancing at her left hand."

"What are you talking about, Luke?"

"Something found only in a jewelry store."

Rachel's eyes began to sparkle and she breathed in with excitement. "Are we going shopping for a ring?"

"Yes, sweetheart—tomorrow—as soon as the store opens."

FIFTY-FOUR

Karla turned the key in her ignition to off, removed her seat-belt, and sat back against her seat. It was Thursday afternoon and she had to set up her weekend plans with George or things would go awry. She went over every detail in her mind once more and then got out of her Mercedes and walked briskly toward the front of the nursing home.

Karla stood at the door of her father's room, breathed deeply, and slowly pressed the handle that would open his door. She glanced over toward his bed and noticed that he was asleep. It seemed that he was sleeping more and more, and the director said that was a little unusual for Alzheimer's patients, as many of them could not sleep. Karla knew George was standing by the window, and she continued to stand beside her father's bed, wondering if he would speak first.

"Did you bring my money?" George asked.

"No, I understood that we would transact at the end of the week."

"Why do we have to wait until the end of the week? You should have brought the money with you today; then we could have made our exchange right here in your father's room."

"You have no idea what is involved in my getting that much money. It does not just fall out of the sky." Karla turned and glared at him.

"You said you might also have some drugs."

"You can forget that. That was nothing but a bluff. You well know that I have no way of getting drugs."

"Then it'll be strictly cash?"

"Yes, I have been working on a loan from my bank. I'll have the money tomorrow, late in the morning. I will have the loan officer give me two cashier's checks. Do you want your money in cashier's checks?"

"No, I told you in the beginning that I wanted strictly cash, preferably in hundred-euro bills."

"I will have the early part of the afternoon to cash the checks at two other banks. I could not ask my bank to give me that much cash."

"Then we can meet later tomorrow afternoon?"

"No, Andre has a weekend trip planned and we are leaving at three o'clock and will not be back until late Sunday—probably around six o'clock."

"We could meet in an elevator at six-thirty."

"Have you lost your mind? The elevators have active cameras. Since your two blunders, there have been more cameras installed in the hallways. I have thought about a safe place to meet and, that would be the swimming pool."

"The swimming pool? Why would you think that?"

"Because they close at six on Sunday evening, and there are no cameras operating at night. Remember, there were no pictures taken of you."

"It will be dark as pitch in there."

"Use the light in your cell—nothing more—we do not want to attract attention."

"Have you forgotten that the swimming center will be locked?"

"Don't worry about that. I've already accessed the code. I'll send you a text Sunday when I arrive home."

"That place is large. Where do you want me to meet you?"

"At the low diving board. We'll meet at the back. That way we can put our wares on the board."

"What time?"

"I'll try to be there at seven o'clock. You come at five after seven."

"You had better be there, Karla. If I thought you were out to double-cross me, well...I promise you, it would be the last time." George's expression darkened, and he turned and looked out the window.

Karla stood only a few moments longer, her eyes narrowing as she stared at George's back. She then turned and quietly left.

FIFTY-FIVE

Rachel glanced down at her hands and then up at Luke and said, "I was always taught that a person's hands should stay in their lap until they are engaged in eating. But, Luke, I'm really having a hard time keeping my hands in my lap. I can't look at my ring with it in my lap."

Luke laughed. "Rachel, I don't think anyone is keeping tabs on your table manners. You don't have to hide your ring in your lap. Put your hand on the table if you want to. I love looking at your ring."

"And so do I," Rachel said, putting her hand on the table in front of her. She tilted her hand slightly up and down to let the diamond catch the light. "Luke, why did you insist that I have such a large diamond? A smaller one would have pleased me just as much. You were far too generous."

"I would have given you a ten-carat diamond if you had wanted it, Rachel, but then that would have been too much weight to carry on your slender finger, and besides that, I know you do not like gaudy things."

Rachel looked up. "What will Susan say when she sees this? She so graciously offered to keep Sarah Beth for me, but I did not tell her we were shopping for a ring. In fact, I did not tell her that we are engaged. I want to surprise her."

"Did you tell her about my decision? The spiritual one, I'm talking about."

"Yes, I could not hold that in. You cannot imagine how happy she and William are for you. She wants to know when you plan to tell Peter and Nancy."

"I haven't decided. I wonder what they'll say."

"They won't be surprised. They told Susan and me that they have prayed for you for years."

"Well, the Lord answered their prayers, didn't He? I'll have to thank them." Luke hesitated a moment and then reached over and covered Rachel's hand with his. "Now, changing the subject, I have something to tell you."

Rachel raised her eyebrows and said, "I hope it's not bad news."

"I'm not sure that it is, but Neumann called yesterday, and he was very excited."

"He found the burial paper?"

"Yes. He said the paper was in the next-to-last box of the thirty that they were searching through."

Rachel sighed and shook her head. "Did he say what his next step was?"

"Yes, he said that Beckle is getting his witnesses lined up and will present his new evidence when Judge Krause calls for the second hearing. I understand that Judge Krause is on vacation, and I'm not sure when he'll be back." Luke gave a short wave with his hand. "And, of course, no one knows how full the docket is. That may have some bearing on the exact date of your case."

"You remember what I told you, Luke. I'm determined not to let this upset me. I'm trusting the Lord to handle it."

"Rachel, I know you are, but I also want you to understand that you do not need the deeds. I have plenty of money. You are going to be my wife. You'll have no need for more money."

"I know you have money, Luke, but I guess it's the principle of the thing. Those deeds were stolen from my grandparents. Can you imagine someone walking into Hartmann Plaza and taking the elevator to the third floor and barging into your office and telling you that you no longer own your commodity business or the interest you own in Hartmann Plaza—that the German government had confiscated it and you would have to step aside and let one of your hired men take charge? That's what happened to my grandfather." Rachel's voice had gained momentum, and she hesitated only a moment. "But it was even worse than that. He and his family were herded onto a train and then transported to a concentration camp and finally murdered."

Rachel frowned at Luke and then sat back, silent, finally dropping her eyes. After a few moments she looked up and said, "I'm sorry, Luke. I didn't mean to take it out on you. You had nothing to do with what happened so long ago. Forgive me."

Luke reached across and took Rachel's hand. "You owe me no apology, Rachel. I doubt I can have the deep feelings that you have, but my sympathy is with you and what happened to the Jewish people. Don't give up. You have not been asked to surrender the deeds yet. Who knows? The Lord truly might step in and right the wrong that happened so long ago. And think about it. You will own the land that my building stands on. Now that should make us a pretty good team, don't you think?"

Rachel smiled. "We will be a good team with or without the deeds, Luke. Marriages are not based on material things, but qualities like love and respect and a servant spirit. I must put you first, and you must put me first. Those are the principles that build a good marriage, and they're from the Word of God."

Luke gave Rachel's hand a gentle squeeze. "I love you so much—how could I not put you first? But look, we have not set a date. Have you thought about when we can get married?"

"Let's wait until after the hearing, Luke. I think marrying before then would put too much pressure on both of us."

"Yes, you are probably right, but I hope the case comes up soon, because I don't know how long I can wait. Marrying you is all I can think about."

"I know. I long for the day I can be your wife."

Susan looked up and smiled when she heard the door open and saw Luke behind Rachel as they came into the living room. "Well, tell me, what have you two been up to? I didn't expect you back this early. I hope you took time out for lunch."

"We had an early lunch and thought we might come on back as we had something to tell you. But first, where is Sarah Beth?"

"Margaret came with Annabelle and asked if Sarah Beth could have lunch with them and then stay for a Walt Disney movie. I didn't think you would mind."

"No. I'm glad Margaret includes Sarah Beth so often."

William walked in from the bedroom and said, "Did I hear Rachel say she had something to tell us? Well, I already know. I've heard through the grapevine that Beckle is prepared for the second hearing. He has two new witnesses lined up." William looked at Rachel and shook his head. "I'm sorry, Rachel. I had hoped he wouldn't find that old burial paper. This is going to complicate everything."

"But, William, that's not what I wanted to tell you."

"It's not?"

"No." Rachel smiled, held out her hand with the ring sparkling on her finger, and said, "This is much more important than cemetery papers, don't you think?"

Susan jumped up from the sofa and hugged Rachel, and William thrust his hand out for Luke to shake, patting his shoulder and grinning. "Yes, I agree—this is wonderful news." William turned to Rachel. "Congratulations to both of you. I know you'll be very happy." William turned back to Luke. "Rachel told us the other good news, Luke. I think we ought to have a celebration. Let's the four of us have dinner with the Grenfells tonight. We'll celebrate under the stars and make Andre a little richer. The treat will be on me. What do you say to that?"

FIFTY-SIX

Luke whispered something to William and then caught Rachel's arm and said, "I see Andre and Karla. Let's stop at their table for just a moment. I want to tell them our good news."

Karla looked up from her menu to see Luke and Rachel approaching and murmured, "Luke must have something to tell us. He has Rachel with him, and he looks as happy as a child on a Ferris wheel."

Andre began to push his chair back, but Luke put his hand on his shoulder and shook his head. "Don't get up, Andre. We can't stay and talk. I just wanted you and Karla to know that Rachel and I are engaged."

Andre beamed. "Well, congratulations to both of you. Now that is wonderful news. When is the wedding going to take place?"

"We have not set a date, but when we do, I assure you that you'll be among the first to know."

Karla smiled at Rachel. "May I see your ring, please, Rachel?"

Rachel nodded and held out her left hand.

"Hmmm. Luke went all out, didn't he? That is a beautiful ring." Karla turned to Andre. "Honey, you might take some lessons from Luke on how to select beautiful diamonds." Karla's smile was a teasing one. "Should I add...beautiful, large diamonds?"

Andre cleared his throat and said, "Pay no attention to Karla. She's just teasing." He gave Karla a warning look and changed the subject. "Rachel, how did you like the music the other night? Luke was instrumental in acquiring that combo." Andre chuckled. "Now, that almost sounded like a pun, didn't it?"

Rachel smiled. "I loved it, Andre. You might consider having the combo on a weekly basis, or at least monthly. This restaurant is so beautiful, and your food is superb. I think music might be the finishing touch."

"Well, thank you, Rachel. I'll seriously consider that." Andre smiled and cleared his throat one more time.

Luke said, "I hope you'll excuse us as we do not want to hold our party up."

"Of course," Andre said.

Luke nodded to Karla, caught Rachel's arm, and guided her away from their table and into the terrace.

Karla pushed her menu to the side and glared at Andre. "Well, aren't you the friendly one? Didn't I hear you say the other night that you wished she would return to America? Why, all of a sudden, the attitude change?"

"I haven't told you the good news, Karla. Neumann called and said he found the information he has been searching for. He's confident that he has the case wrapped up, and as far as we are concerned, the woman is no longer a threat." Andre smiled and looked back at his menu.

Karla sat a minute before commenting. She finally smiled and said, "I'm sure Konrad must be celebrating. I'm surprised you didn't invite him to have dinner with us tonight. We could break out the champagne and toast to the victory that will soon be his."

"You know, Karla, that's not a bad idea. The champagne, I'm talking about. I might get the waiter to bring us a bottle. We can also toast Luke's engagement. He's a good fellow." Andre paused. "But you could have left off that remark you made about the woman's diamond ring. Have you forgotten the forty thousand-euro diamond bracelet I gave you when we married?"

"You know I haven't, Andre. Are you getting so old that you cannot take a joke?"

"It didn't sound like a joke to me, and I doubt Luke took it as a joke. But I have a question. You used to wear your beautiful bracelet all of the time. I haven't seen you wear it lately. Have you grown tired of it?"

"Of course not, Andre. A woman never grows tired of diamonds. How could you think that? I have not worn it lately because the catch seems to be a little loose. I need to take it to the jeweler and let him check it." Karla picked up her menu and said, "I see our waiter coming, dear. We need to decide what entrées we are having tonight."

William glanced at his watch and with a surprised look said, "Can any of you guess how long we have been here?"

Susan said, "Does it really matter, William? Good fellowship has no time limit."

Pete entered in. "But we have small children, and I know Rachel will want to put Sarah Beth to bed."

"Yes, Pete, you're right," Rachel said. "I suspect Sarah Beth has fallen asleep on Nancy's sofa. Luke might have to carry her to his car."

Peter smiled. "With all that has happened and so much to discuss, I'm surprised it's been no longer than three hours. But I do think it's time to say goodnight and thank William for the delicious meal, for surely his thoughtfulness has contributed to this wonderful night of fellowship."

Everyone stood, and Luke shook Pete's hand. "So you're returning to Stuttgart tomorrow?"

"Yes, my week is up, and I must get back to work. It has been a delightful week of making new acquaintances. Luke, I want to say again how happy I am that you and Rachel are getting married. Dad told me all about Rachel's lawsuit, and I'll be praying for the outcome. It's a most interesting case, and I wish I could help in some way, but being out of town makes that almost impossible."

"Thanks, Pete. I think Rachel has made up her mind that she'll accept the judge's decision, whatever that may be, and not contest it should it not go in her favor."

Nancy hugged Rachel and said, "When you come down out of the clouds, Rachel, let us know so we can plan something. Maybe we'll take Sarah Beth on a picnic or something."

Rachel smiled. "Thanks, Nancy. I must confess that I've been floating around in the clouds all day. I hope I made sense with my conversation tonight. Luke teases me and often accuses me of being on the shy side. I probably talked too much tonight."

"No, we loved hearing about some of your experiences teaching school. You might not have noticed, but Luke held on to every word. You and he have a lot to look forward to, getting to know each other's background."

"Luke has promised to take me to meet his parents. I hope we'll be able to do that soon."

"Peter says they are lovely people. I have had the privilege of meeting them, but he knows them much better than I do." Nancy gave Rachel a hug. "I think Luke is trying to get your attention, Rachel."

"Come, Rachel," Luke said. "I've sent for my car, and it should be out front. We might be a bit crowded again, but the Grenfells are ready to go home."

FIFTY-SEVEN

Karla kissed Andre and gave him a quick pat on his cheek. "Give my regards to Mr. Neumann and Mr. Beckle, Andre. You needn't tell them that I am dieting. You might say I have a headache."

Andre frowned. "You're obsessed with your weight, Karla. I don't see where you've gained any, but if you say you have, I'll take your word for it. Now, don't wait up for me. I'm taking Neumann and Beckle to the bar first, and then we'll have dinner. We have a lot to discuss, and I imagine I'll be late coming in."

"Don't worry about me, Andre. I have my green salad and a good movie I've rented. I'll be perfectly fine here by myself." Karla smiled at Andre and then closed the door. She walked quickly into her bedroom and straight to her large walk-in closet where she would change clothes.

Karla looked at her reflection in the long mirror. She had purchased an inexpensive dark pantsuit with pockets in both the slacks and the long-sleeved cardigan top. She had also purchased a cheap, shoulder strap black purse, large enough to hold the bundles of €100 bills that were secured with paper bands. She would put a small bottle of water in with the money.

Karla looked at her watch. It was 6:35. She needed to leave soon if she were to have plenty of time before George came. She patted the left-side pocket in her cardigan and felt the small plastic bag that contained everything necessary to administer the heroin. Her right pocket held the latex gloves, the stun gun, and the code to the swimming center. She had the rubber tourniquet and the newspaper article in her pants pocket. She had worn soft cotton gloves while handling everything. There could be no slip-ups at this late date. One fingerprint could send her to prison for life.

Karla donned her brunette wig, looked once more at herself in the mirror, and left. She hoped to avoid the eye of the camera as much as possible by keeping her face turned downward. She had debated using the stairs but decided that would be foolish as there were also cameras positioned at the doors entering and exiting the stairway. She pressed the elevator button and was relieved to find herself alone as she descended to the first-floor level, where the swimming center was located.

The elevator door opened, and Karla stepped out and walked quickly to the door that opened into a hall that would lead her to the swimming center. The hall was dimly lit, and Karla felt in her right pocket for the code that would open the door to the reception area and the dressing rooms. The code had been changed after Rachel's attempted drowning, but Andre had access to all security measures and Karla knew how to access the information, using his password.

She quickly pressed in the numbers, and using Kleenex on the handle, she opened the door and stepped into the semi-dark room. There was only a small recessed ceiling light above the door that provided minimum light.

Karla first put her latex gloves on, and she then slipped the gun strap over her right hand and above her wrist, allowing the small stun gun to rest in her hand. She pushed the switch to turn on the LED light, walked through the large reception room, and stood at the entry to the swimming pool, sending the beam to the side of the large pool where she would walk. She was glad she thought to wear rubber soles as her footsteps were not audible.

Karla turned her bright beam momentarily toward the pool. She thought how calm the water was and wondered how large of a splash George's body would create when she rolled him into the pool. A shudder went through her body, but she knew she had to stay calm. Killing George was never in the plan, but she could tell that he would cause her trouble the rest of her life if she did not deal with him now. He had hinted at that and bragged one day that he had blackmailed someone when he was younger, finally causing the person to overdose and die. Well, he would never get the opportunity to blackmail or kill her.

Karla stopped at the back of the low diving board and felt the surface to be sure it was dry before putting her shoulder bag down. She pointed the LED light at her watch and noticed that it was ten minutes to seven. She had sent George a text with the code, and he should be coming soon. She kept the beam of her light pointed down, not wanting to penetrate the darkness and create too much light for fear that somehow a tiny bit might find its way under the crack of a door and expose them.

"Why do you have those gloves on, Karla?" George asked, stepping out from the dark shadows beyond the high diving board.

Startled, Karla spun around. Her left hand flew to her throat, and she drew in a sharp breath and said, "You scared me to death, George. You were not supposed to be in here." She stood glaring at him, her heart beating fast with each shallow breath.

"I operate on my own time, Karla." He caught hold of her arm. "Now, answer me. Why do you have on gloves, and why are you wearing a wig?"

"Do you take me for a fool?" Karla spat out, as she pulled her arm from his grasp. "If you get in trouble with this money, I do not want my fingerprints on it or this bag. That's why!"

"And the wig?"

"I told Andre that I was staying in tonight. Are you so stupid as to think I would get caught on camera?" Karla took a deep breath and watched George.

George aimed the small beam of his cell light close to Karla's face, and she squinted and then raised her left hand and shielded her eyes. "Take that damn light from my face, George, or I'm turning around and leaving, bracelet or no bracelet. After all, the bracelet is insured. I can always buy another one," she bluffed.

George dropped the light beam to the bag sitting on the end of the board and reached over for it, but Karla caught his hand. "Don't touch that bag until you show me my bracelet."

George removed, from his pants pocket, a small oblong box bound with a heavy rubber band. He rattled it and slipped it in his shirt pocket, leaving the top third of the box exposed. "You can have your damn bracelet after I make sure all of my money is there. Now, hold your light on the bag while I look inside."

George put his cell down and opened the bag. "Move it over some," he snapped, shifting the bag so her light could shine in. "Why do you have a bottle of water in here, Karla?" He asked, taking the bottle out and feeling the top to see if it was still sealed.

Karla's eyes shifted from the bottled water to George, and she stammered, "Because—because when I get nervous, I get thirsty—that's why! Now, give it to me." Karla held out her hand, but George held on to the water, searching her face. He finally shrugged and handed her the bottle.

George turned again to the bag, then stopped and said, "Give me some more light, Karla, I can't see what I'm doing. This had better be right."

"You don't have to count it, George. It's all there—all twenty thousand. Now, give me my bracelet."

George ignored Karla and continued to rifle through the money, attempting to count it. He looked up and said, "I can't tell if it's all here, Karla. I'm putting it on the board to count. Hold your light there."

"You're wasting my time, George. I can't be gone when Andre returns. This is taking too long."

"Shut up, Karla. I'm in control now. Give me some light." George emptied the bag and began to line up the bundles of money and sort it out, mumbling and counting to himself.

Karla focused her light on the money as she moved closer to George. She held the light high for only a few moments and then dropped her arm and thrust the stun gun into his side. "You should have trusted me, you SOB," she hissed as she pulled the trigger twice.

"What the...?" was all that came out of George's mouth as his arms flew up and his body jerked hard and then fell backward. A low moan ensued as he twitched a couple of times and then lay silent on the hard tile floor. Karla stood staring at George for only a moment before emptying her pockets and turning to the board.

"He might be out cold, but when this stuff hits his bloodstream, he'll be as happy as a baby," Karla mumbled under her breath, as she prepared the heroin and loaded the syringe. Restricting the blood flow with the tourniquet, she quickly injected a large dose of heroin into his vein.

Karla pulled the rubber band from his arm, pushed his sleeve back in place, and buttoned his cuff before stuffing the bundles of money in the bag. She glanced down to make sure George had not moved and noticed the box still protruding from his pocket. Smiling, she removed it and gave the box a slight rattle before placing it with the money.

Karla transferred George's fingerprints to every piece of drug paraphernalia that lay on the board and then quickly deleted her text from his cell. As she stooped to roll him into the pool, she remembered the folded paper and stopped long enough to jam it in his shirt pocket.

She struggled with his large body but finally managed to get him into the deep end of the pool. The splash was as she expected, and she stepped quickly back so as not to get wet. Karla stood a moment watching as George began to sink, but then all of a sudden his arms began to move and he pushed to the surface and frantically reached for the ladder that lay three feet beyond his grasp.

Karla stood petrified, never giving thought to the fact that the water might revive him. She was scared to use her gun again for fear of electrocuting herself. She watched as he struggled in the deep water, his heavy shoes and clothes, along with the heroin, making it impossible for him to tread water, float, or do anything to save himself. Karla could see George's mouth moving, but no words came out. The heroin had not dulled the wild fright in his eyes, though, and she almost felt sorry for him.

He would come up and gasp for air before the weight of his body pulled him under again. Surely he would give up and sink, Karla thought, but George would not give up. His momentum brought him closer to the ladder, and he splashed and flayed his arms, reaching within a few inches of the steel handrail. Karla stood at the edge of the pool and held onto the top of the ladder.

"Why are you making this so hard for me, George?" she murmured as his fingers touched the ladder. She breathed in deeply and then leaned over, put her foot on George's head, and pushed him under. He groped for her foot, but she kicked his hand away and then resumed pushing his head under until she could see the bubbles come to the surface. A few moments later, his arms began to relax, and he finally quit fighting. She gave George's head one last push and then shook the water off her shoe, pulled her foot back, and watched him sink to the bottom.

Karla stood quiet; then all of a sudden she began to tremble, and she walked back over to the low diving board and leaned across it, closing her eyes and fighting the nausea that rose up in her throat. She lay like that for several minutes reflecting on what she had just done. She had murdered a man. Never in her life did she think she would actually kill someone. But it had to be done, she reasoned, and she was glad she did it.

Karla slowly pushed up and looked around. The water was again calm. The drug paraphernalia sat at the end of the board. Everything looked natural, as if George had come to a dark, private place to give himself a fix but in the process had somehow accidentally fallen in the pool and drowned. She looked at her hands. They had almost quit shaking, and she picked up her shoulder bag. She started to walk away but then saw George's cell light. It was still lit, and she debated whether to turn it off or leave it on. Of course it needed to stay on. George would never have turned it off before leaving the dark room.

Karla slipped the strap over her shoulder and walked the length of the Olympic-sized swimming pool, shining her LED light before her. She did not look back, and she felt no remorse. She did regret that she had broken two fingernails tugging on George and struggling to get him into the pool. They were embedded in her latex gloves, and she would dispense with the gloves later. She would be careful not to drop the broken nails at the scene of the crime. She had watched enough crime shows on television to know that the slightest miscue could lead to the incriminating evidence that would send her to prison. She looked down at her wet slacks and almost went into the dressing room to look for a hair dryer but decided that would be too time-consuming and risky. Karla let out a large sigh and then removed her latex gloves and turned off her light as she reached the door leading to the hall outside.

FIFTY-EIGHT

Karla turned over in bed and asked, "Who was that calling so early, Andre?"

"It was Luke. It seems that our cleanup crew found a body in the deep end of the swimming pool. The police are there now doing an investigation, and Luke says the coroner is on his way."

Karla pushed up on one elbow and, with a distressed look on her face, said, "That's terrible, Andre. Who was it? I hope it was not a child who was accidentally left in the center."

"Oh no, nothing like that. Luke said it was a security guard, one who works part time. He worked only on the weekends. He said there was also some drug paraphernalia on the low diving board. The police don't know whether that's connected to the guard or not. They'll have to run some fingerprints."

Karla lay back down and said, "Well, that's so unfortunate. If drugs were involved, he could have lost his footing and fallen while he was checking the center. I'm sure those walkways are slippery in places."

"We'll just have to wait and see what the authorities say, Karla. I hate that something like that happened in our pool."

Karla wrapped her soft terry cloth robe around her body and tied the belt before she came into the bedroom and sat down at her dressing table. She turned to Andre and said, "Didn't I hear the phone ringing, Andre? Who was calling this time?"

"That was Luke again. He said we might have a problem in security. The police were going through the security guard's clothes and found a diamond bracelet in his pants pocket."

Karla's arm jerked, knocking her hairbrush off the table.

Andre waited for Karla to pick up her brush, and after a minute of silence, he cleared his throat and said, "Did you hear what I said, Karla?"

Karla ran the brush through her hair and said, "Yes, Andre, I heard you. Luke said we might have a security problem. Now, tell me the rest of it."

"Luke thinks the guard may have stolen the bracelet. He says the stones look like real diamonds, and if they are, then it's a very expensive piece of jewelry." Andre paused again. "Now the last thing we need is someone who's supposed to be guarding our valuables instead breaking in and stealing them."

Karla ran the brush through her hair two more times before answering Andre. She finally said, "Yes, I agree." She put her brush down, picked up a bottle of body lotion, and began to rub it on her legs. "Did Luke want you to meet with him?"

"Yes, I'm going in just a few minutes, as soon as I finish my coffee." Andre cleared his throat again and said, "I sure hope we can keep this quiet. We don't need publicity of this sort."

Karla didn't comment. Her mind was in her large walk-in closet where she had hidden her shoulder bag—far back behind some sweaters that were neatly stacked on a shelf.

"Damn! Damn! Damn!" Karla said as she stood, locked in the bathroom, staring at the open box on her bathroom counter. She picked up the cheap piece of costume jewelry and held it a moment before putting it back in the box. Looking up at her reflection in the large mirror, she murmured, "Why didn't you look in this box before you pushed him in the pool, you idiot? You should have known he would pull something like this." She balled up her fists and shook them at the mirror. "You never should have trusted him. He made a fool out of you."

Karla gave a deep sigh, sat down on the edge of the large Jacuzzi tub, and wondered what she could do. She could not just race down and claim the bracelet. That would raise too much suspicion. She would have to tell Andre that her bracelet was missing and that she had searched high and low, thinking that she had misplaced it. Would he believe her?

Andre had asked her about the bracelet the other night—why she was not wearing it—and she had used the excuse of the loose catch. That seemed to please him, since he had dropped the insurance policy after the rates had tripled. He would not want her to take any chances with the bracelet.

Karla got up and put the box back in her purse. She did have one thing to be thankful for. She could pay back the loan. But she could not deposit all of that cash at once. She would go to two banks, buy cashier's checks, take the checks to her bank, and pay the loan off today. And she would be sure to drop the pantsuit in the large charitable receptacle on the way to the banks. She had washed and dried it last night to get rid of the chlorine water. Then she would find a Dumpster to put the wig in.

But when would she tell Andre about the stolen bracelet? Karla thought a moment longer, and a smile began to play on her lips. She would call Andre on his cell immediately and tell him that she went to get her bracelet to have the clasp fixed and it was not in her jewelry box. He would hear the alarm in her voice and convey that to Luke. They would assume that the bracelet found on the security guard was stolen from her.

Karla glanced back at the mirror and then down to Andre's hairbrush. She picked it up and threw it against the wall. "Damn George," she whispered to herself, and then a little louder: "Damn his soul forever."

FIFTY-NINE

Richard Wendall shook hands with Luke and then turned the leather armchair slightly to the side and sat down. He put the folder on Luke's desk, reached for the mug of coffee Luke was offering him, and gave a wry smile.

"Well, Luke, I don't want to be premature, but we might have found the answer to the other incidents involving Rachel."

"Before you say anything, Richard, let me tell you the latest development. My partner's wife, Karla Broussard, called after you left and said her diamond bracelet is missing. Her husband thinks maybe the bracelet found on the guard belongs to her. He thinks the fellow George Halford stole it."

Richard looked surprised and set down his coffee mug. "I thought you said he was an outside security guard only."

"Yes, outside and parking garage. That's what he was hired for, and he only worked weekends—actually from noon Friday until Sunday at six o'clock. But what I'm furious about is that our security was so lax in hiring him. We're very careful about who works here, and I have no idea how he made it through the ranks."

"What's done is done, Luke, and now you are rid of him. You'll have to tighten your security."

"Yes, but I still don't have any idea how he could have broken into any of our apartments. The locks are all coded, and no one has the codes but the apartment owners. We do have the codes on file, but no one has access to the file except an absolute trustworthy person who has worked for me for ten years. And, of course, I have access. There's no way Halford could have gotten into that computer file."

"That's interesting. We ran a check on Halford and discovered that he has been working part time for a nursing home. But before that he was working for a computer company. He was fired from the computer company because he was found hacking into other people's computers. The company said he was extremely bright but could not be trusted. I'm not saying he was able to get into your system, Luke, but there is always that possibility."

"Well, I still don't believe he could break into our system, but you mentioned Rachel. What did this fellow have to do with her?"

"We found a folded newspaper article in his pocket. Our forensic team dried it out and used a high-magnification machine to bring the faded print back. It was a newspaper article about the New Progressives. I think I mentioned their organization when Rachel was in the hospital. Are you familiar with them, Luke?"

"Not really. I've heard remarks people have made about them. They're the ones who are harassing the Jews, aren't they?"

"Yes, they use a lot of scare tactics. They are trying to get the Jewish people who are suing to reclaim property stolen by the Nazis to drop their suits."

"Do you think he was the one who attacked Rachel?"

"There is a strong possibility that he was. Being an employee here, he certainly had easy access to her. What we're not sure of is whether he was a member of the New Progressives. We plan to interview the head of this organization. Maybe we can find out if Halford was a member. But I understand that they are real secretive and no one knows much about them."

"Why haven't they been arrested?"

"Because no one has come forth to identify anyone doing the harassing. I can't figure out if they're scared to bring charges or what."

Luke thought a few moments and then said, "Richard, Neumann is certainly not involved in anything like that. I'm talking about hiring someone like Halford."

"Of course not. And didn't I hear a rumor that Neumann has found some new evidence?"

"Yes, and he's preparing for the final hearing. The judge is on vacation but should be back soon."

Richard nodded and opened his folder. "Now, here is the report on the drug paraphernalia that you asked for. I doubt you'll be surprised when I tell you that Halford had heroin in his bloodstream and the drug paraphernalia on the diving board contained his fingerprints."

"No, I'm not surprised. Was there evidence of anyone being with him?"

"Not that we could determine. The only significant fingerprints we found belonged to Halford. We didn't waste time taking prints up and down the side of the pool. We would never be able to identify all of them. It is pretty much like the situation with Rachel when she was attacked in the pool. We did try to lift some prints from the board but gave up there because we didn't have a suitable surface to work with."

"Was there anything on the door handles?"

"No, nothing but a lot of smeared fingerprints. We doubted we'd find anything significant there, but you never know. Some people are germ conscious and wipe everything clean at the end of the day. But it didn't happen in the swimming center. But back to the bracelet. I'm going to talk to Karla Broussard and see if she can shed some light on this investigation. If the bracelet is hers, we'll certainly give it back to her."

"Andre said he has a canceled insurance policy describing the bracelet and also an appraisal describing it."

"We'll want to look at them and get copies. Luke, we'll need to look at some film taken from cameras on Broussard's floor and maybe the elevator, too."

"That won't be a problem. Our security team will help you there. But back to Halford and the drugs. Do you think he injected the drug in his vein and then somehow slipped and fell in the pool and drowned?"

"That's another thing that's rather strange. Being a seasoned addict—and he was definitely one—I would assume that he would stay away from the edge of the pool. We didn't find evidence of any foul play on his body—no trauma to his head or anything like that. Well, I take that back. The examiner said there was a very slight bruising at the back of his head, but nothing that indicated he was hit with an instrument. He said it was probably the result of a fall. Maybe he slipped and fell before he injected himself with the drug. He's a pretty large man. I doubt anyone could have knocked him in the head even if they wanted to. You could be right. He may have slipped a second time and fallen in."

Luke nodded. "Richard, let's hope this is the last time you'll have to investigate anything in our plaza. This is not the type publicity we need."

"I understand, Luke. Now, back to Rachel's two incidents—I cannot prove that this man is the one who attacked her. I think he may have been the one, but we have no concrete evidence. I know you understand that."

"Yes, I understand. Now, let me tell you some good news. In case you have not heard, I have asked Rachel to marry me. We are officially engaged."

Richard sat back, surprised; then a smile broke out on his face, and he quickly got up and thrust his hand out to shake Luke's. "Congratulations, man. This is good news. I thought surely you would stay an old bachelor. I had no idea you and Rachel were forming a serious relationship. When did all of this happen?"

Luke shook his head. "I'm really not sure. Confidentially, I think I was attracted to Rachel from the first day I met her, but I fought it. Richard, she is truly the loveliest woman I've ever known."

"When is the wedding going to be?"

“We have not set a date. Rachel wants to get through this next hearing with Neumann. We think the judge will make a final ruling, and then we’ll decide on a date.” Luke smiled. “I won’t let her prolong it. I assure you of that.”

Richard grinned. “I hope I’ll be included on the guest list.”

“I think you can count on that. With both of us having been married before, the wedding will be small. But yes, you’ll be included. We want our close friends to share in our happiness.”

Luke gave the waiter his and Rachel’s order and handed him the menus. He reached for Rachel’s hand and smiled. “I have not seen or talked to you all day long, and you cannot imagine how difficult that makes it for me.”

“I know. I suspect you’ve been busy with Richard concerning the drowning. William told Susan and me about it. That was terrible.”

“Yes, it seems like we’ve had nothing but trouble with the swimming center.”

“Don’t say that, Luke. I know the attack on me caused you stress, and now there’s been a drowning. But it could have been a lot worse. What happened to me was after hours, and the same was true with this fellow. I think it was fortunate the pool was not full of people. And consider this: an innocent child could have been the one to drown, and that would have been a real tragedy. William said the fellow who drowned had no business being in the swimming center and he was possibly on drugs.”

Luke nodded. “Yes, Richard confirmed that he had heroin in his system. And the fact that he was not authorized to be in the swimming center frees us from any liability.”

“Did Richard determine whether he was alone?”

“He could not be sure but assumed he was. The guard knew the swimming center was closed for the evening, and he apparently figured that was a good place to give himself a shot. Drug paraphernalia was found at the end of the low diving board, and as I said, heroin was found in his bloodstream. We don't know how he managed to bypass our security and get into the center. We're now working on making everything more secure.

"And speaking of security, Rachel, there was another twist to this drowning. The police found a diamond bracelet in the security guard's pocket."

"A diamond bracelet? Was it an expensive one?"

"Yes, very expensive, and do you know whose it was?" Luke raised his eyebrows.

"I have no idea, Luke. Tell me."

"It was Karla Broussard's."

"Karla Broussard's? That doesn't make sense. How did a security guard get in their apartment to steal her bracelet?"

"That's what Richard and I are trying to figure out. But now I have something else to discuss with you." Luke paused. "Richard thinks this man who drowned may have been the one who attacked you in the elevator and also the swimming pool."

Rachel's eyes opened wide, and she withdrew her hand from Luke's and sat back in her chair. "Why does Richard think that? Why would that man attack me?"

"It was a piece of paper found in the man's pocket that led Richard to that conclusion. A newspaper clipping about a group called the New Progressives.

"I remember Richard mentioning them when I was in the hospital. Who are they?"

"They are a group of people, mostly young I've been told, who have adopted some of the old Nazi ideology and are antagonistic toward the Jews."

Rachel frowned. "Are you saying they have targeted me because I'm half Jewish?"

"I'm not the one saying that, Rachel. It's Richard. He thinks that because of the group's tactics. They have harassed some of the relatives of the Holocaust victims who have lawsuits to reclaim their property."

"Oh, I see. They are using extreme scare tactics. Well, he almost succeeded. If it had not been for you, I would be back in Arlington teaching again."

Luke smiled and reached again for Rachel's hand. "I would never let you go back. I love you too much. And if you had, I would have been on the next plane to bring you back."

Rachel grinned. "It seems that my future is sealed. I'm destined to live right here in Berlin." Rachel dropped her eyes a moment and then looked up and said, "If only you could have heard me after the basement incident. I swore to myself that I would never live in Germany—that it could never be home to me."

"Rachel, my love, we often say things we don't mean. I know. I've had to eat my words many times. But now, to change the subject, I called my parents and told them about our engagement."

"I bet they were surprised."

"More like shocked. I think Mother cried. Anyhow, they are thrilled and cannot wait to meet you. I was wondering. Could you and Sarah Beth go to London with me this coming Thursday? I am going to charter a jet. We won't stay long—maybe two or three days."

"I want to meet your parents, but suppose I get a notice in the next day or two about the hearing?"

"I don't think you'll have to worry about that, Rachel. I called and was told that Judge Krause will not be back until this weekend. We'll come back Sunday. I would think the earliest he could give you notice would be Tuesday or Wednesday of next week."

Rachel smiled. "If that's the case, then yes, we'll go with you. I'm really looking forward to meeting your parents." Rachel relaxed against the back of her chair and breathed in a deep sigh. She looked lovingly at Luke and said, "I've always wanted to visit England, Luke, and now you are taking me there." Rachel shook her head and smiled again. "I never dreamed I would see England and meet my future in-laws at the same time. You're determined to make me happy, aren't you?"

Luke smiled and started to say something but the waiter put down his and Rachel's plates and said, "Is there anything else I can get you, sir?"

Karla put the brush down and turned to Andre. "Honey, does Richard or Luke have any idea how that man got into our apartment and stole my bracelet?"

"No, Karla. All Richard said was that the man had worked for a computer company and was very astute at breaking into computers. Though Luke denies it, Richard thinks the guard somehow broke through our security and accessed our code. He may have been impressed by my name, knowing that I am proprietor of the restaurant."

"You could be right, Andre."

"Well, I, for one, am thankful the man had that accident and drowned himself. We won't be bothered by him again, will we, Karla?" Andre cleared his throat a couple of times and watched Karla as she sat, picking a few loose strands of hair from her brush. When Karla ignored his question, a slight look of annoyance crossed Andre's face, and he returned to his paper.

Karla turned back to her mirror and continued to brush her hair, completely unaware that Andre was waiting for her answer. She had tuned him out. Her mind was on the leisurely bath she would take in their large Jacuzzi and the new silk nightgown she would wear. She would remember to dab some of Andre's favorite perfume on. Completely relaxed and finally free of worry, Karla smiled to herself. It had been a long time since Andre had shown any interest in love-making. Maybe, just maybe, she could arouse his interest.

SIXTY

Luke had Sarah Beth in his arms, and she was fast asleep on his shoulder when he carried her into Rachel's bedroom to lay her on one of the twin beds. He turned and whispered to Rachel, "I'll wait for you in the living room. Susan says she's anxious to hear about our trip,"

Rachel smiled and nodded. "I'll put Sarah Beth to bed as quickly as I can and then join you." She leaned up and kissed Luke lightly on his cheek. "Don't tell Susan everything. Be sure to save something for me to talk about."

Luke's chuckle was soft. He pulled Rachel into his arms, searched her beautiful face, and kissed her soundly. "I doubt I'll do that," he said, slowly releasing her. "You women have things to talk about that we men never even consider. Now hurry and tend to your daughter. It's getting late, and you'll be saying it's your bedtime and pushing me out the front door." With that, Luke gave Rachel another quick kiss and left, easing the door closed.

"Where is Susan?" Rachel asked, coming into the living room.

"She's gone to fix us a cup of coffee. I think she wanted to wait for you."

"Where is William?"

"He's in the bedroom taking a call from his uncle. Keep in mind that it's only the middle of the afternoon in Arlington."

Rachel shook her head. "That's the hardest thing about being over here. I don't think I'll ever be able to coordinate time here in Germany with time in the States. Maybe I'm not very technical." Rachel grinned. "I'm glad I'm marrying someone very smart who not only speaks several languages but also can calculate the time anywhere in the world."

"Now who told you I could do all of that?" Luke grinned, pulling Rachel down on the sofa next to him, putting his arm around her, and drawing her close.

"I'm not sure I remember, but it's true, and I confess that I was a little intimidated when I first heard that."

"You mean you were scared of me?"

"Yes, I was."

"You're not scared of me now, are you?" Luke teased.

Rachel leaned her head against Luke's shoulder. "How could I be? Your love trumps your brilliance."

"Coffee's ready, you two," Susan said, coming through the door with a tray in her hands. "I want to hear all about London and if Rachel was accepted by her future in-laws." Susan's dimple was showing, and her green eyes twinkled as she set the tray down on the coffee table in front of Luke and Rachel.

Luke sat forward and said, "I think I can do justice to that question, Rachel. So let me answer it." He first took a sip of coffee and then put the mug back on the tray. "You asked if Rachel was accepted by my mother and father? Susan, I think by the time we were ready to come back to Berlin Rachel and Sarah Beth had not only won their hearts but I believe also outranked me. I confess that I almost got jealous."

Rachel patted Luke on his arm. "Don't be silly, Luke. No one could ever outrank you with your parents." Rachel paused. "Susan, when they look at Luke, you can see the adoration in their eyes. They love him dearly. And I fell in love with Luke's parents immediately. I have never had a warmer reception. And on top of that, Dr. and Mrs. Hartmann treated Sarah Beth like she was their own granddaughter. Sarah Beth loved the attention. She's never known the love of grandparents, with three of her grandparents deceased and the only living one remarried and involved with his second family."

"Sarah Beth can look forward to some wonderful experiences," Susan said. "And pay no attention to me. I was only teasing you a while ago. I knew Luke's parents would love you." Susan smiled. "And it's wonderful to have loving in-laws. I can certainly testify to that with William's mother and David. They are truly like parents to me."

"Yes, I'm looking forward to spending more time with Luke's parents." Rachel patted Luke's arm again. "Honey, tell Susan how they surprised us."

Luke's expression softened, and he smiled. "Where should I start, Rachel?" Luke paused only a moment before continuing. "Susan, I sensed shortly after arriving that my parents had something on their minds. I know them too well. They've never been good at hiding things. Anyhow, we were having coffee and dessert, and Dad said, 'Son, your mother and I want to share something with you.' I could tell he was a little anxious, but I didn't say anything. I nodded and waited for him to continue. He said, 'Do you remember Mr. and Mrs. Young, the neighbors of ours who gave you the Bible when you graduated high school?'

"I said, 'Yes, Dad, and I've been reading it.' My dad looked surprised but didn't comment on my remark. He said, 'They were in town and spent the weekend with us, and to make a long story short, they had a spiritual impact on both of our lives. We have become Christians.' Dad sat back against his chair, looking at me and wondering what I would say. I guess he was remembering some of the anti-God comments I've made through the years.

"I enjoyed the silence that hung in the air. I wanted the moment to be paramount, for it's not often that all the members of a family come to know the Lord within days of one another and that's really what happened as we later compared dates.

"When I shared my spiritual experience with Mother and Father, we all shed a few tears—even Rachel. I think we had Sarah Beth a little upset." Luke chuckled. "But it was a glorious time of talking and exchanging thoughts on spiritual matters."

"I don't know why I would be surprised, Luke. Peter and Nancy said they have prayed for your family for years." Susan smiled. "This is the fruit of their prayers."

"Yes, and I shared that with Mother and Father. They were always fond of Peter Grenfell and are looking forward to our wedding and seeing Peter and Nancy."

William walked in and said, "What's all the commotion about?"

Susan looked up. "Honey, I'm sorry, but you've missed it. I'll have to tell you later. It's getting late, and I, for one, am about ready for a shower and bed."

Luke stood up. "Yes, it is getting late. Rachel and I have had a long day, what with the flight home. I know she's tired."

William said, "Well, I suspect we have an interesting week ahead of us. Neumann is eager for the hearing, and Judge Krause should be back in Berlin by now. I'm planning to spend the morning with Greta tomorrow."

Rachel's expression sobered. "William, do I need to go with you?"

"I don't think that's necessary, Rachel. There's nothing you can add. Greta and I will review everything. I think we'll be ready for Beckle."

"Yes, and in the meantime, we'll all be praying," Luke said.

"Was that the doorbell I heard, Susan?" Rachel asked, coming from her bedroom with her morning coffee in hand.

"Yes, and I think this must be the summons," Susan said, handing Rachel the envelope. "The judge didn't wait long, did he?"

Rachel didn't answer. She stood staring at the envelope in her hand.

SIXTY-ONE

Peter Grenfell put down his cup of coffee and looked at the clock. It was shortly after six o'clock. He got up from the table murmuring, "I wonder who would be calling this early in the morning. I hope it's not one of my members with bad news." He glanced at the name on the small screen and raised his eyebrows.

"Dad? It's Pete."

"Yes, Son, I have caller ID. You're calling mighty early. I hope everything is all right."

"Oh, yes, no problem here. I have a question."

"I'll answer if I can."

"Do you have the name of the Jewish family Rachel was related to? I'm talking about the family who was taken by the Nazis."

"No, Son, I don't remember the name. I'm sure Rachel mentioned it when she told us about the lawsuit, but you know me and names. I have to hear them several times before they're planted in my mind. Why are you asking?"

"Well, we're having our guest room painted, and Liesel asked me to clean out the closet. If you can remember, Mom packed all of my college books and my thesis material in boxes, and when I bought this house in Stuttgart, Mom insisted that I take the boxes with me. I put them in the guest bedroom closet."

"I remember well," Peter chuckled. "She said if she had one more book to deal with, she might lose her mind." Peter stopped and cleared his throat. "Go ahead, Son. I didn't mean to interrupt."

"No problem, Dad. Well, Liesel convinced me that with so much information available on the Internet it was ridiculous to keep all of those books. She suggested that I go through all of the boxes and keep the books that I thought were absolutely necessary and get rid of the rest. So last night after dinner, I was looking through the box with the research material I used for my thesis, and I found a journal written by a midwife. I don't remember seeing this journal before and guess Mom may have accidentally picked it up from your World War II room and packed it with my stuff. Do you remember having this journal?"

"No, Son, I don't. But I have so many things that I've collected through the years that I can't remember everything. A lot of what I bought was bundled together, and I'm ashamed to say I've never cataloged it. Tell me about the journal."

"Well, it was dated 1902 through 1945. I was fascinated with her entries and read several of them. One of her deliveries fits the story you were telling me about that involved Rachel's lawsuit." When Peter didn't comment, Pete said, "Dad, did you hear me? I said–"

"I heard you, Son. This is shocking news because Rachel's hearing is this afternoon, and if you've found the journal belonging to the midwife who delivered Rachel's mother, we desperately need it. Quick–give me the name of the midwife so I can call William."

"Her name is Elsie Graff. But don't hang up. I have something else to tell you. I also found an entry about the birth of Leon Beckle's dad. He was born in September of 1935. Didn't you say Leon Beckle was the lawyer for the other side? The one Rachel brought suit against?"

"Yes, and if this woman is the one who delivered Rachel's mother, do you think you could possibly get this journal to us? It would mean getting on the autobahn within the hour and driving like mad."

There were a few moments of silence before Pete said, "I was thinking, Dad. We have a company jet I could use, but I remember someone saying yesterday that one of our executives has it in London, so that's out. But yes, if Rachel needs this journal, I will leave within the hour and bring it."

"Go ahead, Son, and make preparations while I call William. I'll get back with you as quickly as I can."

Susan turned over in bed and said, "William, why are you up so early? Was that your cell I heard? Who was that calling you so early?"

"It was Peter Grenfell, Susan. He said Pete might be onto something that will help Rachel. He called and wanted to know the name of the midwife who delivered Rachel's mother."

"Why did he want that?"

"Pete's found an old journal with recordings by a midwife. One of the entries is an account of a baby being delivered, and the account reads like the birth of the Weinberg baby. He gave me the name of the midwife who delivered Maria, and it's the same one. I've called Greta and told her. She's excited."

"But Rachel's hearing is this afternoon. Even if this journal is the right one, how is it going to help? Pete's in Stuttgart, and that's over three hundred fifty miles away."

"Peter says Pete will leave as soon as he gets dressed. He'll get on the autobahn and drive up. You know how fast they drive on the autobahn. I think he can make it."

"But William, that's so dangerous. I don't want Pete to get in an accident."

"I don't think he will, Susan. Apparently the Lord let him find this journal and, as the old saying goes, 'right in the nick of time.'"

SIXTY-TWO

William stopped and pulled out his cell. It was Pete. He motioned for Luke to go ahead with Rachel while he stayed behind to take the call.

Luke stepped inside the courtroom with Rachel at his side and stood a moment to look around. Rachel put her hand on Luke's arm and looked up. "I hope this is not awkward for you, Luke. Remember last time? You were seated with the defense."

Luke nodded his head and patted Rachel's hand. "Don't worry about it, Rachel. It may be a little awkward, but I think I can handle it. Remember now, you come first with me and always will. Neumann will have to accept that, and if he doesn't, well, I'm sorry, but it won't change things. Look, Greta's at the table talking to Paul Abraham. I suspect she's telling him about Pete's call and the woman's journal."

"I can't help but be concerned with Pete having to drive fast on the autobahn. We certainly don't need a wreck."

"Don't worry, Rachel; I'm sure he's a careful driver." Luke glanced to the defense's table. "Beckle and Neumann have their witnesses, I see. I suppose they'll authenticate the old cemetery papers." Luke turned around at the sound of the door opening. "Here comes William. Let's see who was calling."

"That was Pete calling," William said. "He's running a little behind because of a bad accident on the autobahn. He thinks he'll be here in about thirty minutes."

Luke glanced at his watch. "Judge Krause will be coming out of his chambers any minute now. I hope you and Greta can stall Beckle for thirty minutes. If I know Beckle, he'll be out for the kill, and he'll do it quickly. Judge Krause is not one to tarry either."

"I think Greta can handle Beckle, Luke."

"Maybe so. I hope so, anyhow." Luke paused. "We need to quit talking and get seated." Luke took Rachel's elbow, guided her down the aisle, and seated her next to Greta just as the judge's door opened and he walked out.

The bailiff asked everyone to stand and announced in English that this was a continuation of the case of Rachel Lewis versus Neumann Development Company with Judge Richard Krause presiding. Judge Krause took his seat at the bench, and everyone sat back down.

The judge peered down at the court reporter and then looked over at both parties. Breaking the silence, he again spoke in flawless English, his voice resonating across the room. "I thought it best to extend the hearing of this case for three months in order to allow both parties more time to produce additional evidence." He glanced at the papers on his desk and looked at the defendant's table. "And as a result I see that Mr. Beckle has submitted new evidence to the court. Is that right, counselor?"

Mr. Beckle nodded and said, "Yes, Your Honor."

Judge Krause turned to Greta. "Mrs. Wineman, I don't see that you have submitted any new evidence. Is that correct?"

"Yes, Your Honor. That's correct."

"Very well." The judge wrote something down and turned back to the defendant's table.

"Mr. Beckle, your first witness, please."

Mr. Beckle nodded and stood up. He gathered his papers and quickly moved to the center of the room. "Your Honor, Neumann

Development Company calls James Albrecht as its first witness." Beckle turned and watched Albrecht as he stood and walked to the witness stand and was sworn in.

Mr. Albrecht appeared to be in his sixties and was rather small with receding blond hair. He wore a navy-blue suit with a striped tie and had a habit of pushing his glasses back up on the bridge of his nose.

Mr. Beckle stood a moment and then cleared his throat and spoke in a loud, clear voice. "Mr. Albrecht, would you please tell the court who you are, where you live, and why you came to Berlin during the latter part of August."

Albrecht nodded and said, "My name is James Albrecht Jr. I live in Frankfurt, Germany. I came to Berlin to bury my ninety-five-year-old father who died in a nursing home. I stayed after the funeral to sell his house."

"Would you please tell the court what you found in your father's attic when you were cleaning out his house."

"I found thirty boxes full of records of deceased people who had been buried in two of Berlin's cemeteries."

"Would you please define for the court more clearly what the records pertained to?"

"Yes. Though the records were scrambled together, they were clearly records of an Aryan cemetery and a Jewish cemetery."

"Mr. Albrecht, would you please tell the court how the records ended up in your father's attic."

"My father was caretaker for the German, or you might say, Aryan cemetery from the time he was in his early twenties until he retired at the age of seventy. During his early years of caring for the cemetery, he became friends with Abe Romansky, the caretaker of the Jewish cemetery. Those two cemeteries resided next to each other.

"It was during the time of the Nazi government and the Second World War that both cemeteries were so heavily damaged. The Jewish cemetery not only suffered from the Allied bombing, but was also vandalized by the Nazis. Many times, as a boy, I heard my father talk about how he saved not only the records from the Aryan cemetery but also the Jewish records for his friend Abe.

"He said that, after the war, when the new Aryan cemetery was established, he wanted to take the old records with him but was not allowed to. I never asked him about the Jewish records. I assumed he had turned them over to a Jewish organization after the war was over. I had no idea they were in my father's attic."

"Mr. Albrecht, would you tell the court what you did when you discovered the thirty boxes in your father's attic."

"Well, naturally I looked in a few of them and was shocked to see that there were burial records dating all the way back to 1850. I immediately notified a member of the Berlin Cemetery Association, and she promised to send someone out to remove the records."

"Mr. Albrecht, you said you looked in the boxes. Would you say this document is typical of the records you saw when you opened the boxes?" Beckle handed Mr. Albrecht a piece of paper.

"Yes, sir. This is exactly like the records that were in all of the boxes. Most of the forms were alike."

"Thank you, sir." Mr. Beckle turned to Judge Krause. "Your Honor, the defendant wants to submit this document as an example of what was in the thirty boxes that resided in Mr. Albrecht's father's attic for as many as sixty-four years."

Judge Krause nodded and made a note and then took the paper from Beckle and handed it to the clerk to be entered in as evidence for the defendant.

Judge Krause said, "You may be seated, Mr. Beckle." He turned to Greta and said, "Mrs. Wineman, do you want to cross examine?"

"No, Your honor."

"Very well." He turned back to the defendant's table and said, "Mr. Beckle, do you have another witness?"

"Yes, Your Honor. The defendant calls Mr. Henry Kramer to the stand."

Mr. Kramer walked briskly to the witness stand and was sworn in. He was a tall, thin man and appeared to be in his late fifties. He also wore a dark suit and striped tie. His bifocals were rimless, and he sat up straight and looked toward Rachel and then back to Beckle.

Mr. Beckle cleared his throat and glanced at the paper in his hand. He said, "Mr. Kramer, would you please tell the court your name, where you live, and your qualifications as an expert witness."

Kramer nodded and said, "My name is Henry Kramer, and I live in Berlin, Germany. After two years of training at the Forensic Science Institute in Berlin, Germany, I was awarded a certificate and have testified as an expert witness in forensic document examination for over thirty years and on as many as one hundred sixty occasions."

Beckle turned to the bench. "Your Honor, I have here in my hand a certified paper from the institute listing the courses Mr. Kramer took and passed. He is well qualified to give an expert opinion on the documents that we are submitting to the court. If it pleases the court, I will submit this paper as evidence of his qualifications and ask the court to accept Mr. Kramer as an expert in forensic handwriting."

"So ruled." Judge Krause accepted the paper from Beckle and gave it to the clerk.

Mr. Beckle handed Kramer the old cemetery document with the information on Maria Weinberg's burial and said, "Mr. Kramer, you have already examined this document along with other documents that were stored with this one. Would you please tell the court what the conclusion of your analysis was?"

"Yes. Well, first, let me explain that I was given a large box of documents to examine along with the one I am holding. Of course I could not examine every one of them, but I picked out random ones from the box. The ink and paper of each document proved to be sixty-four years of age or older. The document I am holding is dated the eleventh of January, 1939. I found the age of the paper and ink to be compatible with the date on the paper, and I testify to the fact that the ink has not been tampered with."

Mr. Kramer handed Mr. Beckle the document, and Mr. Beckle turned to Judge Krause. "Your Honor, may I read this document to the court?"

"You may read the part that is pertinent to this case, Counselor."

"Yes, Your Honor." Mr. Beckle took a few steps back toward the center of the room and turned so his back was not toward the plaintiff's table or the judge's bench. He held the document up and read it out loud and clear. "Printed at the top of the document is *Burial Document*. The city is listed as *Berlin, Germany*. The date is listed as *January 11, 1939*. The deceased member is listed as *Maria Weinberg, infant daughter of Jacob and Rebekah Weinberg*. Cause of death: *stillborn*. The cemetery listed is *Beth Israel Cemetery. Burial plot number one hundred thirty-eight*."

Beckle stepped closer to the bench. "Your Honor, with the court's permission, I would like to reverse my original statement made at the first hearing of this case. After thorough research, I was convinced that the Weinbergs had no fourth child and based my case on that fact. Finding the old cemetery records changed everything. I am asking the court to strike out my closing statement made at the first hearing, and I want to submit this document as the true account of what happened to the fourth child of Jacob and Rebekah Weinberg and ask that it be entered as final evidence by the defendant in the case of Rachel Matthews Lewis versus Neumann Development Company."

Judge Krause reached for the document and passed it to the clerk. He nodded and said, "The court will note the reversal of your statement, Mr. Beckle. The purpose of the law is to establish the truth. Under the circumstances, I am giving instructions to the court reporter to do as you requested. The court will not hold you in contempt. Now, you may have a seat, and we'll continue with our hearing." He looked over at Greta and said, "Mrs. Wineman, you may cross-examine now."

Greta stood up and said, "Judge Krause, I would like to postpone my cross-examination at this time and ask if the court would possibly grant me a short recess. I do have a bit of evidence to submit, but because of an accident on the autobahn, it is late arriving." Greta stood watching Judge Krause. He dropped his eyes as if debating with himself.

There was silence in the court for almost a minute; then the judge looked up and said, "You may have a fifteen-minute recess, Mrs. Wineman, but if your evidence is not here by the time your examination is finished, I have no recourse but to rule on this case. I cannot prolong this case into the evening."

"Thank you, Your Honor."

The bailiff stepped forward and motioned for everyone to rise as Judge Krause returned to his chambers.

Greta turned quickly to William and said, "Quick, William, call Pete and find out where he is."

"I just got a text from him, Greta. He is entering the building now and should be here within a couple of minutes."

Greta closed her eyes and took a deep breath. She opened them, smiled, and said almost in a whisper, "Rachel, I thought for a few minutes that we might be in big trouble, but now I can't wait to see Beckle's face when I read the midwife's journal. He had his moment of drama, and now it's my turn."

After everyone was seated and Mr. Kramer was back on the witness stand, Judge Krause looked at Greta and said, "Mrs. Wineman, your cross-examination please."

"Yes, Your Honor." Greta stood and walked to the witness stand. She smiled at Mr. Kramer and handed him Elsie Graff's journal.

"Mr. Kramer, as an expert witness, may I ask your opinion on the handwriting in this book?"

Mr. Beckle stood up quickly and said, "I protest, Your Honor. Mr. Kramer has already proven that he is an expert witness. I can't see where his opinion about Mrs. Wineman's book is necessary or how her book relates to this case."

Greta turned to the bench. "Your Honor, if it pleases the court, I am only asking Mr. Kramer for a brief opinion. It should not take him more than one minute, or two at the most, to look at three or four random pages and give his opinion as to whether the handwriting is consistent throughout the book."

Judge Krause looked at Beckle. "I'll allow Mr. Kramer to answer Mrs. Wineman's question, Counselor, with the understanding that she won't go off on a rabbit trail."

Mr. Beckle nodded and sat back down amid the sound of a low chuckle from the direction of the plaintiff's table. The judge frowned slightly and then focused back on Greta.

Mr. Kramer flipped through the old journal, stopping on several different pages for only a few seconds. He closed the book and handed it back to Greta. "Yes, I can say with certainty that the handwriting is consistent throughout the book. And I will add that the ink seems to be compatible with the age of the book."

"Are you certain about that, Mr. Kramer?"

Mr. Kramer bristled and a slight look of annoyance crossed his face. "Indeed I am. I have seen too many of this type of book not to know what I'm talking about. The same person wrote throughout the book." Mr. Kramer glanced up at Judge Krause and shook his head.

"Thank you, Mr. Kramer. That will be all," Greta said, opening the journal and slipping a bookmark in it. Mr. Kramer got up quickly and returned to his seat at the defendant's table.

Judge Krause made a note and looked up. "Are you through, Mrs. Wineman, and do you intend to submit that book as evidence?"

"I do, Your Honor, but not at the moment. I want to call Mr. Leon Beckle to the stand."

Judge Krause raised his eyebrows and looked over to Beckle. Beckle stood up and said, "This is highly unusual, Your Honor. I don't know what Mrs.Wineman is up to, but I cannot see where my witness is needed."

"Is this absolutely necessary, Mrs. Wineman?" Judge Krause asked.

"Yes, Your Honor, it's critical to my case."

"Very well." The judge looked over to the defendant's table and said, "Mr. Beckle, you may take the stand now."

Beckle looked down at the papers in front of him and then up at the ceiling. He breathed in and rolled his eyes slightly and then walked slowly to the witness-box, where the bailiff swore him in.

Greta smiled at Beckle and said, "Mr. Beckle would you please tell the court what day and year your father was born."

Beckle's eyes opened wide, and he threw up his hands and looked at Judge Krause and then back at Greta. "Mrs. Wineman, what in the world does my father's birthday have to do with this case?"

"Mr. Beckle, if you will please answer the question, I will be glad to tell you."

Beckle dropped his eyes a moment as if thinking and then looked up and narrowed his eyes at Greta and said, "My father's birthday was the twentieth of September, 1935. Now, would you please tell me the purpose of this?"

Greta ignored Beckle's question, handed him Elsie Graff's journal, and said, "Mr. Beckle, please open this journal to the place where the bookmark is and read out loud the top-entry on the right side."

Beckle frowned at Greta before opening the journal and glancing at the top-right entry. His facial expression changed dramatically, and in a low voice, a little above a mumble, he began to read.

"Mr. Beckle," Judge Krause interrupted, "please read louder. The court cannot hear you."

Beckle nodded and read.

September 20, 1935

I delivered a healthy male child to Annie Kuhn Beckle at 7:25 p.m. this evening. The male child weighed eight pounds four ounces and was twenty-one inches long. The father's name is Leon Anton Beckle and they reside at 1255 Lindenstrasse, Berlin, Germany.

The infant's name is Leon Anton Beckle Jr. The mother's water broke at four o'clock this morning. I was notified at six o'clock. The patient had a hard labor as this is the couple's first child. I left the mother resting well and will check on her and the baby in the morning.

Mr. Beckle quit reading and closed the journal. The courtroom was strangely quiet as he handed the journal back to Greta.

Greta said, "To the best of your ability, Mr. Beckle, is that a true account of the birth of your father?"

"Yes."

"You may be excused, Mr. Beckle." Beckle returned to his seat, and Greta turned to the bench.

"Your Honor, I have in my hands an old journal kept by a German midwife named Elsie Graff. Mr. Kramer and Mr. Beckle have just proven the integrity of this journal by their sworn testimonies. There should be no doubt in the court's mind that this journal is a true account of one woman's midwifery from the years 1902 to 1945, when she retired.

"This journal would have been submitted to the court with the first hearing if it had been known about. The journal was discovered last night by Pete Grenfell, who lives in Stuttgart. He has been on the autobahn since early this morning to bring this journal to the court as evidence in Mrs. Lewis's case.

"Now, if I may have a few more minutes of the court's time and attention, I would like to read another entry in Miss Graff's journal." Greta waited.

"You have not, as yet, given anything pertinent to your case, Mrs. Wineman, but I assume you are getting there, so I will allow this final reading." The judge locked eyes with Greta a moment longer and then finally sat back in his chair, relaxing and glancing around the courtroom.

Greta smiled and murmured a thank you to Judge Krause; then she opened the journal and began to read.

January 11, 1939

It is late at night, and I sit with pen in hand but know not how to start this entry. This has been the saddest day in all my years of midwifery. Maybe I should start back in 1903. I was twenty-three years old and had just completed my first year of practice in midwifery. The Weinberg family had three daughters, the last two being twins, and they were expecting their fourth child. The midwife who had delivered the first three children had retired, and since I had trained under her, she encouraged them to let me take her place.

When I delivered a healthy baby boy to Mrs. Weinberg, the whole family rejoiced. They named him Jacob. He would be the third male child given the family name of Jacob. It was the delivery of their son that endeared me to them and made us become fast friends.

Through the years, I was privileged to see Jacob grow up to be a notable young man. He had the finest education, graduating from the University of Hamburg and afterward entering into his father's business, the prestigious Weinberg department store here in Berlin.

Jacob married his childhood sweetheart, Rebekah Stoltz, and they had three children I delivered: Jacob IV, Aletha, and Samuel. It's their fourth child whom I want to write about.

When Rebekah discovered that she was pregnant, she and Jacob rejoiced and shared their happiness with me and made sure that I would record the due date of the baby in my workbook. I would again deliver a child for them. It would be their fourth. But their happiness was short-lived, sad to say, for Germany is not the same Germany it was when I delivered their first three children. Almost overnight the political situation has become so intensely anti-Semitic, that our Jewish friends no longer have the freedom to live normal lives as citizens here in their own country.

I delivered a healthy baby girl to Rebekah this evening at six o'clock. Her name is Maria, a name they selected early in Rebekah's pregnancy. She is a beautiful baby girl who weighs six pounds ten ounces and is nineteen inches long. I suspect she will grow to be a petite woman, much like her mother.

But sad to say, neither Rebekah nor Jacob will have the privilege of raising their precious daughter. To save her life, they are giving her up at birth to be raised by friends who have graciously agreed to take her as their own daughter. Ernst and Sarah Hoffman will claim to have given birth to this child, register her as pure Aryan, and bestow on her the name of Hoffman. She will always be known as Maria Hoffman.

I asked Jacob why he was doing this, and he said that he knew what lay ahead for the Jews. After Kristallnacht, no Jew in Germany would be safe. Giving up Maria would be the only way for him to save her life and have a living heir.

I watched Rebekah weep as she held her baby for the first and last time. The parents dared not let the other children see her, for they were too young to keep this secret. They were told that their baby sister died at birth and that was why their mother cried so much.

Jacob tried to stay strong for Rebekah, but I could see the tears in his eyes. I signed papers stating that the baby was stillborn. Jacob is friends with Abe Romansky, the caretaker of the Jewish cemetery, and he has provided a small casket for a doll to be sealed in. They will bury the casket in the Weinberg plot in the Jewish cemetery. The Nazis do not scrutinize the Jewish burial ceremonies, for they are quite pleased to see another Jew leave this world.

I left the Weinberg home with a heavy heart and baby Maria in my satchel. She was a good baby and slept all the way to the Hoffman home. I'm sure no one living in the apartment with the Hoffmans suspected that I had a sleeping baby in my satchel. Sarah is a lovely young woman and will be a good mother to Maria. I think

Ernst will also be a good father. Maybe the Lord will let me see Maria from time to time. I surely hope so.

I pray Jacob is wrong about the Jewish situation, but I fear he is right. I suspect his family will disappear one night, never to be heard from again. That seems to be the pattern of late, and especially among the wealthier Jews. I would save all of them if I could, but I cannot. May the Lord forgive my country for what is happening to these dear people.

Greta slowly closed Elsie's journal, walked quietly to the bench, laid the journal down gently in front of Judge Krause, and walked back to her seat. Judge Krause rubbed his hand across the journal and sighed. He finally handed it to the clerk. Words were not needed. Silence had taken command of the courtroom.

William glanced to the defendant's table. The two witnesses and Neumann had their heads bowed, looking at something imaginary on the table. Beckle was tracing his finger slowly on a pad he had written notes on and following the movement of his finger.

Judge Krause tapped very lightly with his gavel, just enough to arouse the attention of the members of the court. He said, "When I usually render a verdict, there is always rejoicing from the side of the victor. But today, I think if we are honest with one another, we will say that the events of this case have brought back memories of something that, as Germans, we have tried to forget. I know that our generation is not responsible for what happened to our Jewish brothers and sisters in the Holocaust, nevertheless, we are responsible today for our attitudes toward those who are still feeling the brunt of anti-Semitism.

"We need to be very careful that we do not let ourselves become brainwashed as the generation of Germans did during the period of the Nazi regime. There is a new movement afoot that seems to be letting that very thing happen, and those of us who are fair-minded will do everything in our power to keep our country honest and fair to all of its citizens.

"I count it a privilege to have been given the opportunity to preside over this case and though I was indecisive after the first hearing, I can say without prejudice or influence from either party that I am satisfied with my ruling today. I hereby rule that the plaintiff, Rachel Lewis, is the true second-generation descendant of Jacob and Rebekah Weinberg and the sole heir to the deeds to the land that Hartmann Plaza resides on."

Judge Krause paused a few moments, giving the members of his court time to absorb his verdict then looked at the defendant's table. "Mr. Neumann, are you aware that the Holderman Company declared bankruptcy and has dissolved, and that you will be unable to recover the money you paid for the deeds?"

"Yes, Your Honor. But at the time it never occurred to me that I would be put in this position."

"Yes, well under the circumstances, the court rules that you may keep the money paid you since leasing the property to Hartmann's Limited Partnership. Furthermore, I see where you close out your year at the end of next month."

"Yes, Your Honor, I do, and thank you for this ruling."

Judge Krause nodded and turned to Greta. "Mrs. Wineman, my office will give you papers to have the deeds transferred to Mrs. Lewis's name with three stipulations: Number one: She cannot sell her lease to anyone but Hartmann's Limited Partnership. Number two: Should she lease the deeds to Mr. Hartmann, it can be at no greater price than is already in force. Number three: She has the option to sell the deeds and that price can be negotiated between her and Mr. Hartmann."

"Yes, Your Honor. My client is appreciative of the court's ruling and will abide by the stipulations."

Judge Krause smiled and said, "Now if our bailiff will adjourn our court, we can all go home." With that pithy statement, he tapped lightly with his gavel and rose to leave.

Karla put the fingernail file down and looked up when Andre walked into the living room. "I know you were talking to Luke, Andre. What did he say? Hurry and tell me the outcome of the hearing."

"You might be surprised when I tell you this, but the woman came up with an old journal at the last minute."

"What are you talking about, Andre?"

"I'm talking about evidence that proved the American woman is truly the granddaughter."

"You are lying to me. Tell me you are lying to me, Andre."

"Why would I do that, Karla? Why are you getting so upset?"

"Well, why aren't you upset? You've lost your deeds. Doesn't that bother you?"

"No. You heard Luke say that...what is her name, Karla?"

"Damn, Andre, why can't you remember her name? It's Rachel. Now don't ask me again." Karla got up, walked into the bedroom, and slammed the door.

SIXTY-THREE

There were seven sitting at the round table under the stars in Andre's beautiful dining terrace. Luke stood and raised his wine glass. "Here's to victory for Rachel." He looked at Pete and smiled. "And also a tribute to Pete for finding the journal."

Peter said, "Are we going to have a speech from Rachel? Surely we'll have a speech from someone this evening."

Rachel laughed. "How about a speech from you, Peter? You are the one who loves to talk."

"Would you have me repeat myself, Rachel? I have said over and over how good the Lord is to have let Pete find the midwife's old journal. I never cease to be amazed at God's timing." Peter put his glass down, and with a twinkle in his eyes, he said, "Now, tell me, Rachel. Have you set the date? Luke said you would set a date for your wedding after the hearing."

"I have not." Rachel caught Luke's hand and looked up at him. "I'm ready whenever Luke is. I have no work schedule to follow or family, other than Sarah Beth. I might let Luke select the date. He's the one working, and his parents will want to come. Yes, since Luke will make most of the arrangements, he should select the date."

Luke sat down and put his glass on the table. "What can I say?" He grinned at Peter. "If I had my way, I would ask Peter to marry us this evening, after our dinner, but I doubt Rachel would agree to that. She will say it's too soon."

Rachel nodded. "Yes, Luke, I think tonight is a little too soon. You must give me time to buy a nightgown. I've never heard of a bride going on a honeymoon with old clothes."

"Would a week be long enough to shop, Rachel?"

"A week sounds just about right, Luke." Rachel turned to Peter. "We've not consulted you, Peter. Since you will be conducting the ceremony, you might want to check your calendar."

"Today is Friday. How about a week from tomorrow? Saturday afternoon would be a good time for me. We'll use the chapel."

Susan spoke up. "I have a better idea. Why don't we have a morning wedding and then come back here to the terrace to have a luncheon with a beautiful wedding cake? We'll have the terrace all to ourselves."

Rachel smiled. "I like that idea. How about you, Luke?"

"I like it, also. I'll call Mother and Father and tell them. We'll get the word to our friends tomorrow. They'll want to come. I know Andre will be flattered that we'll be using his beautiful terrace. My two partners from England might also come with their wives." Luke turned to Rachel. "Honey, are you sure a week is long enough to get ready?"

"Yes, Luke. Any longer, and I may get bridal nerves."

William stood up and held out his wineglass. "I want to make a toast. I want to toast the coming wedding of my best friends and wish them long life and much happiness."

SIXTY-FOUR

"Who was that calling?" Karla asked Andre as she came into their bedroom.

"It was the bank, Karla."

"What did they want?" Karla picked up her brush and focused on her vanity mirror, watching for Andre's reflection.

"They said there was a mistake made on the interest you were charged for the twenty thousand euros you borrowed three weeks ago."

"I don't know what they are talking about," Karla said, running the brush through her hair.

"Are you sure, Karla?"

"Of course I'm sure. I don't owe the bank twenty thousand euros."

"Of course you don't. You borrowed it one week and paid it back the next."

"Who told you that, Andre?" Karla frowned and slowed her brushing.

"That's not important, Karla."

"Well, I didn't want to tell you about it." Karla put her brush down and turned around.

"Why would you not want to tell me about it, Karla? I would think if you needed that much money, you would certainly come to me." Andre cleared his throat.

"You've had a lot on your mind, Andre. I didn't want to bother you."

"You have not told me why you needed that money, Karla."

"Well, if you must know, I thought I had lost my bracelet, and I knew you would be furious with me. I knew I had to buy another one." Karla turned back to face her mirror.

"You were going to buy a forty thousand euro bracelet with twenty thousand euros?"

"I found one with inferior stones. I didn't think you would know the difference." Karla watched Andre's reflection.

"Why are you lying, Karla?"

"I'm not lying. I would never lie to you." Karla picked up her brush again and looked down, slowly moving her fingers through the bristles to remove embedded hairs.

Andre grunted and gave a slight nod of his head. "I wondered what was going on with you—why you have been acting so strange for the last few weeks."

Karla's fingers stopped moving and her head jerked slightly as she looked up to her mirror.

Andre continued. "I know for a fact that the clasp on your bracelet was not broken. Do you know how I know that?" Andre paused, as if waiting for Karla's answer. "When Richard gave me the bracelet, I took it to a jeweler. He said there was nothing wrong with the clasp. You didn't lose your bracelet, did you, Karla?"

"Of course I lost it. Why would I make up something like that?"

"So you would not have to tell me the truth." Andre cleared his throat. "I don't know when you met that guard, Karla, but it's obvious that you were well acquainted with him. And he didn't break into our apartment. You let him in and that's when he stole your bracelet." Andre paused. "You think I don't know about your trips to the nursing home. You were running out there to meet him, weren't you? You were having an affair with him."

Alarm entered Karla's voice. "Who told you I have been going to a nursing home?"

"Konrad saw you leaving one day. He had gone to check on his partner who is there with Alzheimer's disease."

Karla put her brush down, turned around, and gave Andre a pleading look. "I have been a volunteer helping there. I thought you would be pleased."

"How could I be pleased when I knew nothing about it?"

"Why are you doing this to me, Andre?"

"I'm not doing anything to you, Karla. It's just that I'm tired of your lying ways."

"I've always tried to be truthful with you, Andre." Tears welled up in Karla's eyes, and she blotted them with a tissue.

"Tears will do you no good, Karla. I'm wise to that trick."

"What can I do to prove that I love you, Andre?"

"Absolutely nothing, Karla. It's time for us to be honest with each other. You have never loved me. You've loved my money."

"I don't see how you can say that. I've stood by you even with you growing older and ignoring me—you know what I'm talking about."

"Is that why you had an affair with George Halford, Karla? He was satisfying you—sexually? You helped him get the part-time job here at the plaza, didn't you? You wanted him to have easy access to our apartment."

"You know that's not true."

"I'm not going to argue with you, Karla. It's over. I'm through." Andre cleared his throat again and stood silent, watching Karla as she continued to dab at her eyes, her head slightly bowed. He took a deep breath and said, "I might as well tell you that I went to see my lawyer several days ago."

Karla's hand dropped to her lap and she looked up with a bewildered look on her face. "What are you saying, Andre? Are you telling me that you are divorcing me?"

"Yes, I think it's time. You have not been happy with me for years."

Karla pulled another tissue from the box and said, “Well, maybe we need to have counseling, Andre. Have you thought about that?”

“I think it’s definitely too late, Karla.”

“I cannot believe this. After giving you the ten best years of my life...” Karla’s voice began to break and she hesitated a moment, her head slowly shaking. She drew in a breath and continued, “... you are divorcing me.”

Andre’s voice was firm. “My lawyer will have the papers ready for you to sign tomorrow, Karla.”

“Please tell me, Andre. Why are you doing this so quickly?” Karla’s hands had developed a slight tremor, and she abandoned the tissue she was holding and wiped a tear away with her fingers as it began to slid down the side of her cheek.

“Because, Karla, I don’t want Richard asking more questions. If he continues, I might eventually have to tell him the truth.” Andre walked over to the door.

Karla choked back a sob and said, “Are you saying you lied for me?”

Andre stopped and turned. “Yes. And you know what’s so strange, Karla? I have no idea why I did it.”

SIXTY-FIVE

Karla pulled her Mercedes into the parking lot of the nursing home. She pressed the release to her seatbelt and sat back. She would check on her father and then go to the bank and talk to the person in charge of his estate. There was no reason now for her to wait any longer. She had signed the divorce papers three days ago and would have her maiden name, Dowd, returned to her. Her driver's license still showed her maiden name, a custom France adopted many years ago. She wondered what it would take besides her birth certificate to establish that she was Karl Kirsten's daughter.

Karla looked over to the nursing home and cursed. Why did Neumann have to tell Andre about seeing her here? Andre was as smart as he was rich. He had her over a barrel, and he knew it. Only a fool would settle for 100,000 euros, but what else could she do? It was too risky to stay in Berlin. She would have to go back to Paris. Anyhow, she would have plenty of money when her father died. If she were frugal, Andre's settlement would tide her over for almost a year. Her father could not hold on much longer. He would probably die within the next month or two.

Karla walked quickly down the hall to her father's room, relieved that she would not have to confront George but still a little anxious about the whole ordeal. How much did Richard really know about everything? Could he have discovered anything incriminating about her after viewing the film at Hartmann Plaza? Andre implied that he had, but he could have been bluffing.

Karla stopped at her father's door and then pressed the handle and stepped into his room. His bed was empty. Had they taken him to a hospital? Karla turned when she heard the nurse's aide call her name.

"Mrs. Dowd, we are so sorry that we were not able to inform you that Mr. Kirsten died yesterday. We had no way of contacting you. There was a short memorial service held for him this morning in our parlor, and most of our staff was there. You have been so faithful to our patients, especially Mr. Kirsten. We wanted you notified."

Karla stood silent. "You say he died yesterday?"

"Yes, and his body was cremated this morning according to instructions from the bank that was handling his estate."

"I see. I am so sorry. Well, Mr. Kirsten is out of his misery now and at peace. He was a dear man, and I'm glad to have made his acquaintance."

"Will you be passing out magazines today?"

"No, not today. I actually came out to pick up a magazine I left here. It had an article I wanted to keep. But that's not important, now. I can probably look it up on the Internet."

"Yes, well, let me thank you again for your service. Will you be coming next week?"

"That's another thing. My husband is being transferred, and we'll be moving. I did want to tell someone here how much I've enjoyed volunteering my services."

"We'll certainly miss you, and I'll be glad to pass the word around. But before you go, did you hear about the orderly who drowned?"

"No, who was that?"

"Well, his name was George Halford, and I'm sure you met him. He worked here part time."

"I probably did. I'm sorry to hear that. My goodness, you don't hear of many people drowning today. I guess he couldn't swim. Did he fall off a boat or something?"

"No, he was working part time at Hartmann Plaza as a security guard and somehow fell in the swimming pool and drowned. I think it was after hours. He must have been making rounds in the building."

"I am so sorry," Karla repeated and then glanced at her watch. "Oh, I see I'm running late. If you'll excuse me, I need to leave and pick up my husband. Be sure to give the director my regards and tell her that I'm moving and will not be back."

The nurse's aide smiled and nodded. "Good luck with your move, Mrs. Dowd."

Karla located the bank's parking garage and had no trouble finding a parking space. Finding out the name of the bank in charge of her father's estate was the first thing George did for her. She remembered the day she met him in her father's room. She had opened the door and was surprised to see a strange orderly shaving her dad. He was tall and muscular with dark hair and was rather good-looking. He looked to be in his middle thirties.

"Well, you must be new here. I have not seen you before."

George looked up and smiled. "Yes, I've only been coming to work the first of the week." He turned back to Mr. Kirsten and continued shaving him."

"I'm glad you are shaving Mr. Kirsten. I think he was in need of someone who could do that for him."

"Are you related to Mr. Kirsten?" George asked.

"You might say that."

"He's a nice man. He doesn't complain like some of the patients."

"Yes, he's good-natured and even more so with Alzheimer's disease."

"I guess since you are kin, he must be in your care."

"No, he turned his estate over to his bank when his doctor advised that he needed nursing care."

"Oh?"

"Yes, this is a very upscale nursing facility. I think the bank made a good decision when they selected this one."

"Which bank does he do business with?"

"Why are you asking that personal question?"

"Oh, I was just curious. I used to work for a bank and wondered if it was the one I worked for."

"Well, actually, I don't know the name of the bank. I moved to Berlin a few months ago and was asked by a distant relative to check on him."

"And, of course, I can see that Mr. Kirsten is probably unable to tell you anything about his business."

"Yes, you've figured that one out."

"But the director of the nursing home would know the bank in charge."

"I asked her, and she said the law would not allow her to reveal that—patient confidentiality or something like that."

"Oh?" Was all George said, as he turned back to her father and finished shaving his face.

It was the next week when she returned to the nursing home that George slipped her a piece of paper with the bank's name. He had accessed it from the nursing home computer. Karla remembered how pleased he was when she gave him a generous tip.

Karla opened her purse and checked her papers again; then she got out of her Mercedes and took the elevator to the first floor and the bank's side entrance. She was pleased that her father's bank was in West Berlin, far away from the Mitte district and Hartmann Plaza.

The receptionist looked up and smiled. "May I help you?" she said.

"Yes, I'm Karla Kirsten, and I have come to speak to whoever is in charge of Karl Kirsten's estate."

"If you'll have a seat, Ms. Kirsten, I'll see if our vice president can see you. The receptionist picked up her phone, pressed a button and talked only a minute. She hung up and smiled at Karla. "Ms. Kirsten, Mr. Forest will see you now. I'll show you to his office.

"Ralph Forest," the nice-looking middle-aged man said as he held out his hand.

Karla smiled and took his hand. "I'm Karla Kirsten. It's nice meeting you."

"Would you have a seat, Ms. Kirsten?"

"Thank you," Karla said, sitting down in the armchair in front of the large desk that Ralph sat behind.

"Ms. Kirsten, this comes as quite a shock. We here at the bank were not aware that Mr. Kirsten had a relative. I assume you are a relative, and please let me convey my condolences for the death of Mr. Kirsten."

"Thank you. I know this is a little awkward, but I will explain." Karla opened her purse, pulled out papers, and handed them to Mr. Forest. "Sir, I am Karl Kirsten's daughter. This is my birth certificate that you are holding. My mother and my father divorced before I was born, and my mother remarried. Her second husband adopted me before I was two years old. They never told me I was adopted. I discovered all of this after my mother died around two years ago and I found my birth certificate among her legal papers."

Ralph sat quiet, studying the papers. He finally looked up and said, "I see. You were born in Paris and are a citizen of France."

"Yes, that's where I grew up."

"Ms. Kirsten, is this the name you go by now? Did you take your birth name back? I see that your driver's license is in Karla Dowd's name."

"No, I haven't legally taken my birth name back. I'm working on that."

"Ms. Kirsten, I don't think it's necessary for you to have your name changed to Kirsten to claim your father's estate. But since this bank is trustee of Mr. Kirsten's estate, you must provide us a certificate of inheritance. The certificate is issued by the German surrogate court here in Berlin. I see that you have a will signed by Mr. Kirsten and also your birth certificate and other papers relating to this matter. You have what is necessary to obtain a certificate of heirship."

Mr. Forest turned to his computer and began to type. A few moments later, his printer spit out a sheet of paper, and he gave it to Karla and said, "Ms. Kirsten, this is a sheet of instructions to help you obtain what you need. I suggest you file for your certificate of heirship and come back as soon as you receive it. You might call in advance to make sure I'm in my office."

"Yes, I'll do that. I appreciate your time, Mr. Forest."

"No problem," Ralph Forest said, standing and handing Karla's papers back to her.

SIXTY-SIX

The morning of the wedding was beautiful with the sun shining and temperature hovering in the high sixties. There were fifty or more friends gathered at the chapel, all speaking in soft voices.

At Rachel's request, William and Mrs. Hartmann sat on the right side of the chapel in the second row with Sarah Beth sitting in between them. The second row on the left side hosted Pete's family, Rodger and Margaret Springfield and Annabelle. The front-row pews were empty. Luke and Rachel's guests sat in the pews behind.

There was one very large arrangement of white flowers backed with green foliage sitting on the chancel table at the back of the rostrum. The large, white marble urn held long-stemmed stocks, lilies, roses, carnations, and tulips. White candles in tall brass candlesticks flanked the flower arrangement.

A quiet settled over the chapel at the sound of Nancy playing *Canon in D Major,* by Pachelbel. Luke and his father followed Peter as he entered from the back, and they took their places on the rostrum. Susan came in next followed, lastly, by Rachel, and they walked up the four steps and stood with Luke and his father.

Rachel wore a beautiful, long-sleeved, pumpkin-colored original Donna Karan silk suit with the skirt just covering her knees. Luke wore a dark suit, tailor-made especially for him. Peter asked

Luke to face Rachel and take her hands in his, and Susan held Rachel's bouquet while they said their vows.

The ceremony lasted only twenty minutes, with Peter reading scripture, explaining why God created marriage, and reminding the couple of the sacrifices that God expected them to make for each other. After they exchanged rings and Peter prayed, he said loudly, "I now pronounce you man and wife. Luke, you may kiss your bride."

Clapping and laughter broke out in the audience as Luke took Rachel in his arms and gave her a sound kiss. Nancy played *Joyful, Joyful, We Adore Thee,* by Beethoven, and Luke and Rachel stepped down from the rostrum to mingle with, and to receive congratulations from, their friends.

From the chapel, the wedding party went straight to Andre's restaurant and into the beautiful terrace to partake of a luncheon that boasted of the finest of seafood, prime rib, and chicken breast cooked in a wine sauce. The three tiered wedding cake sat on a table by itself, and flowers graced all of the tables. There was a string orchestra nestled back in the corner to entertain the guests. There would be champagne to toast the bride and groom.

Andre asked William where Luke was taking Rachel on their honeymoon. "Where else but Switzerland, Andre? To the finest chalet there is."

"Isn't that where Roger Federer lives?"

"Yes. What made you think about him?"

"I was just thinking about his two sets of twins and how cute they are. Do you think there may be something in the water there...you know, something that promotes the birth of twins?"

"I don't know, Andre. I've really not thought anything about it."

"Now wouldn't it be great if Rachel could have twins for Luke?"

William laughed. "I guess so. He'd be getting a pretty late start, though."

Andre picked up his stemmed glass from the table and took his last sip of champagne. "You can laugh, William, but I still think it's a good idea. Luke's a good fellow, and I know he loves Rachel's little girl, but he needs children of his own."

"I can't believe we're finally married," Luke said, admiring Rachel's voluptuous body through her beautiful pale-blue nightgown. He was propped on his elbow in a king-size bed in the bridal suite of one of the most expensive hotels in Switzerland.

"I know." Rachel stifled a yawn. "It's been a whirlwind of a week, but now it's over, and thankfully, we can relax."

Luke grinned and shook his head. "It's not...*quite* over," he whispered after kissing Rachel.

Rachel laughed. "Luke Hartmann, to look at your face, I would think you were a very young newlywed, experiencing your first honeymoon."

Luke grinned. "Does it really show? I thought I had my emotions under control, but you know what? It was after meeting you that I started losing it. And now having you in bed with me attired in this gorgeous nightgown, well..."

Rachel's lips twitched into a smile. "Are you blaming it on me? I'm talking about your lack of control."

"Yes—you don't mind do you?"

"No, I'm really flattered. But, Luke, why all of this conversation?"

"Are you suggesting—Mrs. Hartmann—that I should turn out the light?"

Rachel's thick eyelashes flicked up and down. "It might not be a bad idea."

Luke reached back and turned the light out and pulled Rachel into his arms and kissed her again. Releasing her slightly, he said, "I doubt we'll get much sleep tonight, Rachel."

"Why do you say that, Luke? This is a very comfortable king-size bed."

Luke laughed, then pulled Rachel even closer and kissed her once more, his fingers sliding up her arm, feeling for the slender strap that crossed her shoulder.

SIXTY-SEVEN

Karla looked in her large Saint Laurent handbag and smiled. All of her papers were there to be executed by the consular officer. She was asked the value of her father's estate, which she did not know, so she gave the clerk at the German Mission a sexy smile and then asked him if he would call Mr. Ralph Forest at the bank for that information. She returned to the mission three days later and was relieved when she was charged a reasonable fee for her certificate.

Karla opened the door to her Mercedes and stepped onto the concrete floor. Pressing her remote to lock her door, she walked quickly to the elevator.

"Good morning," she said to the receptionist. "I'm Karla Kirsten. I called earlier for an appointment with Mr. Forest."

"Yes, Ms. Kirsten. You may go on back. Mr. Forest is expecting you."

Karla smiled and nodded and then walked quickly back to Ralph Forest's office and knocked. Mr. Forest opened the door for her. "It's good to see you, Ms. Kirsten. Please have a seat. I have been looking at Mr. Kirsten's account on the computer along with some printed material. Were you able to get the certificate of heirship without any problems?"

“I was, thanks to the instructions you gave me, and thank you for giving the clerk at the mission the information he needed.” Karla handed Forest the papers.

“I was glad to,” Ralph murmured, dropping his eyes and studying the papers in detail. He finally looked up. “This looks fine, Ms. Kirsten. I see that you have the original for heirship and also a first certified copy of the application. You’ll want to keep the original in a safe place.”

“Yes, I’ll do that.”

“Ms. Kirsten, did your father discuss his estate with you?”

“Not really. He did sign the will, leaving me everything, but as far as details were concerned, I never asked him anything. I’m sure you are aware that he suffered from Alzheimer’s disease.”

“Yes, we were aware of that and were glad to help him. He had banked with us for many years.”

“Will it take long for you to close out his account and transfer his assets into my account? I’m moving to Paris, France, and will open up an account there.”

“I don’t think that will be a problem. You might have your attorney fax us the information we’ll need. We can set up a password for security reasons.”

“Yes, that sounds reasonable. Mr. Forest, would you give me a ball park figure as to the amount of my father’s estate?”

Mr. Forest turned to his computer and scrolled down. He wrote down a figure on his note pad and handed it to Karla.

Looking up with alarm, she blurted out, “Sir, there has to be a mistake. My father was very wealthy. I was told that he had millions.”

Mr. Forest’s brow furrowed slightly. “I’m so sorry, Ms. Kirsten; I thought you knew. Your father was a very wealthy man at one time, but unfortunately he invested most of his money in a company that turned out to be nothing but a Ponzi scheme. It was not until just recently that the owner of the company finally confessed and was indicted.”

Karla's eyes narrowed. "Are you telling me that he died with only ninety-seven thousand euros to his name?"

"Yes, Ms. Kirsten. I have all of the figures here for you to go over. Every euro is accounted for."

"What about his interest in the Neumann Development Company?"

"Yes, he owned forty percent of that company. Mr. Neumann sends in a quarterly report. I'm sure you know that the company was formed strictly to buy East German real estate. The only asset they had was the land they leased to Mr. Hartmann's limited partnership. And I understand that Neumann lost the lease to a woman from the States. I think she was heir to one of the Holocaust victims."

"But, Mr. Forest, I understand that the judge let Neumann keep all of the money he had collected since Mr. Hartmann signed the lease. I would think that is a considerable amount."

Mr. Forest turned again to his computer and scrolled. He cleared his throat and turned to Karla. "I see that, altogether, the Neumann Development Company received four million euros from Hartmann's Limited Partnership. Hmmm. Give me a moment to run down these figures in your father's account."

Mr. Forest once more turned to his computer. "Here is a breakdown of the remaining figures. Your father received one million, six hundred thousand euros from Neumann Development Company. I see here that he paid the German Central Tax Office installments of three hundred thousand a year for four years. There is a notation that most of this was for back taxes owed. That left him four hundred thousand euros." Forest paused a minute and then scrolled further. "It looks as if he spent a great deal of money for nursing home care." Forest picked up his pen and said, "Let me add these figures together. It looks like three years of expenses comes to two hundred seventy thousand euros. If my math is correct, that leaves one hundred thirty thousand euros. Now, take away thirty thousand euros for three years the bank charged for financial management, and that leaves one hundred thousand." Forest paused a moment, glanced to his computer, and then looked back down at his paper. "Hmm—let me see now. There is another three thousand to be accounted for. Oh, yes, your father's body was cremated. We paid for that service. Well, Ms. Kirsten, that seems to take care of all of the charges." Mr. Forest sat silent waiting for Karla to comment.

Karla's eyes narrowed again, and she frowned. "I cannot believe this. I need to sue the damn company that sold my father those useless bonds, or whatever they sold him."

Mr. Forest cleared his throat and said, "Ms. Kirsten, the government is attempting to recover the assets, but unfortunately most of the money has already been spent, and what's left will likely be spent on legal fees. I doubt you'll get a tenth of what he invested, and then it might be fifteen years before you even get that." Mr. Forest looked down and began to gather the papers on his desk, indicating the meeting was over.

"This is devastating! Tell me, Mr. Forest, how can a man go from being a multi-millionaire one day to almost a pauper the next?"

Forest started to say something, but stopped and shrugged. He stood up with her papers in hand and said, "Ms. Kirsten, I wish I could change things, but I can't. All I can do is issue you the ninety-seven thousand euros."

Karla got up and snatched her papers from his hands. "There's no way you can understand what this means to me, Mr. Forest. I've essentially been robbed. It will be impossible for me to live on this meager inheritance." Karla paused and glared at Mr. Forest and then said, "Just write me the damn check."

Karla stood at the side of her Mercedes for only a moment and then drew in an angry breath, got in, and slammed the door. It had all been for naught, she thought, as she sat back against the seat and fought the tears. With Andre's 100,000 euros and now her father's 97,000, how long could she live? Would she have to return to waiting on tables? It was for certain she could never get a job at Andre's Paris restaurant. His son hated her.

She had read in the paper that most people were hiring college graduates, and she had only a high school education. If she could not pass the college entrance exam as a young person, how could she do it at the age of forty?

A tear trickled down Karla's cheek, and she wiped her eyes and looked at the mascara on her fingers and sighed. What difference did smeared mascara make now? Her glamour days were over. She had messed up big time. No more expensive clothes, jewelry or top-of-the-line cosmetics.

But that was not the worst of it. As hard as she tried, she could not erase the murder from her mind. Karla breathed deeply several times and then hooked her seatbelt, turned on the engine, and headed out of the parking garage. Hopefully, she could get George out of her mind like she did those cobwebs. That was the first thing she would work on. If she could get her mind cleared out, maybe she would apply to beauty school. She had always loved working with hairstyles.

Karla reached for the box of tissues and blotted the tears from her eyes; then she turned into the traffic and stepped on her accelerator.

SIXTY-EIGHT

Rachel woke up when she felt Luke's hand on her hip. She turned over, snuggled in his arms and closed her eyes again. In a moment she sighed and said, "What day is it, Luke? I've lost track of time."

"It's Friday, sweetheart. This will be our sixth day. Our week's almost up. Why do you ask?"

"I don't know. I guess I'm thinking about all of the money I spent on those nightgowns."

"Why would you be thinking about that so early in the morning, honey?"

"Because all they do is sit at the foot of our bed on top of your pajamas."

"What's wrong with that?"

"Nothing, I guess, but I keep thinking about how wasteful I've been. I could have saved myself six hundred dollars."

Luke chuckled. "Sweetheart, I'll give you six hundred dollars if it's bothering you that much."

"You wouldn't mind?"

"No."

Rachel slid her hand across Luke's chest and murmured, "I love you so much, Luke. I'm so glad we're married."

Luke rubbed his hand lightly up and down Rachel's arm. "You cannot imagine how happy I am. I could not have waited another day. Do you realize how much I love you, Rachel? Next to God, I love you more than anyone or anything in the world." Luke cupped the side of Rachel's face in his hand and turned it gently toward him and kissed her.

Rachel sighed again. "I'm glad you put God first, Luke. I don't mind playing second fiddle to Him." Rachel adjusted her head on Luke's shoulder and said, "I love lying here in your arms. This has been the most wonderful honeymoon. I hate to see it end."

"We'll come back again, sweetheart. Switzerland is one of my favorite places."

"Yes, I can see why." There was a moment of silence, and then Rachel said, "Luke, I have a question."

"What is it, sweetheart?"

"Well, as we were leaving last Saturday, Andre said I had better be careful about the water here in Switzerland. Why would he say something like that?"

"I have no idea. There is absolutely nothing wrong with the water in Switzerland. You know I would not bring you here if I thought there was."

"I didn't think you would...," Rachel paused a few moments and then continued, "...Andre also said how lucky you were to have married me...you know, with my winning the lawsuit. I told Andre that you would have married me if I had lost the lawsuit." Rachel paused again. "You would have, wouldn't you, Luke?"

"Of course I would have, darling. I would have married you long before the lawsuit was even settled had you given permission. Rachel, pay no attention to Andre. He's always coming up with stupid remarks. That was Karla's influence. He should have gotten rid of her a long time ago."

"I agree with you, and I'm glad he finally did. I never trusted Karla to begin with." Rachel lay back on her pillow. "Luke, do you think Andre will continue to stay in Berlin and live at the plaza?"

"I suppose he will. I doubt he'll move back to Paris. That's where Karla was going. But, sweetheart, I don't want you to be concerned about Andre on the last day of our honeymoon. I want you to be concerned about me."

"I'll always be concerned about you, Luke. You'll always be first in my life." Rachel relaxed with a contented sigh. A few moments later, she said, "Luke? What are you doing?" Rachel's laugh was soft. "You know how that affects me."

"Yes," Luke said, suppressing the laughter in his voice. "I do."

EPILOGUE

"Who were you talking to, honey?" Susan asked, coming into the kitchen.

"Luke called, Susan. Rachel had a sonogram and they have just left the doctor's office." William grinned. "The twins are boys. Identical boys!"

"That is wonderful," Susan exclaimed. "Did Luke say whether they have names selected and whether the due date has changed?"

"No, he didn't mention names, and I forgot to ask that question. The due date is still the first part of July, maybe a week ahead of us. I did tell him that you had an appointment next week, and we will find out the sex of our twins. I promised I'd call as soon as we found out." William walked over, put his arms around Susan, and leaned down and kissed her. "Now wouldn't it be great if we have boys? They can be playmates with Luke and Rachel's."

"William Handel, do you realize what you are saying? Tell me, please, how many thousand miles are we apart? To grow up playmates, I would think the boys would have to play together frequently, at least several times a month."

"Maybe we can convince Luke to move here to Arlington. He can operate his commodity business anywhere. It's all done by computers anyhow."

"Well, what about Hartmann Plaza? He's put so much time and effort into making that successful. I doubt he would give that up."

"He wouldn't have to. He says himself that he has a competent manager now and has been relieved of most of the responsibility there."

"William, Rachel said she wants to move from their apartment into a home with a yard for the children to play in. At least, that's what she told me the last time I talked with her."

"The plaza is a beautiful place, but I can certainly understand Rachel's concern. A high-rise is not an ideal place to raise small children. I guess Luke would have to install a swing set and sliding board in the large exercise room for the boys to play on, and I don't think that would go over well with the adults exercising there."

"I agree. I'm sure Luke is giving it much thought. The babies aren't due for another four and a half months. They still have a fair amount of time to make arrangements."

The low ring caught Luke's attention and he picked up his cell and smiled. Motioning with his hand, he glanced at Rachel and Andre and said, "Excuse me, please. This is William calling. I need to take his call."

"William?" Luke said, the excitement building in his voice. "Rachel and I have been waiting for your call. Don't keep us in suspense now. Tell me what you found out." Luke dropped his head a moment and listened. He grinned, shook his head, and said, "Congratulations, man, that's great." There was another pause. "Yes, she and Andre are here with me. We're having dinner under the stars." Luke chuckled. "You say the due date is still the same? OK. Now don't get ahead of us." Luke chuckled again. "Yes, I'll tell her. Give our love to Susan, and we'll talk later. I know you want to get home." Luke laid his cell on the table.

"Guess what, Rachel?"

"Hurry and tell us, Luke. I don't want to guess. The suspense is killing me." Rachel had a slight frown on her face.

"They're having boys, Rachel. Identical twin boys."

"Oh, that's wonderful, Luke. I'm so happy for them!" Rachel drew in an excited breath and sat back in her chair with her eyes sparkling and a smile on her lips. "Isn't that great news, Andre?"

Andre's nod was slow. "I guess—if you say so." A slight frown furrowed Andre's brow. "But, Rachel, I warned you and that young Handel fellow. He laughed when I told him that he needed to be suspicious of the water in Switzerland, yet he went right ahead and took Susan there as soon as you and Luke got home from your honeymoon."

"But Andre—Susan had never been to Switzerland, and she and William wanted to spend a few days there before returning to the States. Susan said it was a wonderful trip."

"Yes, but look what happened. You can say all you want to, Rachel, but I'm convinced there is something in their water that promotes multiple births. Now, don't get me wrong. I think twins are great—maybe twice the trouble, but at least you get your family all at once." Andre cleared his throat. "But take my advice—don't go back there after your boys are born, unless you and Luke plan to have more children. Who knows? Next time you might have triplets." Andre picked up his glass of wine and cleared his throat again. He sat silent a moment just watching the wine as he swirled it around in his glass. He finally looked up with a sly look on his face and said, "I'm glad I never took Karla there."

ABOUT THE AUTHOR

Eighty-eight-year-old Helen K. Jordan lives in her hometown of Greenville, Mississippi, and is glad to be the mother of three daughters and grandmother of six grandchildren and eleven great-grandchildren. She attended the University of Mississippi and has been a Bible teacher and active member of First Baptist Church for more than fifty years. It wasn't until her daughter gave her a computer after her husband passed away that she embarked on a new adventure as an author and produced her fiction debut, The Journal, followed by the sequel, The Leather Satchel.

Made in the USA
Charleston, SC
24 July 2015